Prais

"Has a lot of things I love in a book: a truly dark and sinister world, delicious tension and suspense, violence so gritty you'll get something in your eye just reading it, and a gorgeously flawed protagonist. Take this one to the checkout counter. Seriously."
—JIM BUTCHER, author of The Dresden Files

"Unique magical concepts, a tough and pragmatic protagonist and a high casualty rate for innocent bystanders will enthrall readers who like explosive action and magic that comes at a serious cost."
—*Publishers Weekly* (starred review)

"Cinematic and vivid, with a provocative glimpse into a larger world. Where's the next one?"
—TERRY ROSSIO, screenwriter,
Pirates of the Caribbean trilogy

Game of Cages

"The fast pacing and over-the-top action never let go. This has become one of my must read series."
—*Locus*

"Connolly fulfills and sustains the promise of his 2009 rural noir debut, *Child of Fire*, with this thoughtful Lovecraftian sequel. . . . Connolly doesn't shy away from tackling big philosophical issues."
—*Publishers Weekly* (starred review)

The Twenty Palaces Series
by Harry Connolly

CHILD OF FIRE
GAME OF CAGES
CIRCLE OF ENEMIES

CIRCLE OF ENEMIES

A TWENTY PALACES NOVEL

HARRY CONNOLLY

DEL REY

BALLANTINE BOOKS • NEW YORK

A Del Rey Mass Market Original

Copyright © 2011 by Harry Connolly

Published in the United States by Del Rey, an imprint of The Random House Publishing Group, a division of Random House, Inc., New York.

DEL REY is a registered trademark and the Del Rey colophon is a trademark of Random House, Inc.

ISBN 978-0-345-50891-1

Printed in the United States of America

www.delreybooks.com

9 8 7 6 5 4 3 2 1

For my son, who isn't old enough to read it yet

It was August in Seattle, when the city enjoyed actual sunshine and temperatures in the eighties. I'd spent the day working, which made for a nice change. I'd just finished a forty-hour temp landscaping job; dirt and dried sweat made my face and arms itch. I hated the feeling, but even worse was that I didn't have anything lined up for next week.

As I walked up the alley toward home, I passed a pair of older women standing beside a scraggly vegetable garden. One kept saying she was sweltering, *sweltering*, but her friend didn't seem sympathetic. Neither was I. I was used to summers in the desert.

When they noticed me, they fell silent. The unsympathetic one took her friend's hand and led her toward the back door, keeping a wary eye on me. That didn't bother me, either.

I stumped up the stairs to my apartment above my aunt's garage. It was too late to call the temp agency tonight. I'd have to try them early Monday morning. Not that I had much hope. It was hard for an ex-con to find work, especially an ex-con with my name.

I'm Raymond Lilly, and I've lost track of the number of people I've killed.

My ancient garage-sale answering machine was blinking. I played the messages. Two were from reporters, one from a journalist-blogger, and one from a writer. They offered me the chance to tell my side of what happened in

Washaway last Christmas. Except for the writer's, I recognized all the voices—they'd called often over the last few weeks, sometimes several times a day.

I absentmindedly rubbed the tattoos on the back of my hands. They looked like artless jailhouse squiggles, but in reality they were magic spells, and without them I'd be behind bars. None of the survivors in Washaway could pick me out of a lineup, and none of the fingerprint or DNA evidence I'd left behind pointed to me anymore. I was on the twisted path.

I erased the messages. There was no point in calling them back. None of them understood the meaning of the words *fuck off.*

The sounds of their voices had triggered a low, buzzing anger that made me feel slightly out of control. I showered, then dropped my work clothes into the bottom of the tub, scrubbed them clean, and hung them from the curtain rod. I felt much better after that.

I wiped steam from the bathroom window and looked out. My aunt had not hung a paper angel in her kitchen window. That meant I could order in a sandwich for dinner. I put on my sleeping clothes: a T-shirt and a pair of cutoff sweatpants. I could eat alone, in silence, without someone asking how I was sleeping, how I was eating, and wouldn't things be better if I went to talk to someone?

I wouldn't have to say *Thank you, but I can't* a half dozen times. My aunt was right; I'd probably sleep better if I could talk about the nightmares—and what I'd done to bring them on—but I'd be bedding down in a padded room.

I opened the bathroom door to dispel the steam, even though an unlocked door felt like a gun at my back. Then I turned to the mirror and looked carefully. Damn. I was wasting away.

A voice behind me said: "You look like shit."

I yelped and spun around. In an instant, my heart was pounding in my chest as my hand fumbled across the sink for something to use as a weapon.

Caramella was standing in the bathroom doorway, and I was so startled to see her that everything went still for a moment. My adrenaline eased, and I could hear my harsh breath in the silence. It had been more than five years, and she'd changed quite a bit. Her skin, which had once been so dark, seemed lighter, as though she spent all her time indoors, and while she still straightened her hair, now she had it up in a bun. She wore orange pants with an elastic waistband and a white halter. She'd gained some weight and she seemed taller somehow.

But she didn't belong here in Seattle. She belonged down in L.A., hanging at the Bigfoot Room with Arne, Robbie, and the rest.

I almost asked her what she was doing here, but I didn't want her to think she wasn't welcome. In truth, I didn't know how I felt about her. "Welcome to my bathroom," I said.

"Thanks. I hate it."

I nodded but didn't respond right away. Her hands were empty, although she might have stuffed a gun into the back of her waistband. Not that I could imagine why she'd want to kill me, but that was how my mind worked now.

"I'm guessing you're not here for old times' sake."

"We don't have any old times, Ray." She turned and walked into the other room.

I followed her, noting that she didn't have a weapon under her waistband. "Then why are you here?" I kept my tone as neutral as I could, although I had less self-control than I used to.

"I'm paying a debt," she said, as though it was the most bitter thing in the world. "I have to deliver a message to you. In person." She stopped beside the efficiency stove.

"Okay. Here I am."

She looked away. Her lip curled and she blinked several times. Christ, she was about to cry. "You killed me, Ray."

I gaped at her, astonished. She turned and slapped me on the shoulder. Then she did it again. That still wasn't enough, so she slapped my face and head four or five times. I didn't try to stop her.

Finally, she stopped on her own. Hitting me wasn't bringing her any satisfaction. "You killed me," she said again. "And you killed Arne, and Lenard, and Ty, and all the others, too. We're all going to die because we knew you."

"Melly, what are you talking about?"

"Sorry," she said with a wet sniffle. I looked for tears on her face, but her cheeks were dry. "That's the message. That's all you get."

She swung at my face again. I flinched, but the blow never struck. When I opened my eyes a moment later, I was alone in the room.

I had been standing between Caramella and the door; she couldn't have gotten around me and gotten out, not in the time it took me to flinch. I walked around the little studio anyway. She was gone—vanished in the blink of an eye.

Magic. She had magic. Damn.

My cheek and scalp were sticky where she'd slapped me, and the stickiness was starting to burn. I went into the bathroom and washed my face and head. I could feel a smear of acidic goop that was so thin I couldn't even see it. Plain water washed it away completely. My clean skin was slightly tender, but the pain had eased.

I checked the washrag, but it didn't have any unusual stains or smells. I hung it over the kitchen faucet.

Crossing the room, I took my ghost knife from its hiding place on my bookshelf. It was only a piece of scrap paper, smaller than the palm of my hand, with a layer of mailing tape over it and some laminate over that. On the paper itself was a sigil I had drawn with a ballpoint pen. It felt alive, and it felt like a part of me, too. The other magic I had, the tattoos on my chest, arms, and neck, were protections that had been cast on me by someone else. The ghost knife was my spell, the only one I had.

Then I took my cellphone out of my sock drawer. After the mess in Washaway, an investigator for the Twenty Palace Society met me on the street and slipped me a phone number. They trusted me enough to give me a way to contact them, which was damned rare and I knew it.

The society was a group of sorcerers committed to one end: hunting down magic spells and the people who used them, then destroying both. They were especially determined to find summoning spells, which could call strange creatures to our world from a place referred to as, variously, the Empty Spaces or the Deeps. These creatures, called predators, could grant strange powers, if the summoner knew how to properly control them. Too often, the summoner didn't know, and the predator got loose in the world to hunt.

I was a low-level member of that society, but except for my boss, Annalise, who had put the magical tattoos on me, I knew very little about it. How many peers were there? How many investigators? How many wooden men, besides me, did they have? Where were they based? Where did their money come from?

I had no idea and no way to find out. The Twenty Palace Society took its secrecy seriously. I hadn't been invited to secret headquarters, hadn't trained at a secret camp, hadn't been given a secret handbook with an organizational flow chart at the back. When they wanted me to do something, they contacted me, and they told me as little as they could.

What I did know was this: peers live a very long time—centuries, in some cases—and the magic they use has left them barely human. Oh, they look human enough, but they have become something else.

And they were bastards, too—ruthless killers who took a scorched-earth policy when it came to predators and enemy sorcerers. As a group, they didn't seem to care much about collateral damage.

They had their reasons. A single predator, let loose in the world, could strip it of life. I'd visited the Empty Spaces once and seen it happen. So maybe the peers were justified in their "kill a hundred to save six billion" attitude, but it was a slim consolation if your loved one was among the hundred.

Which was why I set the cell back on the bureau. Caramella had vanished right in front of me. It was magic, yeah, but calling the Twenty Palace Society and asking Annalise to meet me in L.A. was as good as taking a hit out on Melly and everyone else I knew. Annalise would first determine who, where, and how they had been touched by magic—spells didn't strike people out of the sky like lightning. Magic powers, enchantments, and hungry predators were things people *did* to one another.

After that, Annalise would kill them all just to be safe, and I would be the one who'd hung a bull's-eye on their backs.

God, I couldn't kill more people. It was too soon.

An overwhelming weariness came over me. Too little sleep and a full day's work in the sun had left me exhausted. I smeared peanut butter on a slice of bread and ate it with all the enthusiasm you would expect, then climbed into bed. I wasn't ready for a long trip south. I didn't have the energy for it.

I closed my eyes and fell into a dead sleep. I dreamed of fire, and mobs of people coming at me in the darkness, and brutal violence. I woke screaming at five in the morning.

I grabbed my ready bag, my ghost knife, and my cellphone. I wrote a note to my aunt explaining that I would be away for a few days. Then I went out into the summer darkness, climbed into my rusty Ford Escort, and drove south.

It was a long trip, and I had plenty of time to think. Too much time, really. It had surprised me when Melly had said we didn't have old times. I'd met her when I was seventeen, still stealing cars for Arne and feeling a little cocky about it. She'd been a couple of years older, and I'd tried to smooth talk her. It was the first time a woman had ever laughed at me without making me angry or ashamed. She took me under her wing, sort of, and we became friends.

Until then, I hadn't thought men and women could really be friends—not that I'd become a man yet, no matter what I'd thought of myself. She had been kind to me when she didn't have to, and she had yanked on my leash whenever I got too full of myself. I'd done things for her, too: fixed her car a dozen times, helped her move, and the one time an ex-boyfriend had threatened her, I'd broken his thumbs as an important lesson in good manners.

Never mind the times she'd lifted cash from my wallet. That's how we'd lived back then. I always felt I'd never done enough to repay her for the things she'd done for me. And now she'd denied we'd had good times at all.

Maybe it should have stung more, but it didn't. I'd spent three years in Chino, and the two years after that had been centered on the society and its work. Caramella was like a ghost from another life come to haunt me—a life where we'd told one another we were brothers and sisters but I'd had to sleep with my wallet in my pocket. I could barely remember how that felt.

I drove straight through, taking twenty-three hours with meals and bathroom breaks. Most of the time I was in a trance, but as I approached the city, passing through dry, brown hills wrinkled like unfolded laundry, I could feel my anxieties gathering strength.

Then I was inside the city in the cool, dry predawn, riding on an elevated highway with barriers along both sides. I could see treetops and the roofs of houses laid out around me; I was skimming above the city, and felt it beneath and around me. It gave me the same tingle I got standing outside a lion's cage at the zoo.

I was exhausted. I pulled off the freeway into the parking lot of an IKEA, drove up to the top level, and shut everything down. I slumped in the seat and shut my eyes.

Everything was wrong. I was back in L.A., but I felt like a pod-person imitation of the man I used to be. Stealing cars, getting high, spending hours on the PlayStation or hitting the bag at the gym—none of that matched who I was now. Now I had bulletproof tattoos on my chest, neck, and arms. Now I had tattooed spells that obscured evidence of crimes I'd committed, plus others that did who knows what. Now I was a killer of men, women, and children.

Sleep overtook me and I woke up around ten-thirty feeling sore but without my usual parade of bad dreams. This level of the parking lot was still empty. Already sweating from the morning heat, I started the engine, filled the gas tank at a station on the corner, and drove to the Bigfoot Room.

It wasn't really called the Bigfoot Room. It had changed names several times over the dozen or so years I'd spent as a member of Arne's crew, and the latest name was the Dingaling Bar. I nearly laughed. I couldn't imagine Arne in a bar called the Dingaling. I parked in the lot beside it and walked around to the front. The wall above the door was recessed slightly, and coated with dust. Years ago, Arne had brought a bar stool out front, climbed up, and written BIGFOOT ROOM in the dust with his finger.

"That's our sign, just for us," he'd said. And while the bar had changed hands three times, no one had ever noticed his writing or tried to wash it away.

It was gone now. Someone had swiped a hand through the dust, erasing the words.

I went inside anyway. The place had been remodeled, but there were still booths in the back corner. Arne wasn't there, and neither were Robbie, Summer, or any of the others.

A brief conversation with the bartender confirmed that he didn't know Arne. This wasn't the Bigfoot Room anymore. I recognized the barfly sitting by the jukebox, but he didn't recognize me. He claimed not to remember Arne, either, even though Arne had bought him drinks many times over the years. He had the flat, burned-out eyes of a mannequin.

I ordered an egg sandwich and coffee, mainly so I could use the dirty bathroom. When the bill came, I asked for a phone book. Violet Johnson's name was in there. I paid and left.

Vi still lived in the same place in Studio City. I drove over there, feeling vaguely sick at the idea of seeing her again. Or maybe it was the egg sandwich. Melly had been like a big sister to me, but Violet was the girl I wanted for keeps. I'd wanted us to buy a house together, the whole deal. The three years I did in Chino were because of a punch I threw while defending her kid brother. She was also the one who dumped me just before my arraignment, and I hadn't even heard her name since.

I had to park two blocks from her place, but I managed to find a spot. Her neighborhood was so familiar that it felt eerie. Walking down this same sidewalk felt

like wearing a costume, as though I was disguising myself as a younger me. I went up her same front walk to
her same row of mailbox slots. I even remembered her
apartment code. I buzzed her. Her voice, when she answered, sounded thin.

"Who is it?"

"It's Ray," I said, the way I'd said it many times before. Then I remembered there were five years between
us, and I added, "Ray Lilly."

She didn't answer right away. She did press the gate
buzzer. I pushed the gate open and went inside. The
courtyard and little pool looked the same; no one was
swimming. She was on the third floor, and I headed up
the stairs.

She was already standing in the open doorway, waiting for me. It took me a moment to recognize her. She
looked smaller and thinner than I remembered. Her thick
brown curls were pulled back into a simple ponytail, and
she wore no makeup at all. Like Melly's, her skin looked
lighter than it had, although she'd always been lighter
than Melly. She no longer wore the little stud in the left
side of her nose.

I used to tease her when she looked this way; I'd always liked the hair, makeup, and shoes—what Vi had
called hyper-girly. Now I felt embarrassed by the memory, but I didn't feel much else.

"Melly warned me you might show up here."

Warned her? I didn't have any reaction to that. After
a second look, I realized she had dark circles under her
eyes.

"Ray, you look terrible."

"It was a long drive," I said.

"Do you want to come in? You can't stay, but . . ."

"I can't stay, no, but I would like to come in."

The first thing I noticed was how cool it was in the
air-conditioned apartment. The second thing was the

toys. There were several different types of dolls lying about: rag dolls, Barbies, baby dolls in diapers. A huge dollhouse stood in the corner. Beneath the toys, all the furniture was the same threadbare yard-sale stuff she'd had years before.

I glanced at the couch, remembering all the things we'd done there. Then a little girl came out of the kitchen, a half-eaten peanut butter and jelly sandwich in her hand. Her skin was much lighter than Vi's—nearly golden—and her hair was just a little too dark to be called blond.

"Mommy, can I have a hot dog?"

Vi bent down to her. "You already have your lunch, sweetie. Right in your hand."

"So?"

"Don't answer me that way," Vi said, a note of warning in her voice.

The girl stepped around her mom. "Hi, I'm Jasmin. Who are you?"

"My name is Ray. You're a very big girl, aren't you?" My voice sounded hollow and strange.

"Yes, I'm five."

Vi bent down to steer her toward the kitchen. "Jazzy, eat at the table, okay? If you're still hungry after your sandwich, you can have some raisins. If you behave."

Raisins were the only incentive she needed. She turned and ran into the kitchen.

Vi looked me in the eye. "She's not yours."

I didn't know what to say to that. "No?"

"No. And I know you can do the math, Ray, but it was a long time ago."

If I added nine months onto five years, it was pretty clear that she *could* have been mine. Vi had always been careful with me, saying she wanted to wait for kids, but apparently she'd had someone else on the side. Someone she was not so careful with. "Okay."

"That's it? *Okay?* Two years we were together, and

you're not going to shout at me? Call me a whore with my little girl in the next room to hear? You're not going to take a swing at me? You're not angry or hurt or nothing?"

"When did I ever take a swing at you?" But I knew that wasn't what she meant, exactly. Maybe I should have been angry or hurt—she was the woman I'd planned to spend the rest of my life with—but I was secretly relieved. If Vi had stuck with me, she might have been caught up in the society, too. She'd dodged a bullet when she dumped me. "It's been a long time for me, too."

She crossed her arms over her chest, a sure sign that I was pissing her off. "Fair enough. What did you come here for?"

"Melly came to me and told me she and Arne and everyone was in trouble, and that it's my fault." I almost said *I want to save them.* "I need to find out what's going on."

"Well, I don't know anything about it. I'm not a part of that anymore."

"Fair enough. Where can I find Arne?"

She scowled and looked around the little apartment. For a moment I thought she would throw me out without an answer. Instead, she said: "You could have called me, you know. You could have written me a letter."

"I thought you didn't want me to call" was the only answer I had. I didn't mention the three years I'd spent in jail without hearing a word from her, or that she'd specifically told me to go away.

"You could have tried anyway." When I didn't respond, she shrugged her bony shoulders and dismissed all of it. "He has a new Bigfoot Room. I don't know where it is, though. I have a straight job now, and I'm a goddamn citizen. You should ask Tyalee. I think he's still in touch with all of them."

"Where—"

"Ty has a straight job, too. He's a trainer at a gym now."

"Do you know the name of the place?"

"Nope. But it's across the street from that jungle restaurant. Remember that place you took me to, where everything came with sweet potatoes and mangoes?"

"I remember."

"His gym is in the shopping mall across the street. Don't ask me about the others. I have nothing to do with those people now."

"Thank you." There should have been more for me to say, but I wasn't sure how to come at it. "How's Mouse? I mean, how's Tommy?" Mouse was Violet's younger brother, and I'd forgotten that we weren't supposed to use his nickname anymore.

"Gone," she said. "He skipped town."

I knew her well enough to know she was holding something back, but if she didn't want to talk, I couldn't force her. I supposed I didn't have the right, not after five years, but I was still concerned about her. "Are you doing okay?"

"I'm fine," she said. "You're the one who looks like a hungry ghost."

As I went to the door, Jasmin came out of the kitchen. She watched me leave with a careful expression and, just before the door shut behind me, I heard her say very clearly: "That man scared me."

It was nearly noon, and L.A. felt like a blast furnace. I walked slowly to my car. There was no way I could avoid a ring of sweat under my arms and back, but I could keep it small by going slow.

Unfortunately, my Escort was a Seattle car. The wiper blades were brand new, but it didn't have air-conditioning.

It was a short two miles to the restaurant, and the gym was exactly where she'd said it'd be. The name was EVERY-THING ATHLETIC, and a sign in the glass door announced that it was the home of the founder of the original "Cardio-eira" classes. There were no windows, so I just pushed my way inside.

A sign at the front desk said that all of Justin Gage's Cardio-eira classes had been canceled until the end of the month. As I was reading it, a pale young woman with dyed-black hair at the front desk asked if she could help me. Her eyes were rimmed with red, and her face was puffy. She had been crying.

"What's wrong?" I asked, more out of surprise than concern.

"Oh, I'm sorry," she said. "I just . . . Are you a member?"

"I'm not. I've never been here before."

"Okay. You should know that the Cardio-eira classes have been canceled, and we don't know when they'll be starting again. If ever."

"What happened?" I asked, because she seemed to expect me to.

"Justin was assaulted last night. Right out in the parking lot. He's in the hospital, and we don't know . . . he's in bad shape."

"I'm very sorry," I said. "Did they catch the guy who did it?"

"No," she said. "They have no idea who did it."

A heavily muscled black woman stepped in to join the conversation. "We do have other trainers here." I noticed that her name tag read MANAGER along the bottom. "And while they may not have the same infomercial cachet that Justin has, they're really quite excellent."

"What about Tyalee Murphy? Is he here?"

The manager was carefully neutral. "He's finishing up with a member at the moment. Are you a friend of his?"

"I'd like to talk to him, if I could."

"Why don't you have a seat?"

She gestured toward an overstuffed little couch beside a rack of swim goggles. I sat. The manager typed something into a handheld device without looking at me. The weepy employee handed out keys and towels to people who entered, and collected them from people who left. I heard the sad tale of Justin Gage several more times over the course of five minutes. He was apparently a much-loved figure, and no one had any idea what had happened to him, and wasn't this city just awful?

Eventually, a tall black man rushed into the lobby and said: "You paged me?"

The manager pointed toward me, but I was already standing out of the chair. Ty turned toward me and looked me up and down. He didn't recognize me.

He looked different, too. He'd shaved his head and his chin and, while he'd always been addicted to the gym, now he was almost a parody of fitness. His uniform—a black polyester shirt with the gym logo over the heart—was tight enough to show off all the curves of his muscles.

"Ty, it's me. Ray Lilly."

"Ray!" He almost shouted. He stepped toward me, and for a moment I thought he'd hug me. Instead, he wrapped his gloved hand around mine and pumped, smiling broadly. "Good to see you again, man. Good to see you. What brings you back to town?"

I was almost sorry to answer him. "A little trouble, unfortunately." Melly had said I'd killed him, but he didn't look unhappy. I needed to find out what he knew, especially where the magic had come from, but I couldn't do it in a crowded gym.

"Hey, if there's anything I can do, name it." He glanced back through the door to the workout area beyond, as though he hadn't meant to promise so much. "I mean, things are a little busy *right now* . . ."

I wasn't sure what to make of him. We'd always gotten

along, but I didn't think we were close enough for him to be so glad to see me again. "Ty, I'm looking for the new Bigfoot Room."

"No problem! It's at a place called the Roasted Seal over on Kalibel Ave. Remember that Baja Fresh where Mouse puked in the toilet? Right there. I'm not part of that scene anymore, you understand. I still *know* the guys, but I don't do stuff with them anymore. Not much, anyway."

Everyone had grown up and turned into citizens. Except me. "Thanks."

"Listen, um . . ." He glanced back into the workout area. "I'm a little busy right now. We're short-handed today and I'm covering another dude's clients. Plus, I *really* need the money." He laughed a little at himself, and at the slightly desperate note in his voice. "But I'll catch up with you soon, okay? You're okay, aren't you? You look a little worn thin. Take care of yourself in this heat. And thank you, man. Thank you."

He checked his watch and rushed back inside. I headed out to my car.

I sat behind the wheel and closed my eyes. I'd taken Vi to the Baja Fresh many times and I could picture the intersection clearly, but I needed a moment to remember where that intersection was in relation to this one.

Then I remembered and I opened my eyes. Out of perverse curiosity, I angled the rearview mirror so I could see myself. Jasmin and Ty were right; I looked bad. I needed a week's worth of sleep, but I wasn't going to get it.

Ten minutes later, I was parking outside a church. The Baja Fresh was gone, but the other businesses—a sushi place, a dry cleaners, a shoe store—were the same. The Roasted Seal was just down the street. The front was made entirely of glass, but the view inside was blocked by an amateurish painting of a sad-faced seal perched on jagged rocks. The seal looked at me as if I'd ruined its day with hairspray and car exhaust. In the dust above the door, someone had traced BIGFOOT ROOM.

I pushed the door open and went inside.

It wasn't as dark as I expected. In fact, the place was almost nice. There were circular black tables seeded around the main floor with a surprising amount of space between them. Each table had a little light shining down on it. Ambiance.

There was a row of booths at the far end of the room and a bar against the wall behind me. Everything was polished black stone and hexagonal floor tiles. There was also sawdust on the floor, which didn't seem to fit.

I glanced at the bartender and realized he was watching me with a tight expression. Maybe I didn't look like the trustworthy type. He only had one other customer: a rumpled-looking guy who must have run out of shampoo a month before. He was also watching me, but at least he tried to be subtle about it.

I walked farther into the room and saw him.

Arne sat in a back booth just beside the fire exit. He had a cup of coffee and a smart phone in front of him. He wore a black button-down shirt and chinos, and his curly blond hair was cropped short. Near as I could tell, he was alone and he wasn't surprised to see me.

I started toward him. Lenard suddenly stepped out of a wait station that had been built like an alcove. Before I could react, he had his hands on me, shaking me roughly as he patted me down. I tensed up but held myself rigidly still. I wasn't here to fight.

Time had not been kind to Lenard. He had smoker's wrinkles around his eyes and mouth, and his whole body had gone pear-shaped. "Well, well, Raymundo," he said. "Imagine seeing you here." I looked down at the shaved stubble over his scalp; he was going bald in little patches near his forehead.

He finished by checking for an ankle holster. Of course

he didn't find anything. He stood and shrugged to Arne. I was cleared to go.

"Good to see you, Lenard," I said.

He looked at me sidelong as he backed into his alcove. "You look like shit, baby."

"I know it."

I walked by him. Arne was sitting in his booth with his arms folded across his chest. He wasn't even going to shake my hand.

"Arne," I said. "You don't look surprised to see me."

He smiled without a trace of good feeling. "You always had a pretty good sense of direction, Ray. How'd it take you two years to get from the gates of Chino to me?"

"I got on the wrong bus."

"The bus to Seattle. I heard. I've been following your name in the news. It's very interesting, all the scrapes you've gotten into. What happened in Washaway? You can tell me, buddy."

"Caramella said you were in trouble."

He didn't like that I'd changed the subject. "Do I have to remind you? You used to be smarter than that. I spent two hundred and fifty a month on you while you were inside. Every month, I sent a check to a sweet little lady in Boyle Heights so her son and his pals would babysit you."

And now he was challenging me. The funny thing was that I didn't feel like playing that game anymore. I'd seen too much to be afraid of Arne, and he knew it. "Arne—"

"Because I knew prison would *break* you." He was letting his anger show openly now. "I knew you couldn't handle the misery. You were never tough enough up here for that." He tapped his temple with his index finger.

I let him have his say. After he finished, we stared at

each other for a second. Then I said: "Caramella said it was my fault."

Arne laughed. There was something desperate and helpless in it. "Jesus. Ray. *Ray.*" He looked at the phone on the table, then slipped it into his pocket. "Okay. It's time. Come on, Ray. You're going to do a job for me."

CHAPTER TWO

Lenard came up behind me. "You're taking *him*?"

"He's here and Ty isn't," Arne said, "so yeah. I sure as hell can't take you. Stay here just in case. He only has to drive a car—as long as he doesn't point the grill at Seattle and take off, he'll be fine. Besides, if I show up with you, they'll probably make us mow the lawn or something."

Lenard laughed. "Fuck you. Those guys have Japs do their landscaping. They'd make me patch the roof."

"I'll be two hours at least. Probably three. Go into the kitchen while I'm gone and wash some dishes. Make yourself useful."

"Hey, I was born in this country, just like you. I'll do a day's work when I see you do one."

"Don't hold your breath," Arne said. "No shit, Lenard. Be careful."

"Always."

Arne turned to me. "Let's go for a drive, Ray. You owe me."

He started toward the front door, and I followed. I'd always trailed after him, going from one place to another. It felt natural to let him lead me around, and the feeling— that if I did what he wanted he'd eventually give me what I needed—was startlingly familiar.

And he was right. I did owe him.

We went into the street. Arne was more watchful than he'd ever been, and I wondered why. We walked to a Land Rover, and he circled it carefully before he got in

I sat in the passenger seat and aimed the air-conditioning vents at my face. He pulled into traffic.

"Where are we going?" I asked.

"You'll see."

"No. Seriously. Where?"

"You know what I always liked about you, Ray? Timing. You always had good timing. For instance, here you are today of all days. Remember Rufus Sceopeola?"

I did. He was a weight lifter and amateur boxer who'd tried to take over the Bigfoot Room some years ago. He was used to intimidating people with his size, but he wasn't as tough as he'd thought. "Of course."

"You remember how you took him out?"

"A couple punches."

Arne laughed at me as he swerved onto a freeway on-ramp. "You don't even realize you do it, do you? Anybody can throw a couple punches, Ray. You threw the right punches. Rufus thought he had defenses—I ran into him later, and he talked about you. He said he'd never been taken apart so fast, in the ring or out. He said you had a good eye. When I told him you were in jail, he dropped into a deep funk. I think he wanted to invite you to his gym."

None of this interested me, but I asked anyway. "Whatever happened to Rufus?"

Arne slapped his hand on my chest, then crumpled my shirt. I couldn't feel anything where the tattoos covered my skin, but I didn't like being searched anyway. "I'm not wearing a wire, and Lenard already checked me once."

He finished searching anyway. "The asshole is doing a stint at Corcoran. Some bastard took his gun and mailed it to the LAPD in a shoe box. Funny thing. They had his fingerprints on file, and the gun matched a shooting in North Hollywood from the year before. Attempted homicide." He glanced at me. "That's what I heard, anyway."

I didn't answer right away. For Arne, *asshole* had a

specific meaning. Assholes were criminals who liked to hurt people—or who tried to mess with his business—which was pretty much every criminal we met.

Arne hated assholes. He had always kept us low-key—we dressed like college students and did "safe" jobs—but there was always someone who heard about the money he was making and tried to muscle in. Arne hadn't blustered or threatened, but those guys generally never came back a second time. We'd always wondered what he'd done to drive them off. Had he been turning them in to the cops? The idea made me a little sick.

But I hadn't come here to talk about old times. "Arne—"

"No questions, Ray. You don't have the right."

"Yes, I do. I'm in this car. I came down here to find you, and I can help, maybe."

"Maybe," he said. And laughed to himself. "Do you know why I asked you to go to the bar with Mouse that night?"

That startled me. I'd forgotten that he'd asked me to watch Mouse's back. "No."

"Okay. Do you know why I paid that protection money for you while you were inside?"

"Because you thought I would try to make a deal for a lighter sentence."

"Ray, Ray. You're such a beautiful idiot. And now I'm glad you took off for Seattle. At first my feelings were hurt, but now I think it's better you weren't around when everything went to shit."

He wanted me to ask him about Mouse and the protection money, but I wouldn't give him the satisfaction. "How did things go to shit?"

"We got old," Arne said, sounding annoyed. "When you're stealing cars and getting high at sixteen, it's like an adventure. Hell, even when you're twenty-two you can tell yourself you're a hard and dangerous dude, out on the streets taking what you want. But as you get older, it changes. The life starts to go sour. Even I wanted a house, a wife, and a kid, Ray."

I noticed he said *wanted* instead of *want*. "Caramella said someone had killed you."

"Well, here I am," he said. His tone was difficult to read. I'd always found Arne hard to read; maybe that was why I'd always been willing to follow him.

"She said it was my fault." But I'd said this already, and it didn't pry the truth out of him this time, either. Arne stared into the harsh desert sunlight, staying with traffic. He never drove faster or slower, preferring to hide in the crowd.

We were heading east. Las Vegas? But he'd said three hours at most, so it couldn't be. "Where are we going?" I asked again.

"Ray, have you noticed that I'm not answering your fucking questions?"

I looked over at him. He was shorter than me and built heavier, but he was quick. And I knew he was tough, but I was a wooden man with the Twenty Palace Society. I'd faced scarier things than Arne Sadler. "That's why I have to keep asking."

He smiled at me then, and I truly couldn't read his intent. Then he turned his attention to the road. We drove in silence for a while.

For more than ten years, Arne had been the most important person in my life.

I met him in juvie, when I believed I was going to spend the rest of my life in prison. He was three years older, and while he wasn't the first person to tell me that the shooting wasn't my fault, he was the first one I believed even halfway. And he told me to come find him when the time was right.

I did. Arne taught me to steal cars, to fight, to live as a criminal without being an asshole, to tell victims from non-victims, and how to treat them both.

But I'd turned my back on him. When I walked out of Chino, I couldn't go back to that old life. I just couldn't. I wouldn't have chosen the society in its place, but that didn't change how I felt about being in L.A. again.

And yet, here I was. Worse, I had already gotten swept up into one of Arne's jobs.

I was seriously considering cutting him with my ghost knife—he'd tell me whatever I wanted to know after that, and he'd apologize for making me wait, too—when he suddenly sighed.

"Ray, how about this? You help me finish this job, and I'll help you with your thing. Okay? Melly was right. Things are in a bad way for me, and for Robbie, Summer, Lenard, even Bud, if that matters. But this job we're on is too important, and if I start talking about this shit, I'm going to lose my game face. You get me, don't you?"

"I get you."

He smiled at me. "Thanks, man."

We cruised the freeway eastward. The houses and strip malls gave way to warehouses and industrial, which eventually gave way to rough, low desert hills. The car was silent. Arne hated to play music when he was on a job.

The hum and movement of the car had lulled me to a dreamless sleep. I heard the tires roll over gravel and jolted awake. "This is it," Arne said. The sun was in my face; we'd turned around, and I'd slept through it.

Arne pulled off the highway onto a flat gravel path. There was a dry streambed directly beside us—if the car swerved a foot to the right, we'd tumble into it. Directly in front of us was a low hill, no different from any other low desert hill in Southern California. I honestly had no idea where we were, or even if that was the 15 back there. The gravel gave way to a dirt track as we drove northwest, following the trail around the hill.

At a wide part, nearly out of sight of the freeway, Arne

did a quick two-point turn. "Get behind the wheel and wait here for me," he said. "I have to pick up a ride from just around the bend there." That meant he was about to steal a car. I held out my hand. Arne smirked at me, then took out his key ring. He had dozens of keys, along with a little flashlight, carabiner, Swiss Army knife, and who knows what else. He detached the Land Rover key and gave it to me.

He got out of the car into the scorching desert heat. The Land Rover was pretty roomy, but I was too tall to climb over the shifter. I got out, too, and walked around the front. "Expecting trouble?" I asked.

"We'll see." I must have reacted to that, because he smirked again and said, "The place should be empty. It's a hell of an August out here. But if someone's home, it won't be a problem. Wait here and be ready to pull out fast, just in case." He turned his back to me and walked away. After a few steps, he glanced back. The expression on his face suggested I was not doing my job. I climbed into the car and shut the door.

It was cool inside. I rubbed the sleep out of my eyes. Considering the way I'd been sleeping, it shouldn't have been a surprise that I'd nodded off, but I felt pissed off and ashamed anyway. If something dangerous had happened—hell, if Arne had decided to shove me out of the car at freeway speeds—I couldn't have done much about it.

I watched Arne as he moved away. He didn't look tense, but maybe he'd gotten more relaxed when he stole cars in the years I'd been away. Maybe he'd lost his edge. Or maybe he didn't expect any trouble out here at all.

After forty yards or so, he disappeared around the side of the hill. Without really thinking about it, I opened the driver door as quietly as I could and slipped into the afternoon heat. I shut the door gently, hoping the sound of car tires on the nearby freeway would mask the noise.

Arne didn't peek back around the edge of the hill at me. I felt absurdly like a disobedient teenager as I followed after him, walking on the dry, hard ground to avoid the crunch of footsteps on gravel.

At the bend in the path, I crouched low behind an outcropping of rock and spied on Arne. He had stopped at the end of the gravel path and was fiddling with a padlock on a gate. The hill concealed a fenced area, and inside the fence was a prefab sheet-metal building.

The gate was on the western part of the property. The building faced south, with a peaked roof and a row of closed windows set high on the walls. The huge front doors slid open on runners.

The building was deep enough that a tractor trailer could have driven through the front and pulled all the way inside without turning, and it was three times wider than it was deep.

Whatever Arne was doing with the gates, he got them unlocked and pushed them both all the way open. Then he started toward the big front doors. He moved casually, but his head turned back and forth as he scanned the area, making sure he was alone.

He spent much less time fiddling with the latch at the two big front doors before sliding them open and walking into the darkness. Damn, it must have been like an oven in there. Sweat prickled on my back at the thought of it.

There was a sign on the open gate, but I was too far away to read it. If the society had brought me in as an investigator, I'd probably have a pair of binoculars, or maybe a camera with a telephoto lens that would not only let me read the sign but would record it for the benefit of the people who recovered my body.

But I was just a wooden man, and this was not even an official mission.

Still, I couldn't help but wonder what Arne was doing all the way out here in the middle of nowhere. When I'd been with him, we'd stolen cars and driven them to a dealer in Long Beach. He'd fake up papers for them and ship them out of the country for resale. It hadn't made any of us rich, but it had been better than throwing trash into the back of a municipal truck, or mopping floors, or clearing dirty plates from restaurant tables. At least, we'd thought so. Maybe we'd have made more money if Arne had been more willing to take risks, but he'd kept most of us out of jail.

A car rolled slowly out of the big double doors of the building below. I didn't recognize it for a moment. Then Arne got out to close the hangar doors.

A Bugatti. Arne was stealing a Bugatti.

They were worth a quarter million dollars, and they were completely out of the range of cars we usually handled. Hell, he'd told us not to steal Ferraris because they were too high-profile. But a Bugatti?

He shut the building. I'd seen enough. I slipped away from the outcropping of rock and hustled back to the car. It was several minutes before Arne pulled up alongside me.

I rolled the driver's window down, but he only gave me a thumbs-up as he crept by. I followed him back to the freeway, watching him drive at a crawl. The Bugatti scraped its bottom on the gravel, but it had made it in, and it made it out, too. Arne gunned the engine and zipped into traffic. I hurried after him. Together we headed west again toward the setting sun.

I made note of the first sign that told me how many miles we were from L.A. Figuring quickly, the sheet-metal building was almost as far as Bakersfield, but not quite. That meant the desert on the other side of the highway had to be the Mohave.

I hoped Arne would let me drive that damn Bugatti, just for a few miles.

That didn't happen, of course. Instead, we drove

through the last remaining hours of the evening rush and swung over to Bel Air.

Arne pulled up to a white marble mansion ringed by a black iron fence like a wall of spears. The lawn was as neat as a putting green, and the driveway was lined with white pillars. As L.A. mansions went, it was nearly moderate in its splendor. The place across the street was little more than a long driveway with a gate at the end. Nothing of the house itself was visible except for the Mediterranean-style roof.

I'd always liked driving through the rich neighborhoods of Los Angeles to look at the houses. There's a kind of sick fascination about it, like looking at a car accident.

Arne honked the Bugatti's horn and stepped out of the car. I rolled down his window as he came over. He dropped his fat roll of keys into a little pocket on the driver's-side door. "Wait out here, okay?" He was rubbing his hands together. "I'll be a couple minutes." He'd never been this excited on jobs in the old days, and I didn't like to see it now. I didn't trust it.

"What are we doing here?"

"Recovering stolen property," he answered. "Some guys have been operating out of the Valley, mostly, crowding my turf. I made a point of learning all their wheres, whens, and hows, and now they're going to make me a couple of bucks."

"That doesn't sound like your style."

"You've been gone a long time, baby. Things change."

He got back behind the wheel as the gate rolled open. He drove through the pillars while I shut off the engine and settled in.

I didn't stay settled in for long. After about three minutes, four men walked through the gate toward me. The one in the lead was a white man of about fifty, with a bull neck and a face like a plate of lumpy mashed potatoes. One of the men behind him looked familiar, but I couldn't place him. He was a black man, my height but bigger in the shoulders. His broad forehead was furrowed with a resentful scowl.

I rolled down the window a few inches. Potato Face crooked his finger at me, signaling me to come with him. There was nothing bullying or arrogant in his expression, but I didn't like being treated like a misbehaving first-grader.

"Why?" I asked.

Mr. Familiar didn't like my question. He tried to come around Potato Face at me, but the old man laid a hand on his chest to stop him, and Familiar stopped. Nice to know who was in charge.

Potato looked at me again. "Your buddy needs your help."

I didn't believe that for a second, but I opened the door and climbed out anyway, mainly because I could see they'd force me out if I didn't. There was no sense in scuffling in the street.

Potato walked toward the house, and I fell in behind him. Familiar walked on my left, and the two other guys, both bulky, pale-skinned, and as expressive as boulders, flanked me on my right and from behind.

"I recognize you," Familiar blurted out. "You're the Flower." Suddenly I recognized him right back. He was Wardell Shoops, a former wide receiver for the Chiefs. He'd been drafted out of UCLA and, during bye week of his rookie year, he'd flown home to have dinner with his mother and to beat the hell out of his business manager, who'd lost half his money on a Louisiana alligator farm. He'd pleaded guilty and did a year in Chino while I was there.

I looked at him and at his aggressive smile. He looked at me like I was an apple about to be plucked and eaten. I didn't like that look. "I remember the man you used to be," I said. "What happened to that guy? He was something else."

Wardell's smile vanished. He cursed and stepped toward me, but Potato stopped him with one backward glance. We all walked up the driveway while the gate rolled closed behind us.

The inside of the house was bright with natural light. Nearly everything was white—the carpet, the chairs, even the narrow hall tables with white princess telephones. White picture frames with no pictures hung on the walls. The ceiling was made of squares of glass with black framework in between.

Potato led us into a sunken living room at the back of the building. Arne was there, standing by a pair of French doors, with two more heavyset creeps next to him. Through the doors, I could see a broad lawn with a flower garden along one side and a little Jacuzzi on the other. Two men were on their hands and knees digging in the garden, but I couldn't see them well enough to tell if they were Japanese, Mexican, or something else.

"Come on," a man said impatiently. "There's no reason to be afraid."

Potato led me down into the room, and there, seated on an overstuffed couch in the corner, was the man who thought I was frightened of him. He was narrow-shouldered and as thin as a boy, and just about as tall, too. His face was weathered by sun, but his two-hundred-dollar haircut and open-necked linen shirt suggested he'd gotten his tan in a deck chair. His blue eyes were watery, and his thin hair was the color of sand. A tall, bony Asian woman in a purple bikini lounged on a couch beside him, a magazine in her hand.

Potato jerked a thumb back at me. "This is him."

Linen Shirt was about to speak when Wardell said: "I know him. His last name is Daffodil or something. Something flowery. He was in Chino a couple years back, and someone on the outside had to pay for his protection, 'cause he couldn't do it himself."

Linen waited for Wardell to finish. Everyone else was silent, and I had the impression that Wardell had stepped on his boss's line, and not for the first time. Then he glanced at me. "What are you doing here, Mr. Daffodil?"

Arne spoke up. "I needed someone to drive my car."

"I wasn't asking you," Linen said, his voice sharp. He turned away from me. "Well? Is this him?"

The Asian woman regarded me with a sleepy, careless self-confidence. Her skin was dark and her face broad and beautiful. "Nope," she said. She took a swizzle stick off the table beside her and began moving it through her hair as though she was stirring her scalp. "I told you it was a spic."

Linen sighed. "Don't say *spic*. It's low-class." She shrugged and went back to reading.

"I told you before," Arne said, "I didn't steal your car. I thought I knew who'd done it, and I was right. I took a real risk retrieving it for you."

Another one of the interchangeable beefheads came into the room. He held up a DVD inside a paper sleeve. "It was right where you left it."

Linen opened a cabinet, revealing a little screen. The beefhead loaded the disc and pressed PLAY.

Swizzle Stick found the energy to stand and look at the screen. We all watched the video of her and Linen naked and grunting on a white bed in a white room— probably one right upstairs. No one seemed the least bit embarrassed or awkward.

"I look hot," Swizzle said.

Linen sighed again and turned the show off. "Did you see this?" he asked Arne.

"No, I didn't." Arne sounded very casual.

Linen turned toward me. "You?"

"No, but maybe if you play more, I'll recognize it."

Arne laughed suddenly. It felt so good to have him smile at me that I almost laughed with him. We had been friends once.

Linen turned to Potato Face. "Make sure."

Wardell grabbed my arms and held me while one of the other men patted me down. Arne got the same treatment. Potato stood watch over us. They found my ghost knife and cellphone, but no one objected when I took them back. No one found any discs, so Potato took Arne's satchel and dumped it out onto the table.

"Hey!" Arne shouted. I heard the dangerous tone in his voice, but no one else seemed to care.

They picked through his things, bending them and ripping the pockets of his bag. Linen opened the French doors, and one of the men pitched Arne's laptop into the Jacuzzi.

Arne glowered at them.

Linen took a checkbook from a little drawer, filled out a check, and gave it to Arne. I noticed a wedding ring on his tanned finger. Swizzle Stick didn't have one.

Arne glanced at the check. "What's this?"

"That's your payment," Linen said. He sounded bored with us, as though we'd stayed too long at his party.

"Half the price," Arne said. "That was the deal. I'd get the car back for you, and you would pay me half what it cost."

"But did you get that in writing? That disc was valuable; the car . . . meh. The Bugatti is insured. My marriage isn't. That check will buy two laptops to replace the one that just took a swim, with a little left over for a lazy day's work."

"Are you sure you want to do this?" Arne asked, his voice quiet. "Are you sure you want to break a deal with me?"

Linen turned to Potato. "He sounds feisty."

Wardell immediately sank a hard right into my midsection, while one of the other men did the same to Arne. It didn't hurt me; I could barely feel the pressure of it through the protective tattoos Annalise had put on me.

I threw a quick uppercut at Wardell, but one of the other men tangled my arm with one of his punches, blunting the force.

I caught another painless shot in the guts, then the men on either side of me drove their knees into the outside of my thighs. The pain was intense, and I fell onto the cool tile floor. The beating continued.

I didn't have to take this shit. My ghost knife was in my pocket. All I had to do was cut one of these bruisers with the edge of my spell to take them out of the fight. In less than a minute, I could take control of this room and everyone in it.

I took the beating anyway. I wasn't going to use a spell in front of Linen; he might decide to search for magic of his own, and I was sick of the messes that came of that.

A punch grazed the edge of my chin—nothing serious, just a scrape—and Potato stepped in and backed Wardell off. "Not the face," he said. "You know better."

That was the end of the beating. Arne rolled onto his side, cursing, but he didn't look too bad. Linen picked the check up and stuffed it into Arne's shirt pocket. "No need to be feisty anymore, right? Because now you know how lucky you are. Be glad our deal is the only thing I'm breaking. Get out, and tell your car-stealing buddy he was smart to stay away from me."

The guards lifted us to our feet. One of them swept Arne's things into his satchel, being careful to get everything but not being careful in any other way, then hung it around Arne's neck like a gold medal. We were hustled out of the house and down to the street. I could hear Wardell behind me, laughing.

Once released, Arne stripped the satchel off his neck

and collapsed onto his hands and knees. He puked onto the street. There was no red in it. I picked up his satchel. A few things had fallen out when he'd dropped it, and I examined each as I put them back, hoping I'd find something useful.

"What's this?" Wardell said. He was facing a wall of bodies. Potato Face and his men were barring Wardell from returning to the house. One of the men held out a tan sports jacket for Wardell to take, but he wouldn't accept it.

"You have the wrong temperament for this work," Potato said. "You think this is about you. It ain't. You're fired. Don't let me see you again, or you won't be happy about it."

Wardell stared at them, simmering. I hadn't known him personally in Chino, but everyone had known who he was: a pro athlete who'd done a TV commercial or two. He was used to being the big man in the room, and he didn't seem to be adjusting to his new life all that well.

"Come on, Arne," I said, helping him up. He staggered as he went toward the driver's door, but I wanted him to move faster. "Let's get out of here and find a place we can talk."

"I don't think they broke anything," Arne said. "Jesus, can you believe that guy called me a liar?"

I glanced back. Wardell was still staring at Potato. Potato stared back. Beefy guy still held his arm extended toward Wardell, jacket in hand. Finally, he got tired of waiting for Wardell to take it, so he tossed it. Wardell was forced to catch it against his chest or let it fall into the street. Potato and his men went back through the gate and shut it with a sharp *clang*.

Arne made his key chain chirp and popped the locks on his car. Wardell turned his head toward the sound. Shit.

Arne got behind the wheel. "I don't have time to talk to you right now, Ray."

"Arne, no. This is too important—"

"No." Arne glanced through the windshield at Wardell, who was stalking toward us. "After the job, remember? The job isn't over until I get paid. Besides, your boyfriend wants to talk to you."

"Hey!" Wardell shouted. "Flower!"

Damn. I hated being called that.

Arne started his car. He gave me a crooked smile. "Take care of this, would you, Ray? I have work to do."

Wardell grabbed my shirt and shoved me against Arne's car. I tipped back over the hood, my feet coming off the ground. Christ, he was strong.

I drew my ghost knife from my back pocket.

Arne's car began to back down the street, and I slid along the hood of the car until I dropped backward. I heard my shirt tear just a little in Wardell's grip.

"You just cost me a job, Flower. A good job that paid okay. There ain't a lot of places a guy like me can get paid to have my fun. So now you're going to hire me."

Arne backed away down the street. I saw him grimace as he twisted to look through the back window, but he didn't glance at me at all.

"Don't you look at him," Wardell said. "You look at me now. Just like you paid those barrio motherfuckers to watch your back in Chino, you're going to pay me to watch your back out here."

"I wouldn't pay you to watch a pot of chili," I said, and slid the ghost knife through his ribs.

According to the spell book I'd cast it from, the ghost knife could cut "ghosts, magic, and dead things." Its edge could split a steel door, destroy the sigils that made spells work, and on living people, it could cut their "ghosts."

Whatever that meant. I'd never seen an actual ghost, but trial and error had taught me that the ghost knife took away a person's anger and hostility, turning them docile and apologetic but without doing them any physical harm. At least, no harm I could see.

Wardell was no exception. He gasped as the spell passed through him and his eyes went wide like deer eyes. He lifted me to my feet—the spell didn't take his strength away. "I'm sorry," he said. "I shouldn't have said those things."

"You're right. You shouldn't have." Arne was long gone. I sighed and turned to Wardell. "Where's your car?"

He led me to it. It was just around the corner, parked beneath an old oak. It was an older Nissan Pathfinder, and it had probably been his run-around-town vehicle before he went inside. He asked me if I wanted to drive.

I did. Traffic was heavy on the way back to the Bigfoot Room. Wardell talked most of the way, mostly about what he was doing now that he was outside and people we'd known inside. An unsurprising number of them had gotten themselves out and gotten themselves thrown right back in again. Wardell was of the opinion that that would happen to him soon, too.

He also told me that Linen's real name was Steve Francois, and that he'd inherited his money from some South American paper mills and banks in Texas. Mostly banks. Steve liked having badasses around, and Wardell was an ex-con and ex-NFL, so he was hired.

I couldn't even begin to guess why Arne was running errands for a guy like Francois.

I liked Wardell better when he wasn't desperate to be alpha male, but not much better. Even with his aggression cut out of him, he was still arrogant enough to think he should dominate the conversation. I was tempted to make him turn himself in to the cops until he said he had a wife at home who was sticking by him—so far. "She wants me to go to anger-management classes," he said.

"Why haven't you?"

"I didn't want to," he answered. "I'm sorry about the buttons on your shirt. Do you want me to ask her to sew them back on? She would, I think."

I looked down. He had popped off a button from my shirt, second from my top. "No, thanks," I said, being polite because of the ghost knife, and I didn't feel like taking anything else from him. "Do you beat on her?"

"No! I would never hit my lady." He sounded honestly surprised that I'd asked.

"Good. You should take her advice." I remembered waking from nightmares in the middle of the night. "If your shit isn't under control, you should get help."

I pulled up to the curb at a corner near the Bigfoot Room and climbed out. My legs and back were getting stiff and achy from sitting so long. I was glad Potato and his men had landed most of their punches on my chest and stomach, where I was protected. My car was still where I had left it.

"Thanks for the ride," I said.

Wardell climbed into the driver's seat. He was a big guy, but he was limber enough to make it without knocking the stick shift out of PARK.

"Thank you," Wardell said. I shut the door. He hit the turn signal and pulled into traffic.

I watched him go, wondering what I could do if my own stress got so bad I lost control of it. Not therapy; as soon as I talked about predators, the therapist would think I was delusional. And if the therapist found out about the people I'd killed . . .

It didn't matter. None of it mattered.

Wardell disappeared into traffic, so I crossed the street and entered the Roasted Seal. The sawdust was still on the floor and the rumpled guy was still sitting at the bar, a beer and a cup of coffee beside him.

And Arne was sitting in the same booth. He was tapping at a different laptop.

I moved toward him, holding out my hand to block Lenard as I came around the wait station. "Are you going to pat me down again?"

Lenard slammed a little locker door shut and spun the combination lock. Then he glanced at Arne. Arne shrugged. Lenard backed toward the booth, and his body language told me not to approach.

"I hope," Arne said, "you're not pissed that I took off without telling you what's what or caring one shit what was going on with you."

"Of course not. What kind of petty bastard do you think I am?" And it was true. I wasn't pissed. In fact, I'd expected him to abandon me somewhere—that's why I'd held out my hand for the Land Rover keys when Arne asked me to drive it. It's one thing to be stranded in Bel Air and another to be stranded in the middle of the desert. "Bought yourself a replacement already?"

"Oh, no. This is my real computer. The other was the one I take on jobs, just in case."

"Arne, what happened to Melly? What happened to you?"

"Just a minute. Busy." He turned back to the computer and started typing.

"Busy with what?" My voice sounded sharper than I'd intended. I wanted to say more, but everything I could think of sounded ridiculous.

"Destroying a man's life," he said. "Ray, what do you know about porn on the Internet?"

"There's porn on the Internet?"

Arne laughed loudly, and I could feel some of the tension going out of the room. I needed him on my side, but somehow I'd lost the knack of winning people over.

"My favorite is where people make their own and put it up online. It's crazy popular, even if most of the content is videos some dude made with a hooker or revenge postings by the recently dumped. Sometimes it's even weirder. Check it out."

He turned the laptop toward me. A video was playing, and it took me a moment to realize it was the same video I'd seen in Francois's house. Except that someone had added a timer to it.

"Why is there a . . ." Then I saw why. By the time the counter reached 27, Francois had finished.

"See, Francois has a wife somewhere—Park Avenue or something—and she is a litigation powerhouse. Her whole clan is. Once word starts to spread about this video, he's going to have a very expensive divorce on his hands. Plus the twenty-seven-second thing."

He turned the laptop toward himself again. There was a jangle of keys, and I noticed that his big key ring was hanging off the side of the machine. Arne pulled at it, unplugging a memory stick, and pocketed it. He must have found the DVD in the Bugatti right away, copied the file during the drive back to the city, and put the disc back.

But that was his deal. I had other problems.

"Arne, Melly said you were dead. She said you'd been killed and it was my fault."

Arne gave me a steady look. This was it. He was about to break down and give me what I needed. "Well, he was your buddy, wasn't he?"

I didn't have any buddies. Not anymore. "Who?"

"Wally King."

Oh, God. Wally Fucking King.

CHAPTER THREE

LENARD touched ARNE's shoulder as though he'd just seen something they'd both been waiting for. "Hold that thought," Arne said.

I heard a foot scuffle behind me. Arne glanced at the floor behind me. I turned, but there was no one there.

A heavy metal canister clanged near my feet and let out a wet hiss. A plume of tear gas billowed around my legs.

I turned to shout a warning to Arne, but he was no longer in his booth. I shut my mouth and clamped my hand over my nose before I caught a whiff, then soccer-kicked it toward the front door. Damn, it was hot already—I could feel the heat of it against my ankle. It struck something on the floor I couldn't see and skittered sideways toward Rumpled Guy.

I shut my eyes just as the stinging started. Something moved very close to me, and the gunfire started.

I dropped flat onto the floor. The tattoos on my chest and the outside of my forearms are bulletproof thanks to a spell called the closed way, but my head, back, legs, and sides were completely exposed. The guns sounded very loud and very close, but nothing hit me.

I crawled blindly toward the fire exit. Sawdust stuck to my skin, and my chest felt tight. I hadn't caught a good breath, and my oxygen was running out. Fortunately, the gunfire had already stopped. It takes very little time to empty a magazine.

I heard the sounds of clips being ejected from pistols and slammed back in. There were two gunmen, at least, and now I was sure they were close. Someone was hacking and choking on the gas, but it didn't sound like anyone near me. Were the gunmen wearing masks?

I was sure they could see me—the gas couldn't have been that thick—and I expected a bullet in the back. I hoped they'd have the decency to shoot at my head; at least it would be quick.

But I didn't stop crawling, and the bullet never came. I finally made it to the wall and, reaching to my right, found the doorway. Arne was right about my sense of direction. The door was open, but I was barely across the threshold when it swung shut, slamming against my head and making me gasp.

I crawled into the alley, gagging on the wisp of tear gas I'd inhaled. I didn't know if it was heavier than air, but I wanted to be on my feet; I stood and stumbled against a dumpster. Time to live dangerously; I opened my eyes.

Immediately, they started to burn. Tears flooded my cheeks, and I couldn't stop coughing.

Arne and Lenard weren't there, but Rumpled stumbled through the door just behind me. He was coughing so hard I thought he'd convulse.

My eyes were burning stronger now, as though the tears were washing the chemicals into my eyes rather than out, but he had it worse. He kept saying: "Ah, God! God!" between retches.

We were helpless. If the shooters inside the bar came out here, they could have put bullets into us without breaking stride. Of course, they could have done that inside, too.

I blinked through my tears and saw a short, slender figure knock Rumpled to the ground. A second, larger figure stepped up close to me. "Well, well," he drawled. "If it ain't old Ray Lilly himself. Howsdoin', Raymond?"

"Bud?" I asked, suddenly recognizing his voice. "Someone just tried to kill Arne. I didn't see who, though. Is he around?"

"I don't see Arne," Bud answered. "He musta lit out." Again.

I could almost hear a smile in Bud's voice. I blinked to clear my vision, and it worked a little. The slender figure moved toward us. "He's gone," she said. "We should go, too." That was Summer, another member of Arne's crew.

Bud and Summer each grabbed one of my sleeves and steered me down the alley toward the sidewalk. I let them. While I could see—barely—I couldn't see well enough to drive. And my tears were still flowing, my nose was running, and I was still trying to blink the pain away. If the cops found me here, they'd snatch me right off the street.

I heard Bud reassure a passing pedestrian that I'd just had my heart broken. I didn't know where we were going. "Someone tried to kill Arne. We have to look for him."

"Oh, we'll look for him, all right," Bud said.

Something was wrong. Bud and Summer were part of Arne's crew, just like Lenard, and just like I used to be, and right now they were being too casual.

A bad feeling came over me. I turned toward Summer. She'd let her hair grow out so that it almost reached her shoulders. Her face was broad and tanned, her pale blue eyes sullen in the heat. Her sleeveless jogging shirt was damp with sweat and hung untucked over a pair of shorts with an elastic waistband. Had she been one of the shooters? She could certainly conceal a gun at her back, but a gas mask, too? I didn't believe it.

Bud was the same. He had a loose T-shirt over belted shorts, and while he'd cut off his mullet, he still wore that stupid bolo tie. He could have hidden a gun at the small of his back—or maybe under his growing beer belly—but not a gas mask.

Arne had taught them better than to dump something like that right at the scene of the crime, so I figured they weren't the shooters. Of course, they could have been lookouts or backup. "Where are we going?" I asked.

"Tear gas is toxic," Summer said. "There's a Ralphs up the street. We'll pick up some stuff that will help there."

"At a supermarket?" I asked. "How do you know—" A fit of coughing cut off the rest of my question, and a rolling drop of sweat suddenly blinded my right eye.

"Are you seriously asking me how I know what to do about tear gas?" I'd forgotten that Summer's hippie parents—her hated, hated parents—had marched in dozens of street protests over the years, and Summer herself had probably been dosed with the stuff several times.

"Then we'll get out of here," Bud added. "Robbie is going to want to talk to you."

Robbie was Arne's second-in-command, and we had always gotten along well—better, in fact, than I'd gotten along with anyone. I wanted to talk to him, too.

But first I needed to get away from Bud and Summer. Arne had said Wally King's name, and that meant bad things were happening. He was the reason I was mixed up with the Twenty Palace Society. The spell book he'd stolen, the predators he'd summoned, and the deaths he'd caused almost two years before had ruined my life.

I needed to call the society, and I needed to do it in private. Those bastards take their secrecy seriously. And I needed my boss. I needed Annalise. I didn't want to face Wally King without her again.

"We're parked just up here in the lot," Bud said as we turned a corner. I blinked my eyes clear again and saw a field of colored metal gleaming in the sun. They led me to a white pickup and let me sit on the gate.

Summer stepped away from me. "Bud, go inside and get what he needs."

"You sure?" he asked, as though nervous about leaving her with me.

"Go." She sounded irritated. He went.

I squinted in her direction. I wanted privacy to make my call, but she didn't seem ready to give it to me. "I'm glad you and Bud are still together," I said.

"We're married now," she answered, her voice flat.

"That's great." There was nowhere for the conversation to go after that, so it just sat there. Now that we had stopped moving, my eyes began to sting even more. I raised my hands to rub them but thought better of it. "I need to make a call," I said. "In private."

She didn't move. "To who?"

"Nobody you know." Since she wasn't moving away, I hopped off the gate and walked along the side of the truck to the wall. Then I started toward the sidewalk.

She trailed behind me.

"Wait by the truck, Summer," I said. "I'm not kidding. This is a private call."

"You're calling the cops, aren't you?"

Out of reflex, I cursed at her. If that's who she thought I was now, she couldn't be trusted. It was the same as saying *We are enemies*.

My reaction must have mollified her a little. She sulkily stepped back, but not because she was afraid of me. I'd never known her to be afraid of anyone.

A young mother came toward me, navigating her baby stroller through the narrow space between the whitewashed wall and parked cars. I stepped around her, then looked toward the truck.

Summer wasn't there. I glanced around the lot and inside the truck. Nothing. I dropped to the ground and peered under the cars. Nothing, again. She'd vanished.

I walked to the sidewalk, darting through a line of

cars pulling in from the street. The store was too far for her to have gone inside, but where was she? I didn't like that she seemed to have blinked out of existence within ten feet of me. Just like Caramella. Had she transported herself far away? Where?

Even now, as evening was coming on, the traffic noise was ever present. I stepped into a bus shelter for some relative quiet and took out my phone. It had speed-dial buttons, but none had the number I needed. That was only in my memory.

I was feeling jumpy as I dialed. Something was wrong, but I couldn't figure out what. The phone picked up after four rings.

"Hello? This is Mariana." She had an accent I couldn't place, but I was never good with accents.

"This is Ray Lilly. I need my boss."

"Mr. Lilly, this isn't how you are supposed to make this request. What is the situation?"

I knew I was breaking the rules, but my instincts were ringing like fire alarms, and I couldn't ignore them. "I can't go into it on the phone."

"Mr. Lilly," she said in a tone that was almost scolding, "you aren't calling from an unsecure location, I hope."

"Considering what I've been seeing here, I don't think a secure location is possible."

"I understand." She had dropped the scolding tone. "The phone GPS has given me your location. Return to that location at this time each day for the next four days." I glanced at my watch. It was just after seven-thirty. "You will be met."

She hung up and so did I. There was a trash receptacle right next to me, but I was supposed to ditch the phone where no one would notice. And while I couldn't see anyone nearby . . .

I swept my right arm away from me and struck something invisible a foot from my elbow. It was sticky, just like Caramella's slap. I heard a hiss and the scuffle of shoes on concrete.

I grabbed the invisible shape, shoving it toward the bench and knocking it off balance. It suddenly darkened, becoming an outline with a misty blackness inside, just like the Empty Spaces.

Damn. That's exactly what it was. I was looking into the Empty Spaces.

I would have freaked out if I'd had the time, but the vision vanished suddenly, and I was holding Summer by the shoulders. She was staring at me with wild, dangerous eyes. "Let go of me, Ray," she said, and grabbed my wrist with her bare hand. My skin began to itch and burn under her grip.

I pulled her to her feet and spun her around. She tried to resist—and she was strong—but she wasn't as strong as me. I yanked a pistol out of the back of her waistband, then patted the pockets of her gym shorts. They were empty.

The urge to run was unbearable, but I knew it would be useless. They still had Bud's truck. "Keep away, Summer." My breath was coming in gasps. I barely recognized my own voice. "Don't make a bigger mistake than you already have."

I backed toward the lot, holding the gun on her. My mind was racing. There were no other pedestrians nearby, but someone in a passing car might see me and call the cops. For a moment I tried to imagine what I would say if a patrol car suddenly pulled up to the curb, but I couldn't focus on it.

Summer stood in the bus shelter with her arms at her sides, watching me. I bolted back into the lot.

Bud was standing beside his pickup, scanning the lot for us. He had a little shopping bag in his hand. I ran toward him. Once he spotted me, he patted the truck bed.

"Back here, Ray. You're giving off fumes. We'll get you showered and changed as soon as we can, but first"—he held up the shopping bag—"we'll mix these and—"

I came up next to him, and he saw the gun in my hand. "Give me the keys, Bud."

His good-ole-boy grin twisted with disappointment. "I thought you were out of the car-stealing business."

"Keep back. Don't touch me. Give me the keys. I'll drop your truck within a few blocks of the Bigfoot Room, but I'm not going anywhere with you. And don't touch me. Get it? Don't touch me! I'm not going anywhere with you!"

"Don't get all wigged out, Ray. All right? Don't. Here's the stuff you need for your skin." He tossed the grocery bag onto the passenger seat. "Just mix it one to one. And don't scratch my truck." He set his keys on the hood.

While he backed away, I picked them up. I wondered where Summer was—I should have made her come with me. I should have made her stay visible. I imagined her behind me, knife in hand. I imagined the point digging into the back of my neck or into my kidneys, and my skin prickled all over. My breath rushed in and out of me, and even though everything was different I felt that same urge to scream that I'd felt that last night in Washaway, just before the killing started. My finger tightened on the trigger.

No. No, I wasn't going to shoot Bud. I was in control of myself. I was in control.

I climbed into the truck. Bud stood with his hands at his sides. If he'd been one of the shooters inside the Bigfoot Room, and I was ready to believe he was, he had a gun on him that I'd forgotten to take. I was screwing up, and that was going to get me killed. Either that, or I was going to have to kill him. I wasn't ready for that. I started the engine and lurched out of the spot.

In a mild voice, Bud said: "My apartment keys are on that ring, you know."

"Within a few blocks," I told him, fighting the urge to *flee flee flee*. "You fucked up, Bud."

"Robbie will still want to talk to you."

"And I want to talk to him," I said, and raced out of the lot. Summer stood by the entrance, watching me impassively. She was still there when I drove down the street.

I forced myself to take long, slow breaths. I looked down at my wrist. My skin had turned red and gotten inflamed where Summer's little hand had touched me.

An idea occurred to me, and I lifted my arm toward the rearview mirror when I stopped at the next stoplight. My shirt was a henley, three buttons at the neck, no collar, and sleeves that reached just past my elbow. Both Summer and Bud had grabbed my arm where the sleeve covered it, but I couldn't see any effect on my clothes. They weren't sticky, discolored, or slowly dissolving.

The light turned green and I drove on. Could Bud turn invisible? I hadn't seen him do it, and I hadn't touched his skin, but something about the way he'd acted—as though he'd expected my reaction, just not so soon— made me think he could.

And Caramella. I thought she'd transported herself out of my room after that last, aborted slap, but maybe she'd hung around for a while, watching me sleep.

The idea gave me the shivers, and I almost blew through the next red light. Instead, I forced myself to calm down. Potato Face and his men hadn't triggered this kind of response when they'd swarmed around me, but why should they? They were men. All they could do was kill me.

When the light changed, I parked the truck. I was only a block and a half away from the Bigfoot Room, and that was close enough. I didn't like the idea of driving Bud's truck when another drop of sweat could blind me.

I wiped my fingerprints off Summer's gun. There was no reason to—the twisted-path spell on my chest altered the physical evidence I left behind, like fingerprints and DNA, making it impossible to pin me to a crime scene. It still felt good. Then I stuffed the weapon under the seat.

I opened the glove compartment. Sure enough, there was Summer's purse. I flipped through it. There was no makeup—the only thing she had in common with her mother was her refusal to wear it. There was an address book and a billfold with a little cash inside. I was tempted to take the money to teach her a lesson about fooling around with magic, but I didn't. Class hadn't started yet.

I did take her address book. I flipped to the *H* and read the entry for Caramella Harris. She lived in Silver Lake.

There was only one more thing to do. I still had the cellphone the society had given me. If I turned it on and stuffed it into the back of the seat, the society would be able to locate them the same way they'd located me.

I didn't do it. The risk that Bud or Robbie or someone else in the crew would find it and press REDIAL may have been slim, but I still wasn't going to take the chance. Secrecy came first. I pocketed it, tossed the keys under the front seat, and picked up the grocery bag. Then I climbed out, leaving the driver's window rolled down.

I walked back to the church and my car. There were police cars with flashing lights parked in front of the bar, and plenty of yellow tape on the sidewalk. I stopped at the corner to gawk a little; it would have looked suspicious if I hadn't. A patrol cop looked at me, then looked away, uninterested.

I went to my car and drove away before a cop came close enough to smell the tear gas.

Summer and Caramella could turn invisible. Probably Bud could, too. I tried to figure who else should be on that list, but I didn't know enough yet. I was sure Arne knew about it, even if he couldn't vanish himself. I suddenly understood why there was sawdust on the floor of the Bigfoot Room.

But that wasn't the worst of it. The worst part was the way Summer had looked when she'd dropped her invisibility—she'd looked like a doorway into the Empty Spaces. Nearly two years earlier, when I'd first come face-to-face with predators, magic, the Twenty Palace Society, and all the rest, I'd cast a spell that let me look into the Empty Spaces.

That had only been a peek, though. I'd learned enough to scare the hell out of myself, but not much more. And it wasn't like the society was going to explain things to me; they didn't exactly offer night classes.

What little I understood about the Empty Spaces was this: it surrounds the world we live on and is, at the same time, beside it. It's a void of mist and darkness, and *creatures* live there.

The society calls them predators, but they aren't like the animals you find here on the earth. Coming from this other, alternate space, they have their own physics and their own biology. Some are living wheels of fire, some swarms of lights, some massive serpents in which every scale is the face of one of its meals, some schools of moving, singing boulders. When they come to our world, they are "only partly real," as my boss once explained. They're creatures of magic, and can be used to do all sorts of strange and dangerous things . . . if the summoner can control them.

So they're out there in that vast expanse, right beside us but unable to find us. And they're hungry. One of them, allowed to run loose on our planet, would feed and feed and feed, possibly calling more of its kind, until there was nothing left but barren rock.

The entire reason the Twenty Palace Society existed,

as far as I could tell, was to search out and destroy the summoning magic that called predators to our world, along with anyone who used that magic. They also kill predators when they find them.

But a human taking on a predator is like a field mouse trying to kill a barn owl. That's why the society uses magic of its own. They don't call predators—summoning magic is a killing offense, even for them—but as far as I could tell, everything else was fair game. The spells tattooed on my body and the ghost knife in my pocket were prime examples of that.

A car behind me honked, and I realized I'd been sitting at a stop sign for nearly a minute, lost in thought. I pulled through the intersection, blinking my eyes clear.

And although it had been nearly two years, I'd instantly recognized the Empty Spaces when Summer had dropped her invisibility. If she'd gotten this ability through non-summoning magic like mine, that would be bad enough. The society would want to check her out and hunt down the spell book she'd used. And . . . damn, I hated to think it, but they would probably kill her just to be safe.

When people learned magic was real they often became obsessed with the power it gave them, and they did dangerous things to get it, like summon predators they couldn't control. I'd seen it more than once, and it was why I was so alarmed when Arne had said Wally King's name. Wally hadn't just summoned predators; he'd killed people to steal spells from them.

But were Caramella and Summer his accomplices or his victims?

In the end, that might not even matter. That vision of the Empty Spaces suggested that Summer got her power from a predator. Maybe it was inside her body like a parasite, maybe nearby, but it was connected to her somehow. I'd seen both. Maybe she didn't know how dangerous it was, or even that it was there.

That predator, if that's what it was, had to be destroyed. The big question was: could I destroy it, whatever it was, without killing my friends?

I kept driving west and pulled into the second park I saw. The grass was dead brown, but what did that matter to me? I carried the Ralphs grocery bag to a bench beneath a tree. There were two bottles inside: a liter bottle of water and a little blue bottle of liquid Maalox. The first thing I did was pour water over my wrist, washing away whatever acids Summer had left there. It didn't stop hurting, but it stopped getting worse.

Then I guzzled some of the water. The heat was oppressive, and the sweat on my face made my eyes sting.

Once the water bottle had as much fluid as the Maalox did, I poured the antacid in and shook it up. It worked surprisingly well, and soon I'd rinsed off my face and hands completely.

I stood. It wasn't enough. The faint, choking stink of tear gas still clung to my clothes, and my skin was beginning to crawl.

I used a clean shirt from my jump bag to wipe the drying Maalox from my face. The empty bottles went back into the grocery bag along with the cellphone. I wrapped them up and dumped them into the trash.

I drove back toward the freeway until I came to a Best Western half a block from an exit. The vacancy sign was lit.

My shirt still stank, but the clerk didn't care. I don't think she cared about anything except her air-conditioning. I rented a room on the second floor and trudged upstairs.

The room was clean and plain. I stood by the bed with the TV remote in my hand for a full two minutes and tried to convince myself to shower. The temptation to sit in front of the tube in a trance state was so strong it was like a death wish. I closed my eyes and tried to imagine myself watching TV while predators spread through the city, killing people. I couldn't do that, no matter how much I wanted to rest. I carried my bag into the bathroom.

I stripped down and threw my clothes into the bottom of the tub. I had brought a small bottle of laundry detergent, and I scrubbed the sweat, stomach medicine, and tear gas by hand. The cold water felt good on my hands. Then I hung them by the window, turning off the air just below them.

Then I took a shower of my own. My skin was raw and red where Summer had touched me. I switched to cold water. It was uncomfortable, but I wanted it that way. I'd seen a predator on Summer and I'd backed off. I had to stand up and stay in the fight. I had to endure.

My clothes were not even close to dry when I finished. I took my last clean shirt, a white button-down, from the bag and put it on. Then I looked at myself in the mirror. I didn't look like a hungry ghost anymore, just a guy who needed a good night's sleep. At least I had cleaned the sweat off my face. I've always hated the feel of dried sweat.

I got back into my car and drove to Silver Lake, giving a wide berth to the Bigfoot Room and the street where I'd parked Bud's truck. I wasn't ready to run into them again.

Caramella's place was a little house, which surprised me. It had a lawn about the size of two postage stamps and a lot of Spanish stucco on the outside. As on just about every street in L.A., the houses on the block were a mishmash of styles, but hers was a basic A-frame that had been troweled over with a pueblo exterior. I took out my ghost knife.

A Corolla was parked in the driveway. There were two tall windows at the front of the house, and I nearly walked into the tiny flower garden to peep through the glass. It was just after 9 P.M., and I was planning to break and enter a friend's house.

Instead, I pocketed the ghost knife and rang the door-bell.

No one answered. I fidgeted a little, then rang it again. Again there was no answer. My Escort was parked at the curb, but the idea of driving away felt like defeat. Where would I go after this? I didn't know where Caramella worked. I didn't know where she hung out. A detective might have started walking around the neighborhood, asking about her at every diner, deli, and bar, but I wasn't a detective. I was a criminal.

I took out my ghost knife and slid it through the lock. The front door opened easily, and I let myself in, push-ing the door closed behind me.

The house looked even smaller on the inside, but it was nicely furnished. Everything I owned had come out of a yard sale, but Melly's tables and chairs were new if not fancy. The plaid couch and recliner matched the cur-tains, and there were tiny white throw pillows every-where. A pair of lamps on either side of the couch threw a pale blue light around the room, and the ceiling light in the bathroom was on.

But while the room looked tidy and homey, it was swel-tering hot and stank of garbage. The smell made my eyes water. It wasn't a dead body, I didn't think. I'd smelled bodies before.

It felt strange to stand in Melly's empty house, but what the hell. She had walked into mine without knocking.

First, I wandered around the room. I was concerned that the garbage smell would hide the stink of a dead body, but I didn't find one behind the furniture and there were no blood splashes against the walls. The bedroom was empty—the bed was neatly made, in fact, and the little desk in the corner was tidy.

Then I went into the bathroom. The medicine cabinet was standing open. I pushed it closed, getting a glimpse of the dark circles under my eyes. The shower curtain was drawn, and a couple of the rings had been pulled free. I peeked through the gap into the tub. I couldn't see anything in the bottom of the tub, not even droplets of water.

I went back to the living room and noticed a mail slot just beside the front door. Below it there was a small wicker basket full of mail. It looked like a couple of days' worth, but I couldn't tell exactly. I fanned through it and saw that most of it was addressed to Luther Olive.

There was a list of phone numbers on a notepad by the phone. I picked up the receiver and dialed the one at the top, labeled WORK. The woman who answered announced that it was a hospice-care facility, but she wouldn't answer any questions about Caramella and she wouldn't transfer me to her voice mail. I left my real name and a fake call-back number and hung up.

Finally, I went into the kitchen. There was a pink ceramic bowl full of rotting chicken on the counter, but most of the stink was coming from the open garbage can. I looked around without touching anything, then went back into the living room.

I was alone and it was obvious that I was the first person to stand in this room for a couple of days. I picked up a framed photo on the end table.

It was a picture of two faces close together. One was Melly and she was laughing. She looked older than I remembered, and more beautiful. She had little wrinkles at the corners of her eyes, and seeing her openmouthed smile brought back the memory of her laugh.

The man laughing with her, his cheek pressed against hers, was a black man with a short haircut, a scar below his eye, and a crooked nose. He had a beefy, solid look about him—the kind of muscular guy who would get fat at the first sign of comfort. He also gave the impression of puppy-dog earnestness, as though he was eager to please out of habit. That must have been Luther.

I liked the friendly roughneck look of him, and I was

a little jealous, too. Not because I wanted Caramella—we hadn't had that sort of relationship—but because he had happiness and love and a home. I hoped I would be able to save whatever he and Melly had.

There were other pictures on the mantel, and I studied them one by one. Here were pictures of Melly and her guy with her mom and sister in a lush forest somewhere. Next was an old bridal picture of a black couple, both looking heavenward. Next was a picture of Luther with Ty, Lenard, and Arne. They were all smiling. Most of the rest were Melly and her guy at various events—parties, picnics, carousels. The last showed Melly and Violet laughing while they baked Christmas cookies. I was surprised to see them together. They hadn't been close when I was around, but apparently things had changed.

Suddenly, I couldn't stand it anymore. I rushed into the kitchen, dumped the rotting chicken, bowl and all, into the trash can, then carried the garbage out the back door.

There was a plastic bin in the little backyard. I up-ended the trash can into it, letting a plume of stink blow over me. I tossed the can onto the parched lawn and went inside, leaving the back door open. I went to the bathroom and threw open the window, then opened the bedroom and living room windows. A mild crosscurrent blew across me. It wasn't enough to clear the stink, but it was better than the stale, oppressive heat.

Then I got to work.

I searched the house from top to bottom, taking special care to put things back where they belonged. I was careful out of respect for Caramella more than a desire to trick her, although if she never found out I'd broken in, I'd be happy.

I was looking for spell books, of course. Barring that, I wanted to find single spells, either instructions for casting them or a spell itself—a sigil drawn, carved, or stitched onto another object. If I couldn't find that, I hoped to find something to tell me where to look for Caramella next. An open phone book with a secluded Big Bear resort circled in red ink, maybe. I wasn't that lucky.

I searched every drawer, beneath every cushion, inside the pocket of every jacket and pair of pants. I opened every box and chest, looked inside every lamp, and ran my hand along the underside of every piece of furniture. I even unscrewed the grates over the air vents for their central heating. Nothing.

Caramella had a laptop on a tiny sewing desk in her room, but I hadn't done more than search around it so far. I didn't have a computer of my own, and I didn't know much about them.

I opened it and it came to life. I was surprised that it was sitting there, already turned on. Had Caramella been here recently, using it? She could have come and gone invisibly, of course. In fact, she could have followed me around the house while I searched it.

I felt a surge of anxiety as that thought grew larger in my mind, but I took several deep breaths. No one was there. Not with that garbage smell. No one was there.

Once the computer had fully come to life again, it began to download four days' worth of emails. It had been sitting there, switched on, for several days, and no one had used it recently.

I read the five dozen new emails as well as a couple of days' worth of old ones. Most were useless: supposedly funny stories about squabbling married couples, ads for natural Viagra, and attempts to organize a group of friends for a Friday movie date.

Only in the last day's messages did I notice anything unusual. Her mother had sent a note asking where she was, and telling her to please call. She had similar notes from her supervisor and co-worker, and from Arne.

I tried to find out more, but everything I did on her

computer caused something inexplicable to happen, so I closed it.

I went back into the living room and looked at the clock. It had been just over two hours since I'd snuck in, and I had nothing to show for my time. Predators were on the loose, and I had no idea what to do next. Tomorrow at seven-thirty I'd go back to Ralphs and hope to meet Annalise, but until then I had nothing.

But there was nothing left to do here. If I went back to my motel, I could have another shower and sleep—maybe—but I would have run out of options. There was nowhere else for me to go but back to Arne, and I wasn't ready for that yet. I needed to talk to Caramella first.

So I stood there, my indecision making the choice for me. Finally, I decided I might as well wait. I wanted to talk to her, and I was more likely to find her here than at my motel.

I dug out the remote and turned on the local news, hoping there would be a segment about a mysterious invisible assailant, but I was out of luck there, too. The first segment covered the president's plan to visit L.A.

Then the newscasters switched to extended reports of a break-in at a movie star's Beverly Hills home. Her name was Ellen Egan-Jade; she'd been in Minnesota filming her latest romantic thriller, but her live-in housekeeper had been beaten, raped, and left for dead. The only thing the asshole took was her Oscar. The cops didn't have any leads.

There was a pizza box with three slices of pepperoni in the fridge. The house didn't smell so bad anymore—or maybe I'd gotten used to it—so I took the pizza into the living room to eat at the coffee table. It was dry and tight, like jerky.

The announcer started speculating what would have happened if the actress had been home at the time of the break-in, while they showed pictures of her beautiful

face. The whole thing made me feel a little sick, so I
turned it off and ate in silence.

After finishing the pizza, I leaned back on the couch.
My eyes started to fall closed, so I jumped up and walked
around. I peeked out the front window, then the back.
No one was in sight.

The heat and food were making me drowsy. I shut the
front and back doors and propped a chair under each
knob. I shut all the windows and turned the thermostat
to eighty-five. Cool air hissed into the room. That would
help with the heat. I just needed to keep myself awake.

I paced until I grew tired, then sat on the couch with
my arms folded. Just as I told myself I could stay up as
late as I needed to, I nodded off.

I dreamed I was standing on a ship on a stormy sea.
Everything below deck had been taken over by a huge
beehive—the buzzing was incredibly loud—and waves
against the wooden hull were making it groan and crack.

Then I realized I was sleeping and that the sounds were
coming from outside my dream. I snapped awake in a
living room full of noise. I jolted to my feet, looking
around.

The buzzing, cracking sounds were coming from the
bathroom.

CHAPTER FOUR

I raced to the bathroom door. The windows were dark; it was still nighttime, but how late was it? I took my ghost knife out of my pocket.

I glanced around the room. No one else was here—not that I'd expected Caramella or Luther to come home and leave me sleeping quietly on the couch. I rubbed my eyes, trying to get them to focus.

The buzzing became hollow, as though it was echoing down a long tube, and was followed by a series of cracks that sounded like the bathroom was falling off the building. I pushed the door open just as a terrible silence fell.

The bathtub seemed to be full of darkness. I took a step into the room so I could see the bottom, but there didn't seem to be one. All I could see was swirling black, and slightly darker shapes moving far, far away.

An opening to the Empty Spaces had appeared in the bathtub. It wasn't a vision this time; I could feel the *absence* there.

Something floated through the opening into our world. It was little more than a colorless, shapeless shimmer, strung out like pulled taffy, and it hovered seven feet off the floor.

A bad feeling came over me, and I backed out of the room while lifting the ghost knife. A second form began to rise out of the tub.

The first shimmer rushed at my face. I instinctively held up my empty hand to ward it off. It struck my palm and flowed around it like a thick jelly. Tendrils struck my mouth and nose. It was sticky, just like Summer's hand when she grabbed my wrist. I kept my mouth tightly shut, but it seemed to be trying to squirm into my nostrils.

My iron gate, one of the spells Annalise had put on my chest, suddenly felt burning hot. For a moment, I felt a strange, heavy blankness in my thoughts, as though something was erasing my mind.

I slashed my ghost knife through the tendrils, splitting it apart. The blankness vanished. I yanked the bathroom door shut. Whatever the hell I was dealing with, I wanted to face them one at a time. I slashed again, and the stuff let out a strange keening that bypassed my ears and went directly to my guts.

This goop was alive. It was a predator and it was after me.

My ghost knife can kill predators, though. I slashed it across the shimmer again, dragging it along my face and around my mouth and nose. More keening, which was just what I wanted. I cut it again.

But I had to be careful: I know little about magic, and only slightly more about this spell I'd cast. My ghost knife has a powerful effect on living creatures, and I'd never cut myself with the spell, for fear of what might happen. At best I'd lose my will to fight, like Wardell. I didn't want to imagine the worst thing.

So I held the laminated edge of the paper close and smeared it through the sticky liquid slime spreading over my neck and shoulder.

The creature flexed, twisting me off balance and knocking me to the carpet. I reached out to the table to break my fall, stupidly dropping my ghost knife. The predator wrenched me flat on my back. I could still feel it pushing despair into me, trying to make me surrender. With a quick exertion of will, I *reached* for my spell and called it back into my hand.

The creature flowed over my face, and I squeezed my eyes shut. I blasted air out of my nose to clear it, then clamped it shut with my free hand. My skin . . . Everywhere it touched me, my skin burned. The thing was like acid.

My iron gate flared again. The despair grew stronger and my thoughts were sluggish and dull. Without that protective spell, I would have been comatose.

The creature flexed again, trying to pull my hand away from my face. Damn, it was strong. It took everything I had to hold my fingers over my nose. Eventually, it would realize it could bend back my fingers until they broke. For now, though, I was new prey and it wasn't quite sure how to deal with me.

I brought the ghost knife toward my face, but the predator pushed it back, slamming my wrist to the floor. I couldn't move that arm.

It had me pinned, and eventually it would find a way inside my body. Then the acid burning would be on my insides. With the right leverage, I might be stronger than it, but I was on my back, my air was running out, and I couldn't see. I had to do something quickly—I had to think quickly—or I was going to die.

I flexed my right arm with all my strength, trying to bring the ghost knife near my face with a sudden burst of power. It almost worked, but I couldn't quite reach. I moved the paper back and forth along my wrist as much as I could. It made tiny cuts in the predator, but I felt it peeling away from my hand and the spell.

Then my burst of power was over, and the predator slammed my arm back against the carpet.

I was failing. Bad enough that I was going to be killed by this damn predator here on the floor of Melly's pretty little house, but Caramella would have a predator in her home, waiting for her. God, no, I could not do that to her. I could not be responsible for that.

I *reached* for my ghost knife again, even though it was already in my hand. I could feel it, like a part of me, ready to do what I wanted it to do. I'd learned months ago that I could "throw" it without moving my body at all; the spell went where I wanted it to go—there was no other way to explain its uncanny accuracy. But while the throwing motion helped me picture where I wanted it to go and made the spell faster, I didn't need it.

I willed the spell out of my hand, imagining it zipping across my body and over my face. I felt the edge of it strike the predator several times, and the creature keened in its soundless way again. Its body peeled back where it had been cut, and the tension suddenly went out of it.

I kicked out, rolling myself onto my knees while *calling* my ghost knife back to me.

There was a sudden pressure against my ears; it was trying to get inside me by going through my eardrums. I scraped the ghost knife over one side of my head, and the creature suddenly leapt away from me.

I gasped, taking in air. My hands and head stung all the way up into my nostrils. I opened my eyes, feeling my eyelids burning where they folded.

The predator moved away from me, dragging parts of itself on the carpet. Instead of being a liquid shimmer, it was frayed, like torn rags blowing in the wind.

I threw my ghost knife at it, willing it to hit the center. It did. The thing split apart, turned pallid gray, and fell to the carpet with a *squerch*ing sound. Dead.

I felt a sudden rush of triumph and fury. I'd faced another creature from the Empty Spaces, and I'd beaten it. My mind seemed to rev into overdrive, but after a moment I realized I was just coming back to myself—the predator had tried to take my mind along with my body, but my iron gate had partly blocked it, and now I could think clearly again.

My whole body was drenched with sweat, and I gasped in heavy, ragged breaths. Damn, my whole head was really starting to burn.

I moved toward the bathroom. I'd definitely seen a second predator coming out of the tub, but was there a third, and a fourth? Was there a thousandth? As much as I was ready to take my victory and retreat, there was no one else here. I was the only one who could stop these predators. I had to open that bathroom door and fight.

The knob trembled slightly as something on the other side moved against the door. I reached out just as I saw a flicker of movement near the floor.

I jumped back. Another predator had pushed under the door, flowing through the narrow crack and protruding toward me. And I'd nearly stepped in it. I'd been so focused on the doorknob that I had missed the threat below me.

It struck at me like a hungry snake.

There was no time to think. I grabbed hold of the creature's farthest end—it felt strangely like a muscle—and slashed the ghost knife through it. The predator collapsed, almost splashing onto the carpet, then vanished.

In a panic, I fell to my knees, gouging and slashing with my spell. I'd thought it had escaped somehow, and that I'd let a predator get loose in the world. Then the strange keening returned. The thing was still below me, but it had turned invisible. I kept cutting. After several more slashes, it turned a pallid gray and died.

Were there only two? If I opened the door, predators might flood out at me like a breaking dam. I crouched low, waiting to see if another predator would try to squeeze under, but I didn't see anything. I swiped my ghost knife through the crack but didn't connect with anything.

Fine. If there were more inside, they weren't coming out.

The stinging on my face and hands had become worse—it felt like every patch of bare skin the creature had touched was coated with a film of weak acid. The pain grew and grew, and eventually I had to act, because waiting made me think about the pain too much.

I shoved the bathroom door open, darted inside, and slammed it shut. The predators weren't fast enough to have gotten out—at least, I hoped not. I yanked a towel off the rack and kicked it against the bottom of the door.

In the tub, I saw only a faint bath ring. The vast, deep darkness of the Empty Spaces was gone. Good. I didn't have a way to close a portal into another universe.

But had more predators come through? I couldn't see anything, but I hadn't seen that second one after it went flat on the floor.

I bent down and swiped my ghost knife against the floor, barely splitting the linoleum, then I did it again and again. The marks spiraled out one from another, covering the whole floor and moving up the walls and cabinets. I made long vertical slashes six inches apart, then I stepped up onto the toilet and did the same to the ceiling.

I was especially careful with the window. I didn't want to cut it open, in case a predator was looking for a way out. I did scrape through the wooden jamb and latch, though.

Then I fell to my knees and opened the cabinet under the sink. I cut through all of it, including the drainpipe. There was no keening sound, and while one of these predators might have escaped down the drain, I doubted it. The space under the door was much larger than the pipe, and it would have been a struggle to squeeze through.

Two. There had only been two. I was blearily glad that I'd turned on the air-conditioning and closed the bathroom window.

And I couldn't stand the burning on my skin anymore. I'd forced myself to stay and search the bathroom carefully, but the pain had become unbearable.

I ran into the kitchen, stuck my head in the sink, and sprayed cold water into my hair. The effect was sudden and wonderful—my skin was still hurting, but the acid film dissolved and washed away on contact with the water.

I did my hands, my neck, and my face. Finally, I got a turkey baster out of a drawer, filled it with water, and sprayed the water into my nostrils several times.

Better. Better. I still felt the pain, but at least it wasn't getting any worse.

I wandered back into the bathroom. It was all ruined, of course. Melly would need a contractor to come in here to fix what I'd done, but I couldn't bring myself to feel sorry. The pain was still there, and my fear was too recent. I picked up a bottle of aloe gel and began dabbing the stuff onto my face. It dulled the pain even more.

I glanced down at my sleeve. It was wet but perfectly clean. The predator had wrapped itself around my arm, but it hadn't left a stain on my clothes.

The predators had hurt my skin in exactly the same way that Summer's handprint had, and Caramella's slaps. They were hard to see, too. When they were attacking they looked a lot like heat shimmers in the air. But the predator that had squeezed under the door had gone flat and vanished. I'd looked right at it and hadn't seen it.

It was invisible. Just like Summer.

Summer had to have one of these predators on her, and she must have been protected from it somehow. Well, "somehow" wasn't really much of a mystery. Someone had cast a spell on her. She was wrapped up by a predator that wanted to devour her but couldn't.

The thought gave me shivers.

My face felt a little stiff and I looked like I had a bit of sunburn, but that was all. I'd gotten off easy.

Back in the living room, the pile of goop on the floor looked smaller. Was my mind playing a trick, or was the dead predator dissolving? I took a sock from a drawer in the bedroom and laid it beside the gray mess. Slowly, the goop receded from it. It was vanishing on its own. How considerate.

I took a chair from the desk and sat beside it. My hands were shaking. It was strange that my hands were shaking so long after the fight. I kept control. I breathed as slowly and as evenly as I could while the predator's corpse vanished in front of me.

Under normal circumstances, I would have burned Melly's house to the ground. These weren't normal circumstances because *this was Melly's house*. When she and her guy returned . . .

I looked around. The faint garbage stink was still there. The place felt empty. They weren't coming back—I knew they weren't—and to hell with this pretty little house.

I fetched a cotton robe, a candle, and a lighter from the bathroom, then closed all the curtains. I lit the candle and arranged it and the robe beside the edge of the couch. Then I lit the robe. The flames spread down to the throw pillows, and I knew that it would soon spread to the curtains and carpet.

The lock on the front door was still broken. I went out the back way, walked down the block, and got into my car. I didn't drive by Melly's house. I wouldn't have been able to see the flames behind the curtains, and I didn't want to try.

Five years ago, Melly had been a good friend to me. We'd been part of the same crew, had joked and laughed together. Now, as a wooden man in the society, I was burning her house down.

I didn't want to think about that, but I felt like a complete bastard.

What to do next? It was after three in the morning; the sun wouldn't rise for hours, and I'd never be able to sleep. There was no use going to Violet's place. If Arne had gone out looking for cars to steal, he would have already quit for the night. At best, he'd be at Long Beach, loading stolen SUVs into shipping containers. The very early morning hours were no good for boosting cars, he'd always said. No one else was on the street, and it was too easy to get noticed.

I drove back to the Bigfoot Room. The bar was closed, of course. I parked down the block and walked by the outside. There were no bullet holes in the glass front. None of the shots had gone in that direction. I checked the top of the door; someone had already wiped the words BIGFOOT ROOM away.

I walked around to the alley, half expecting to find stinking clouds of tear gas there, but of course there weren't. Even the smell was gone.

The security light above the bar's back door gave me enough light to look around, but first I waved my arms and kicked my feet along the walls in case an invisible person was standing there. I didn't find any.

The fire exit had a half dozen bullet holes punched through it. My eyes had been closed for most of the gunfire, but it appeared that the bullets had gone in one direction—toward Arne.

Then I noticed my name. I stepped closer to the door and saw that someone had written my name in black Sharpie. It read: RAY LOVES TO HANG AT THE QUILL AND TYRANT ANY TIME OF DAY OR NIGHT.

I touched the ink; it wasn't wet. It could have been

graffiti written by a disgruntled customer, but the way it was phrased made me think it was a message for me, in case I came back. Arne would never have been sloppy enough to leave a message right where the cops would see it, but maybe Bud or Robbie would.

I returned to my car. I knew people could look up addresses with their computers or with more expensive phones than the one I'd thrown away, but I was going to have to make do with the yellow pages.

I went back to my motel room and looked up the Quill and Tyrant. The address was in North Hollywood; I had to drive back the way I'd just come.

The Quill was just a door in a cinder-block box, and of course the lights were out. It was after 5 A.M. I went up to the door anyway and looked through the window. Everything was pitch-black inside, except for one lone beer sign.

When I turned around, there was a cop car at the curb, with a cop inside it asking me what I thought I was doing. I told him I'd lost my credit card and started looking around on the sidewalk. He grunted, looked me over once, and drove away without wishing me luck.

When he'd turned the corner, I walked around the building to the back. There was a dumpster back there along with a row of recycling bins. Behind that, by the cellar door, was a heavily tattooed Mexican man with a crooked nose and full beard. He was smoking a reefer, and he had a .45 S&W in his lap. He looked so stoned he was nearly comatose. "You got lost," he said.

"I'm looking for Robbie. Is this the right place?"

He laid his hand on his weapon. "Ain't no Robbie here."

"My mistake," I said, and started to leave.

"Hey! I didn't say you could go. Who're you?"

I turned back and looked him in the eye. It had been a

couple years since I left prison and this life behind me, but I knew better than to show fear or try to make friends. "I'm Ray," I said, keeping my voice flat.

He pursed his lips in a parody of thought. He really was amazingly stoned. I wondered, briefly, if I could rush him if I had to. "Ray Lilly?" he asked.

"That's right."

He rolled his eyes. "Well, you should have said so. Go ahead down. Fidel is waiting for you."

Fidel? I didn't know anyone named Fidel. But Stoned had waved at the cellar door, so I stepped toward it and lifted it open.

Light and music came through the opening, but no voices. I walked down the stairs, letting the door fall closed behind me. There were two more young guys on my left, both tattooed and bearded like Stoned. Bud and Summer sat on a low couch on my right. Robbie stood at the far end of the room with a very short, very muscular man with a shaved head. He was covered with jailhouse tattoos, including one along the side of his neck that said THUG in Gothic letters.

And everyone was watching me.

Robbie smiled. "Ray! You got my message."

He didn't walk toward me, so I walked toward him. "Good to see you again, Robbie."

His smile faltered a little. "That ain't my name anymore, dude. It never was. It's Fidel Robles."

"Really?" I said. "All those years we knew each other and you never told me your real name?"

He shrugged and smiled more broadly. His teeth were straight and white, his face full. He looked healthier than anyone in the crew, myself included. "I used to be embarrassed, man. My parents named me after an enemy of America! Oh no! The shame!" He laughed, and I laughed with him. "Then one day I realized I had brown skin just like Castro, and a nasty habit of taking things from rich people. Then I realized, hey, I'm an enemy of America, too. And proud of it."

I laughed and held out my hand. "It's good to see you again, Fidel."

He glanced down at my hand but didn't take it. His expression told me that he thought it was a test he didn't want to take, which it was. "I know you know," he said.

CHAPTER FIVE

I let My hand and my smile drop. "We gotta talk about this," I said.

"I agree." Robbie waved toward the room. It was just basement storage—a couple of stools with torn seat covers in the corner, a massive beer fridge against one wall, with stacks of whiskey crates beside it. There was a tatty carpet on the far side of the room, and a yard-sale couch set on it. Bud and Summer were all alone over there. "Humble beginnings, huh? But we're tired of being humble. We're ready to move into the big time."

Arne had looked at me with resentment and anger. But Robbie looked ready to thank me. "What happened to you?" I asked.

"I got a super power! Want to hear my origin story? It's pretty fucked up."

"Actually, I do. I really, really do."

"That's cool, Ray, but later. I need something from you first. Okay? We got more important things to talk about. What did Arne say when he called you back to L.A.?"

"It wasn't Arne," I told him. His smile became a little strained, as though he didn't believe me. "It was Caramella. She said she was in trouble."

"Come on, Ray. Are you kidding me?"

"Of course not. Caramella came to see me in Seattle. She said everyone was in trouble and that it was all my fault."

"Well, she was wrong. I'm not sure I'll ever be in

trouble again." He rubbed his chin, thinking of a new way to come at me. "Ray, you know that Arne was never really your friend."

"I know it." Robbie had been the closest thing I had to a friend. Still, though: only the *closest* thing. "And you were his second-in-command."

"Yeah, but he *trusted* you. He always thought you were smart."

"And he kept food in our bellies and games in the PlayStation. So why aren't you with him anymore?"

"I already told you, dude. We're through playing it safe. No more stealing cars, no more tiny payouts. We jumped the fence. No one can touch us now, so we're moving up."

"To what?"

"Anything we want! If I want to rob a bank, I can do it. If I want to kill a guy—even the best-protected guy in the world—I can do that, too. How much you want to pay me to kill the royal family in England? I could fly over there and fly back in a couple days and the job would be done. Me, I'd have the money in my Swiss bank account."

I stared at him, trying to decide if he was joking. I was pretty sure everything Robbie knew about being an international hit man came from the movies.

"You don't look all that convinced, Ray."

"Can I hear that origin story now?"

"Don't you get it? You could be in with us. I'm going to take my cousins over to see your boy later, and you could come with us."

"Wally King isn't my boy."

"Oh yeah? He told us he was your friend."

I couldn't talk for a moment because my jaw wouldn't unclench. Wally had murdered a woman to steal spells from her. He'd claimed to be able to cure any disease or injury, when all he could really do was implant predators into people—including the oldest friend I had in the world. He'd turned my friend Jon into a monster, and God help me, when Annalise came to put a stop to it, I'd fought her.

And now he was telling people we were friends? "Rob—I mean, Fidel, the last time I saw Wally I tried to kill him." And I'd try again, as soon as I could.

"Does he know about that? 'Cause he's still talking about you like you're his bestest pal."

"Can I hear that origin story now?"

He sighed, sounding a little irritated, then turned into a silhouette. I caught a brief glimpse of the Empty Spaces, and he vanished. I held myself completely still, listening. What the hell should I do?

Before I could come up with a good idea, he suddenly reappeared in the same spot, but now he was pointing a gun at my face.

I jumped back and ducked low, my heart pounding. The door was too far for me to run to with a gun on me, and there were too many of them for me to start swinging. I had to fight an overwhelming urge to *attack! attack!*

Fidel laughed and his cousins laughed with him. Summer and Bud watched me quietly from the couch, their expressions closed. The laughter made me furious, made me want to blow myself up like a bomb, but I swallowed it. It was time to stop thinking of him as Robbie, the guy who could never beat me at Mortal Kombat but always made me laugh. This was someone else.

The jeering laughs slowly died down. Fidel seemed sorry they had to end. "Damn, Ray. Living easy up in Seattle has made you soft. You're jumpy. I was just showing you my new piece. It's a SIG Sauer, just like those Blackwater guys in Iraq use." He slid his gun into the waistband of his pants. "But I'm not sure you can really appreciate it from all the way down there."

I was still crouched down. It took all the willpower I had, but I made myself stand straight. "Guess so."

"Are you joking about trying to kill your pal Wally? 'Cause I was hoping you could help me out with him."

It took me a second to catch up. "I get it. You want super powers for your cousins, and you want me to talk Wally into giving them an origin story of their own."

"Not just that, Ray. I want you on my side. Arne was right about you. You're a sharp guy. You always got your eyes open. I want you on my team, not his."

"What about that origin story?" I asked.

Fidel shook his head and came close to me. He still wore that broad, perfect smile. "Didn't your boss tell you all of that? You came to town and ran straight to him. We saw you there."

"Caramella contacted me, not Arne," I said again.

"He was never really your friend, Ray," he said, as if trying to convince me to stop lying. "You were his loyal guy, and look how he paid you back with Violet."

I stepped back, startled. Violet and Arne? So Jasmin—

"That's right, dude." Fidel stepped close to me, but not close enough to touch. "You did everything he told you to do, and he went behind your back with your girl."

I flinched. I couldn't help it—the image of Arne and Vi together in her bed was sudden and sharp. Fidel could have been lying, but I didn't believe it. Arne and Vi—I knew it was true. It was like a secret I was keeping from myself.

I closed my eyes and imagined Annalise beside me. Would she think this mattered? Those relationships were five years in the past. I'd come out of prison and turned my back on all of it. Did it matter? Of course not. It hurt, yeah, but I wasn't here to settle that sort of score.

"Fidel," I said. "Where can I find Wally?"

Fidel smiled and turned sideways. "I don't think that's

such a good idea, Ray. You haven't even signed up with me yet. You're still on Arne's side."

"Sign up with you, Fidel? Wally King already killed you."

He didn't like that, but he smiled through it. "I don't think so."

"You think I've been living easy in Seattle? Wally King put a curse on my oldest friend up there, and . . ." I wasn't sure how to say this next part, so I just said it. "And now he's dead."

Fidel's cousins were focused on me. They didn't like what I was saying, and Fidel didn't like the attention I was getting. "C'mon, Ray. Don't try that shit with me. Are you ready to make your choice? Me or Arne?"

I absentmindedly rubbed the back of my hand. The tattoos there made my skin dead to the touch. I had a new boss now, and I couldn't talk about her. "I'm here for both of you, Fidel. Against Wally King. I'm here to save your life, if I can." I glanced over at Bud and Summer. "All your lives."

The short, muscular cousin stepped close to Fidel and said something in Spanish. I couldn't understand him, but I knew it wasn't friendly. "No, no," Fidel said to him, then turned to me. "Ray, why don't you go visit Arne? Talk to him about Violet and about his plans for the future. Then you can decide if you want to come back to me. Tell me what he has planned, and decide if you want to be safe with him or rich with us. Go ahead, and think about what I said."

I started backing toward the door. "You should think about what I said, too."

Fidel watched me with a look on his face that I'd never seen before. He looked confident and wise, like a king sending a messenger on a particularly clever errand. I wanted to hit him. His cousins glared at me, but Summer and Bud had peculiar expressions. Had I gotten through to them, at least?

I backed to the stairs, then forced myself to turn around and walk away. No one shot me. I went outside. It was still cool, and the sun wasn't up yet, but I could see a faint glow along the horizon. Traffic had already started to pick up.

It was nearly 6 A.M. I should have been tired. It was unfair that I couldn't drive back to my rented room and close my eyes for a little while. I'd been in L.A. barely a day, and I was already back on a car thief's schedule.

Where could I go next? Was it late enough to stop at Violet's place to ask her about Caramella again? Probably not, but I didn't know where to find anyone else, so I thought I'd try it.

I drove back through the Valley with my windows down. The temperature was perfect, but I knew the heat would roast me later. I had no idea what to do about Robbie—Fidel, I meant. He had magic, almost certainly from a predator—he and Summer and Bud, and probably Arne and Lenard, too.

My boss, Annalise, would know what to do. She would have killed everyone in that room just because they had magic and wanted more. And having worked against her on one incident and with her on two, I could see where she was coming from. People could be crazy about magic. I'd seen it.

But I didn't want to kill them. Not if I could avoid it. In fact, even if I couldn't avoid it, I didn't want to do it. I hoped Annalise would be there to meet me outside the Ralphs tonight, so I could hand off the job to her. Maybe it was unfair, but there it was. I'd done my share of killing in Washaway, and I wasn't ready for more.

If it was not a predator that gave Fidel his invisibility—if it was just a spell, like the spells on my chest that blocked bullets or obscured evidence I left behind—then I was sure I could take care of it without killing anyone. My ghost knife cuts "ghosts, magic and dead things," and I could slash it through whatever spell they had on them and put an end to it.

The odds that their magic came from a spell were so low they were practically nonexistent, but I had to have hope, or I wouldn't be able to keep going.

Aside from that, I'd have to find Wally King. I owed him something, and it was long past due for him to get it. Him, I didn't feel squeamish about killing. Not at all.

The lights in Violet's apartment were dark, which didn't surprise me. I found a parking space just a block away, pulling in behind a woman who was obviously on her way to work, and closed my eyes for a while. I was ready to sleep after all.

The sun woke me around 8 A.M. I rubbed my face, climbed from the car, and rang the doorbell.

Jasmin answered. I introduced myself again, reminding her that I'd visited the day before, but she buzzed me in before I could finish.

It wasn't Violet who answered the door; it was her mother. "Raymundo," she said, squinting at me from behind her drugstore glasses. "Vi isn't here. But come in! Come in! Have a cup of tea."

"Thank you, Mrs. Johnson. I'd love some."

I followed her into the kitchen, where Jasmin was sloppily spooning cereal into her mouth. Mrs. Johnson put the kettle on the burner. "Please," she said. "Call me Maria. You are a grown man now. You can talk to me like one. I don't mind."

"Thank you, Maria." I was careful to keep my tone respectful.

She leaned against the cutting board and looked me over like an unexpected second chance. "So how have you been? Where are you working?"

"Things have been difficult," I told her. That was true, but the next thing I said was a white lie: "I got laid off from one job and haven't been able to find another." She looked disappointed at that, and I suddenly remembered that she could talk about jobs and the finding of them endlessly. I changed the subject. "How have you been? How is Mr. Johnson?"

"Oh," she said, and waved my question away. "I'm the same as always, but older. Mr. Johnson, he is off in Florida now, fighting for the unions. I tell him, 'Why go there? They hate unions!' but he don't listen. So, Ray, can you tell me what happened to my Tommy?"

That startled me. "Vi said he left town, although the way she said it made me think there was more to the story. I'm sorry, Maria. I haven't heard a thing about him."

"Can you ask around for me? I tried, but nobody does anything for an old Mexican lady. You're the only one who ever showed me any real respect. And Tommy . . . He don't call me or his father. Mr. Johnson, he blames me. He thinks I drove Tommy away from the family. You went to jail for Tommy, yes? You'll do this for me?"

"If I can, I will," I said. "But I'll need to talk to Violet again. Where—"

From the other room, Jasmin shouted: "*Abuela,* the ghost is still here!"

I hadn't realized she'd left. I rushed into the other room, Maria close behind me. Jasmin was kneeling on the couch, looking down into the space behind it.

"Jazzy! You come away from there and finish your breakfast. Then we can go to the park. And stop this foolishness about ghosts."

I went close to her. There was nothing behind the couch except dust bunnies. "What kind of ghost is it?" I asked. The window was right beside us; I glanced through it and saw a man in a red shirt with long camo pants standing on the sidewalk, looking up at the building.

"It's a fire ghost," Jasmin said. "It burns you if you touch it."

I knelt on the cushion beside her and reached into the space between the couch and the wall. I touched something wet and sticky that I couldn't see. Almost immediately, my fingertips began to burn. I yanked my hand back and pulled the little girl off the couch. "Hold her," I said to Maria, and the tone of my voice surprised her. She took the little girl in hand.

I rushed to the kitchen and ran my fingers under the tap. The pain washed away quickly, leaving my skin a little red. I filled a tall glass with water and went back into the living room.

Maria had pulled the couch away from the wall. "Go to your room, Jazzy," she said, but she didn't object when the girl ignored her by jumping onto the couch and peering over the back.

Maria reached into the space in front of the wall. "Ah! Holy Maria!" She held up her fingers, trying to see what had hurt them.

"Don't wipe it on your clothes," I told her. "Dip your fingers in here, quickly. That will help." I gave her the glass and she wet her hand, cleaning it off.

"And I didn't believe Jazzy when she said she saw a ghost. What is it, Raymundo? What's in my daughter's home?"

"I don't know yet." But that wasn't true. I knew damn well it was one of the predators that had attacked me at Caramella's house, but why was it lying inert behind Violet's couch?

I knelt and poured the water behind the couch. It struck something, then flowed over it onto the carpet. Water could wash off the burning effect but not the invisibility.

"What is it?" Maria asked.

I didn't know how to answer. It was an irregular

shape, and rounded. Was it lying in wait? "You have to get Jasmin out of here. Right away."

"But what is it?" Maria asked again. "You didn't tell me."

"Because I'm not sure, but you're not safe here. Please."

"You brought this, didn't you?" She looked at me with narrowed eyes. "Is this some fancy plastic you put here?"

Jasmin hopped off the couch and ran into the back of the apartment. I turned to Maria, incredulous. "How could I have put something behind the couch? And why?"

"You should know already we don't have nothing to take," she said. "I know that's what all of you boys do. You and Arne and the rest—I know you got Tommy into it, too, before he vanished."

There was nothing I could say to that. I was good enough to search for her son but couldn't otherwise be trusted. Maybe she would have liked me more if I'd lied about having a job.

Jasmin ran back into the room with a roll of toilet paper, the loose end trailing behind her like a streamer. She leaped back up onto the couch and offered the roll to me.

The end of the paper fell onto the invisible whatever-it-was and stuck there. Damn. Smart kid. I took the roll and laid the paper over the invisible shape, doubling it back when it reached the end closest to me.

The paper stuck into place, showing the contours of the object. All at once, I realized what I was looking at. It was a human face, its eyes closed, its mouth open in a soundless scream.

Maria gasped. "Oh, my Melly!"

I jumped back, nearly knocking Maria over. Christ, she was right. It was Caramella. I stared at her, stunned. What had happened to her?

"You brought this here," Maria said. The way she

said it made me think she was trying to convince herself rather than accuse me. "This is because of you!"

I felt a sudden flash of anger. "You don't know what you're saying!" Her eyes went wide, and she stepped away from me. I took a deep breath, pulling back my anger. Of course Maria wasn't accusing me of feeding Melly to a predator. Of course not.

I swallowed my anger and panic, trying to get a rational thought out of my brain. "Do you really think I brought invisible acid plastic here? Sculpted to look like Melly?"

"I—"

"Take your granddaughter out of here. Something dangerous is going on."

"That's really . . . her, isn't it?" Maria looked back over at Caramella. Jasmin was still kneeling on the back of the couch, but she was now laying toilet paper along the invisible form on the floor, outlining Caramella's breasts, belly, and arms. I didn't even realize I'd dropped the roll.

"Hey!" Jasmin said. "Her lips are moving."

My guts turned into a tight knot. I knelt close to Melly's face. It was true; her lips were quivering as though she was in tremendous pain.

She was still alive.

"Why is she doing that?" Jasmin asked.

I lunged at her, caught her by the arms, and lifted her off the couch. I felt like I was violating a taboo—*never touch someone else's child*—but I wanted to startle Maria. I wanted her to get the hell out.

As I pivoted to hand the little girl to her, she was already moving to take her. I pressed Jasmin into her arms, then forcibly steered her toward the door. She let me. "I can't tell you what's going on because I'm not sure myself. I only know that, whatever it is, it's not safe for little girls."

Jasmin pleaded as they left. "I want to see Melly some

more! I want to see!" I closed the door but didn't lock it in case I needed to get away quickly.

I went into the kitchen and grabbed a sheet of cheesecloth from the bottom drawer by the oven, silently thanking Violet for keeping everything the way I remembered it. Back in the living room, I tore the toilet paper away; Caramella didn't deserve to have that stuff over her face. I laid the cheesecloth in its place. Then I laid a second sheet over her neck and chest, then a third over her stomach. I could see it move very slightly as she breathed.

My throat felt tight and my breathing was shallow. Melly was obviously in agony, and I was sure I knew why. This predator had draped itself over her and started to feed. Whatever had been protecting her when she'd visited me in Seattle—whatever was protecting Summer right now—must have worn off or been taken away. Now she was feeling the full extent of the creature's acid touch. It covered her entire body, was up her nose and down her throat, and it was slowly dissolving her while she was still alive.

As if I needed another reason to hate Wally King.

I took out my ghost knife. When I killed the predator in Melly's house, I'd had to cut it ten or twelve times before it died. Maybe it had a weak spot, but I didn't know how to find it.

I took a deep breath; I'd need steady hands for this. Judging by the cheesecloth, the creature was spread thin over her skin. There was no way I could cut it without also cutting her. That was okay. The ghost knife wouldn't hurt her while she was alive—it would just alter her personality for a while. The predator—this drape—was made partly of magic, so it *would* be hurt.

I heard movement somewhere nearby—this was an apartment building full of people. I imagined the Twenty Palace Society arriving and airlifting Caramella to a secret base in the desert somewhere, where a team of scientists in hazmat suits waited to save her life. Too bad I didn't have a copter or a desert lab. I didn't even have a pair of safety goggles. And the society, even though it was still hours away, would rather burn her to cinders than try to save her.

It was just me, and if Melly was going to come through this, I would have to cut the predator off of her by myself.

No more stalling. I moved the ghost knife close to her face, thinking I would scrape it along the skin of her cheek, possibly over her lips to clear her airway. How long had it been blocking her mouth and nose, or was it breathing for her?

The drape seemed to tense as I came close, and when the ghost knife plunged into it, the cheesecloth over Caramella's rib cage suddenly jerked upward. I heard her bones crack, and beneath the cloth her mouth opened in a silent scream.

Then she seemed to sag, and her lips stopped trembling. Her head rolled slightly to the side. It wasn't a big change in position, but it looked as though the strength had gone out of her. The predator had killed her.

I closed my eyes and lowered my head. Melly had just died in front of me—had just died *because* of me, in fact. I had failed her. I remembered her slapping my face just two days before, her face twisted with misery but without tears. Had the drape taken those from her, too?

I wanted to tear the cheesecloth off her—she deserved a more dignified shroud, but if I did that, there would be no evidence of her at all. I heard more voices outside, and I quashed the urge to yell at them to shut up. People shouldn't be shouting at their kids. They should have respect for the dead.

A strange buzzing voice spoke from somewhere near me. Then I heard a second and a third. Something groaned and creaked like a ship in heavy seas. Then there was another crack—this time not coming from Caramella's body. This one sounded like the world was breaking open.

I slashed the ghost knife through Caramella's head. A pale gray line appeared where I cut the predator.

I felt that strange keening again, and I took a savage joy in it. I slashed a second and third time, as the buzzing voices grew around me until they became that furious beehive noise I'd heard in Melly's home. Was this drape calling to others like it?

There was a sudden thump on the couch above me, and for one terrified moment I thought another predator had landed beside me. But it wasn't a drape; it was Jasmin. She'd broken away from her grandmother and run back inside.

"What's that noise?!" she shouted.

Beneath Caramella, the floor vanished, revealing an opening into the swirling black mists of the Empty Spaces.

CHAPTER SIX

The shrouded figure of Melly dropped into the darkness, and I fought for balance at the edge of the portal. The back legs of the couch were also over the void. The couch tipped downward and began to slide into the opening, scraping the edge of the wooden floor.

Jasmin screamed as she pitched forward. I lunged at her, throwing all my weight over the gap. I didn't think about it; I had no plan or courage. I just moved.

The couch pitched over backward as the front legs caught on the edge of the floor. I clamped my hand on Jasmin's wrist, my knee slamming onto the arm of the chair, my ghost knife slipping from my grasp and tumbling into the darkness.

I wish I could say I'd been graceful about it, that I'd grabbed her arm and hopped lightly to safety. But in truth I scrambled across the tumbling couch, snagging my shoe on the arm and trying desperately to throw some of my body weight onto the solid part of the floor.

It didn't happen. The couch floated away from me as my weight pressed on it. I slammed my left hand down on the carpeted living room floor and tried to keep my left foot in the solid world, too, but it slipped free and I swung out over the void.

My hand pressed down on the floor, stopping my fall. Once my body weight dropped below the level of the room, I wasn't falling anymore. Like the couch, I had momentum, but the void didn't pull me downward because there was nothing to fall toward. The friction of my left hand against Vi's carpet held me in place, and I started to pull myself back up. I glanced down at Jasmin. She stared at me with huge, terrified eyes.

Suddenly, a strange pulse pulled me downward. It wasn't like the tug of gravity—this felt as though something huge was trying to breathe me in. My mind only had room for one gigantic thought: *Hold on hold on.* The pull subsided, then came back again, and again, and again, with the regularity of a beating heart. *Hold on.*

Something grabbed my left wrist, and I cried out in panic. I pulled myself high enough to see Maria on her knees holding my forearm like a baseball bat. For a moment I had an absurd fear that she was going to lift my hand and fling me into the void, but instead she pressed down, anchoring me in this world.

"*¡Santa madre de Dios! ¿Que pasa aqui?*" she shouted.

"Here!" I lifted Jasmin as high as I could.

Maria let go, snatched her granddaughter, and dragged her into the world. She pushed the little girl toward the door and, bless her, started toward me again.

"Get out of here!"

She grabbed my wrist again. "What's happening? What's happening?"

I glanced down and saw pale, shapeless forms swirling in the darkness below. "Get out of here and close the door behind you! Run for your lives!"

It was a ridiculous thing to say, but it worked. Maria rolled to her feet and scooped Jasmin off the floor. With both hands free, I lifted myself halfway into the room. The door slammed shut.

My ghost knife was gone. I tried to *reach* for it with my thoughts the way I've always *called* it back to me, but I was scrambling out of the hole in the floor, and the shapes below were getting closer, and I was frightened, and I hated myself for my fear. I couldn't concentrate.

I'd lifted one leg out of the void and onto the solid floor when one of the sudden pulses dragged me back. They hadn't let up the whole time, but just as I was about to be free I was hit with one so much stronger than the ones before that it nearly sucked me in.

I cursed and scrambled upward again. I had one leg out when something heavy and soft struck my trailing foot. I rolled onto the floor, outside the void, just as another, even stronger pull started. I'd made it back into the world, but I wasn't safe.

There was a pale glob on the lower half of my left leg, like a small blanket bundled around my foot and ankle. And it was creeping upward.

I leaned over the opening into the Empty Spaces. The shapes were closer than ever now, and two were very, very close. I held my hand over the darkness and closed my eyes. *There*. I could feel my ghost knife in the darkness below. I *called* for it, desperately.

God, I had a predator on me, and it was already making the skin on my leg burn. I didn't even have to watch it move; I could feel it.

One of the drapes rushing out of the void faltered, and a moment after that I had my spell in my hand again.

Just as I rolled away from the opening in the floor, a drape rose out of it and rushed at my face. I shut my eyes and slapped my free hand over my nose and mouth.

The predator hit me and knocked me back; my iron gate suddenly burned white hot. A sudden rush of despair sapped my strength and my thoughts became confused, but I knew it was something the drape was doing to me, and I did my best to shake it off.

The first one creeping up my leg suddenly *squeezed* so hard that I almost gasped in a mouthful of slime. They began to pull in opposite directions. *Christ, they're fighting over me.*

I laid the edge of the ghost knife against my cheek and

began to slash at the drape. It flared back, clearing a space from my mouth and nose, but I didn't dare take a breath. Not yet. I could feel it holding on to my head and neck, burning my already tender skin.

If one broke my neck, would another opening appear in the floor?

I scraped my spell across my throat just as the predator tried to squeeze. It pulled away, releasing me, and the one on my leg began to drag me across the floor. I opened my eyes in time to see the drape float away from my face. A third came through the gap in the floor, then the gap closed. The opening to the Empty Spaces was gone.

There were still three predators in the room with me. The third one moved unsteadily. It took me a moment to realize my ghost knife had already passed through it once when I *called* it from the void.

I twisted onto my stomach and slashed my ghost knife through the one that had just let go of my face. I swiped through it four, five, six times, but it wasn't dying fast enough. It retreated along the floor, too badly wounded to fly.

But the first drape around my leg was still pulling me in the other direction. I scrabbled with my elbows after the second one, then dug my untrapped foot into the carpet and launched myself after it.

I plunged the ghost knife into it. The drape tried to wrap itself around my hand, but I was already twisting and wiggling my spell, cutting it with every tiny move, and it quickly turned to sludge and died.

I spared a second to look at it closely, hoping to see a brain or an eye or some other vulnerable spot on its now visible body. I wanted a way to kill the thing in one shot, but I couldn't see anything

I rolled onto my back. The first predator had reached higher than my mid-thigh, but the effort it had put into dragging me away from its competition had slowed its progress. Still, it was much too close to my crotch. There was no way I was going to let this damn thing crush and dissolve my nuts.

I scanned the room for the telltale shimmer of the other one, knowing that it would be invisible if it had landed on something solid.

It hadn't. It hovered at the edges of the apartment door as though trying to figure out how to get through. I had to kill the third predator before it reached open air and a victim of its own, but first I had to give this first one something to think about. I sat up and slashed at it with my ghost knife.

But pain and panic had made me sloppy. I saw the edge of the spell cut through the thin flesh of the drape, and I saw my pants split apart, and I felt the ghost knife cut my leg.

My iron gate flared with white-hot pain—every tattooed spell on my body, even the two tiny ones on my neck that I never think about, suddenly burned as though they were made of napalm. A scream erupted from my throat.

My head was filled with roaring: *Cut cut cut cut* it screamed, over and over. It was a compulsion—a fury—to slash and splinter and tear and slice. The ghost knife had a desperate hunger to cut and destroy, and it ached to cut the spells on my chest, the spells Annalise had put on me.

I moved the spell toward my stomach.

A tiny voice in my head resisted. Those spells were precious. They'd saved my life many times, and I wouldn't last long without them. The burning of my iron gate slowly brought me back to myself.

But the compulsion from the ghost knife was unbearable. It had a powerful will of its own, and it needed to destroy *everything*, especially the magic on my body and in the predators.

One of those predators was getting away. I turned my attention toward it, trying to turn the will of the ghost knife toward it, too. I couldn't hold out much longer against the compulsion; I had to distract it. The spells on my body weren't going anywhere, but that predator would escape if I didn't destroy it first.

The ghost knife turned toward the drape. I threw it. It flashed across the room faster than I'd ever seen it move and cut through the creature.

I *called* it back immediately. I couldn't deny its hunger for the predator, and now that I'd opened myself to its will, it ran wild. The spell returned to me and I threw it again. *Called* it back. Threw it. I struggled to my knees, scrambling clumsily toward the drape, suddenly feeling as though I was as hungry as the predator I was destroying. *Called* it back, threw it.

The drape collapsed onto the carpet. I grasped my spell and fell on the creature, slashing and tearing at it in a mindless frenzy. I might have screamed, but I wasn't aware of myself at the moment, only of the growing pain of my iron gate and the ghost knife's unbearable urge to destroy.

Finally, the predator was dead, and my attacks against it felt empty and useless. The urge to *cut* was still strong, but the iron gate under my collarbone was blocking it with pain.

It would have been so easy—so easy!—to surrender to that need and slash through all the spells on my chest.

Instead, I turned to the drape on my leg. My hand trembled as I laid the edge of the spell against it. The predator wrenched at me and squeezed, but I didn't even notice. All my perceptions had narrowed to a tunnel, with the compulsion of the ghost knife at the center and pain everywhere else. It wanted to jump out of my hand and cut me, but I held on to it like it was a rattlesnake. It slashed into the drape.

The predator recoiled, and I felt the ghost knife's hunger for it. I couldn't fight my own spell, so I let it pursue the drape, using all my will and strength to redirect it from my body.

The drape peeled off me, and I cut it until it died. At the end, I could barely feel the ghost knife's compulsion anymore. The pain from my iron gate had grown large enough to fill my whole mind and will. It burned away the spell's influence, and I was in control of myself again.

I rolled over onto my stomach, gasping for air, waiting for the pain to ease. My mouth lay open against the carpet, and I inhaled enough dust and hair to make me hack. The pain wouldn't subside—my iron gate kept burning and growing, and I finally cried out pitifully, feeling tears running down my cheeks. Maybe it would never stop. Maybe it would go on and on until I lost my mind or ate a bullet or I really did slash it with my spell.

Then, finally, it began to subside. I struggled to my knees, not ready to stand yet. My ghost knife lay on the carpet beside me. It was mine. I'd created it. I'd used it against other people.

I shuddered. The pain from my iron gate had been so overwhelming that I thought it would destroy me, but I'd needed it to scour away the influence of the ghost knife. The spell hadn't affected other people the way it affected me, but I had no idea why. I also didn't have a coherent thought in my head; this was something I'd have to puzzle out later, if ever.

But my own spell had been just as hungry as the predators I fought, and by cutting myself I'd let it take control of me. I could never let that happen again. Never.

The pain wasn't entirely gone. My face, neck, and head were burning, just as they had the first time a drape attacked me, and so was my leg. I struggled to my feet. Exhaustion made me unsteady, and my leg felt stiff and swollen. I needed to wash away the sticky acid the pred-ators left on their victims. Maybe a shower?

I stepped onto the section of the floor that had closed over the gap, feeling miserable enough to risk my life. It felt solid—I didn't fall through into the Empty Spaces, at least. Was it safe to bring Maria and Jasmin back into the room?

I glanced out the window. The big guy in the red shirt and camo pants was back, and he was looking right up at me. He took something long and thin from a hockey bag at his feet. One end was vaguely spear-shaped.

He lifted it to his shoulder and pointed it at me.

Oh, shit. I spun and hustled for the apartment door. It was seven or eight strides away—too far. I was never going to be able to run that far before the explosion hit. I ran anyway, because the only other option was waiting to die.

My stiff leg made me lurch across the room like a wounded drunk. I was halfway there and the explosion hadn't come. Then I had my hand on the knob, then I was pulling the door open, knowing that would only make it easier for the flames to blast out into the hall. Then I shut the door behind me, threw my leg over the railing, and jumped toward the pool below.

The explosion, when it came, was loud but not as loud as I expected. The flames never reached me; I struck the water with a painful slap and was shocked by how cold it was.

The pain on my face and leg eased immediately, and I struck the bottom gently. For one disorienting moment, I lost my bearings, but I saw light above and struggled back to the air.

The building was burning. Fire alarms blared and doors around the complex swung open. What were all these people doing here so late in the morning? Didn't they have jobs?

I saw Maria and Jasmin standing beneath a set of concrete stairs. They both had a shell-shocked look about them. I paddled to them and pulled myself out of the water.

"Take her out the back way," I said, straining to keep my voice low.

Maria grabbed my hand. "What—"

"Don't ask me questions!" I snapped at her. "It's not the time! Take Jasmin out the back way and get her someplace public. She's still not safe here."

Maria snapped her mouth shut. Jasmin tugged at her arm. "*Abuela*, I want to go."

They both hustled toward the little door on the far side of the pool, leaving me dripping water onto the pavement. People were charging around the complex, shouting at one another, demanding to know what had happened.

Me, I turned toward the front gate. I should have been exhausted, but my anger gave me a surge of energy. Someone had just fired a grenade at me, and I was going to kick his ass.

I ran out to the sidewalk. The asshole in camo pants was nowhere in sight. I looked up the street both ways; a Jeep Cherokee was driving away in one direction, a Dodge Ram truck in the other. Which one should I chase?

I had no reason to choose either, then the choice was gone. Both vehicles turned corners and vanished. Neither had been driving fast, like they would if they were fleeing the scene of a crime. Which meant the asshole could still be here.

And I was standing out in the street like a target at a gun range. I ran toward the spot where he'd stood, but I wasn't quite sure where it was. I turned around and surveyed Violet's burning building.

The flames were already shining through the windows of the apartment above, and the smoke was billowing out in two heavy black columns. I heard sirens in the distance, and people were rushing out of the courtyard with cats in their arms, or baby gear. One woman ran across the street toward me and set a milk crate full of paperbacks on the lawn, then sprinted back to the building.

Things would get very crowded soon. I tried to remember everything about Camo Pants that I could. I had seen the hockey bag at his feet, so I moved away from the line of parked cars. Had the telephone pole been on the right or the left? Had he stood on grass or the pavement?

I walked around the area, looking for something that looked like a clue. In Chino, I knew a guy who'd left his wallet on the front seat of a Lexus he'd jacked. Camo Pants wasn't so considerate. I couldn't find anything but cigarette butts and food wrappers. Maybe TV cops could spend hours going over all this trash in some lab and finger the guy, but it was useless to me. And I'd forgotten to ask where I could find Violet.

The sirens were getting closer, and that made me itch to leave the scene. But as I turned toward my car, someone behind me said: "Hey, Mr. Lilly."

I turned slowly and saw a homeless man walking toward me. His clothes were tattered and stiff with dirt, and even at this distance I could smell a year's worth of cheap cigarettes on him. "Hey, Mr. Lilly," he said again, his pale blue eyes wide and blank. "Your sick friend asked me to give you this." He held out a cellphone.

I didn't move to take it. "Who gave it to you?"

"Come on," he said, "he paid me ten bucks." He sounded a little nervous, as though he'd have to give back the money if I didn't accept it.

The phone rang.

"Who?" I asked again. I still didn't move to take it.

"I don't know his name, but he looks like a cancer patient or something. He said he's your friend. Come on."

Okay. I can come on with the best of them. I took the phone from him. He bustled away, looking relieved.

The phone was a cheap flip-closed type. It stopped ringing as the call went to voice mail. I opened it and looked at the number. It was an 818 area code, so it was coming from somewhere nearby. As expected, it started ringing again a few seconds later. I answered. "This is Ray."

"Ray! It's been so long. Remember me?"

"I remember you, Wally. Why don't we get together? We can talk about old times."

"Heh. I'm sure you'd like that, Ray, but I haven't forgotten that you tried to kill me. I mean, some stuff is hard to remember, but not that."

He sounded different, almost dreamy. Wally had never been the sharpest guy, but he'd never sounded like this. "I'm a different person now," I said.

"I'll bet. Listen, Ray, I do want to meet with you. Right now. Walk west about three blocks. There's a little diner that serves a nice breakfast. My treat."

I didn't know what to say to that. "Do you think I'm stupid, Wally?"

"Not at all, buddy. I know you still want to kill me. But I haven't forgotten what you did for me over the years. I still owe you. So we'll meet in a public place, and you'll give me a chance to talk for, say, sixty seconds before you try to kill me again. Okay? After that, we'll see what happens. The place is called the Sugar Shaker. Okay?"

"Okay." I closed the phone and started walking west. The fire engines drove by me as I went, and I saw bystanders and lookie-loos helping tenants unload their apartments or stand guard over their stuff.

At the corner I dropped Wally's cell into a trash can. It was painful to throw away resources, but it was Wally's. I didn't want any gifts from him.

I had three blocks to figure out what he wanted, but I couldn't put it together. In junior high, a couple of guys from the baseball team had picked on Wally until I told them to lay off. It wasn't that I liked him, but I hated to see the misery they were making.

Then I'd played with a handgun, and my life changed forever. I never went back to school and didn't hear from Wally again until just before I got out of Chino. He wrote to me, offering me a joe job at his copy shop. I tried to remember how it felt to be grateful to him, but it was too long ago. Too much had happened since.

So I wasn't sure what Wally owed me. An apology for what happened to Jon? For the predators he'd unleashed? As far as I was concerned, all Wally King owed me was his spell book and his miserable fucking life.

The Sugar Shaker turned out to be a storefront café with a counter along the back wall and ten round tables.

I took hold of my ghost knife before I walked through the door. The spell was quiet—just a sheet of laminated paper that I could sense—as it had always been. But if it still wanted someone to cut, Wally would do just fine.

A man sitting by the wall near the newspaper rack waved to me, and it took me a moment to recognize him. It was Wally, and he looked bad. His sallow skin sagged off his body. His skull seemed slightly misshapen, and his body was a formless mass. He'd always been fat, but now he looked lumpy, as though he was riddled with tumors. He wore green sweats that needed to be thrown into a hamper, but he'd spent a long time brushing and blow-drying his hair.

There were a dozen other people inside, talking, eating breakfast, or just reading. My adrenaline was still running, and I was jumpy and pissed off. Annalise, if she were here, would have smashed in Wally's skull and burned him down to cinders without a second thought, and she would have written off anyone killed in the crossfire as an acceptable loss. I wasn't ready to do that. While Wally needed killing—oh, how he needed killing, no one knew that better than I did—this wasn't the place.

Unless it had to become the place.

Wally held up his pale, flabby hands. "Sixty seconds, right?"

"You don't deserve sixty seconds."

"But they do." He gestured toward the crowd around him.

"You look terrible."

"But I feel fantastic." He rubbed at a piece of peeling skin on the end of his ear. "Ray, I know what you want to do—it's written all over your face and I can see it in your glow—but I'm a different person, too. If you make your move here, all these people are going to suffer."

I stared at him, picturing him with a split skull. Could I do it quickly enough? My ghost knife felt alive in my pocket. I remembered how it had felt when it tried to control me, and the killing urge dimmed just a little.

"Can't we just talk?" Wally asked. "Have a seat."

I sat and placed my hands on the table. "My friend died today because of you."

"Which one?" I nearly snatched a knife off the table and stabbed him in the eye, but he kept talking, oblivious. "Was it the cute one with the big butt? I knew we were getting close to her time. She gave you my message, right? I mean, you're here."

"Why, Wally? What are you trying to get out of this?"

He sighed. "I'm not much for schemes, Ray. I think you know that. Some guys can come up with complicated plans to get what they want, but I'm not like that. I need things to be simple."

A waitress stepped up to the table. She was a tall Asian woman with a broad forehead and long, straight black hair. She did her best not to look at Wally and didn't seem all that impressed by my soaking wet clothes. "Can I take your orders?"

"I thought this table was in the other waitress's section," Wally said. He sounded a little whiny about it.

"Nope, I'm your waitress," she answered in a tone that suggested she wasn't happy about it and didn't want to argue.

Wally sighed again. "I'd like three hard-boiled eggs, a side of bacon, and a side of sausage. And water. Ray? It's on me."

"Black coffee," I said, knowing I wouldn't drink a drop of it. I didn't want to accept anything from him.

The waitress hurried away. "I thought this table was in the other waitress's section," he told me, as though I hadn't heard him the first time he said it. His lips were rubbery and his teeth were gray. "I'm not into Asian chicks. I know some guys are crazy for them, but I like curly hair."

I closed my eyes. I was not going to sit here and talk about women with him. "You need things to be simple," I prompted.

"Right. I needed invisible people for my thing, and I wanted to do it in a way to get your attention."

"What 'thing' are you talking about?"

"I'm trying to get my hands on a puzzle. . . . Actually, never mind about the thing," he said. "I blew that, anyway. This is about you now. You remember what I told you last time, right before you tried to kill me? Well, nothing has changed. Bad shit is coming, Ray. Really, really bad shit."

"But why is this about me?"

"I owe you, for all the good things you did for me growing up."

"That doesn't make us friends."

"Oh, no. I'm well aware of that. Still, you did good

things for me when no one else would, not even the actual friends I had at the time. Besides, I like knowing you. It's like being pals with Stalin's deadliest assassin or something."

Even I knew who Stalin was. "What the hell are you talking about?"

"The Twenty Palace Society, natch. They used to be really scary, you know, back in the day. I've spoken to some of the people who were around back when. Everyone was terrified of them, and hid like field mice. But they lost their spell books—the original spell books—and can't produce primaries anymore. They've been in decline ever since."

I knew all this. Zahn had bragged, and Annalise confirmed, that the society had once had and had lost two of the three "original" spell books. According to Annalise, they were the source of all magic in the world, and they weren't really books with spells written in them.

Why they were still called spell books was beyond me. I learned the names of two of them—the Book of Grooves and the Book of Oceans—during the disaster in Washaway. I had no idea where they were, and as far as I could tell, no one else did, either.

Annalise said that anyone who read them had visions. The visions turned them into a "primary"—the most powerful kind of sorcerer—and they recorded their visions by writing them out as spells in an actual book. Those secondhand spells were what everyone thought of as spell books, and they were traditionally named after the primary and the source: Smith Book of Oceans or Jones Book of Grooves.

I'd seen one of those secondary books. Well, in truth I'd stolen it. I'd cast my ghost knife out of it and nearly died in the attempt. Annalise had taken it back, but I had a copy hidden away. In fact, it was so well hidden that I hadn't gone near it since.

When a second person laid hands on the Jones Book of Whatever, that person became a "secondary." The third person became a "tertiary." Every time a book of spells passed from one hand to the next, the spells became weaker, because each new person was further and further from the original vision. It didn't take many generations for them to become useless.

That's why sorcerers guarded their spell books so carefully, because sharing them made them decay. Unfortunately, the spells that held on to their potency the longest were summoning spells.

I knew the society was losing power as their sorcerers died and their spell books were handed down, but it didn't really matter to me. That was long-term thinking. I was in this game for the short-term fight. I was here for this enemy, and this danger. Someone else would have to worry about the next few centuries.

Wally watched my face, waiting. For a moment, I thought he might try to sell me something.

I said: "You're not telling me anything new."

"You're the first real threat they've been able to put into the field in decades."

I looked away. Annalise, my boss, was ten times more dangerous than I was. She could tear my head off with one hand, and she wasn't the most powerful member of the society by any means. I was a guppy in a shark tank. "That's bullshit and bullshit won't work on me."

He laughed. "You would think so, dude, but I'm one hundred percent serious. You killed Ansel Zahn, man!" The rail-thin old woman at the next table looked up from her book at that, but Wally was oblivious. "You killed the last of the Hammers. You took out a whole swarm of cousins, too. And those were just the top-of-the-marquee names. Do you understand how badass that is?"

I glanced at the woman beside us. She watched us warily and looked about to bolt from her seat. "He's talking about videogames," I said. She sighed and returned to her book.

Wally grinned at me with his gray smile. "And then there are all the *regular* folks. I didn't know you had it in you. I tried to get my hands on the police report—"

"Shut up."

"No, really! I wanted to find out how many bystanders you killed in Washa—"

"*Shut up.*" I wanted to hit him so bad I could barely breathe, but I didn't know what would happen to the people around me. They would be just like the people I'd killed in Washaway, innocent victims—only this time it wouldn't be self-defense, it would be sloppiness.

Luckily, Wally wasn't interested in pushing me. "Okay, dude. Be cool. I'm just saying it's like I went to grade school with the Seahawks' quarterback. People are talking about you."

That, I didn't like. "Tell me about the 'thing' Melly was supposed to help you with."

"Why else would you want an invisible person? I wanted to steal something that's moderately well guarded."

"A puzzle," I prompted. He smiled and shrugged. "But you couldn't get it." His gaze became a little distracted, as if I was boring him. Either he didn't want to talk about it or there wasn't anything to say. "You're TheLast-King,' right? That was you last Christmas in Washaway, right?"

He focused on me. I had his attention again. "I was never in Washaway."

"But you were the one feeding information to . . ." The faces of dead people came back to my memory, and I stopped talking. I couldn't say the names of those dead men out loud.

Wally held up his hand, his thumb and index finger almost touching. "Teeny, teeny bits of information, but it was enough to get them running out there with their checkbooks and shotguns. They didn't matter, though. Not really. They were in the way."

"Wally, tell me about the thing you're planning. What part did Caramella have in it?"

He laughed. "Forget about the thing. I wish I could. Anyway, she already did her part."

"You . . ." I'd almost said *killed her,* but the woman with the book was still too close. "The drape already took her, and it almost got me, too."

"That's the risk we face when we call these things," Wally said, absentmindedly touching a lump on his chin. "But wait, what did you call it?"

I shrugged, feeling vaguely embarrassed. "I had to call them something, so I've been thinking of them as drapes."

"Hah! In the book, they're called Wings of Air and Hunger, but I like your name better. Less ridiculous."

The word *book* pushed one of my buttons. "Wally, I want you to turn over your spell book and all copies—"

"Ray! I can't believe you'd try that shit with me."

"Excuse me," the waitress said. She set a plate in front of Wally and a cup in front of me. "You can't use that language in here. If you do it again, you'll have to leave."

Wally beamed up at her with his sickly face. It was a nasty smile. "I hear you."

She left. Wally picked up a hard-boiled egg and popped it into his mouth—he didn't even peel the shell off first—then gulped it down like a snake. "Ray," he said, as he cut his sausage patties in quarters and stacked them. "Don't try that 'turn over your books' crap with me, okay? It's insulting. First of all, I'm not one of the power-crazy jagoffs you're used to dealing with. I'm trying to do some good here."

"Tell that to Caramella."

"And her boyfriend, too, probably." He looked at his watch. "Should have happened for him first. And the rest of them soon enough. But I'm sorry about that. Seriously. I know that drapes are painful, and I'm not looking to cause a lot of pain."

I laughed at him. He shrugged and looked sheepish. I said: "They're bringing more of their kind."

Wally stabbed the stack of sausages with his fork, stuck them into his mouth, and swallowed them all without chewing. I wondered how his throat could squeeze them all down. "Good thing I brought you and your buddies down to take care of it, then."

"I'm going to take care of you, too."

The lumps on Wally's face suddenly shifted position, as though something under his skin was moving around. His body hunched up, bulking around his neck and shoulders.

"Whoa," he said. "Hold on, let me deal with something." He closed his eyes and took deep breaths as though fighting the urge to puke. After a few seconds, he smiled again. "My passengers didn't like that you said that. Don't, okay? It'd be embarrassing to call you here under a white flag and break the truce myself."

"Christ, Wally. You have predators inside you."

"Oh, yeah, Ray. You'd be surprised by how many. I'm a different thing than you're used to facing. Man, the whole world looks different to me now. Literally. Did you know that some outsiders don't use light to see? Now I'm sharing that gift, too, and it's wild."

"You're carrying predators for their abilities? Are you fucked in the head? What could be worth that?"

"Oh, well, they let me fly like Superman, and I can hork Chubby Hubby ice cream through my nostrils. Right? Dude. Come on. You expect me to just *tell* you? We're not exactly pals—for now, anyway—so I'm not going to tell you everything I can, you know, *do*. That would be showing my hand."

"Showing your . . . Have you looked in a mirror lately? You look like you're dying right in front of me.".

"Looks bad, feels good; that's what I say."

"Christ. You're so fucking stupid."

"Hey now," Wally said. He didn't seem offended at all. "I have power, Ray. Not Ansel Zahn levels, but I don't have to take the risks his type takes, either. All I had to do was put a protective spell on myself—a permanent one—and summon a couple something-somethings into myself. I keep them fed, and they share their little tricks with me."

My hand twitched as I resisted the urge to grab my ghost knife and start cutting. It could destroy the mark that protected Wally from his predators—wherever it was—turning them loose on him.

Except that was absolutely forbidden. No one in the Twenty Palace Society was allowed to feed a predator, ever. When I killed Wally, I was going to have to do it some other way.

He kept talking, oblivious. "Ray, I'm sure *you* could find a way to kill me if you really tried, but it would not be easy. Then, if you survived, you'd have my little buddies to deal with. But you shouldn't try. You want to know why?" He gestured toward his face and neck. "Because I'm making sacrifices to do some good here."

"You're trying to kill everybody."

"Everybody dies anyway, Ray. I've seen it. If things keep going the way they are, what happened to Caramella will look like passing peacefully in your sleep. And you know what? Drapes and cousins and sapphire dogs—that shit is really painful and scary for people. But I'm not about that. Just because I plan to euthanize the world doesn't mean I want to be a dick about it. My plan is supposed to make things easier. Make it, you know, quick and painless."

"Don't do me any favors," I said.

"Too late. I already decided. Ray, do you want to know why the outsiders are so anxious to get here, to our world? Do you know why they're desperate to escape the Deeps?"

"What outsiders are you talking about?"

Wally touched a lump on his face. "The society calls them predators, which is correct but doesn't really describe everything they are, and calls their home the Empty Spaces, which is a pretty stupid name for a place that's so full of weirdness. Ray, do you know why they want to get here so badly?"

I didn't like being instructed by Wally, but no one else ever wanted to explain things to me. Certainly not Annalise. "Tell me."

"Because there's no death there. I'm serious. The Deeps are teeming with outsiders, but they can't feed on each other because they can't kill and eat each other, because nothing there can die. So they're stuck out there, desperate and *starving*. You think what happened to your friend was bad? She probably had a couple days of pain before she died. Maybe less. The outsiders hurt for decades—centuries, maybe—waiting for a chance to feed again."

"And you want to help them to a snack."

He sagged and looked disappointed. "No, Ray. I'm trying to save everyone from . . ." He stopped and looked around the room. The woman with the book had left, and no one had taken her place. In fact, the diner was only half as full as it was when I entered.

Wally sighed again. "Never mind. I had to try, okay? I owed you that. I know the Twenty Palace Society has brainwashed you, but I still think of you as the guy who stood between me and Rocky Downing at the edge of the basketball court. I know you have your heart in the right place, you just need to get your head there, too. Keep your eyes open, Ray. That's all I'm saying. You can't trust those society people. And you may decide soon that you want to stand between me and the bullies again."

Wally swallowed the remaining two eggs, again without peeling them. Then he folded his soggy bacon, speared it with his fork, and gulped it down, too.

"Don't get up," he said as he stood. "I'm serious. You're a great guy, but the truce only lasts while we're here. I'm skipping town now anyway, so you should deal with the, uh, drapes. We'll see each other again." He laid a couple of bills on the table. It was more than enough to cover the check. "And I wish Curly-Head had waited on us. That was supposed to be part of the plan."

Damn. He was leaving, and I hadn't gotten anything truly useful out of him. "Wally, at least tell me how to stop the drapes."

He snorted. "Is that how you've been doing it? *Please please tell me what to do?* Come on, I want to see some of your mad skills."

I stood out of my chair and turned toward him. He stepped back, looking up at me in surprise and delight as though I was a plot twist in an exciting TV show. I reached into my pocket for my ghost knife.

But Wally had already placed his fingers in his mouth. He pulled out something small, wet, and red as blood. It was round like a Ping-Pong ball and gleamed like metal. Then it unfolded legs as long and slender as needles.

Wally tossed it over the counter into the kitchen. "Choices, choices," he said and took one step backward. He passed through the wall like a phantom.

CHAPTER SEVEN

Damn. I was tempted to run out the front door after him, but a scream from the kitchen changed my mind. I vaulted over the counter.

The tile on the other side hadn't been mopped recently. I landed on grease and nearly fell on my ass. I heard a clatter of shell on stone and a man's cry of fear and disgust from the kitchen. I pushed through the door into the back.

It was a kitchen much like any restaurant kitchen. Everything was stainless steel, and the three Hispanic men at the stove were dressed in white with black hairnets. The tallest of them shrieked like a little girl and staggered back, away from the creature that was scuttling across the floor at him.

A short man snatched a huge pot of water off the stove and dropped it onto the creature. Boiling water splashed into the air, and the heavy pot clanged like a muffled bell.

Then it fell on its side. Steaming water rushed at me, and I jumped back too slowly. It sloshed through the fabric of my shoes, scalding my feet.

The little predator wasn't affected. It charged at the man who'd dropped a pot on it and jumped onto his leg. Then it began to dig.

The man screamed and grabbed a ladle. He hit the predator with all his strength, trying to knock it away, but the ladle crumpled and the predator didn't move an inch.

Blood splashed onto the floor and the predator burrowed deep into his flesh. The man fell, screaming full-throated now. His co-workers backed away in terror, screaming themselves.

I charged through the scalding water, grabbed the cook's torn pants, and ripped them up to his thigh. The predator was visible as a bulge moving under his skin. I took my ghost knife and slashed through it.

My spell passed through the man's flesh without damaging it, but the creature inside him was another matter. It exploded into a fireball as large as a basketball.

The cook, mercifully, fainted. I snatched a pot off a hook and filled it at the sink. Then I poured it over his burning clothes. The other cooks stared at me, dumbfounded. I said: "What do you think? Ambulance?" One of them blinked and lunged for a phone.

Wally's waitress was standing at the edge of the kitchen, her body hunched in shock, her mouth hanging open. Behind her, also dressed in a waitress uniform, was Violet. "Vi, check your voice mail!"

I didn't wait for a response. I ran out the back door into the parking lot, desperate to find Wally again.

I sprinted to the side of the building where Wally would have come through the wall, but there was no sign of him. I scanned the area, looking for a blob of a man in green. Nothing. The predator he'd thrown into the kitchen had distracted me, but not for more than a minute or so. I didn't think he'd had enough time to get into a car and get away.

Unless he'd brought a driver. That would have been a smart play, but I didn't believe for a moment that Wally had a friend in the whole world. Which would mean he was still on foot. Was he in one of the other stores, watching me? Was he walking through them, building after building, wall after wall, down the entire block in a place I couldn't see him?

Did you know that some outsiders don't use light to see? Now I'm sharing that gift, too, and it's wild. Maybe he was watching me through a brick wall, waiting to see what I'd do. My skin tingled at the thought of it.

Violet came outside and edged toward me. She looked afraid of me. "Ray, what the hell is going on?"

"How well do you know the guy I was sitting with?"

Under other circumstances, she would have snapped at me for answering a question with another question. I wondered what my expression looked like. "Not at all," she said. "He's just a creep who's been coming around lately."

She was lying again, but I didn't have time to press her on it. "All right. Listen: I think he's still nearby, watching. I think he's going to make sure he lost me before he goes back to wherever he's staying. So I'm going to walk away, and you're going to stand in the window of the café and watch for him. Understand? I'll be back in five minutes or so."

"What happened to my apartment, Ray?"

"I'll explain what I know later, but I can't let this guy get away." She didn't look convinced. "Vi, all you have to do is stand in the window and watch."

I could see she didn't want to do it. She didn't want anything to do with Wally King at all, and I didn't blame her. But then she nodded and looked away from me. Thank God.

I ran to the sidewalk. If Wally had kept going in a straight line, he would have gone back toward Vi's apartment and my car. After one quick look around, just in case I got lucky, I headed in the opposite direction.

I wasn't sure how far I should go. I wanted Wally to have enough time to feel safe and hit the sidewalk again, but not so long that I couldn't catch up to him. As long as he didn't have a car stashed nearby . . . I didn't want to think about that.

I'd planned to jog two blocks, but I'd only gone a block and a half before I felt too anxious and tense to continue. I hurried toward the Sugar Shaker, sweat prickling my back.

Violet met me at the door. "He was just here, not a minute ago," she said. "The creep walked by the window and winked at me." She shuddered a little and pointed down the street toward her apartment. "Then he took off that way and turned right at the corner. Ray—"

I ran off before she could finish that thought. Whatever she had to tell me, it would have to wait until after I'd found Wally. Found him and killed him.

"Ray!" Vi followed me onto the street. "Ray! You wait for me!"

"Vi, dammit, he's going to hear you."

"Don't you tell me to shut up! You're going to tell me what's going on!" So much for being afraid of me.

"If Wally hears you, he'll come back here and kill us both."

"You don't play that shit with me! You're going to tell me who this asshole is, or you're going to regret it."

We couldn't stand out on the sidewalk hashing this out while Wally walked away. "Come on, and keep your voice down."

I led her down the sidewalk. In the distance, I could see a column of black smoke stretching into the sky. It gave me a weird, jangly feeling to see the destruction that was following me around.

"I'm waiting," she said.

"Wally is from Seattle."

"Duh."

I remember this mood very well. She wanted me to talk to her, and she wanted to be nasty about it. If I let her turn it into a fight, I'd lose my shot at Wally. "Don't, okay? Just let me finish. I knew Wally from school. We weren't friends, but I made a couple of bullies leave him alone, so now he likes me. But we're not friends," I added quickly, because I could see she was about to talk.

"That's not what he says."

"Fuck him." We reached the corner and I peeked around it. Wally was almost to the end of the block, walking with a strange, stiff-legged limp on the other side of the street. He wasn't moving very fast, and I figured he'd be easy to catch on foot.

And I was ready. I was ready to kill him right there on the sidewalk, if I could. But not in front of Vi.

"He did something to a friend of mine," I said. I didn't want to explain further, but I knew she wouldn't be satisfied with that. "He hurt the oldest, best friend I had in this world. Understand? Nobody in my whole life ever meant as much to me as that friend did."

She seemed taken aback, but I pressed on. "Wally . . ." *Wally put a predator inside him.* "Wally poisoned him. He gave him some kind of experimental drug that drove him crazy—"

"And he ate people. Right? That was all over the news."

Of course. "I tried to save my friend . . ." *From the Twenty Palace Society.* "I tried to bring back the old him, the guy I knew. I protected him. But in the end, he wouldn't stop, so . . ." *I killed him.*

No. I couldn't say that. I didn't believe in confession.

She didn't need me to say it. Something in my voice had blunted her anger. "So Wally's after you and you're after him, and me and my daughter are caught in the middle."

"At least you're still alive," I said. "So far."

She turned her back on me and walked away. Finally. I peered back around the corner and saw Wally farther up the street, close to the intersection. Maybe I'd do something for Vi later, if I survived, but I couldn't imagine what. I couldn't think about her, not when Wally was right there.

I took out my ghost knife. Wally didn't change his pace or turn around as I crossed the street and fell in behind him. Whatever X-ray vision he might have had, he still couldn't see behind him. Good. If he was as full of predators as he said, I was going to need to ambush him.

And God, it felt so good to have that clarity. It was calming, almost, even as I felt my heartbeat quicken and my body grow warm. I was going to rush at this bastard, and I was finally going to kill him.

I walked faster. My spell would hit whatever I wanted it to hit, but I'd have to call it back between each attack, and the distance between us meant there would be a lot of time between hits. I had to get closer.

He crossed the street and slumped up the next block. Suddenly, all the doors of a 4Runner opened just as Wally came near it. Five guys piled out and stepped up to him, blocking the sidewalk. Wally didn't seem startled by them at all.

I had been about to cross the street, but I ducked into the loading dock of an appliance store at the last moment. I peeked at them from behind a stack of pallets.

One of the men who'd stepped out of the 4Runner looked up and down the street warily. I recognized him immediately as the shortest and most muscular of Fidel's cousins. Then I immediately recognized the others, including Fidel himself.

I couldn't hear what they were saying at this distance, but I could see their body language. Fidel was smiling and making broad gestures with his hands—he was trying to look like a magnanimous gangster, the guy who asked for things in a friendly way while the gunmen around him made sure you knew what the correct answer was supposed to be.

Something Fidel said made Wally throw back his head and laugh. He didn't seem nervous or intimidated at all.

They were standing in front of a hotel, and Wally waved for them to follow him up the walkway. They did, glancing around warily as they went.

"Hey! What are you doing there?" a voice behind me said.

The man who'd challenged me had a belly like a wine barrel, a wiry beard, and tiny round glasses. He'd just come out of the back door onto the loading dock. "Duh," I said. "I'm spying on someone."

He opened his mouth to respond, then shrugged and went back inside.

Wally, Fidel, and all his people were gone. I crossed the street, approaching the building slowly. There was an arched opening in the middle of the building and a driveway for cars to pull through. On one side of the arch was the lobby and reception area, and on the other was a diner.

The building was stucco, with tall sliding glass doors, and even from the street I could see how dirty it was. The little diner was mostly deserted, with a few scattered people-watchers on plastic furniture eating out of red plastic baskets. None of them looked like Fidel's crew.

A sliding glass door opened somewhere above me, and I glanced up. The stoned guy from the alley last night stepped onto a balcony. It was the lowest floor and nearly at the north end of the building. I quickly turned my back.

I walked away from him until I heard the door close again, then risked a glance back and saw that the balcony was empty. Thank God for a criminal's paranoia. I'd never have found them otherwise.

The windows and balconies alternated along the length of the building—window, balcony, balcony, window, window, balcony, balcony, window. That meant there were four units on each floor in opposing pairs that let the architects set their bathrooms back-to-back.

How to get there was the problem. I wasn't keen on the idea of kicking the door down, and no one had left a ladder conveniently leaning against the building. I went into the office.

The man behind the desk was small, dark, and narrow-shouldered; he had a thin mustache like a movie star from the thirties. "How may I help you?" He had a slight British accent.

"I need a room."

"Of course, sir. Do you have luggage?"

"In my car," I said. "I'm looking for something specific. I need the lowest room you have, and I need it to be in the northeast corner of the building."

"Ah. Are you concerned about feng shui?"

"No, I'm interested in the flow of energy in my living space." He couldn't quite suppress a smile, and I was happy to let him laugh at me. Being underestimated has saved my life more than once.

"We do have such a room." He brought out the paperwork.

"Can I check it out first? For a few minutes alone? I'd like to meditate on it."

He pursed his lips and shook his head. I wasn't *that* amusing. I paid for the room and promised to get my luggage after I checked out the flow. He gave me a plastic card to unlock the door.

I went up the stairs, gambling that if Fidel didn't place a guy in the diner, he wouldn't have one in the hall. And I was right. I paused at the door to Wally's room and heard Fidel say that he couldn't use that place anymore and they needed a new place. His voice was raised, as though he was arguing.

I didn't listen for long. Getting caught with my ear at

the door would be a bad thing. I walked quietly down the hall, feeling the sweat prickle on my back. The gold-painted walls and wine-colored carpet made me feel stifled, even if it was cooler inside than out.

I let myself into my room. It was two steps above utilitarian, with a floral print on the covers.

My hands started shaking. I clenched them into fists and pressed them against the dead flesh over my heart to control them. Wally was just on the other side of that wall, and my chance to kill him was coming soon. I had no idea what he was capable of, aside from walking through walls and puking a tiny monster onto me. I took a deep breath, trying to calm myself down. It would have been nice to have a better plan than *Move fast hit hard,* but what the hell. I would give it a shot, and if I failed, so be it. I just hoped I wouldn't see any more of his *tricks*, if he had them.

I went to the balcony and looked across at the adjacent one. I could jump it and be close enough to eavesdrop, but I knew someone would catch me.

The ground was about fifteen feet below. If I missed the jump, I'd land just outside the manager's office. I think he'd find me much less amusing after that.

I hurried into the bathroom to splash water on my face, then grabbed a glass off the sink and returned to the main room.

By my standards, the room was comfortable, but the walls were not terribly thick. I laid the glass against the wall and pressed my ear to it.

I'd seen this work on TV, but it wasn't doing me a bit of good here. The voices in the next room were too muffled to understand, although I could tell that the argument was over.

"Seriously, Ray? A glass against the wall?"

I pivoted in surprise, dropping the glass onto the carpet. Arne was standing just behind me. He sat on the edge of the bed. "If you want to spy on people, you ought to order the right tool for the job. On the Internet you can get a pretty good listening device for a hundred bucks."

My heart was racing, but I did my best to act calm. "Sure, but can you drink iced tea out of it, too?"

"You got me there."

"I guess you finished your job?"

He rubbed his hands on his thighs. "No. This is just a quiet moment while I wait for the stupid people to catch up, so I thought I'd check on other things. What happened with that big guy?"

"Wardell? We're best buds. He invited me over for a *Golden Girls* marathon."

"I'll bet." He sighed. "You've developed a knack for slipping out of trouble, haven't you? Didn't you get snapped up by Uncle Sam a few months ago? After Washaway?"

I became very still. "Yes."

"And what? They let you go?"

Not really. "Yes."

"I guess they had to, huh? How'd you manage that?"

I'm on the twisted path. "They caught the real assholes. Nothing to do with me."

Arne seemed amused by that. "You know what turns people into monsters, Ray? Knowing they can get away with anything. Once they realize they aren't going to be punished for anything they do, the masks come off, baby, and the devils run free."

I didn't need anyone to tell me this. This was my life. I said: "It's time to help me with my thing, right?" Arne spread his hands to say *Why not?* "Tell me how this started. Tell me about Wally."

"But it didn't start with Wally. It started with Luther."

"He's the guy you brought in to replace me, right?"

"Nobody replaced you, Ray. Your spot was open and

waiting for you. Luther was just extra help. He was big, strong, and friendly—not that bright, but how many bright people do the work we do? Mostly he was loyal, as long as you put a couple of bucks in his pocket.

"Luther was hanging at the Bigfoot Room all by himself when Wally walked in. Wally dropped your name, which Luther recognized. After I don't know how long, Luther called all of us at once: me, Fidel, Summer, the whole crew. Everyone but Vi and Melly met up at the Bigfoot Room. Wally made his pitch—he offered us a super power—and Luther was the living proof that it was real. He vanished right in front of us. All we had to do in return was a single favor. Luther's excitement was infectious.

"I had a bad feeling about it, though, and I put him off for twenty-four hours. You know why."

"Wally looks like a walking tumor and you didn't want to end up like him."

"Hell yeah. I'm a good-looking man. I can't throw away a face like this. But Luther said that the powers Wally had were different from the invisibility thing. Bigger. He said Wally couldn't vanish himself, which was why he needed our help."

My mouth suddenly felt dry. "What powers does Wally have?"

Arne shrugged. "I don't have a lot to tell you. You'd have to ask Lenard."

"Why?"

"Well, Lenard doesn't like victims to feel too comfortable around him. He likes them wide-eyed and sweating, right? And he starts thinking that your buddy Wally is too cheerful, so out of the blue he rushes the guy and knocks him over, right into the dirt. Then he starts screaming at him like a nutcase, 'Don't you dare smile at me! Don't you fucking smile!' And the rest of us are rolling our eyes at him.

"But your buddy just got to his feet and smiled at Lenard again, like a big *fuck you*. And Lenard, now he has to step up or he'll look like he wimped out. So he gives Wally another shove.

"Except this time, your boy was ready and it didn't even move him. It was like Lenard was pushing against an office building—he couldn't even make a dent in the guy's flabby man-titties. Almost like . . ."

I remembered the way the cook had hit the little red predator with his ladle, and how the creature didn't move an inch. *I keep them fed, and they share their little tricks with me.* "Almost like nothing could move him if he didn't want it to."

"Yeah, and then there was this wave that came out of him—I'm not sure what to call it. It was like one of those old kung fu movies, where one dude shoves another without touching him. Lenard had his ass lifted off the ground and dropped into the dirt ten feet away. He didn't know what to do about that, but Ty and Fidel took the heat off by making a joke of it. You'd have to talk to Lenard to find out what it felt like. I was just standing there watching."

"Right."

"Not much, is it? It's like he's the patron saint of shoving. He acted like he could do more, but then, he would."

I nodded. I didn't want to thank Arne; he might have told me I was welcome and walked out. "What favor did Wally want?"

"He hasn't asked for one. Not from me. By the time Luther came to us, his debt was paid in full. I asked him what he'd done, and he took me to the—"

A gunshot popped in the next room. Arne's expression became weary, and he vanished.

Damn. My questions would have to wait. I ran into the hall and cut the lock on Wally's door with my ghost knife.

The door swung inward. A bearded man pivoted toward me, raising his arm. I threw myself to the floor, but there was no gunfire. Fidel laid a hand on the gunman's shoulder, and he lowered his weapon. Fidel had his SIG Sauer in his other hand.

"Ray?"

They all had the same gun. I left the ghost knife on the floor and raised my hands to show that they were empty. Then I got to my knees, letting my hand fall on my spell and picking it up. Wally lay on the bed, his arms wide, his feet on the floor. There was a single bullet hole in his chest. He looked like a lumpy bundle of old clothes.

Was he dead? I'd assumed he'd be as hard to kill as a sorcerer, especially with normal weapons. Ansel Zahn had been reduced to a bloody mess by an amateur firing squad, and he'd laughed about it. And Wally had said he was full of predators.

But now he had a hole in his chest, and he wasn't moving at all. Had they done my job for me?

I didn't believe it. I couldn't believe it.

"That's not cool, man," Stoned said. He pointed at me. "This guy's a witness."

"You saved me the trouble," I said. My hand brushed against something on the table. It was a wallet, bulging with paper receipts and cash. One of those scraps of paper might lead me to his spell books, and damn if I didn't want to steal his money.

"He laughed at me," Fidel said, staring down at Wally's body. The hammer of his pistol was cocked. I looked at the other guns, but their hammers were all uncocked. Stoned rolled his eyes and shared a glance with the others. The three of them looked disappointed.

In the moment they looked away, I pocketed the wallet.

Fidel chewed his lip as though he was trying to work out a tough math problem. "First, he refused me. Then he laughed at me."

"What now, Fidel?" The short, muscular man with the heavy beard stepped close. "You promised us something. How you gonna deliver now that this guy is dead?"

Wally's shirt moved.

"You guys should get out of here," I said.

Muscular pointed his gun at me again. "You ain't calling the shots here."

"It's not about who's the shot caller," I said. I pointed to Wally. "This guy isn't as dead as you think."

Wally's shirt twitched and shifted. One of the guys cursed in surprise, and they were behind me all of a sudden, because I'd moved toward Wally's body without even realizing I was doing it. The clean, cold certainty I'd felt while I was stalking him had evaporated. More predators were about to get loose, and there was nothing between them and the world except me. I raised my ghost knife.

A gleaming red ball pushed its way out of the hole in Wally's shirt. Then another, then four, five, six more were coming out as if they were being pushed through the opening. They tumbled down the sides of Wally's body like golf balls and stopped in the folds of the blankets or in the nest of his crotch. A couple struck the floor with a heavy thunk.

Spiny metallic needles extended from their bodies, and they began to scramble toward us. I gripped my ghost knife tightly and moved forward to meet them.

Pop-pop-pop-pop-pop-pop came from behind me, as Fidel's family cut loose with their SIGs. Bullets zinged around me, some punching through the floor, others ricocheting in unpredictable ways. I turned to shout at them to stop, but as I did I saw Muscular lean down to fire at the closest predator.

The sound of the shot, the spark on the creature's shell, and the bloody wound on his leg all seemed to appear in the same instant.

He fell back against the wall as the predator advanced on him. The bullet's impact had as much effect as it would against a bank vault.

There were a dozen predators fanning across the room toward us and more coming every moment. Three were a second or two away from my own ankle, and I swept my ghost knife through the lead.

It burst into flames as I leapt back. The fire touched the two behind it, and they burst apart as well.

The sudden flares stopped the gunfire, at least. Fidel and his cousins backed toward the door, leaving Muscular cut off against the wall. Stoned drew back his leg and kicked at one of the scuttling little balls, but it was like kicking a metal post anchored into the ground.

I had to move away from the burning spot on the carpet. Stoned fell backward toward the doorway, cursing. Fidel and one of his cousins grabbed at him, but they were so spooked and frantic that they worked against each other. I could hear Muscular behind me, shouting in Spanish, his voice going high with fear.

Everything was loud and bright and hot. The carpet was burning, streaming thin black smoke that smelled like burned plastic. It was all too much. I couldn't think clearly.

I moved toward Stoned, Fidel, and the others and cut through one of the predators pursuing them, then drew back. The creature burst into flames, then the others began to go up in a chain reaction, spreading the fire from the wall to the dresser and cutting off my path to the door. I turned my back on the popping sounds and the growing firelight.

Muscular had scrambled into a corner. He'd tucked his injured leg behind him and hammered at the closest of the predators with the butt of his pistol, but there was no effect at all. His teeth were bared in raw terror, and I rushed toward him, ghost knife in hand.

The nearest of the predators began to tear through his leather shoe with its needle-sharp forelegs. I saw blood, but Muscular didn't do anything more than grunt. I swept my spell through the creature, and this time I saw that the predator didn't split apart—its shell and limbs seemed to vanish, revealing the expanding fire from inside it.

Now Muscular screamed as the flames engulfed his leg. A second predator burst into flames nearby, and I fell away from the heat. There were no other creatures close enough to go up with it.

Christ, the things were still coming through the hole in Wally's chest, as though he had an inexhaustible supply of them. The flames blocking the way toward the door had spread with startling speed; the front half of the dresser was wrapped in fire. Black smoke flowed along the ceiling and out into the hall through the door that Fidel had left open. The smoke alarm shrieked out in the hall, but I could still hear predators popping like caps in the fire.

The way out of the room was blocked by burning carpet, so the predators were trapped on the far side of the bed, piling up against the wall, testing it with their sharp legs. Apparently, they didn't like digging through something that wasn't flesh.

Another stream of predators came toward us from the balcony side of the room. Muscular tried to pull farther back into the corner. He slammed his elbow against the wall, trying to break through to safety, but he had no leverage and no time.

I stepped over him and crouched low, swiping my ghost knife through the lead predator. It burst, igniting the other creatures beside and behind it. The fire spread backward along the sliding glass door and ignited the polyester blankets hanging off the bed.

The flames had already reached the other side of the

bed. I dropped to my knees, beneath the thickening cloud of black smoke. The fire on the carpet was only as high as my calves, but the doorway was already wreathed in flames. The covers, still just starting to burn, dripped liquid fire onto the carpet.

And damn, it was so *loud*.

I lifted Muscular to his feet, but we both stayed well below the billows of smoke. The fire moved toward us, and the carpet at the edge of it was giving off white smoke. God, it had gotten so hot in the room so quickly. I felt like I'd been thrown into an oven.

But predators were still pouring out of the hole in Wally's chest. They were tumbling away from the flames, swarming in thick piles along the headboard and wall. I could see some of the predators digging at the drywall, trying to escape into the next room.

The only real weapon I had was my ghost knife, and it was just a piece of paper—covered by laminate and mailing tape—but still just paper. I'd been hitting the predators as quickly as I could—like flicking a finger through a candle flame—to keep the fire from damaging it, but I couldn't hold back anymore. My spell was precious, but stopping these predators was more important.

I threw my ghost knife toward the opening in Wally's chest. At the same time, I willed it to move as fast as it could, putting my fear and adrenaline behind it. It zipped away from me like a rocket.

I lunged across Muscular's body toward the curtain.

The ghost knife passed through the bulge in Wally's stomach. Fire blasted out of his body like water from a fire hose. I tore the curtain from the rod, letting it fall over us. Predators went off like little firebombs. I slapped my hand across Muscular's mouth and nose as the flames roared around us.

God, the heat! Muscular's face was inches from mine,

and his eyes were bulging with terror. I'm sure I looked the same.

The roar of flames subsided. The curtain scorched my back, so I threw it away, letting it fall on the carpet between the sliding glass door and us. I'd hoped it would smother the flames a little, but actually it added fuel.

At the other end of the room, fire climbed the wall and rolled against the ceiling. The bed was completely aflame, and I couldn't see anything of Wally except his feet.

I hefted Muscular onto my shoulder. He was heavy, but my adrenaline was flowing. Time seemed sluggish, my chest felt tight, and my skin was steaming as sweat poured out of me. There was no way I could get to the door, but the balcony was only three feet away. I just had to walk through the fire.

Eight thick midnight-blue tendrils suddenly rose up out of the flames where Wally's body lay. They arced and pressed down against the floor, lifting Wally's corpse toward the ceiling. He was still on his back, his arms flopping loose, his nasty green sweat suit burning against his skin. A thick sludge bubbled out of the hole in his chest and flowed over his body, extinguishing the flames. He—it—something turned so its face was toward me.

Wally's eyes were open. "Damn, Ray. That actually hurt."

Moving like spiders' legs, the tendrils walked him through the wall as though he were a phantom.

My blood was rushing in my ears, and Muscular was clutching at me, digging his fingers into my shoulder blade. I ran through the flames, staying as low as I could. The heat against the bottom of my shoes and up my legs was intense, but it was just pain. Just pain. I slammed my elbow against the door handle, and thank God it opened. Then I was through the doorway and onto the concrete balcony.

I swung Muscular off my shoulder, setting him on the far side of the iron rail. We both gasped for fresh air, and he suddenly began slapping at me. For a moment I was furious and drew back my fist, but then I realized he was beating out the flames on my clothes.

I stood still, listening to the roaring fire behind me and the sirens in the distance. My legs and feet didn't hurt anymore, which was a huge surprise.

Muscular stopped swatting the flames out and looked me directly in the eye. *"Mi hermano,"* he said.

Adrenaline buzzed in my head and made it hard to focus on what he'd said. We gripped each other's wrists as though we were actors in a sword-fighting movie, then I lowered him to the grass below. I bent over the rail as far as I could, but just as I thought it was still too high, he let go.

He struck the ground with a cry of pain, rolling on the grass and clutching at his burned and bloody legs. Then he struggled upright and began hopping toward the sidewalk.

The wind changed, blowing the choking black smoke toward me. The temptation to follow Muscular down to the grass was strong, but I couldn't flee the scene yet. My head still buzzed; it was hard to think, but I knew I needed to look for predators. I had no idea what I'd do once I found them, but that had never stopped me before.

I swung my leg over the railing. I felt stiff, but it didn't register why. The other balcony was only about six feet away, but when I jumped for it, my legs had no strength in them. I barely managed to catch the top of the rail opposite and pull myself up onto the ledge.

Something was wrong with my legs. No, not something. I was burned, and worse than I realized. Maybe I was in shock, too. I staggered into my room. The wall between mine and Wally's was dark at the top and giving off wisps of smoke. I felt the door; it was cool. I pulled it open and staggered into the hall.

Just a few feet to my left, the doorway to Wally's room was open. Black smoke flowed out and the flames ran all the way up to the ceiling. The smoke alarm blared an awful noise. Where were the other guests? Long gone, I hoped.

There was a staircase on the other side of the flames, but I knew it led down to the front office. Instead, I turned to the stair at the other end of the hall. The door was propped open. As I stumbled toward it, choking and coughing, I saw that it was blocked by a pair of legs.

I pushed the door open. Stoned lay on his back on the stairs, his head hanging down and his mouth open. His face was bloody, as though he'd puked blood on himself, and there was a ragged hole where his windpipe was supposed to be. His shirt rippled—something moved under there.

Damn. I had screwed up again. At least one of Wally's predators had escaped, and Stoned had died. I dragged him by the belt into the hall and let the metal door close. Fidel and his other two cousins were nowhere to be seen.

I stood over Stoned's body, feeling dizzy and weak. I couldn't breathe deeply without gagging. The sirens were getting closer, but they didn't sound close enough. Stoned's pant leg rippled then, and his shirt in two places. Did he have three of those nasty little bastards in him? I reached for my ghost knife, but it wasn't there and I couldn't remember where I'd left it.

To hell with it. I pulled him down the hall by the pant cuff. The dragging on the carpet caused his green plaid shirt to slide up, and I saw lumps under his skin moving down his body toward my hand, as though they could smell living flesh where it brushed his. I moved faster.

By the time the nearest predator was at Stoned's knee, I was close enough to the fire to feel it scorching my back. I let go of his ankle and shuffled around to the other side of him. The bulges under his skin stopped moving toward his foot as though they'd lost the scent.

I didn't want to give them the chance to find it again. I grabbed Stoned under the armpits and hoisted him up and through the doorway. I had to get so close that it felt like being on fire again, but I managed to drop him well into the flames.

I staggered back against the wall, coughing and choking. I crouched there, staying low where the air was still breathable, and watched to see if any of the little iron creatures came scuttling out of the flames. There was nothing I could do about it if they did, but I had to know.

My back and legs began to hurt in earnest now, and my wooziness grew stronger. I wanted to puke and take a nap but forced myself to wait and watch.

The flames spread, the sirens of fire trucks roared outside, and the smoke grew thick. No creatures came out of the fire toward me, but did that mean they'd been destroyed? I couldn't think about it. My head was too muzzy.

Time to go. I crawled along the wall toward the metal door at the end of the hall. Saturday-morning public-service announcements had told me that I would find clean air at knee level, but I coughed and hacked on the stink of burning polyester. Just as I reached the edge of the door, it swung open.

Two firefighters rushed by me. They wore helmets and bulky masks, and I suspect they didn't even see me there on the floor. I slipped into the stairwell and let the door close behind me.

The stairs were difficult. What smoke had gotten

through rose up to the top of the stairwell, making the air breathable, but my legs did not want to move. I didn't know how I was going to get to my car, or what I would do after that. A sudden wave of nausea almost made me slide down the final six steps.

On the ground floor, I fell against the door and went out into the sunlight. The heat of the day was raw against my burns. I didn't look down at them, though. I didn't want to see how bad they were, because then the pain would hit me like a tidal wave.

Not that it wasn't already coming on. I tried to breathe slowly to control the pain, but every breath caught in my throat. I circled around the back of the building, leaning on parked cars while I passed between them. A firefighter yelled at me to get out of there, and a slender black woman in gray pinstripes rushed by me with car keys in her hand.

Suddenly, Bud was beside me. "Hey there, Ray."

I staggered away from him and fell against the hood of a Lumina. "Damn," I said, my voice slurred. "Scared me. Give me a hand, Bud."

He laughed. Summer was standing beside him. She never laughed. Neither moved to help me. "You said you were going to save us, Ray." There was a touch of contempt in her voice. "How you gonna manage that?"

I didn't have the energy to spar with them. I was helpless, and that made me furious. "Vanish!" I shouted. The word made me choke. "VANISH!"

Summer sneered at me. Bud smirked. Both of them turned their backs and walked away.

I didn't care, because my anger had given me focus and I'd suddenly remembered what I'd done with my spell.

I'd thrown my ghost knife but hadn't *called* it back,

not through those flames. It should have passed through the wall, but I didn't know how far it could go. I staggered toward the far end of the building—the south? I was all turned around—determined that I would not leave a magic spell lying around for anyone to find. I had to get it back.

At the far side of the building was a narrow alley with a high fence. The chain-link fence had plastic slats threaded through it, so I couldn't see what was on the other side. The pain grew stronger, stealing my life force away.

There was not very much trash in the passageway, but I didn't see my ghost knife anywhere. The only places left to go were back into the building and out to the front, where the fire trucks had gathered.

I didn't need to do that. I closed my eyes and *reached* for my ghost knife. It was nearby—still inside the building and above me, and as I focused on it, I felt myself wavering. My body wanted to shut down, and I was barely able to feel my spell and *call* it to me. The world seemed to be growing dark, but I did see the ghost knife slice through the wall to land in my open palm.

I slapped it against my chest and fell against the side of the building. Whatever it was and whatever it wanted, it was part of me, and I was glad to have it close. I slid it into the back pocket of my pants, miraculously hitting the target on my first try.

I was about to fall when I felt a pair of hands grab me roughly. Damn, I had been caught by one of the firefighters, which meant an ambulance, then cops, then jail. I tried to convince myself it was better than dying, but I couldn't make those thoughts come together in my head. The hands were strong; they lifted me and propped me against the fence.

I looked up but didn't see a firefighter's jacket and helmet. It was the guy in the red T-shirt and the camo pants.

He seemed happy to see me. "Hey!" he said. "Here you are!"

I punched him in the mouth with all my strength, but I knew it wouldn't be enough. The whole world turned dark, and I went down into it, knowing that I might never see daylight again.

CHAPTER EIGHT

Pain woke me. I was lying on my stomach in a darkened room; my legs were stiff and my back felt like it had a turtle shell attached. I put my arms underneath me and raised myself slowly—I couldn't see any people, but if Camo Pants was nearby, I wanted him to think I was fall-down weak right up to the moment I jumped him.

Unfortunately, I *was* weak. My back and legs hurt beyond belief. Every movement I made was like being burned all over again.

Still, I had to move. I didn't know anything about this place except that Camo Pants had brought me here, but that was enough. I had to get out.

Most of my burns were below the knee, so I lifted my feet off the bed and did my best to roll over into a seated position.

I didn't make a sound. It took every bit of restraint I had, but I didn't make a single sound.

When the spots faded from my vision, I looked around. In the dim light from the window, I could see a little lamp on a table by the bed. I snapped it on. I was in a little room—a hotel room, by the look of it—with white paper on the walls, gleaming silver in the fixtures, and pale, ghostly furniture.

I wasn't wearing a shirt. My clothes were gone and my lower legs were covered with gauze and gauze pads. Now that I was finally ready to look at my burns, they were hidden. I glanced around the room again and saw burned, ragged black cloth on the little table by the window. My pants.

My head was pounding and my mouth was parched. I peeled the edge of the gauze away from my leg just enough to peek underneath. It looked red, swollen, and wet. Had they smeared some kind of gel on me, or was that a huge blister? I hoped it was gel.

I stood. The pain was blinding. I gritted my teeth to hold back a scream and dropped back onto the bed. God, the power of it made me nauseous. What the hell had I done to myself?

I had only walked a few steps through a fire. A magic fire.

Dammit. I was out of commission. How was I supposed to help Arne and the others with these drapes on them? How was I supposed to find Wally again? How was I supposed to find out what happened to Mouse?

I put my feet on the floor. They felt swollen and the pain was agonizing, but it was only pain. Only pain. I staggered to the little table and searched my pants pockets. I found my wallet, my keys, and my ghost knife. The wallet even had my money inside. What this said about Camo Pants, I didn't know and didn't care.

I put my wallet in my teeth, biting down hard on it to distract myself from the pain. I slid the key ring over the little finger of my left hand and used my ghost knife to cut the corner of the table. The table leg came free, with enough of the top still attached that it made a dull wooden pick. I stared at my ghost knife for a few seconds, wondering how I was going to take it with me. Eventually, I slid it inside my wallet and put the wallet back in my mouth. It didn't fit but I didn't care. I just needed to get to a place where I could call an ambulance.

I used the table leg as a cane while I crossed the room, then I pushed the door open and staggered through.

It was a hotel suite, as I'd thought, and an expensive one. There was more white, silver, and platinum out here. My feet felt like they were soaking wet through the gauze, and I was sure I was seeping onto the snowy carpet.

A gleaming silver phone sat on a tiny table at the far side of the suite. My original plan had been to get out of the building to get help, but suddenly I wasn't sure I could cross the room. My vision was swirling and my head throbbed. I nearly lost my balance, which would have gotten me off my feet, but I didn't think I could get back up.

Then I noticed a small figure sitting at a marble-topped table in the center of the room. Its back was turned to me, and it was wrapped in black lace and hunched over like a vulture. It couldn't have been Camo Pants, could it? He was too large for this small shape.

It didn't matter. I couldn't get to the phone without passing him. I hefted the table leg like a club and moved forward. The pain made it hard to think, but maybe this little person all wrapped up in black fabric was Camo after all.

It was just pain. Just pain. It made me dizzy and sick, and it clouded my vision at the edges, but I could push through it. I raised the table leg, feeling bleary and angry. I was hurting and I was ready to share that hurt.

"Ray."

I stopped, confused, and turned toward the voice. Annalise stood beside a small desk in the corner, watching me carefully.

Annalise Powliss was my boss, a peer in the Twenty Palace Society, and she was incredibly powerful. Although she was just barely over five feet tall and as thin as a rail, she was covered with tattoos—spells—that gave her extraordinary strength and toughness. She could tear a car door off its hinges with one hand and could shrug off a bullet through the eye. I'd seen her do both.

She wasn't wearing her usual gear—there was no outsized fireman's jacket, no vest covered with alligator-clipped spells. She wore a pair of plain blue drawstring pants and a white button-down shirt. Her tattoo-covered feet were bare. I'd never seen her dressed in such flimsy clothes.

Like mine, her tattoos were spells, but hers covered her whole body from her collarbones down—I'd seen them one time after her clothes had burned on a job.

Finally her face, which was pale and delicate—almost childlike—was set in the most curious expression I'd ever seen. She had always been difficult to read, but for the first time since I'd met her, she seemed nervous.

"Ray," she said again in her funny high voice, "that's a peer in the society you're threatening."

I turned back to the shrouded figure. It had turned toward me, and I saw that it was a little old woman with olive skin and gray streaks in her hair. Her face was impassive and her eyes were dreamy.

How had I mistaken her for Camo Pants? I let the table leg fall from my hands, then immediately wished I had it back so I could lean on it again. The little old woman was a peer? If so, she was probably just as powerful as Annalise—maybe more so. Hitting her with a hunk of pine wouldn't have done more than tear some lace.

The world began to go dark.

"Talbot!" Annalise called. Her voice seemed to come from far away. Suddenly, I felt hands lift me up and steady me. I leaned against a body—not Annalise's, a large one—and fought my way back to consciousness.

"Hey hey now," a man beside me said. He smelled of Old Spice and dry sweat. "You shouldn't be out of bed yet. You ain't ready."

I looked up at him. He wasn't wearing his red shirt anymore, but it was Camo Pants. I was happy to see he had a fat lip. He was holding my wallet and ghost knife; I reached for them and he let me take them.

"Get off me," I said. "You tried to kill me."

"Is that right? Maybe I did, although most of the guys I've tried to kill were wearing a keffiyeh at the time."

"You fired a rocket at me today." Had that happened today? I had no idea how long I'd been out.

"Guess I should apologize then. Guess I should be glad I missed." He must have guessed wrong, because the apology never came. He led me back into the small room and eased me into the bed facedown. "My name is Talbot, by the way. I'm a wooden man, just like you. Do you want some kind of painkiller?"

"*Yes.*"

"No," Annalise said from somewhere behind me, and in that moment I hated her and everything about her. "Talbot, go out to the fridge and bring the blue container."

Talbot left the room. My face was turned toward the window. I didn't want to look at Annalise. I was badly hurt, helpless, and ashamed of it.

"Ray, what the hell am I going to do with you?"

I almost said *Put me out of my misery,* but I was afraid she'd do it. "Water, boss. I need water."

"No, you don't." She took my wallet and ghost knife. Damn. I thought we were past that. I didn't have the strength to object.

The door opened again. I turned my head and saw Annalise intercept Talbot and take something from him. He left, closing the door behind him. I felt my ghost knife getting farther away from me, until I could no longer sense it through my pain and misery.

Annalise pulled up a chair and sat by the bed. She looked absurdly small, but I was glad she was nearby. She held a big plastic bowl in her lap. "You know you belong to me, right, Ray?"

I didn't like the sound of that. "I'm your wooden man,

boss." She didn't respond. "You're not going to sell me, are you?"

"No, I don't want to sell you," she said, as if it was a legitimate possibility that didn't interest her for the moment. "But I have changed you."

I almost laughed. Yes, a lot about me had changed since I met her.

"Ray, you're not paying attention." She popped open the lid on the plastic bin and held it close to me. Inside were tiny cubes of raw, red meat. Beef, probably. They smelled like blood—I'd been cooked more than they had. The smell made me dizzy and sick.

I stared into the bin and at her. She moved them closer to my face. Carefully, I reached in and picked up one of the cubes. It was cold.

"Don't bother chewing," she said. "It doesn't help. Just swallow it down."

I put it in my mouth. It felt wrong. Wrong wrong wrong, as though it were a dog turd. I spit it into my hand.

"No, Ray. Try again."

I didn't like the way she was looking at me. I put the cube back in my mouth. Was it poison? No, and I knew it wasn't. Annalise would crack my skull open or throw me through a window before she'd poison me. I tried to swallow it three times, but it wouldn't go down. The fourth time, it finally slid down my throat.

Annalise quickly set the bin down and lunged at me. She clamped one hand over my mouth and grabbed the back of my head with the other. Her strength was enormous; she held my head in place, my mouth closed, while my guts wrenched and my body bucked. My legs scraped against the sheets, bringing out a whole new level of agony—fierce and wild and utterly in control of me. Blisters burst and flooded the gauze. The pain was so overwhelming that it felt like madness.

Eventually, whatever was happening inside me eased. My body stopped writhing and I lay on the sheets, soaked in sweat and exhausted.

Annalise had a spell on her body somewhere that healed her when she ate meat, especially meat that was raw and fresh. Not only had I seen her do it, I'd saved her life once by cramming tiny slices of raw beef down her throat.

But it hadn't been like this. She hadn't tried to puke up what she ate. Her body had accepted it. Mine didn't. Mine wasn't healing. If she'd put a spell on me like the one she had, she'd screwed it up. It didn't work.

I lay still because I didn't have a choice. Annalise let go of me and picked up the plastic tub again.

"No."

"Yes, Ray. Another."

"No. I don't belong to you."

"Yes, you do, Ray. You wanted to be my wooden man, so you do. You're mine."

She held the bin closer to my face. I swatted at it, but I was too weak to knock it away. I doubt I could have knocked it out of her grip if I'd been at full strength. "Fuck you."

"Ray," she said, leaning close to me. Her voice was still absurdly high, like a cartoon animal. "Ray, you gave yourself to me. You're mine. The golem flesh spell is on you because *I* wanted it there; you don't get a say. If I have to, I can break your jaw open and force this crap down your throat. Why not? Enough meat would just heal you again. Now, are you going to take it, or am I going to make you take it?"

God, I hated her. She scared the living hell out of me, and I hate to show my fear. "Boss, go fu—"

In a blink, her thumb was in my mouth. It tasted gritty—of course she hadn't washed her hands—and she forced another cube of meat past my teeth. I tried to bite down on her, but it was like biting the tread of a tractor tire. If it hurt, she didn't show it.

She forced that cube down my throat, then another, then another. After a while, I didn't have the strength to buck and thrash anymore. I sprawled on the bed, sweating and miserable. When I tried to puke, Annalise clamped her hands over my mouth and nose. I choked. I shuddered. Finally, I wept like a child.

She forced it all down me. It took almost two hours, but she put the whole contents of the tub into me.

When she was done, she tossed the bin onto the carpet behind her.

"Boss," I said weakly. I wanted to die, and I thought I could make her do it for me. "Annalise. I'm going to kill you for this."

"That wouldn't surprise me at all," she said as she sat back in the chair. She took a white ribbon from her pocket and held it up. I knew what her white ribbons did, and I was hungry for it. I looked at the sigil at the bottom and fell into unconsciousness.

When I awoke, it was daylight. Annalise was sitting beside me.

And my pain was gone. I sat up and looked down at my legs. There were no bandages on them, and the skin looked pale and healthy. And hairless.

"We have clean clothes for you," Annalise said. "Still want to kill me?"

"Boss, I . . ."

"Forget about it. You handled it better than I did, that first time."

"Golem flesh?"

"I hate the name," she said. "I don't know who called it that, but it's the name that stuck. Remember when I took that bullet in the eye?"

I did remember. She'd gone on talking and walking around with a huge hole in her head. My throat felt thick at the memory. I nodded.

"Well, you won't be that tough. Not for a long time. Golem flesh takes a while to have its full effect. The spell is still changing for me, too. But here's the deal: you need to eat meat every day. Your body will break down if you don't. Also, you can heal injuries by eating flesh—the more recently killed, the more effective it will be. Over time—over decades, really—you'll have less pain and less impairment from each wound. Eventually, massive injuries won't do much more than make you look like an extra in a shitty horror movie. That'll take a long time, but when it happens you'll be like a person made of clay. Sort of."

I didn't say anything to that. My hands were resting on my bare legs, and I pinched myself. Annalise noticed.

"You aren't dreaming. And I didn't put this spell on you. Csilla did. I don't have the power for it." She took a long breath. "I called in a favor for this."

She had put another spell on me. She'd healed me. It had been hellish, but it wasn't as bad as skin grafts, physical therapy, and a lifetime of scars. "Boss, we have a lot to talk about."

She gave me a quick nod and stood briskly from her chair. "Your new clothes are on the table. Put them on and come out to debrief us."

They were white briefs, faded blue jeans, a green T-shirt, and white socks and sneakers. The briefs would cramp my style, but what the hell. Beside them was a brand-new cellphone. Annalise hadn't said it was mine, but she hadn't said it wasn't. I slipped it into the pocket of my new jeans; if she didn't want me to take things, she was going to have to put them away.

My room had a little bathroom, so I went inside for some water. I thought I really ought to be shaking and unsteady, but I felt strong. I felt like a man who'd slept. I touched my bare face and leg; it felt like skin, not clay. For now.

There was a drinking glass on the sink, and when I unwrapped it, I realized it was made of actual glass, not plastic. I filled it, drained it, and filled it again.

In the mirror, I found the new mark on my ribs under my left arm. It was in black, like my others, and the swoops and curls suggested images of . . .

I looked away. It was dangerous to study magic too closely.

My face was covered with dry sweat, so I brought my new clothes into the bathroom and took a quick shower.

When I finally went out to the main room, Annalise, Talbot, and the old woman in the black shawl were sitting at the table under the chandelier. They were serving themselves from a platter of bacon, hard-boiled eggs, sausage patties, fried potatoes, and toast. No one spoke to me as I approached the table and began to serve myself, too.

"Thank you, Csilla," I said to the old woman.

She looked up at me with a vague expression. "You'd better be worth it."

Worth what? I didn't know what it had cost her to cast the spell on me, and I squelched the urge to ask. She had already started staring dreamily at an empty spot on the wall. I sat, cut a small piece of bacon, and put it into my mouth. I didn't vomit or have a seizure. The flavor seemed muted, but I didn't have the urge to spit it out.

While I chewed, I tried to decide what to tell Annalise and the other peer. I knew them well enough to know what would happen if I told them about the drapes. It'd be like putting out a contract on Arne and the others.

But what could I leave out? It wasn't just that Annalise would kill me if I tried to shield another friend—she would, but that wasn't the important part. The important part was that protecting my friends would almost certainly unleash more predators on the world.

And there was the thought that had been lurking in my mind ever since Melly was carried away. Luther had been lying at the bottom of the tub in his house the whole time I'd been there, and when he died, his drape carried him away and two more came through.

That had to have been what happened, because that's what happened to Melly. The only difference was that three drapes had come through when she died. Did that mean four would come through when the next one died? Five for the one after that?

I tried to do some quick math, but the others were staring at me and the numbers jumbled in my head. Damn. I'd been lucky that the first two victims had died indoors and close to me. If Summer, Ty, or one of the others keeled over in a subway station, or outside a Starbucks, the drapes would be free to hunt in secret. In no time, people would vanish by the thousands until the whole world was empty.

My friends were important to me, but were they more important than the survival of every living thing on the planet?

I told Annalise, Csilla, and Talbot everything. I didn't sugarcoat it, and I didn't hold back any names. I even told them about the Bugatti, Wardell, and Steve Francois.

While I spoke, Annalise stared at me the way a cat stares at a mouse hole. Talbot kept eating; he was paying careful attention, but he was trying to be casual about it. Csilla stared off into space and didn't seem to know I was there.

When I was done, I realized I still didn't have my ghost knife. I asked for it. Annalise nodded at Talbot, and he resentfully fetched it for me.

"These 'drapes' are minor stuff," Annalise said.

I was startled. "What do you mean, boss?"

"The big question is this: Why is your old buddy Wally King making operatives in L.A.?"

It was hard to imagine Arne or Fidel as an operative of Wally's, but they owed him, and he could collect at any time.

"He's trying to end the world," I said.

"Seriously?" Talbot said, a crooked, swollen-lipped smirk on his face. "I'm sitting here squirting ketchup on home fries, and we're talking about a guy who wants to destroy the world?"

"He thinks it's a mercy killing," I said. "He thinks something worse is going to happen to us. He thinks the whole world is going to be—" Talbot was still smirking. "Is this funny to you?"

"No no!" he said, smiling wide enough to show teeth. "It's just . . ."

"I know." Talbot didn't have to say it. He felt like a hero, fighting to save the world, and he loved it.

"There is a dream in my eye," Csilla suddenly said. "I see strangers and darkness and a thought as large as the universe."

After a moment of awkward silence, Annalise said: "We know what he wants. Why does he think he can make it happen here, in Los Angeles?"

"I pressed him to find out what he was doing, but . . ." What was I supposed to say? He started calling me a rock star and I got distracted? "I'm sorry. I was focused on the predators. All he told me is that he needed people to get a puzzle. He had a simple plan to steal it, but he blew it."

Annalise put down her fork. "He had a *simple* plan?"

"He's not a smart guy, boss. I don't think he could plan a meal, let alone an elaborate crime."

"Have you seen this?" Talbot asked between bites of toast. He slid a newspaper across the table toward me. At the top was a notice about security preparations for the president to speak at the L.A. Convention Center about renewable energy or something. But below that was a follow-up article on the movie star break-in. Ms. Egan-Jade's spokesperson said the actress was going to sell her house without returning to it. She'd also set aside a trust fund for the murdered housecleaner's children. Apparently, the woman had died. To Egan-Jade's credit, she also blasted unnamed media personalities who had expressed relief that "only" a housekeeper had been killed.

I liked her just for that. At the bottom of the article, it stated that police had no leads but were investigating puzzling aspects of the case.

I glanced up at the others. They were watching me, waiting impatiently for me to finish. "Puzzling aspects?" I asked.

Csilla narrowed her eyes. "So many dreams that they come to life. Puzzling." I couldn't tell if she was responding to me or not.

Talbot smiled. If it stretched and hurt his fat lip, he didn't show it. "See, that's what *I've* been doing. It's surprisingly hard to get information out of the cops in this town. Easy to get them to crack you on the head with a stick, but hard to get them to take a bribe." He spoke like he was giving a performance, and he was so snide about it that I wanted to punch him again.

"We are beautiful children swimming in the belly of the great fish," Csilla said.

"I found out some interesting things, though," Talbot continued. I glanced at Annalise; she watched Talbot carefully, absorbed by what he was saying. Not two years ago, she had refused to tell me anything about the job we were on, and now I was allowed to sit at the grown-up table for the grown-up talk. It was a big change, and it felt good. Talbot kept talking: "For instance, Ms. Egan-Jade's home had a state-of-the-art security system. Cameras everywhere, and even a guard with a twelve-gauge to look over things. The cameras were running, too. The cops have a digital video of the break-in."

"Who did it?" I asked.

"Nobody," he said, and he smiled as though he was pleased with himself. "I've seen the video. The lock on the front gate breaks apart and swings open a few feet, but no one is there. When the guard shows up to check it out, he collapses from no apparent cause. It was an hour before the cops found him, stretched out in some bushes. He's in a coma now. Brain damage. They don't think he'll wake up, and you don't hear anyone talking about him on the news, or his kids, but hey, he's just a white male.

"Anyway, the cops don't have a recording of the attack, but it's not the only one. There have been several different break-ins around the city—women's homes, banks, jewelry stores, all sorts of places."

"Where? Do you have a map or something?"

Talbot snorted. "No. I don't have pushpins, either. But some of them take place at different locations at pretty much the same time, so we know it's more than one of your friends doing it. The cops think someone has a new, superfast version of Photoshop, and the burglars are bringing a laptop to erase themselves from the video files, somehow. There were two break-ins last night, in fact. A jewelry store and a convent. Two women were killed."

I nodded. Was this Wally's plan? To create people who could break in anywhere, stir up the cops with these crimes, and . . . And what? What would he get out of that?

Nothing. Wally wasn't the type to create chaos. Events were hard enough to predict under normal circumstances, and I couldn't imagine him drawing more danger to himself.

But he had brought me down to L.A., knowing I wanted to kill him. Caramella had said she was doing a favor by visiting me, and Arne said favors were what Wally expected in return for his "super powers." Wally wanted me and the Twenty Palace Society to take care of the drapes, yeah, and the drapes allowed people to break in anywhere without getting caught, but what if Wally expected to be long gone by the time we got here?

"Where was the first break-in?" I asked.

CHAPTER NINE

For once, we didn't drive in Annalise's battered Dodge Sprinter. Csilla had a black Grand Vitara, which was a little embarrassing, but at least Talbot had to drive. I sat in back.

We skirted a country club, got lost for a short while as Talbot drove in circles, then finally pulled up to a house in Hancock Park. There were iron gates along the front, with heavy green foliage blocking the view of the house.

"This is it," Talbot said, sounding relieved.

"What's the story?" I asked.

"This one we don't know as much about, because my source wasn't that interested. There was a break-in, same as the others, but the video was shut off two minutes in, which no one bothered with in later invasions. Another difference was that there was no one home at the time; the guy who lives here was in San Diego. The cops checked him out like they always do but couldn't find anything suspicious. They think the invaders hit the wrong house, waited around for the person they expected, got bored, and finally split."

That sounded like crap to me. I opened the door.

Csilla roused herself. "Where are you going?"

"Where do you think?" I turned to Annalise. She had put on her fireman's jacket and heavy boots; they were her fighting clothes, and they made her look a little wacky. "Um, boss—"

"Ray, I'm going to wait here. I'll keep Csilla company."

"Go with him," Csilla told Talbot. She seemed almost lucid.

"Ray." Annalise stared at me intently. "Be extremely careful in there." I nodded, wondering what the hell was going on.

Talbot followed me to the front gate. The lock had been broken—I could see the marks of the crowbar—and it hadn't been repaired yet. A blue supermarket twist tie held the two halves of the gate together.

I undid them and pushed the gate open. The heavy bushes and trees were as thick as a jungle. I was sure the owner received regular visits from the city to discuss his water use.

"Smells nice," Talbot said. "Big-money Los Angeleeze house. Comes with its own perfume." He sounded as though he disapproved, but I didn't know why and I didn't care.

The house had a stone foundation and green-painted wood above that. I couldn't say exactly why, but the place looked like a haunted house. There were pry marks on the doorjamb by the dead bolt. That hadn't been repaired yet, either.

The trees and bushes were growing close enough to the house that I could have climbed up and broken in through an unlocked window upstairs. There was a thin trail that led to the side of the house. I didn't circle around. Instead I knocked four times with the knocker, then looked up into the camera above the door. I didn't feel like smiling.

After a few moments, the door creaked open a few inches and a man put his face in the gap. He was short, with a trim black mustache and a flabby face. He squinted at us a bit, his dark eyes straining against the sun.

"Can I help you?" he asked. He sounded nervous.

"We'd like to talk to you about the break-in that happened at your house," I said.

"Are you police?" he asked, but it was clear he already knew the answer.

Talbot started to say something that might have been *yes*, but I cut him off. "No. Can we talk? It could be important."

He looked uncomfortable. He didn't like the idea, but he opened the door anyway. We followed him inside.

Instead of opening into a room, the door led to a narrow hallway. The place was underlit, making everything seem dark and faintly unclean. The air smelled of unvacuumed carpet and Szechwan spices. "Thank you for giving us your time." I extended my hand. "I'm Ray Lilly." Someday, I was going to have to come up with a decent alias for society missions.

He shook it. "Lino Vela. I don't understand who you guys are or why you're here. The police are already working on this."

This time, it was Talbot who cut me off. "Anyone else in the house?"

Lino was startled and alarmed by the question. "What?"

"That's not important," I said to Talbot.

He gave me an annoyed look. "Experience tells me it is. So how about it? Anyone else here?"

"No," Lino said out of politeness, but I could tell he resented it. *Victim*, I thought, but I shook that off. Those thoughts were a habit I didn't need anymore.

I tried to steer the conversation back to the job. "I understand nothing was taken?"

"Who are you guys? Why are you here?"

"That's not important," Talbot said.

"We've been asked to look into these break-ins. We're not with the police, and you don't have any obligation to talk to us. But we're hoping you'll help us put a stop to this."

He'd been about to ask us to leave, which would have ruined my chance to get information from him, not to mention that I couldn't tell how Talbot would react. Now he hesitated.

"Who are you working for? Is it Jade?" The familiarity of his tone threw me for a second, until I realized we were talking about a movie star. He probably thought of her as a part of his extended family.

"That's not something we can talk about. I'm sorry. And if the police knew we were asking questions, that would make things hard for certain parties."

"It's not her, I guess. Or is it?"

I made an expression of regret. "Will you help us?"

He sighed. "Let's go sit down."

He led us into a front room. The lights in there were brighter, and there was so much furniture—chairs, shelves, desks, cupboards—that the room felt cramped. All of it was old, made of dark wood, and just about every horizontal surface had something on it. I walked past hand-painted plates, battered oil lamps, fabric dolls, hand-stitched leather balls, and an antique sewing machine with a foot pedal. It was all crammed together as though this was a showcase instead of a home.

Lino offered us tea, but we declined. "Why don't you guys take the sofa?" he said. He settled into a creaky wooden rocking chair beside the curtained window. Talbot and I sat on the red couch. The velvet had been worn shiny, but it was comfortable. Opposite us were the only modern touches in the room: a flat-screen TV, a mini-fridge, and an Xbox. A tiny end table was covered with coasters but nothing else. In the back corner was a desk littered with papers and stacks of books.

"Thank you," I said. "It's our understanding that nothing was taken?"

"That's right."

"Are you sure?"

"Well, as I told the cops, if I'd been robbed, there'd be

someplace to put down a drink. But it's not just that. I double-checked against the list."

"The list?"

"The list of antiques," Lino said, waving reluctantly toward the room as though he was obligated to show it. "It's what I do."

"What do you mean?" Talbot asked. "How is it what you do?"

He folded his hands over his little paunch as though holding his guts in. "I'm something of a curator—a historian by training. I earned my Ph.D. at a little Texas college you probably never heard of, then fell off the tenure track. I came to L.A. for . . . actually, I'm not sure why I came. Hope, I guess. Hope for something better. Not that I found it. I was about to take a job teaching for the L.A. Unified when I noticed an ad in the paper for this place.

"This is my home, but I don't own it. It's the official residence of another man—I just live and work here. His inheritance is in the form of a trust—it's a great deal of money, but to access it, he has to maintain this family antique collection in his own home."

"He lives here, too?" Talbot asked.

Lino looked a little uncomfortable. "As I mentioned, this is officially his home. In reality, he spends three hundred sixty-five days out of the year traveling, often to his vacation home in Bel Air. The trustee turns a blind eye to it, if you understand my meaning. The owner visits once a month to check on things. It's my job to keep the house and make sure the antiques are maintained."

"That's it?" Talbot said.

Lino spread his palms as though he couldn't believe it, either. "The terms of the trust require my services, so I am here. I'm not paid very much, but my duties give me ample free time to work on personal projects—"

"That's what you do for a living?" Talbot let his scorn show. "Dust all this shit and play the latest Splinter Cell?"

"Talbot," I said, trying to cut in.

"Oh, I'll bet the chicks just love you, Mr. Inheritance—"

Lino sprang to his feet, and so did Talbot. I found myself between them, right in Talbot's face.

"You get out of here *right now*," I said. My voice was low, but every other part of me was burning adrenaline. Did he have a gun? A spell like my ghost knife? I imagined myself going for his eyes and balls—hell, I had golem flesh now. I could lean in to his throat and start chewing. Anything—*anything*—to get him to shut up and back off.

"You don't scare me." He tried to stare me down. There was something odd in his expression. He seemed angry and confused, as though we were doing something dangerous he didn't understand.

"You are fucking this job up," I said, "and you don't even know why. Get out of here. This part isn't for you."

He stepped back and held up his hands. "You know what? You're right. Sitting around chatting isn't what I'm on this job for. I'll leave that to you."

He walked out of the room. I followed him into the hall and watched him slam the door behind him.

He was gone. I took deep breaths, trying to pull in my anger.

"I do not have an inheritance!" Lino said. "No! I worked very hard for my degrees. Many hours! Many late nights! I still work hard on other work!" He waved at the desk in the corner. "Is it so wrong to have a good job? I'm asking you. Is it wrong to have a good job and to own a game console?"

"No," I said. My voice sounded strangled. Lino's raised voice was making my adrenaline pump harder. It took all my concentration to not punch him in the mouth so he would *shut the fuck up*. But I couldn't do that, because I needed information from him and because he had a right to be angry.

"Yes, I play games sometimes. It's a very relaxing thing to shoot zombies in the head." A note of humor came back into his voice as his anger subsided. I kept my mouth shut. I kept my control. "What I shouldn't do is jump from my chair when I'm insulted by someone bigger, fitter, and fifteen years younger. Thank you for getting between us. I think you saved me from a thorough beating."

"I'm sorry for bringing him here. I didn't know."

Lino looked at me and his whole expression changed. "Are you all right? Do you want a glass of water?"

I said yes, so he would leave the room for a couple of moments while I got myself together. When he returned with a tall glass of chlorine-scented water, I took a long pull. He gestured for us to return to our seats, and I made a point of using the coaster.

"Thank you," I said. "And thank you for not throwing me out."

"You're welcome. We were talking about the list, weren't we? Would you like to see it?"

"I don't know yet. I don't think so. Did the burglar take any money?"

Lino sighed heavily. "I wish I had money to take."

He had gone right back into the interview, which helped me steady myself again. I was grateful. "Does a woman live here with you?"

"What?"

"You know that some of these . . . odd break-ins have been attacks on women."

"Rapes, you mean." He said it with the air of a man who didn't like comforting euphemisms. "No. There are no women here. The trust has provisions for spouses and such, but I live alone. I'm an introvert and I find the quiet soothing. I don't even open the curtains that often. I do have a partner, but he doesn't like the collection. He finds it unsettling."

That made things clear enough. "Does the owner ever have people stay here? Friends or relatives visiting from out of town, maybe?"

"Not here. Mr. Francois doesn't even bring his wife here. He has nicer accommodations across town."

"Wait. What was that name?"

Lino stood and crossed to the mantel. "Mr. Steven Francois," he said. He took down a framed photo and handed it to me. "That is him there, with his wife. He keeps personal items here as part of the ruse that this is his home."

The photo showed Linen—Steve Francois—on a beach somewhere with a towel over his bony shoulder. The woman beside him, his wife, was tall, thin, and blond, with a Doris Day haircut. Her smile had the cool superiority of self-righteous affluence.

"I don't know where that was taken," Lino said as he returned it to the mantel. "I don't like to ask personal questions of my employer. His manner doesn't encourage it."

I tried to imagine how Swizzle Stick fit in. "Do they travel together a lot?"

"Sometimes. Not always." Lino shrugged. "They are both quite rich—her more than him, even. They live unusual lives."

I gestured toward the picture. "She looks tough. Are they having any problems? Money or marriage?"

He gave me a look. "I don't pry into his personal life."

"I have to ask," I said. "If she wanted to hurt him, could she do something to violate the terms of the trust? Hire someone to steal something and break up the collection?"

"I don't believe so, but I don't know all the details of the trust. Also, I don't see why she'd bother. Her family runs a successful law firm, and she is one of the top litigators in the country. If there was a problem between them, it would be played out in a courtroom, I think. Not here."

I could see that he was uncomfortable with the subject, so I changed it. "What about the video? I saw the marks on the door out front and the camera."

"Yes." He sounded grateful to talk about it. "The police collected the disc and the machine as evidence. The camera isn't plugged into anything anymore. Sorry. I did watch the video before I reported the break-in, obviously."

"Tell me what happened."

"Nothing to tell. I came home from my trip. I was surprised to see the front gate standing open. I didn't even realize it had been broken until later; I thought I'd forgotten to lock it. The door was open slightly. I saw the scratches and pushed it wide. When I walked in . . . it felt weird, you know? I was suddenly really afraid, as if I would find a burglar waiting for me. I went inside anyway. Only one . . . nothing was missing. I checked the security camera, and it had been turned off. I played the last fifteen minutes that it had recorded and . . ."

"What did you see?"

"Nothing. The video showed the front stair and front walk, but there was nothing to see. After a while, the door burst inward suddenly as though it was hit by the wind. A minute or so later the video ended."

Something was off about this story, but I couldn't figure what. "Can I see where the machine was set up?"

Lino shrugged and led me into the hall. On the other side of the house was a small library, although it had more knickknacks than books. He opened a little closet and showed me a bare shelf with a bundle of wires running out of the wood. "The insurance company lowered the rates when the trustee put this in, for all the good it did."

"Could someone have been standing to the side when—"

"No," Lino answered, as though he'd answered that question many times. "The video showed the whole door. You saw how the camera was placed. I haven't moved it since it was installed."

"What did you see that made you afraid? Why did you say 'Only one'?"

He looked uncomfortable for a moment, then shuffled his feet. "Come with me."

He led me to the dining room at the end of the hall. There were cupboards along each wall, with more plates and odd objects displayed on shelves. There was a place setting at the table, with a bowl of pita chips sitting out. Lino snacked on one as he walked by.

"See this?" He indicated a not-quite-square mirror about two feet wide. "The frame is walnut with gold leaf."

I expected him to tell me he had seen a reflection in the mirror, but it wasn't positioned where he could see it from the front hall. Next he showed me a surgeon's kit—a wooden case filled with knives, saws, and needles. Then he showed me a battered copper kettle, a drum with an eagle on the side, an apothecary balance that predated the Revolutionary War, and a daguerreotype of a husband and wife who had been friends of the owner's great-great-grandfather.

Why was he giving me the tour? I leaned close to the picture and studied the faces. I half expected to recognize them. "They don't look like anyone's friends."

"Dour, aren't they? And over here—"

"Lino, you were going to show me something." He was standing next to a wooden object that I could never have guessed the purpose of. He looked both confused and secretive. He glanced down at the shelf beside him, and I followed his gaze.

There was a little metal sculpture on the shelf near the items Lino had been describing to me. It showed a seated man with an open book in his lap, while a second man behind him chopped off his head with a sword. In fact, the figure was in midstroke, and only a little bit of the seated man's neck still connected his head to his shoulders.

I leaned in close, even though it seemed like an unbearable imposition on Lino's privacy to do it. The swordsman didn't have a face—was he wearing a hood? It didn't seem so. The seated man's face looked serene. I guessed he'd finished the book.

"When I came into the house after the break-in," Lino said, "this little statue had been moved into the hall. Someone had taken it off the shelf and set it down right in the middle of the floor over there."

Lino offered me another glass of water, and I gratefully accepted. I wasn't thirsty, but it felt good to follow him into the kitchen away from the statue—it felt profoundly wrong to pay attention to it.

This had happened to me before, I suddenly realized. Some kinds of magic—very powerful magic—could make you think certain thoughts. Every time I looked at that statue, I felt like I was intruding on someone's privacy, and it was unbearable.

Which was ridiculous. I used to be a car thief, after all. I've intruded on quite a few private spaces in my time, and I never gave a damn. I'd also spent time in prison, where guys did every private thing you can imagine in full view, from crying like a baby over a letter scrawled in crayon to beating off to rape. Now that I was outside, I was protective of my privacy and happy to let others have theirs, but I didn't have shame. Not that kind, anyway.

Which meant I was being magically controlled. I reached up and touched the space under my right collarbone where Annalise had put an iron-gate spell. It was supposed to protect me from mental attacks, but it hadn't even twinged. I didn't know what that meant, but it made me nervous.

And it told me that damn statue was important.

"Tell me about the statue," I said. It took an effort.

Lino turned away from me and picked up a little pot on the stove. He moved to a makeshift plastic funnel by the side window and emptied the pot into it. I heard the water run through the pipe and out the window.

"There's a drought on," he said. "I have a rain barrel in the back and a drip irrigation system for the plants. All my tea, pasta water, and such flows into the yard. Very water-efficient. I even have a pump for the bathtub."

"Lino," I said, keeping myself focused and my gaze direct. "Tell me about the statue."

Lino glanced at the door, as though the little statue might be standing there watching him. "It's part of the collection."

"Nothing unusual about it?"

"I don't like it," he said. "Some of the antiques are gross or disturbing. There's a room in the upstairs back that has some ugly stuff in it: pictures of lynchings, heads in jars . . . weird, awful stuff. I enter that room only when the maintenance schedule requires. This statue . . . I would have put it up there, too, but it fits better where it is."

That was it. We talked about his friends, whether he thought the statue was put there as a threat, who might want to threaten him, new people he'd met recently, and so on. It was all an excuse to find out if he'd met Wally King, and what he might know about him, but he never mentioned Wally, and with the way Wally looked, he would have. He did admit that he wondered if the statue had been moved to frighten him, because it had worked. He couldn't imagine who would do that, though.

I thanked him for his time, and he led me out. As I passed the statue, I wondered why it was so heavily enchanted, but really, that was none of my business, was it?

Outside in the car, Annalise was still sitting in the back, with Talbot behind the wheel and Csilla beside him. I had the impression they had been silent for a long time. At least they had air-conditioning.

Talbot pulled into the road before I could buckle up. Annalise turned to me. "Well?"

I almost said *I didn't learn anything,* but the way Annalise was staring at me let me know that was a bad idea. And that was the enchantment at work, still controlling me. I didn't like to be controlled. "Steve Francois has a little statue with a spell on it. Actually, I should say I noticed one statue with a spell—the spell may be on his whole collection. You know I'm no expert, boss, but it seemed really powerful."

Csilla turned to look at me, then at Annalise. She seemed impressed. Annalise said: "That's right, but not everyone makes note of it. We've known about that statue for years, but there isn't a lot we can do about it. It can't be stolen, bought, or given away."

"How did you get him to talk about it?" Csilla asked.

"It wasn't too difficult," I said. "He was nervous about it. Someone had moved it during the break-in."

Csilla and Annalise looked at each other, and I could tell I'd just said something important.

No one spoke for a while. Csilla seemed to drift off into her own thoughts. Finally, Talbot said: "Where do I go?" No one answered. "Ms. Foldes?"

Csilla didn't answer him. She just stared at a spot on the dash. Annalise spoke up. "Back to the hotel."

I stared out the window while we drove. Steve Francois

was mixed up in this mess, and I didn't think he knew it. Just before the gunshots started in Wally's motel, Arne had said, *By the time Luther came to us, his debt was paid in full. I asked him what he'd done, and he took me to the—*

Took him where? It had to have been Lino Vela's house. Before Wally even offered the predators to Arne and the rest, he'd sent Luther into Lino's house to shut off the video surveillance system, then he'd tried to steal that statue. Tried and failed.

Later, Luther had brought Arne to the house. They probably saw Francois show up in his damn Bugatti to check on the break-in, and Arne, buzzing with the idea that he was about to get a super power, threw away all his usual cautions and went after him.

In the underground hotel parking lot, Talbot had to help Csilla out of the car. She didn't seem infirm, but she moved like a sleepwalker. Annalise hung back and so did I.

"What's going on with her?" I asked.

"Nothing," Annalise said. "Not really. She's just very old. Peers that survive a long, long time sometimes begin to withdraw from the world. She has lucid moments and can still do magic—I couldn't have laid golem flesh on you; it's not in my book and it would have been such a weak spell that it would have been useless. But it's hard for her to stay engaged. I don't know if it's because of the spells or because they're centuries old, but it happens."

"Should she even be out here?"

"No. I'd planned to ask her to help clean up Hammer Bay, but now that I look at her . . ."

Uh-oh. Hammer Bay was the first job Annalise and I had ever gone on. She'd been injured and I'd been forced to leave a huge, scary predator alive, trapped in a circle, because I had no way to kill it. That was nearly a year and a half ago. "Boss, what needs to be cleaned up in Hammer Bay?"

"The predator there is still alive, obviously. No one in the society is quite sure how to kill it without a risk of escape."

My stomach suddenly felt like it was full of lead. "Really?"

"Really. And that's not the only one." She sighed. "The society isn't what it used to be. Which reminds me: don't ask Csilla any questions. Be careful around her. If she doesn't recognize you during one of her bad moments, she might attack. You don't want that." Before I could respond, she asked: "How did Talbot do?"

Time to change the subject, apparently. "He's a smacked ass. I don't like him and I don't want him around. He insulted the guy in that house for no reason and almost blew my chance to find out anything."

"And you kicked him out."

"Yeah. I was surprised he went, too. I didn't take him for the type to knuckle under."

"He's not, but he's worried about you. He knows you're the reason he's here, and he wants your approval."

"Um, what's that again, boss?"

"You, Ray. You're a wooden man, and you're still out here fighting."

I looked away from her. A wooden man was a term the Twenty Palace Society used for low-powered underlings who distract the enemy while peers hit them from behind. We were supposed to have the longevity of an ice cube on a hot desert rock.

And I had volunteered for the position. I hadn't really known what I was doing, but when do I ever? "Boss, how is this guy my fault?"

"Because you're successful at a time when the society has been struggling. We've been falling behind in this fight, Ray, for a long time. You've given us some rare victories lately. The peers never thought they could get this sort of success from a mere wooden man, but here you are. And they want more of you."

"And they picked Talbot? The guy's an asshole."

"They're peers. What do you expect?"

True. When it came to the society, I couldn't keep my expectations low enough. They were killers—vigilantes, really—hunting for the Wally Kings and Caramella Harrises of the world, and they didn't care what sort of person you were. All that mattered to them were the predators; the people killed in the crossfire were acceptable losses.

Naturally, they recruited a guy willing to fire an RPG into a crowded apartment building in L.A.

"Boss, I've been . . ." *I've been having trouble sleeping. I have nightmares.* I couldn't say it, not to her. She wasn't here to listen to my problems.

"I know, Ray," she said. She kept her voice low, as though afraid someone might overhear. "You have the look. You're constantly afraid. It's hard to control your temper. You continually think about the things you've done and will have to do again."

I nodded. Annalise wasn't nice to me all that often. I thought I should pay attention.

She studied my face, then turned away. "Lots of things in this job will kill you, not just predators, sorcerers, or mundane threats. You can win every fight and be destroyed by the victories. A guy like that doesn't last long."

I took a deep breath and let it out slowly. The garage smelled of damp concrete and exhaust. That was a perspective I hadn't considered. *Of course* the society was full of assholes; those were the only people who could stand it.

"Did Vela say anything else important?"

"I don't think so, boss, but there's magic there, and I may have heard something important without realizing it." I remembered Steve Francois saying *He sounds feisty*. "The guy who owns that collection, he's not a sorcerer, is he?" Annalise snorted as though the idea was ridiculous. "Who is he?"

She gave me a measuring look. "Remember when I told you that the society used to have two original spell books but lost them? Well, Georges Francois was one of the peers who went missing with the books."

"Meaning what?" I wasn't sure how far I could push the brand-new Share Time aspect of our relationship, but I was going to find out.

"Eleven peers vanished overnight along with the original books. No one knows what happened to them. Most people think two of them stole the books and betrayed the other nine. Maybe they were killed and their bodies dumped somewhere. Maybe they were banished from the planet altogether. Then each of the two took a book and went into hiding."

"But no one knows which two."

"No one is even certain that's what happened. It's possible that one or more rogue sorcerers took the books and killed all eleven peers. Or that one peer killed the other ten. Or that a predator took them. Or maybe the books left our world in some way and dragged the peers away with them. No one believes that one, though, because they don't want to.

"What we do know is this: the peers who vanished left behind odd objects and secrets—these were damn powerful sorcerers, you know—and the Francois collection is just one of them. Some people think it contains clues to the locations of the books."

"And these would be which books?" In Washaway, I'd heard the names of a couple of these spell books, but nothing more. "The Book of Oceans, right? Because that's your book. And the other is the Book of Grooves?"

"I cast spells out of the Mowbray Book of Oceans,

yes, but the society never had the Book of Grooves. We could never find it. We had the Book of Motes."

"Uh, Moats? Like a castle?"

"No, motes. As in *And why beholdest thou the mote that is in thy brother's eye, but considerest not the beam that is in thine own eye?*"

I had no idea what she was talking about. "Okay."

"Like dust motes, Ray."

"Oh. Boss, has anyone ever come across the Francois Book of Motes or something?"

She squinted up at me. "No. No one ever has. As far as anyone knows, there hasn't been a new primary since those books vanished. In fact, there don't seem to be any primaries left."

"And Wally wants to be the next. Could Wally get what he wants as a primary? Could he destroy everything?"

"He's a dipshit, Ray. Any of us could destroy everything. All it would take is a summoning spell. You don't have to be a primary for that. That's the whole point."

"But he doesn't want to kill us all with predators. He wants to be gentle. He wants to euthanize us."

"And he thinks becoming a primary would give him the power to wipe the world clean. All these assholes are like that. They have power, but it's never enough. If they could just find one more spell, if they could just become a quinary, a tertiary, a secondary, if they could just find the real Book of Grooves, they're sure they could do whatever they want. All they think about is their limitations, and they're sure they'd be able to do anything at all if they could just get a little more power.

"Except it's bullshit. There's never enough power, not for that kind. What's more, primaries were damned scary, but they weren't powerful enough to make us all extinct. It's not like they crapped A-bombs."

"Okay, then." I scratched at the spells on the back of my hand. "I guess that means that Wally already has the power to kill everyone, but he wants the power to do it a certain way. So his euthanasia plan is on hold. But if he becomes a primary, he's going to realize he's wasting his time and fall back on option b: summoning one predator after another."

"Except by then he'll be really hard to kill. So let's hope he doesn't wise up." She glanced at her watch. "We should get back to Csilla. We don't want to keep her waiting. But . . . go easy on yourself. Okay? Remind me sometime to tell you the story of how I got into this life."

She started toward the elevator doors, and I followed. I wanted to hear that story. I just hoped I lived long enough to have the chance.

In the room, Csilla was back in her place at the table. Talbot hovered over her, draping a shawl over her shoulders, then setting a plate of crackers and cheese before her. She was oblivious to him, staring blankly into space. Talbot smeared a blue-and-white-speckled cheese on a cracker and passed it back and forth under her nose. She didn't react.

He dropped the cracker onto the tray in disgust. He was trying to be a loyal flunky, but he was beneath notice.

Annalise waved him away as she sat opposite Csilla. Talbot suddenly had nothing to do, and I turned my back so he wouldn't approach me. The suite had a balcony. I went out onto it.

A breeze off the ocean made the sun and dry heat tolerable. We were getting toward the middle of the day, but the air was actually pleasant.

Talbot ruined it by joining me. He closed the door behind him. I had the idea that he was going to tip me over the rail, and I backed away from the edge.

"Whoa," he said. "I'm not your enemy here."

"Okay."

"I got off to a bad start, didn't I?"

"Twice."

"Yeah. Sorry about the RPG. I knew there was magic in the apartment, and I wanted to really take care of it."

I didn't respond to that. It would be great to have a way to destroy predators by hitting them from a safe distance, but I didn't have a weapon that could do it. And neither did Talbot, probably. Predators were part real, part magic. Normal weapons didn't hurt them—most of the time, anyway. Would the drapes be vulnerable to shrapnel or concussion? What about fire? It was possible, I guessed, but not likely.

Never mind that he could have killed Jasmin, Maria, or Violet. Never mind that I should be tipping *him* over the rail.

Talbot exhaled through pursed lips. I guess I should have responded right away. "I don't know if an RPG would affect those predators," I said. "I mean, we'll never know until we try, but from what I've seen, most predators can only be killed with magic. Did they give you any?"

"Nope. Not a weapon, anyway. I got these, though." He lifted his shirt and showed me a circle of tattoos on his chest centered over his heart. I didn't recognize them, but I knew the same spells could look different depending on which spell book they came from. He dropped his shirt and looked at me. He seemed to be waiting for something.

I lifted my shirt, too. My spells were more extensive than his, but they were also darker and thicker, making my torso look like a nest of black lines. He looked down at them with a calculating expression, like a batter studying the positions of the opposing team's fielders.

I dropped my shirt and turned away. I wished I had resisted the temptation to share my spells with him. No way was I going to show him my ghost knife.

"Hey," he said. "A few years ago, do you know where I was?"

"No."

"Iraq. I was serving over there. We had some real scary shit go down, stuff you don't even want to think about. One time— Do you mind if I tell you this?"

"Go ahead."

"One time, we had word that there was a dude with bomb-making equipment in his house. Not that he was making it himself, supposedly he let insurgents visit him for tea and explosives lessons, right? So we made a forced entry in the middle of the night, the way we do, and we're shouting at them, scaring the crap out of them to intimidate them. Which is for their own good, really, because if they're not intimidated, they might do something stupid, and that'll get them killed.

"Anyway, we drag them out of their beds, and they're screaming and pleading with us, but we have no fucking idea what they're saying. And the mom is yelling at the kids, and it's all the usual chaos.

"But one of the guys on my squad, a dude from Oregon named Park, was trying to control a fifteen-year-old kid, and the kid suddenly did a jumping, spinning kick at him. I saw it, and it surprised the hell out of me. Park lost his grip on his weapon—it didn't fly up in the air like in the movies, but he did let it get out of his hands. Crazy, right?

"And see, when I come across a snobby fag like that Vela dude, who earns a living by wiggling a feather duster back and forth, I get pissed off. He's doing nothing, and I'm out here feeling like a fucking teenage hajji in my pajamas taking on trained soldiers with nothing but moves I learned from a cabinetful of Jackie Chan DVDs."

"Talk to Csilla about that."

He smiled, measuring me. "You didn't like my story, huh?"

"At least you got some Jackie Chan movies out of it, right?"

"Damn straight," he said. "The reason I tell you that story is that I'm ready to do whatever now that I'm in this society. I'll be that hajji. I'm ready to do whatever it takes."

"To accomplish what?"

His head quirked to one side. "To live forever, man. Well, I know it's not forever, but it's what, five hundred years?"

Great. Now the society wasn't just hunting down people looking for magic and power, they were recruiting them. I took a deep breath to ease the anger building in my gut.

Talbot laughed a little at himself. "That was the wrong answer, wasn't it?"

"Pretty much, yeah."

"Well, I figured the whole 'I'm happy to be saving the world' thing was a given. Guess not."

I started toward the doorway. The balcony felt very cramped. "You'll meet some of the people we're going against, and you'll see why it's not a given at all."

"Hey." Talbot caught my elbow. "You don't have to tell me. I was there. I saw it. Some guys, you take away all consequences, and they turn into monsters. Like being a human being is just a mask for them. I saw it."

"I believe you."

"Listen." There was a hunger in his expression that I didn't trust. "I just want you to know I'm committed. If these guys"—he tilted his head toward the inside of the suite—"do things the smart way, they'll make you a DI, and I want you to know where I stand."

"I don't even know what a DI is."

"DI? It's a drill instructor."

Goose bumps ran down my back. I yanked the door open and went into the hotel suite. No way was I going to teach anyone anything, least of all a roomful of Talbots. Let the society make them into a useful part of the crew—it would be easy to find people who knew more about hunting, fighting, and killing than I did. The only real difference was in what we cared most about, and I'd spent too long in prison to think I could change that part of a person.

Annalise stood across the room, holding the fancy silver phone to her ear. She held up her hand to signal for me to wait a moment. The platter in front of Csilla had a long hunk of salami on it, and I had a sudden craving for it. I cut it in half and began eating it like a bread stick.

Annalise hung up the phone. "Gear up, both of you," she said. "The plane is prepped and ready, and we'll have a boat waiting for us at the other end."

"Okay. Where are we going?"

"Your friend Wally said he was skipping town, didn't he?"

"Boss, don't call him my friend. But yeah."

"Well, thanks to you, we know where he's going." She pointed to a wallet on the corner of the marble tabletop.

I walked toward it. It was brown leather and stuffed with paper. It was also singed at the edges. I felt I should remember it, but I had no idea where it came from.

"It's Wally King's wallet," Talbot said. "We took it out of your pocket when we brought you here."

I suddenly remembered snatching it off the dresser in his room. "I forgot. I was distracted by being on fire."

Talbot laughed. Annalise picked it up and dropped it into an envelope. "He had a punch card from a lunch cart in there. It belongs to a little place on Slostich Island. If King left town, it's likely that he went there."

"Boss, how big is this island? Because I never heard of it."

"It's in *Canada*," Talbot said, as though it was something shameful.

Annalise added: "Thirteen months ago a cabin on the

north end was bought by a man named Walter Roi. With a wire transfer."

"That's it? You have an address and a name?"

Annalise shook her head. "There isn't time for anything else. We don't even have time to send an investigator. We're going to follow up on it ourselves. You know that *roi* is French for king, don't you?"

I didn't know that. Something about this felt wrong. Wally knew he was being hunted, and although the guy was no genius, he wasn't *entirely* stupid, either. Was he stupid enough to use a comic-book alias?

"Gear up," Annalise said again. My jump bag was still sitting on the floor by a bed at the Best Western, but it had nothing I needed, except maybe a toothbrush.

Someone knocked on the door and pushed it open. Talbot started talking about the drapes. He thought we should take them on first, then move on to the next target. His back was to the door and he was blocking Annalise's view, so neither noticed the housekeeper as she entered. She looked to be middle-aged and of Southeast Asian ancestry, maybe Vietnamese.

Talbot's voice was loud; I couldn't hear what she said to Csilla. From her body language, she appeared to be asking if she could come in to clean up.

Csilla stood without answering and walked around the corner of the table. The maid stood politely with her hands folded in front of her. Csilla didn't move fast, but it didn't take more than a few seconds for her to stagger up to the woman.

In one quick move, Csilla clamped her small hand over the maid's windpipe. The woman's face twisted in sudden pain and shock as Csilla twisted.

"Hey!" I shouted stupidly. Talbot and Annalise turned toward the center of the room.

Csilla yanked the maid onto the floor, then took something out of her pocket with her free hand; it was small—

about the size of a raspberry—but dark and shiny like a stone. She stuffed it into the maid's gaping mouth.

I started forward, ready to throw myself at her, ready to slash into her with the ghost knife, but Annalise caught my wrist. I struggled, but she was too damn strong.

The maid bucked and her eyes rolled back. Csilla leaned down onto her, pinning her to the white carpet. A horrible wet rattle came from the maid's throat.

I couldn't stand it anymore. I twisted against Annalise, using my body weight to knock her off balance. She was strong as hell, but she weighed as much as a pile of brooms. I'd carry her across the room, if I had to.

But it was already too late. The maid's body burst as though she'd swallowed a grenade. Her legs, arms, and head split open in a ragged confusion, but there was no blood. In fact, there was no red in it at all, just a strange charcoal gray and smudge brown, and her body held together like a shredded blanket waving in front of a fan.

The maid's body was gone, transformed into something that fluttered to the ground as Csilla's spell spent itself. Her flesh, bones, clothes, and shoes had vanished, and in their place was a pile of something I couldn't make out. My brain was looking for a corpse; it couldn't recognize the dark, shiny stuff on the carpet.

I wasn't struggling against Annalise anymore—what would have been the point?—but she was still squeezing my wrist, much harder than she realized.

Csilla stood without letting go of what had been the maid's throat, lifting something that shimmered like raw silk. It hung from her hand like fabric, splotchy and wet-looking. She draped it over her shoulders as though it would keep her warm, and among the discolored blotches and ragged ends of that cloth, I could make out the shadow of an agonized face. Csilla returned to her chair and stared into space.

My hands were shaking and I felt sick to my stomach.

A fury was building in me, and I didn't know what to do with it.

I turned to Annalise. "Boss." I looked down at my wrist and so did she. She let go. Her face was pinched and pale. I didn't want to think about what my expression looked like.

Talbot was breathing heavily. "That was fucked up."

"We're going to be fucked up if we don't move quickly," I said. I moved toward the door. The housekeeping cart was parked just outside the room, but there was no one else in the hall. "Talbot, pull that cart all the way back to the elevator. Then get back in here and close the door."

He looked jumpy. "What if . . ." *What if I get caught?*

I held his gaze with my own. "If someone sees you, tell them it was in the way. Just be cool."

He hurried out the door, taking a tissue from a silver box by the phone. He laid the tissue over the handle before pulling it away.

I spun on Annalise. "Boss, aren't predators just magical beings that kill people?" My voice was a harsh whisper, although I felt like shouting.

She understood what I was saying right away. "No." Her voice was low and urgent, as though she was afraid she'd be overheard. She glanced at Csilla. "Predators are a new link in the food chain. They're alligators in the rabbit hutch. The society doesn't hunt down *murderers*."

"I can see why."

She stepped close to me, her teeth bared. "Don't you *dare* talk to me about killing. Do you think I've never killed an innocent person by accident? What about you? Are you sure your hands are *completely* clean?" Talbot hurried back inside. He shut the door with both hands and his shoulder, as though it weighed as much as a bankvault door.

"This isn't even her fault," Annalise said. "It's mine.

The peers wanted her out here for him." She pointed at Talbot. "I was supposed to look after her."

Don't ask Csilla any questions, Annalise had said. I paced back and forth. Wally King, Arne's crew, and the drapes were all running around the city, and I had Csilla on my side. I felt just as dirty as the people we were after.

Csilla was still sitting in the same chair on the other side of the room, staring at the same piece of nothing. "The universe . . . we think its thoughts and . . . ," she said, her voice trailing off. "We . . . we . . . we . . ." She seemed agitated. Maybe she knew she'd done something wrong.

Annalise said: "We'll have to move her."

"What about me?" Talbot asked.

Annalise scowled at him. "You're with me now. Don't fuck up."

We packed quickly, throwing all the clothes into suitcases without folding them. Annalise checked us out, and a valet brought the Grand Vitara to the front door. We moved to a Best Western in Canoga Park, throwing all Csilla's things onto the bed and parking her in a little chair by the window. Annalise went into the bathroom to make a call.

When she emerged, she said: "An investigator will be here before tomorrow morning to escort her home. Let's go."

We went straight to the airport in Burbank, boarded a private jet, and lifted off. Predators were on the loose with more coming anytime, but we were leaving for Canada to go after the guy who was bringing them here. I was sure we were making a terrible mistake.

During the flight, Talbot tried to talk about the mission, but Annalise didn't answer any of his questions, and I certainly didn't know anything. Eventually, he stopped talking and stared out the window. I closed my eyes and slept heavily for an hour and a half. We landed at a small airport in Everett, Washington.

At the airport, we were met by a woman who didn't want to know our names. She was nearly my height, and was as skinny as a mop handle. Her hair was a nest of tight black curls with a good bit of gray mixed in, and her muscles were long and ropy. Annalise handed her an unsealed envelope, which she tucked into the satchel she carried.

She piled us into a pickup truck—Talbot and I sat in the bed. I peered into the cab to see if Annalise had something to say to the driver, but I didn't see them talking.

The truck ride ended at the docks. We had to detour through waterfront construction, but we eventually pulled into a long parking lot and stopped at the back.

Annalise followed the tall woman, and Talbot and I followed Annalise. The driver unlocked a gate and we followed her down the dock. The boats on either side of us were pleasure craft of one kind or another—some sailboats, but mostly they were tall motorboats with enclosed cabins and tinted windows. They looked like expensive condos with a hull, or maybe oversized SUVs. A little thrill went through me. I had never liked the ocean, but I liked a high-class ride as much as any car thief.

Unfortunately, the boat we stopped at was the smallest of the bunch. It was a little more than twenty feet long, I guessed, and completely open to the weather. BAYLINER was written along the side, but it looked like a brand name, not the name of the boat.

Annalise stopped short. "This isn't a sailboat."

"There wasn't time," the tall woman said.

"Wasn't time for what? This is a deck boat."

The woman sighed in exasperation. "Wasn't time for you to find someone else. I'm not doing this for you people in a sailboat. Not again."

I had an uncomfortable moment waiting for Annalise's reaction, but after a few seconds she nodded. "You're the expert."

The captain led us aboard. She cast off and carefully motored out of the slip.

"Do you have our folder?" Annalise asked.

"After we pass Jetty Island," Captain answered.

It was about thirty minutes before she opened her satchel and handed Annalise a folder. By that time, we were all stretched out on the long cushions that ringed the small deck area. Talbot went to sit out at the bow, but Annalise and I stayed near Captain.

Annalise opened the folder and took out three sheets of paper in plastic slipcovers. She handed one to Talbot and one to me. It was a map. I laid it flat on the cushion beside me to make it easier to read—we weren't going that fast, but there was enough of a breeze that the ride was rough.

"This is Slostich Island," Annalise said. "The little *a* is Walter Roi's cabin. That's where we expect to find Wally King. For once, there are no other residences nearby, although it's not *completely* isolated. The southern end of the island is where all the people are. The north end is scattered cabins, a few retreats, and protected forest. Memorize that map, because we're not bringing it ashore. With luck, we'll reach the cabin, kill the target, and be back on the water in two hours with no one the wiser."

There was a little mark on the paper where we were coming ashore. It was some sort of park, and it looked to be about a mile from the cabin. "Will there be a car for us, boss?"

"Not unless we steal one. There was no time to arrange it."

I nodded, but I didn't like it. A mile wasn't far to walk if you're going for pad thai, but fleeing the scene of a murder—and probably an arson—was another thing entirely, especially on a long strip of land with what appeared to be two north/south roads running through heavy woods.

Talbot looked at us, irritated. He waved the plastic sheet cover at me. "In the service, we had blue-force tracking. We had computers and . . . not fucking Google maps! We flew here on a private jet, but we can't afford a GPS?"

"Who's 'we'?" Annalise snapped. "The jet is Csilla's. She spent a couple of centuries killing people and taking their shit. You haven't. We're lucky we have someone in place to take us by boat."

"We could do better, is all I'm saying. Do we really have to go the whole way by boat?"

"Did you bring your passport?" Captain asked.

Talbot took a deep breath. "No."

"I'm a convicted felon," I said. "There's no way they'd let me through a checkpoint."

Annalise scowled at Talbot. "So we cross the border. We surprise King in his home, hopefully while he's asleep. We kill the hell out of him. We cross back into U.S. waters and fly east before anyone even knows about the body."

East? I almost corrected her, when I noticed Captain take the unsealed envelope out of her satchel. She opened it and unfolded the single sheet of paper inside. I couldn't read it, but I saw that it was a short, printed letter. Captain looked it over grimly, then put it back into the envelope and shut it inside a compartment below the steering wheel.

We cruised for about an hour. I studied the map off and on. I'd never been much for learning things off paper, but I went back to it several times until I was sure I had it down.

Finally, Captain turned off the engine. We floated a thousand feet off the Washington coast, gently rolling with the waves. Talbot looked alarmed. "Why did we stop?"

"We'll cross into Canadian waters after dark. Sunset's just after eight P.M., which is . . . two hours from now. Try to act like we're out for some summer sun. Maybe no one will pay attention to us."

I closed my eyes and lay back on the cushions. I was going to see Wally King again. Did he sleep with all those predators inside him? I hoped so. We could destroy the creatures and him at the same time.

How simple that seemed. How right. I closed my eyes, but I couldn't sleep.

After night fell, Captain started the engines again. We puttered forward, obviously in no hurry. She told us we had another five hours, more or less, before we reached our target.

We rode in silence. After three hours, Captain brought out a cooler and slid it to Annalise. She took out four bags of fast-food burgers, fries, and soda. The drinks were watery and the food was cold and greasy. I was hungry enough not to care.

I kept my eye out for patrol boats, but no one approached us. The trip was smooth and easy right up to the moment Captain pointed out our landing spot, and Annalise took out the guns.

CHAPTER TEN

They were revolvers, old Magnum .44s like the ones Clint Eastwood used to carry, and they were sealed in gallon-sized Ziploc baggies. There were two speed loaders in the bag, too. Talbot looked at his as though he'd been asked to dig a grave with a soup ladle, but I took mine without comment. I didn't expect it to be much use, but I appreciated the thought.

There were only two, of course. Annalise didn't need one.

Captain killed the engines and let momentum carry the boat toward the shore. There was a steep beach ahead and a line of trees at the top of the hill. Captain turned the wheel, letting the boat swing around. Annalise, Talbot, and I jumped off the port side into water up to our thighs—on Annalise it was up to her navel. Damn, it was cold, but no one else complained, so I kept my mouth shut.

Talbot ran ahead, yanking the gun out of the baggie as he left the water and charging up the sand as if he was storming the beach at Normandy. I hissed at him, but he ignored me.

I was surprised to come out of the water onto a flat, grainy tan rock. In the starlight it had looked like a stretch of sand, but it was actually solid and smooth like a boat-launch ramp. Annalise and I walked slowly up the hill, as though it was the most natural thing in the world, and Talbot came out of the trees to join us.

I took the gun from the baggie, folded the plastic and put it into my back pocket, then stuffed the speed loaders into my hip pocket. I wasn't wearing a jacket, and no way would I slip this blaster into my waistband. Life was too chancy. I carried it by the barrel instead.

It was about three hundred feet to the road, then we turned toward the south. It was almost midnight, and of course there were no streetlights. The starlight was bright enough for what we were doing, but flashlights would have been better.

We jogged along the side of the road. Talbot ran ahead, although I'm sure he thought of it as taking point. There was no sidewalk, of course, so we trotted along the asphalt. I turned around every ten steps, watching for headlights behind us. Not that it mattered: the gully along the road was choked with bush and brambles. We couldn't exactly dive for cover.

We didn't need to. No one came. The moon rose over the trees, lighting the roadway. I ran toward my own faint shadow.

At the mouth of a driveway, Talbot stopped and looked back at us. He made some sort of hand signal I didn't recognize, but Annalise beckoned him toward us impatiently. When he came close, she said: "This is it, isn't it?"

I'd forgotten that Annalise was hopeless with maps. Talbot said: "Yeah. Shouldn't we get off the road?"

Annalise shrugged, and the three of us started moving up the drive. I felt a twinge on my right collarbone.

"We shouldn't be here," Talbot suddenly said, rubbing the top of his breastbone with two fingers. "This is the wrong place."

I felt it, too. I was suddenly sure this was the wrong path. Why hadn't I studied the map better? My iron gate throbbed.

Talbot began backing down toward the road. "Let's try somewhere else."

"Talbot," I said, "are any of your spells hurting?"

He was still rubbing the spot on his chest. "Yeah."

"There's a spell on this place," I said. "Some kinds of magic can make you think or feel certain things. Pay attention to the spells on you. They're painful for a reason."

Talbot looked embarrassed and walked with me toward Annalise. "Want me to lead the way?" he asked.

A cloud moved across the moon, and things were suddenly very dark. "Is that how you want it?" Annalise asked. She took a scrap of wood out of her pocket and lit a Bic lighter. I recognized the scrap as one of her Geiger counters for magic, but the sigil was dark and inert.

The cloud moved away from the moon. I looked around. Everything seemed completely normal. "Shouldn't you be getting a reading from that thing, boss?" If magic was making my iron gate throb, her detector should show it.

"Yeah," she answered. "Unless I'm not."

"Boss, let me take the lead here," I said, without even realizing I was about to speak. "I owe this guy."

"No offense, Ray," Talbot said. "But I was the one kicking down doors for Uncle Sam. I should lead the team into the house."

Annalise turned to him. "We don't work that way. We don't bunch up; we don't charge in together."

"But . . . what about covering each other?"

"These are sorcerers," she said. "Taking them down is like taking down a suicide bomber, except without the suicide. This is how we do it: one wooden man comes at them from the front, and the others hit their flank."

"Boss, you know I have history with this guy. I want him."

"Ray, if you have history with him," Talbot said, trying to be reasonable, "if it's personal, you should probably not even be on this mission. Just saying."

Annalise waved that off. "With Ray, everything's personal." She turned to me. "Go ahead."

I started up the gravel driveway, wondering if I should feel stung. I shifted the gun to my left hand, holding it properly now. With my right, I took my ghost knife out of my back pocket. The revolver was loud, clumsy, and very, very solid, but the ghost knife was my weapon.

I wanted to head back to the boat. I wanted to be in L.A. Nothing was right and everything was wrong. My iron gate was aching like an old bruise. The spell on this property, Wally's or not, was getting stronger. I lowered my head and bulled forward, determined not to let feelings I couldn't control drive me away.

The brambles on either side of me were tall, well over my head. The path curved to the right, and after following it a few dozen yards, I saw a light in the trees up ahead. It was bright, not a lamp in a window—probably a security light.

I suddenly hit a spot where my iron gate flared with sharp pain. I flinched, bending over slightly as the pain hit. "Something is different here."

Annalise hurried forward, and I could see she felt it, too. Talbot also flinched, but less than I had. Annalise took out her scrap of wood and held it in front of her. Immediately, the design started moving. A shower of dull gray sparks shot out, along with a jet of black steam.

Something had changed drastically in just a few steps. I had stepped from a magic-free area into one that set off Annalise's detector like a siren. When I moved toward the house, my iron gate eased. I backed toward the spot where the pain had first started and moved side to side, trying to find out if whatever was hurting me was a single spot or if it had a shape.

It turned out to be a line that went across the driveway, down the stony gully into the brambles.

"The plants look thinner here," Talbot said. He was

right. Not only were the brambles thinner, they were shorter. They had been cut or burned away some time ago up. I knelt in the rocky dirt and tried to peer through the underbrush, but it was too dark even with this bright moon.

"It's a circle," Annalise said. "He surrounded the house with a circle and buried it."

I scraped at the ground at the base of the gully, dragging my fingers through the loose and not-so-loose stones. Eventually I came to a piece of brick. I dug around it, exposing it and the two next to it. They had been broken at odd angles and fitted together . . .

"Leave it," Annalise said. "We have more important things."

I stood and brushed the dirt off my pants. "Are you sure it's a circle, boss? It seems like a straight line to me."

"It's some kind of closed shape," she said. She held up the scrap of wood. "It has to be to do this."

We looked through the trees toward the single lonely light. It was about fifty yards away up the hill. Did Wally really make a circle this huge?

"Boss, do you want me to destroy it?"

"I told you to leave it. There's no telling what he has trapped in here. Let's go."

Talbot bent his knees to lower his center of gravity as he raised his weapon. I started back up the driveway, my grip on my ghost knife tight.

After a few seconds, I heard Annalise say something to Talbot, and they both left the driveway, pushing through a stand of trees. I could hear their shoes quietly scraping on a wooden walkway.

Sound traveled far at night. I kept moving toward the house, trying to empty my thoughts of everything except what I could see, hear, and smell. When my iron gate twinged at the bottom of the drive, I'd been sure a sorcerer of some kind lived here. I was less sure it was

Wally; it would have been just like him to lead us here to collide with some jackass he didn't like.

But now that I'd crossed the circle—and knew what it could do—I felt more certain that this was Wally's place after all. A huge buried circle a hundred yards across seemed like just the kind of crazy move he'd make. He was lazy and obsessive in nearly equal measures, and I believed a guy who would load himself with predators would set aside a private reserve for them, too.

I was letting myself get distracted. I focused my attention outward. I didn't see or hear anything unusual as I approached the house.

He wasn't here. The house was small, with a space beside it for a car and trees growing close behind it. The parking space was empty, and I couldn't imagine Wally walking all the way here from the nearest ferry.

The real question was whether he had left predators behind to guard the place or taken them all with him.

And there was something else. During our little talk, Wally had said *Don't try that "turn over your books" crap with me, okay? It's insulting.* He'd said "books." Plural. It had taken a while for me to realize what that meant, but I wasn't here just to find him and pay him back. He had spell books, and spell books had to be destroyed.

The cabin had wooden walls that had been painted the color of bricks. It was bigger than I'd expected. The outside light was a floodlight, one of the newer ones that use very little electricity but give off a thin, bluish light. It lit the front door and two windows. One of the windows was shuttered, and the other was boarded over.

I almost knocked at the door, which was absurd. Instead, I held the gun so my index finger rested beside the trigger, then I pushed the corner of the ghost knife into the door between the knob and the jamb and slid it up and down.

My spell cut through the door and locks as though they were made of smoke. I pressed gently on the wood, and it swung inward a couple of inches. The physical locks had been cut, but did Wally have magical protection, too?

I forced myself to take a deep breath. Whatever was going to happen to me here would happen, and I'd live or I'd die, and there was nothing for me to do but get started.

I pushed the door all the way open. The light from the security lamp showed no one else was in the room. I turned on a table lamp by the couch.

The lamp was expensive, and so were the couch, table, and rug. I'd expected yard-sale furniture like the castoffs I had in my room, but the end table was made of solid dark wood. The couch was plump and new, and the rug was a mix of deep, beautiful colors. I supposed if I ever learned how to walk through walls the way Wally could, I'd have as much cash as I could carry.

Sometimes an empty house *feels* empty. Everything seems inert, like a vacant tomb. But I couldn't tell with Wally's place. It didn't feel empty or full; it was just a space.

A quick scan of the room didn't show any sigils or other signs of a spell. I kicked over the corner of the fancy rug, but it was just unmarked floorboards underneath.

To the left I saw a doorway to a room with counters and a tiled floor. I went in. It was a small kitchen, but it wasn't lacking for gear. It had a four-burner gas stove top and a full-sized fridge. I went through and opened another door to a little mudroom, complete with washer and dryer.

The only other door here obviously led outside. I wasn't ready to leave yet, but I did peek out the window. Having light sources close by made the darkness outside look like black paint on the glass. If Annalise and Talbot were out there, I couldn't see them.

On my way out of the kitchen, I opened the fridge. Part of me was convinced it would be full of human heads, but all I found were spoiled chicken parts and discolored steaks still in the packaging. The unit was just as cold as it should be; Wally hadn't been here for a while. This was the second abandoned home in as many days, and it made me feel like I was in a race but so far behind the pack that I couldn't see the other runners.

I went back into the living room, and more details jumped out at me. There was no TV, but there was a stack of newspapers in the corner and a pile of magazines beside that. A small stack of mail sat on the table, but when I flipped through it, I didn't see anything interesting. No brochures for Vegas hotels or train schedules, at least. It was all addressed to Wally King.

I lifted a framed photo off the table. It showed Wally at about eighteen, wearing a life jacket and standing next to a wide stretch of white-water rapids somewhere. He was smiling and giving a thumbs-up, as though excited about his new adventure. There was no one else in the picture, and there were no other photos in the room— not family, not friends, nothing.

In the back corner there was another doorway. It led to a short hallway with a door at the end and another just on my left. I figured the one on my left was a bathroom, and opening it proved me right. I looked around quickly but didn't find anything unusual, unless you counted a bottle of Vicodin with no doctor or patient's name on it, which I didn't.

When I put my hand on the knob of the other door, though, goose bumps ran up my arms and back. I've learned to trust those sudden intuitions, and I held both my weapons at the ready as I opened it.

This was the bedroom, naturally. It was empty. I stood

in the doorway, my heart pounding. No one was there. I flicked the light switch.

The bulb in the center of the ceiling struggled to life. It barely lit the room. The dresser against the back wall was made of mahogany, and the sheets on the bed were satin. Between the dresser and the wall was a pair of sliding closet doors.

I crossed the room to the dresser, hearing the floor creak under my feet. I took each drawer out of the dresser and dumped the contents onto the bed. All of his clothes were triple-X sweat suits in various colors, plus gray boxers and white socks. There was nothing else in the drawers or taped to the bottom. There was nothing in or under the bed, either.

Then I opened the closet.

The only thing hanging inside was a heavy winter coat. I took it off the hanger and tossed it onto the bed. I'd search the pockets, but that could wait.

Because inside the empty closet, Wally had drawn something on the wall in black Sharpie. I couldn't see the whole thing at once because the sliding doors blocked half the closet. Gripping the bottom of the door, I lifted it up and out like the door to a DeLorean until the wheels burst out of the tracks. Then I did it again, tossing both onto the bed.

I squatted low, because the light was weak and I was throwing a shadow. "Well, well," I said aloud. The sound of my own voice surprised me.

In the upper left corner of the closet was a drawing of the earth. There was a crude energy to it—it wasn't pretty, but I could see Florida and the eastern edge of South America along one side of the circle. On the other, I could see West Africa and southern Europe. Two heavy black lines ran along the continents and oceans like cracks in an eggshell.

To the right of that drawing and a little lower on the wall was a second drawing of the earth, but while the first was made by someone who couldn't form a perfect freehand circle, this one was obviously meant to be bulging and malformed. Billows of steam shrouded most of the planet like a blanket of clouds, but something was just coming through them—something alive. Wally had drawn a single eye on a face that might have been liquid, or partially liquid, and in other places something else was rising out. Were they tentacles? The curves of a serpent?

To the right of that drawing and still lower on the wall was a crude image of a city. In the foreground, people fled toward me, their arms over their heads in a stick-figure depiction of blind panic. In the background was a towering *something*—a thing so huge that the city sky-scrapers looked like pencil stubs next to a grown man's leg. I had the impression that it was dragging across the ground like a tongue licking a lollipop, and inside it I could see objects rising up: buildings, trees, and tiny screaming people.

The last image was almost down at the carpet, and at first it was difficult to make out in the shadowy corner of the closet. I got onto my hands and knees to peer at it.

The sun—our sun, presumably—was way down in the bottom right corner. There were a few broken specks to the left of that, and it took me a moment to realize that they must have been asteroids or loose rock. Maybe the broken pieces of the earth?

On the left edge of this picture was a drawing of something obviously meant to be very much in the fore-ground. It was a ragged piece of something that was mov-ing out of sight on the left, and all I could see was the rear part trailing behind like a corner of wet laundry. Inside it, as though trapped in an amoeba, were people, and they were screaming with all their might. I got the impression that they had been screaming for a long time, and would still be screaming an eternity from now.

I took out the cell Annalise had left for me. I had to noodle with it a little, but eventually I figured out how to take a picture of all four pictures together, then I took a close-up of each one. What the hell. Someone might care.

On the floor by this final sketch was an open book. It was a thin hardcover, one of those kids' books that come in series with each featuring a different animal. This page showed a wasp laying eggs inside a caterpillar, and what I could read of the caption in the bad light said the eggs would hatch inside the living animal and begin to feed.

There was a Post-it note sticking out of the book. Wally must have bookmarked a page. I grabbed the book off the floor and flipped through it.

Immediately, the darkness began to deepen as though someone was dialing down a dimmer switch. At the same time, I heard a sound that was part hiss, part electrical crackle.

Damn. When I'd moved the book, I'd uncovered a small sigil on the closet floor. Now, with the spell exposed, something around me was waking up.

CHAPTER ELEVEN

I slapped the book back down over the sigil, covering it again. It didn't work. The room kept getting darker, and the hissing grew louder.

I swept the edge of my ghost knife through the sigil, cutting the spell in half. It came apart in a jet of black steam and iron-gray sparks—for all the good it did.

The darkness started to feel solid, like a thickening gel. I put my back against the wall, desperately afraid of being trapped. A dark line hovered in the air in the center of the room, as though something I couldn't see was blocking the light. It was dull black at the top and progressively lighter gray down toward the floor, and it was between me and the door. Things were getting darker every moment, and the line was moving slowly upward toward the bulb.

Inside the line, something moved. Then, from the very darkest spot, an arm reached into the room.

I squeezed off two shots at it, as much to sound the alarm for Annalise as to injure it. One of the bullets must have struck home, because the thing drew back.

Incredible. A predator that could be hurt by a mundane weapon. I turned back to the wall and slashed my ghost knife through the plasterboard in one large circle. I shoved at it, trying to bull my way through, but the air was so thick I could barely use half my strength on it. I held my breath. Whatever this stuff was, I didn't want it in my lungs. The darkness pressed against me; it had weight.

Something suddenly clamped down on my right biceps. It looked like an eagle's talon, but it was huge—easily bigger than my own hand—and it was mottled, greenish, and flaking. It squeezed, and the pressure was enormous.

My ghost knife was trapped in my right hand. I placed the revolver against the thing's wrist and fired off another shot. The sound of the gunshot near my face was like a whole new kind of punishment, and burning gunpowder struck my lips and ear.

The bullet deflected off the thing's bones, but not before tearing through its thin flesh. The pain must have startled it, because it released me. I pivoted into the corner of the closet. The room was still dim and gray at the edges, and I could see the talon where it had reached out of the darkness. I swung the ghost knife up at it, but my arm wouldn't work right, and I struck it along one talon instead of straight through the leg.

The end of the talon fell away, clunking onto the floor, and the crackling hiss turned into a sort of grinding shriek.

The darkness was flowing around and against me now, and I could barely see. The weight of it held me against the wall and made it difficult to lift my arms. The section of the wall I'd cut burst with a loud *crack*, and I felt the darkness moving toward it like a current of water. I pushed toward it, almost blind now, desperate to get out into clean, breathable air. As it grew heavier, the shadow around me began to feel like worms crawling on my skin. The darkness was not an effect, like a squid's ink cloud. It was part of this thing's body.

I grabbed the edge of the hole, but the plaster broke off in my hand. At that moment, I heard and felt the whole wall buckle outward. The predator, whatever it was, was entering our world, and it was too big to fit in Wally's bedroom.

I reached the hole in the wall just as a talon scraped along my back. I cried out; each talon was like a slashing knife, and I could feel the darkness inside my nose and sinuses, wriggling and alive. I shot at it again, but my grip was all wrong and the recoil knocked the gun out of my hand.

Then I was through the hole, stumbling across the back of a toppled shelving unit and falling to my hands and knees. This predator had gotten inside me, and it *hurt*; I had to get outside. At least I'd be able to breathe out there, and run.

A talon caught my right ankle. I spun immediately to swipe the ghost knife through its wrist, but it was so strong that it was already dragging me back. Fast, so fast—I knew I'd be pulled into that dark line before I could cut myself free.

The back door burst open and Talbot charged in, revolver at the ready. I could barely see him through the gray, but I shouted: "It's got me! Shoot it!"

There was nothing to shoot, not really. There was only a hole in the wall and a growing shadow spreading through it, but Talbot aimed his weapon into the darkness and squeezed off five shots, handling the recoil better than I had, and sending each round at a slightly different angle.

The talon released me after the third shot. "Let's go!" I shouted. He pulled me through the door, my injured ankle banging painfully across the back of the metal shelves. I struggled to get my good left foot under me and hopped along beside him, fleeing the house as fast as I could.

Annalise was running toward us. "Boss—" I yelled, but I didn't get to finish because just then the washing machine smashed through the wall and flew by me like it had been flung by a tornado.

Talbot jumped away, even though it had already gone

by. I lost my balance, stepped onto my injured foot, and fell.

All the windows along the front burst outward, shutters and boards along with the glass. The whole cabin buckled out like an aboveground pool overfilled with water. I heard the groans of straining wood along with the bursts and cracks of breaking beams. The roof split and began to spread apart.

Annalise plucked a green ribbon from her vest and threw it into the open doorway.

At the same moment, that claw came rushing out of the darkness. The ribbon fluttered between the predator's fingers and disappeared into the darkness. With her left hand, Annalise caught the middle of the creature's three talons, holding it at arm's length.

But although she had the strength to hold the predator off, she didn't have the mass. Her boots slid in the gravel as the thing pushed at her. The other talons tried to scrape at her.

Green light flared inside the house. Annalise leaned back, pulling on the predator's talon just as it tried to retreat. She braced against the crooked doorjamb with her right hand, holding the creature in place while the fire burned. The hissing crackle became a grinding shriek again, but this time it was three times as loud.

The green light shone on her face, and I'll never forget her expression. She was fierce and joyful, her eyes wide and wild, her teeth bared.

Then the darkness spilling out of the doorway retreated back inside. The talon went limp in her hands, and the limb it was attached to dropped as though someone had let go of the other end. Annalise tossed the talon behind her without looking back, and it nearly landed on me. The thing had been burned off above the elbow. The talons twitched, scraping at the gravel, and for a moment I was sure it was going to start crawling at me, like a hand from an old horror movie.

But it didn't. Annalise walked into the house. The building groaned and shifted, but it didn't collapse on her. Yet.

I turned and saw Talbot standing at the edge of the gravel lot. He stared at the house—at us—in amazement, his mouth hanging open. If this was his first real experience with spells and predators, he was having pretty much the same reaction I'd had—stunned disbelief.

Of course, I'd been a citizen. Talbot was already a wooden man; he should have been better prepared. Had the society warned him what this was going to be like? I doubt Csilla would have, but somebody should have.

Something moved in the woods behind him. "Talbot!" I said in a harsh whisper. "Come here!"

He stared at me as if I was a talking dog. A shadow behind him moved against a darker shadow.

"Wake up! Get over here!"

He didn't want to come any closer to the house than he already was. Then he realized I was glancing over his shoulder and turned, taking a few tentative steps toward me. The wind hissed through the trees, but suddenly it didn't sound very much like wind at all.

Damn. There was another one out there.

Talbot hurried to me and crouched low. "Call your boss out here," he said, as though he wasn't allowed to talk to her.

"Shh!" I struggled to my feet, using Talbot as a support. I hadn't seen any eyes on the one inside, but that wasn't necessarily unusual. Did it hunt by sound? By smell? Maybe it could feel its prey with its expanding shadow. Then again maybe it saw "with something other than light." Whatever, I wanted to be as still and quiet

as possible until Annalise finished whatever she was doing inside.

The security light at the front of the house flickered
and went out, making the whole area clear in the moonlight. To the left, I saw another dark patch moving against
the faintly lit background. Then another and another.

Christ, how many of these damn things had Wally
summoned?

I watched them, hoping they were moving away from
us. Maybe there was a deer or something they could hunt.
It wasn't happening. The darkness was getting larger,
blocking out the moonlit leaves and underbrush. Were
they growing or just moving closer to us?

Either way, to hell with keeping still and quiet. "Boss!"
I shouted. "There are more out here!"

Talbot backed toward the house, and I hopped to keep
up with him so I'd have someone to lean on. I didn't trust
my ankle enough to walk on it. Annalise still hadn't come
out. "Boss!" I shouted again.

The creatures were close to us now, blocking the
woods as they glided out of them. There were three—no,
four. That I could see, at least.

I readied my ghost knife.

Talbot pivoted away from me, and I had to step on my
injured ankle to avoid a fall. I hissed in pain as he broke
into a sprint, running for the driveway.

Damn. I hopped in place, ghost knife in my hand. One
of the predators changed direction, moving toward Talbot. I threw the ghost knife just as a claw reached toward him.

The spell sliced through two of the creature's fingers.
That horrible grinding shriek sounded out again, and
the limb retreated into darkness. Talbot juked toward it
to avoid another of the predators, then leaped over a
low wall and sprinted down the gravel path toward the
edge of the circle.

The bastard. I hoped he'd make it.

I closed my eyes and cleared my mind, then *reached* for my spell. Annalise came up next to me just as the spell returned.

"Ray, how badly are you hurt?"

"I can't put any weight on that foot. Sorry, boss."

"There are five that I can see, and one of them followed Talbot. I only have four more of these." She held up the green ribbon with the sigil drawn at the end. It was the spell she used to call up her green fire, and I'd never heard her call it by name. Was it a secret?

The predators hovered at the edge of the forest. The darkness that shrouded them stopped expanding when they touched. "You can see them better than I can, boss. Do you know what they are?"

"Claw-in-Shadow. There are only a couple of predators that we could call common, but this is one of them. The summoning spell for it turns up in a lot of spell books, and it's a popular guardian predator among a certain sort of sorcerer."

"But . . . six of them? With only four more ribbons? Are you, um, going to carry me outside the circle?"

She turned toward me suddenly, scowling. "Run? Now?"

"So they're not . . ." *Dangerous?* I almost said.

"Oh, they'll kill you. They'll hunt you like a pack, tear you apart, and drag the pieces into the Empty Spaces. And they're not stupid. They know what I did to the one inside. That's why they're hesitating."

The predators were trapped inside the buried circle, and if Wally was right, they were starving. They wouldn't pass up a meal, but they were being careful. I needed to make them a little reckless.

I hopped away from Annalise, nearly falling over. I took a deep breath to relax my shoulders and kept my balance better as I went out in front of the house. I'd played decoy for Annalise before—that's what a wooden man was for—but I'd never done it in full wounded-bird mode.

The predators at the edge of the gravel seemed to be moving back and forth. I was no expert on living spots of darkness, but they looked agitated. Their hunting instincts must have been screaming at them.

I hopped toward them again and almost lost my balance. The predators moved toward me, then stopped. I needed to draw them in, so Annalise could take out more than one with each ribbon. As long as they were careful and keeping their distance, we were never going to kill them all.

It occurred to me that I might have been thinking of this all wrong. What if Wally's spell had simply created an opening between our world and the Empty Spaces? What if it wasn't six predators we were facing but one?

One of the talons emerged from the darkness ahead of me. I could see them better now as my eyes adjusted—there were five curving shapes, blotting out the moonlit landscape behind them. And they were getting closer. I tried to spot the one I'd mangled with my ghost knife, but I couldn't.

Five? The edge of the circle wasn't *that* far. Talbot should have reached freedom by now—or been killed—and the predator should have had enough time to get back up the hill.

Goose bumps ran down my back. I turned to Annalise just in time to see a dark shape come over the top of the ruined cabin and fall on her. I didn't even have time to shout a warning.

The hissing sound grew louder. I turned again and saw the other predators rushing at me. Instinctively, I reared back and, having only one good leg, fell sprawling onto the stones.

A predator clamped down on my wrecked ankle, and the pain made me scream with a high, shameful voice.

I sat up, reaching for that claw with my injured arm and wishing I'd switched my ghost knife to my left, and another predator clamped down on my other ankle.

Just as they were about to tear me apart like a wishbone, I swept my spell through the talon on my injured leg, severing it at the wrist. If the predator shrieked with that metal-grinding sound again, I couldn't hear it, because I was too full of my own screaming—the pain wouldn't quit, and my fear was tearing through me.

Before I could swipe at the claw on my left leg, another grabbed at my left arm. I swung the ghost knife at it, feeling something long and sharp slash through my right biceps as another talon barely missed me. I cut my arm free, but the pressure against my left leg was hurting like crazy and I couldn't see a damn thing.

Something slammed down on the left side of my chest, pinning me to the ground. Another talon caught my right wrist. I could still throw my ghost knife with a flick of my fingers, but I had to concentrate to aim it, and damn, they were already pulling me apart. The talon on my chest slid up onto my face and neck, and it was too much all at once; I couldn't concentrate. They were going to kill me, and my brain was screaming at me *This is it this is it oh thank God . . .*

Then green firelight flooded around me. The iron-gate spell beneath my right collarbone flared with pain as it protected me from Annalise's spell. The predators released me immediately, and I slapped my spell against my chest. It was only made of laminated paper, and Annalise's green fire could burn a human being down to the bones in seconds.

Then the fire was gone. There was no hissing and no grinding shriek. I blinked at the darkness around me, but my vision was full of spots. Were they all gone?

"How badly are you hurt?" Annalise asked. Her high, funny voice startled me, although it shouldn't have.

"Boss, I . . ." I started to shake. I'd come close to death yet again. Damn, did people really get off on this?

I pushed myself to my knees. "I think I'll live, boss, but I'm going to need some help."

She grabbed my left arm and raised me up. Her grip hurt, but I hid the pain as best I could. My left ankle was going to be bruised, swollen, and stiff by morning.

Annalise led me to a tree at the edge of the tiny gravel lot. "Did you get them all?" I asked. My vision hadn't quite cleared, and I wasn't sure if I should still be on alert.

"Yep," she said as she walked toward the house. "We'll get you fixed up soon. Good job."

Well. A compliment. I nearly fell over from the shock.

My ghost knife was still in my hand, and it appeared to be undamaged, as best as I could tell in the moonlight. I tried to consider what that meant, about her spell and mine. Was the ghost knife protected by my iron gate? Did her green fire affect everything but spells? Or was something else going on?

I kept turning it over in my head, anything to avoid thinking about that moment of relief I'd had when I thought I was going to die.

Annalise set a fire in the cabin, then I leaned on her while we returned down the long gravel drive. I hopped, she stayed close to me, and we went very slowly. It was exhausting, and it would have been so easy to fall flat on my face, but to hell with that.

Of course, Annalise could have carried me as easily as I'd carry a loaf of bread, but to hell with that, too.

On the way down, I showed her the pictures I'd taken of the drawings in Wally's closet. The phone's screen lit her face, but I couldn't read her expression. I wanted to ask if this was news to her or if it was goofball conspiracy stuff, but I was afraid she'd give me an answer I didn't want to hear.

Instead I asked what we should do about this place.

She said she'd file a report and let another peer check it out. We'd leave the circle intact to deter locals from coming up to investigate, just in case there was something we missed in the darkness. She put my cellphone into her pocket.

Then we crossed the circle. Talbot hurried out from under the cover of a stand of trees and came toward us.

"I tried to lead them away," he said. Annalise laughed at him, but I didn't have the heart. If I'd had two good legs, I might have run with him. Well, probably not, but that didn't mean it was a bad idea.

He looked at me closely. "I saved your life."

Before I could respond, a pair of headlights swept around the corner. Police lights flashed on the roof. I had my ghost knife ready, but Talbot's hand moved toward the back of his waistband, a gesture I recognized immediately. As the driver's door opened, Talbot drew a gun.

I slammed my left arm across his hand and nudged him off balance. His gun went off, the bullet striking the stony dirt in front of the car, and he stumbled. I would have fallen over completely, but Annalise had a tight grip on my shirttail. With my right hand, I flicked the ghost knife.

A normal piece of paper would have fallen at my feet, but my spell went where I wanted it to go. It fluttered upward and passed right through the space between the car and the open driver's door just as the silhouette there drew a weapon.

He didn't get off a shot. I couldn't see him clearly, but I'd managed to hit him anyway. The gun fell from his hands, and he reached into the car and switched off the headlights. Annalise let go of my shirt, and I hopped toward the car, bracing myself on the hood.

"Put that away," Annalise said. I knew she wasn't talking to me.

I hopped around the front of the car. "I'm sorry," the silhouette said.

"Turn around and close your eyes," I told him. He did. "Did you get a good look at us?" I picked up his gun, a Glock, and tossed it into the car. My ghost knife was nearby. I *reached* for it and it zipped into my open hand. I put it away.

"I did," he said.

"That's all right. Just don't do it again. Call in to the fire department. They'll be responding to this fire soon, and you should warn them that ammunition inside the building is cooking off. Tell them to keep well away for now. And tell them there's no one here."

"Okay." He did that while I turned to Annalise and Talbot.

I patted the roof of the car. "This is going to be our ride back to the beach."

Annalise shrugged. It was all fine by her. Talbot stared down at the cop. "What did you do to him?"

We piled into the car. I couldn't drive with my injured ankle, so Talbot drove instead, and I sat in the back with Constable Shayholter.

That was how he introduced himself. He was a little under six feet and built like a high diver. He had a thick head of black hair and the kind of face you see on the covers of romance novels. And he sat beside me, obediently keeping his eyes shut tight.

The drive back to the park was so quick we almost missed the turnoff. Talbot drove us into the parking lot and parked at a wooden rail. The weird stone beach and night water lay open before us.

Annalise and Talbot got out. I turned to the constable. "Don't open your eyes yet. But listen carefully. I'm not going to cuff you or take your gun. In fact, I'm not going to do anything that would give you an excuse for letting us go. I want you to wait for a slow count of six hundred, then drive back to the fire and do your cop thing. Don't tell anyone you saw us. You'll remember all this tomorrow, but you won't be able to explain to anyone why you let three suspects leave the scene of an arson. You certainly won't be able to explain it to yourself. Think how it would look if you tried."

"I understand."

"Start counting," I said. He did. I hobbled out of the car. Annalise led me down to the bay, and it was a relief to float out into the cold, cold water.

Captain was waiting for us. Annalise muscled us into the boat and we sped away. I lay back by Captain, stretched out on the padded bench, and let the cool night air blow my clothes dry.

After about an hour, Captain turned to me and asked if I would hold the wheel steady. "Don't turn at all," she said as if talking to a child. "Like this." I struggled into the pilot's seat, my ankle stiff and screaming, and did as she asked.

She went to the front of the boat to fuss over something. While her back was turned, I opened that cabinet beneath the wheel and took out the envelope in there. I took out the note Annalise had given her. It was printed on generic printer paper. I held it up to the lighted dials. It read: DO WHATEVER THE BEARER OF THIS ENVELOPE TELLS YOU TO DO IF YOU EVER WANT TO SEE YOUR SON ALIVE AGAIN.

Oh, shit.

CHAPTER TWELVE

The SUN was rising when we docked in Everett. By that time, my ankle was swollen and unbearably tender. It had to be broken. Walking was impossible; Talbot and Captain had to practically carry me to the truck. They laid me in the bed, and Talbot sat beside me. He looked as though he wanted to talk but wisely kept his mouth shut.

We stopped off at a supermarket on our way to wherever we were going. While we waited in the parking lot, I closed my eyes and fell asleep almost immediately. I woke again instantly when we pulled out of our parking space.

Not long afterward, we were back in the plane and in the air, heading south. I wanted a chance to talk to Captain—to apologize—but I never got it. Then it was too late, and I knew I'd never get another chance. I didn't even know her real name.

I sat on the plane, miserable and tired. I wanted to lie down, but there was no space.

Annalise sat next to me. She held a plastic bag full of sliced meat. "Remember how bad it was to heal those burns?" she asked. "Broken bones are worse."

She was right.

When we landed in Burbank again I was shaky and sick to my stomach, but I could walk again and my bruises were gone. I rode back to the hotel with Annalise and Talbot, but I couldn't look at them. I was wrung out and tired, and pissed off at the world.

Annalise had Talbot drive us to my Escort. "Stay here," she told him. Talbot gave us an unhappy look as we climbed out and went to my car. There was no pain in my ankle at all. It was completely healed.

Annalise stood beside the driver's door. The heat roasted us. "Well, he was useless."

"He wasn't wrong to run, boss," I said. I sighed. This wasn't a conversation I wanted to have. "Csilla didn't give him a useful weapon. He'd have fed a predator, and there would have been two victims to draw them in. You might not have gotten them all with your green fire." She shrugged. I was boring her. "What's next?"

"Same thing we've been doing: find your buddy Wally King. I want you to get out there. Here." She gave the cellphone back to me. A quick check showed that the pictures I'd taken had been erased. "My number is in there. Call me when we have some killing to do."

"What about the predators he's been summoning?"

"Wally King is our top priority. If I find out anything about those pictures, I'll let you know. The predators . . ." It was her turn to sigh. "You knew these people, yeah? If you confirm they have predators in them but you can't bring yourself to cure them, give their names and addresses to me." I knew what she meant by *cure*. "I can make it quick, Ray." There was no kindness in her voice, and I was glad of it. The woman who'd given Captain that note shouldn't play at kindness.

She turned and walked back to her van. Did I want to see Annalise burn Fidel down to a pile of bones? Did I want to sit alone in a motel room, TV blaring, while I knew she was out there killing him, or any of them?

Hell, no.

I drove back to my motel.

Annalise had promised to tell me what she learned about Wally's pictures. She had never offered to pass me information without prompting before. Now, just as she was trusting me, I wanted to be far away from her.

My duffel was still in my room; I was glad I'd paid for the week. Then I showered and lay on the bed. I dreamed of a huge mob of women, all of them clones of Captain, weeping on their knees beside tiny caskets.

When I woke up, it was just six o'clock. The air-conditioning had turned the place into a fridge. My throat was raw from the dry air. I went into the bathroom and ran cold water over my hands.

I'd nearly died the night before.

It seemed like such a small thing. *I nearly forgot my keys. I nearly bought new shoes. I nearly died.* I looked at my face in the mirror, remembering the way the talon had clamped down on me, and trying to picture how it would look in the light.

I also remembered the Iraqi kid with the Jackie Chan DVDs—maybe he would have made it if he'd had an Annalise of his own at his back—an Annalise who threatened a woman's son.

I left the room and got into my car. The filling station was packed; cars were lined up three deep at each of the pumps. After I topped the tank, I drove aimlessly for a while.

Annalise had offered to kill my old crew for me. I knew she thought she was doing me a favor, but I couldn't turn the responsibility over to her. I had come here because my old crew was in trouble. I wanted to save them.

That was the hard part. I wanted to be a guy who saved people. I wanted to protect them from sorcerers and predators, but that wasn't how this game was played. Arne and the others were being eaten alive by predators, and I had no idea how to save them. In fact, I was nearly certain it couldn't be done.

I knew what I had to do. I had to kill them. Because it didn't matter what they'd done, and it didn't matter if they had people who loved them and kids to look after. Only the predators mattered. Not the people.

I said it aloud in my car: "Only the predators matter. Nothing else." It was easy to say when I was here alone. It was a lot harder when I was holding a gun to someone's head, or swinging a length of pipe in a crowded room. I had killed people to get at predators, and if I had to be honest with myself, I knew I'd do it again.

But I couldn't kill a woman's kid because she refused to give me a boat ride.

The Twenty Palace Society had changed me, but maybe I needed to do more to change the society.

I parked a block away from the Roasted Seal. I didn't have a conscious reason to go there, but it was as good a place as any to take the next step. I walked through the back alley to confirm that it was empty before I went to the front.

The bar was busier than it had been, which meant it had ten or twelve people in booths or sitting at the bar. The bartender was new, but he looked enough like the other guy to be his brother. A pair of middle-aged women gave me the once-over as I scanned the room, but Arne wasn't there, and neither was Lenard, or anyone I knew. One thick-necked guy with a crew cut looked vaguely familiar, but I couldn't place him. He was talking on his cell and looking down at his beer, not at me at all.

Most of the crowd were watching Mexican soccer on two flat-screen TVs mounted high on the wall. The surging white noise of the crowd was the loudest sound in the room.

Three tall, slender men occupied Arne's booth. They wore waitstaff black and had stylish haircuts. They were victims; they wouldn't know where to find Arne.

The back door had already been replaced, and the

wall was patched with fresh spackle. Soon it would be painted over, I was sure, and all traces of that incident would disappear.

Behind me was the alcove Lenard had been standing in. It was a wait station, but there were no waiters here. The plastic tub was dusty, and the notepad on the counter had yellowed at the edges. Only the bar stool looked as if it had been used lately.

Lenard's small locker was there, painted the same dark color as the wall. The lock had a little slot for a key, but I had something almost as good.

The urge to look around the room to check who was watching me was powerful, but I knew it would just draw attention. I took the ghost knife from my back pocket and sliced through the lock. The door squeaked as it swung open.

Right at the front was a Nintendo DS; Lenard liked his videogames, especially when he needed to kill some time. Beside that was a roll of cash no thicker than the cord of a vacuum cleaner. But in the back, hidden in the shadows, was a foot-high gold statue of a hairless man standing on a black base. The base was made to look like a spool of film, and a nameplate had Ellen Egan-Jade's name on it.

Oh, shit. Was this what Lenard did when he thought he could get away with anything? This?

I snapped up the roll of cash. If he'd been standing beside me, I could have beaten the hell out of him. I could have kicked him in the nuts. I even, for a few moments, considered calling the cops. But no. I couldn't do any of that. I took his money—let that be an expensive lesson. Then I'd tell Arne one of his people was keeping evidence of a rape and murder at the Bigfoot Room. I'm sure that would go over beautifully.

"Hey, what are you doing?"

It was the bartender. I shut the locker as I turned

around. "I'm looking for a guy," I said, unsure if I should use Lenard's name or how best to describe him.

"Try a bar in West Hollywood," he said, to general laughter. "This place is for people who want drinks."

Now every face in the room was turned toward me. Only Crew Cut wasn't smiling. Suddenly, I recognized him. He had been the one who tossed Wardell's jacket at him in front of Steve Francois's fancy white house. He shut his cellphone off and put it into his pocket.

At that moment the front door opened, and I saw several large figures backlit by the desert sun as they entered. Crew Cut slid off his stool.

I sprinted to the back door, slamming it open. This time an alarm sounded.

The alley smelled of garbage and concrete. I vaulted onto the dumpster, then jumped for the edge of the bar roof. Crew Cut and the rest of Potato's crew weren't idiots, even if they looked like they were. I was sure they'd have someone at the mouth of the alley.

I scrambled onto the roof, feeling like a coward. Which I was. Ghost knife or not, I didn't want to tangle with anyone in Potato's crew. The door banged open a second time, and I heard heavy treads scraping against the ground.

"Dammit," a man said. Despite the alarm, I recognized the voice as Potato's. "Gone."

"He didn't come this way," a second voice shouted. It sounded farther away.

Another voice came from a good distance away. "Not this way, either." I'd been right about the entrance to the alleys.

Someone opened the dumpster lid and let it fall shut again.

"How do they *do* that?" Potato didn't sound annoyed at all. In fact, he sounded almost admiring. "Okay. This fucking alarm is going to bring cops. Let's get gone."

I risked a peek over the lip of the roof and saw them moving away. Good. Just as they turned the corner, I threw my leg over the sheet-metal roofing and hung by my fingers. It was a three-foot drop to the concrete, and when I hit the asphalt, I was face-to-face with the bartender. He scowled at me from the open doorway, the Oscar statuette in his hand like a bell.

"What the hell do you call this?" With the door open, he had to shout to be heard over the alarm.

"Evidence," I shouted back. "And you're putting your fingerprints all over it."

His hand sprang open and the award clattered to the ground. I turned and ran toward the end of the alley that Potato and his men had not taken. Once I hit the sidewalk, I slowed to a casual stroll.

I should have asked Wardell to drop me off a mile from my car and walked back to it. I should have realized that Francois would send Potato and his men after me once he found out about the video Arne posted, and that Wardell could tell them where he'd dropped me off.

But had they already grabbed Arne off the street? Judging by what I'd just heard, I'd bet against it.

Still, if Arne wasn't at the Bigfoot Room, I didn't know where to find him, and I didn't have as many friends as I used to.

I unrolled Lenard's money and spread it flat under the floor mat. A cop would find it two minutes into a determined search of the car, but this was the best I could do. I drove back into Studio City and parked outside Ty's gym.

Six people pushed through the doors in a rush just as I reached them, but the last, a muscular woman who couldn't seem to stand up straight, held them open for me. The front desk was swarmed with people turning in locker keys and receiving plastic cards in return. I waited for things to thin out, watching people get processed at the desk and exit. Leaving work, rushing home to make dinner, pick up their kids, or go on dates, they were nothing like me. And God, there were so many of them.

When things had slowed enough that the supervisor could pay attention to me, I stepped forward. She was the same one I'd spoken to a couple of days before, but she didn't recognize me. I had to explain myself again. Ty wasn't here, she told me, and no, I couldn't have his address or phone number.

A customer at the counter turned to me and said: "You mean Tyalee Murphy? He's just around the corner. I'll show you."

I followed him outside. We stood at the edge of the parking lot together. He gestured toward an intersection like a man karate chopping an imaginary opponent. "That street there beside the pct-supply store is Cartwell. I think. Whatever the name, you go that way one block and take the very first left. Ty lives on that block, on the left side, in a building with two beautiful jacarandas out front."

I had no idea what a jacaranda was, but I could figure it out. "That's great. Thanks."

"No problem. You're a friend of his?"

"Actually, I'm a hit man hunting him down."

We laughed and went our separate ways.

It was early evening, so parking on Ty's residential street was impossible, but I did luck into a space around the corner. There were three buildings with two trees out front, and I found Ty's name in the second one. I rang the buzzer and spent a few seconds studying the tiny fernlike leaves of the whatever tree out front. The security gate squawked at me like a mechanical crow, without anyone trying to speak to me first.

I went inside and up the stairs, then knocked on the

apartment door. It was yanked open by a short, slim Korean man. He had small features on a broad, smooth face, and he was so fit his collarbones showed at the opening of his polo shirt. Like the client who'd given me directions, he had hair that had been cut very recently, and it had a lot of mousse in it.

Something about me startled him, and he laid his fingertips next to his throat. "You're not the guy."

"No," I answered. "I'm a different guy."

"I mean the pizza guy." He looked me over, as though I might be hiding a pizza box somewhere.

"I'm looking for Ty," I said. "Is he here?"

He moved his weight onto his back foot and put his hand on his hip. His expression suggested he thought I had a lot of nerve saying that to him.

"It's not like that," I said. "I'm an old friend and I think he's in trouble."

He started to say something but stopped himself to think about it. Then he let out a long, relieved sigh. "Come in come in," he said, as though I was a doctor making a house call. "What's your name?"

"Ray."

"I'm Dale. I'm glad you came here and said what you said. I've been thinking something has been wrong for days, but . . . Ray Lilly? Tyalee told me about you."

All my old crew were talking about me. It made me feel odd; I never talked about them. "What did he tell you?"

Dale looked around the room as though he was going to offer me a chair, but my question had made him rethink it. "He said you were the most honest thief he had ever seen, and that he could never trust you. What does that mean, anyway? Are you really some kind of thief?"

Ty and I had been thieves together, but I wasn't going

to be the one to break the news. "Let's stay focused on Ty. Why do think something has been wrong?"

"He won't touch me," Dale said, looking distinctly uncomfortable. "He wears those gloves, and when I touch his skin . . ."

"It burns."

"Yeah. And he gets angry, like he's afraid for me. What happened to him?"

I wasn't going to go there. "Is he here?"

"I don't know where he is."

That wasn't a good sign. Ty could have been lying somewhere in the apartment the way Caramella had.

The buzzer sounded. I stepped aside to let Dale access the intercom, but all he did was press the security button. He was a victim waiting to happen, and I wondered what Ty saw in him.

"Oh my God," he said. "I haven't even asked you to sit down. Come in, please, and be comfortable. Can I get you something? Beer?"

"I'd rather have water."

"Of course, it's so hot." He hurried into the kitchen and filled a glass. I looked around the room. Their apartment had been furnished right off the showroom floor of IKEA, which made the place feel like a robot habitat. On the end table beside me there were two little spaceships facing each other. One was from *Star Trek,* but I couldn't recognize the other. I had the sudden urge to smash them both.

As Dale handed me the glass of water, there was a knock at the door. He opened it without looking through the peephole first, signed the pizza guy's slip, and shut the door. I took the pizza box from him.

"There's something we need to do first."

Together, we searched the apartment. He looked in cabinets and cupboards, and above them, too, searching for a clue to Ty's odd behavior. I went through the motions with him, but what I really wanted to do was check every corner and behind every bit of furniture for a shape that could be touched but not seen. We didn't find that, but in the bedroom, Dale showed me something else.

"I wasn't sure if I should, but . . ." He dragged a stainless-steel suitcase out from under the bed. I knew what was in it even before he opened it.

Cash. It was bundles of twenties and hundreds, all thrown in randomly, and all bound up in paper wrappers.

I shut my eyes and took a deep breath. The urge to slug Dale, hard, and run out the door with this money was incredible. So many of my problems could be solved with this suitcase. And he was a guy who didn't even look through the peephole before opening his door. It would be a useful lesson for him. . . .

"Look at this! It's just like a *movie*!" Dale made that sound like an insult. "I don't even know where it came from!"

I held up one of the bundles. The name of the bank was printed on it. "Yes, you do."

He plopped down onto the corner of the bed. "Okay. I do. But Ty, he . . . Okay. Once, about a year and a half ago, I had a flat on my car, and I couldn't afford a new tire. I was really, really broke, and he and I had just gotten together, okay? And I was upset because I'm in frickin' L.A. without a car, okay?

"The next day, Ty had put four new sidewalls on it. He thought I would be happy, but he had even less money than I did. He hadn't even started to cover his facility fee at the gym. I'm not stupid, okay? I knew he hadn't bought them. But I made him promise not to steal again."

"But you kept the tires," a voice behind us said. I spun around, my pulse already racing. Ty stood in the doorway, his hands empty. He looked at Dale, then at me, then back at Dale again, as though he wanted to make us unmeet each other.

"Why is this here?" Dale demanded. "In my home!"

Ty glanced at the suitcase without much interest. "I need it," he said. "I need to offer it to someone to get him to do something for me."

"Who?" I asked. "Wally King?"

"Yeah," he said to me. "You've been putting it together."

"I still have a couple of blank spots in the story. Help me with the rest of it." He laughed at me. It was a cynical sound; he wasn't so glad to see me anymore. "All right, then," I said. "Help me get the guy who did this to you. No one else can."

"You're the one who did this to me."

"That's bullshit, Ty."

"Well, *what do you expect from me*?!"

His shout echoed in the tiny room. Dale bolted to his feet and retreated toward the corner. I held myself absolutely still, and I knew right then I would have to kill him.

"What do you expect from me, Ray? This guy shows up out of the blue at the Bigfoot Room saying he knows you. He says he can do things for us, and Luther is right there to say it's true, it's all true. He promises us power, and he delivers, too. All he asks is one favor in return, and he hasn't even collected from me yet."

"I don't think he'll bother, Ty." *You're just a distraction. You're his wooden man.* "Tell me what happened."

He sighed. "What's the use?"

I thought about Wally's cabin and my iron gate. Maybe I didn't need him to explain it all to me. "I'll tell you, then. You went somewhere secluded. Wally had a circle or square or something painted on the floor—maybe it was drawn in chalk—and it had symbols around it. Then he put a symbol on you, too, and you got into the circle.

What was next? Chanting? Music? Did he draw another symbol?"

Ty wasn't in the mood to answer questions. "How did you know he drew a symbol on me?"

"Because he put a *thing* on you. Something alive, and the only reason it hasn't killed you yet is that you're protected."

Ty lifted his shirt, exposing ab muscles that gave me a twinge of envy. And a sigil.

It wasn't large, barely as wide across as seven quarters arranged in a circle, all touching. Three squiggles had been drawn inside a slender ring, but this time I couldn't figure out what those squiggles might represent.

Then I realized that the ink was fading. The outer ring especially was wearing away.

Dale had leaned in close to me so he could look, too. "It's henna," he said. "But fading."

Ty dropped his shirt to cover the sigil. It occurred to me that I had Annalise's cell in my pocket. I took it out and lifted Ty's shirt again. He went stiff and awkward when I touched him. I snapped the picture quickly and backed away. Ty frowned at me and straightened his shirt. "Yeah. The ink was diluted, I think, and when it wears out, I'm history, right?"

I looked him in the eye. "Caramella is already dead."

"Damn." He turned his back and stepped over to the bureau. There was another unrecognizable spaceship on it. Ty flicked it with his fingers. It slid across the painted wood and fell to the carpet with a fragile plastic sound.

"Ty," I said, pointing my thumb at Dale. I chose my words carefully. "Do you care about this victim?"

Dale looked at me, shocked. "Victim?"

Ty laughed sadly. "Oh, Ray, you have no idea. You don't know how many times I've had to pick up a credit card he's left forgotten on a restaurant table. Or car keys. You don't even know. But yeah. I love him."

"Then you have to get away from him."

"No!" Dale shouted. "Ty, I don't know what's going on, okay, but—"

"Shut up," Ty said. His tone wasn't unkind, just sad. "I mean it."

"When Caramella went," I pushed on, "she nearly took Vi's daughter with her."

"Vi's daughter?" he said, as though it was hilarious that I'd called her that.

"Yes. And not just her, either. When this thing takes you, it's going to take whoever is nearby, too. Ty, I can—"

"You can what, Ray? What? Tell me what you can do?"

"I can get you away from people—"

"Fuck that. I want to live." Ty bared his teeth at me as he said it, letting anger give him strength. "I'm not going to give up now! I'm going to find this Wally King, and I'll offer him the money. If that doesn't work, I'll offer him his own damn life. He'll show me a way—"

"Ty—"

"No, Ray, shut up! He'll show me how to take it off and put it on when I want, and—"

"Ty, it's not a goddamn jacket! It's down in your lungs, isn't it? It's breathing for you, and it's up your nose and in your head. And it's strong, I know. It's not going to let you put it on and take it off like a hat."

"What can you offer that's better, Ray? I wouldn't even be in this mess if it wasn't for you, and you want to take me somewhere quiet to die?"

My ghost knife was in my pocket, but if I used it, the drape on him would kill him, and who knows how many more would come through. Ty wouldn't be happy to see me reaching into my pocket just then, either.

"You were wrong about one thing, Ray. Wally King *did* ask me to do a little something for him, but I wasn't going to do it. I think I changed my mind."

He turned into a silhouette, giving me a glimpse of the Empty Spaces, then he vanished.

I spun and tore the covers off the bed, throwing them at him. I didn't have to bother; he wasn't hiding from me, he was charging. The striped sheet flopped over Ty's head just before he slammed me off my feet into the wall.

I was pinned, the wooden bedpost digging into my low ribs and kidney. Damn, he was strong. I felt his right hand release my shirt, saw the blanket flutter as it slid off him. I raised my left hand to protect my head.

His first punch glanced off my triceps and the top of my head. It probably hurt him as much as it hurt me. His second struck the part of my forearm protected by spells. That one didn't hurt me at all.

His weight shifted and I twisted to the left. His third punch landed right on my solar plexus. He might have killed me with it if not for the spells there.

My feet were off the floor, and I didn't have room to lift them onto the bed. Instead, I kicked low, hoping to hit Ty's knee. I missed. I had no idea where he was. All I could see was Dale standing in the corner with a horrified expression.

I tucked my chin and protected my face as well as I could. Even though I couldn't see him, I could feel him. He was still holding me with his left hand. I reached out with my right, trying to find his eyes, but he wrenched himself away and slammed me down on his bed.

I could hear his breathing, ragged and furious, but I looked straight through him at Dale. While he rained down punches on me, I curled my legs and kicked at him again. I needed to get him off balance. I needed leverage.

Ty switched his grip on my shirt so his knuckles would grind into my throat. I finally managed to get a good kick against his knee and made him stagger. He didn't let me up, but the pressure eased, and I had a moment's break from the beating I was taking on my ribs and my left arm.

His grip on my throat loosened. I caught his thumb in my right hand and started to peel it back. He wouldn't let me break it, though. He ripped his hand away and backed off.

For a moment I was afraid he'd gotten smart. If he'd let go of me and hit me with a bit more distance, I'd never have been able to protect myself. I pushed my way off the bed toward him, determined to keep him close.

I hadn't yet gotten all the way upright when a fat ceramic lamp floated off the bedside table and rushed at me. I swung at it with my protected forearm and shattered it. Broken bits of clay clattered against my face and chest, and the heavy base struck my lip painfully.

I felt something kick against my feet, and I was on my back again. Ty fumbled at my shirt, trying to get control of me and pin me again—he could turn invisible, but he couldn't break his fighting habits. He had to stick with what he was comfortable with.

Shards of broken ceramic jabbed painfully into my back, and the twisted metal workings of the lamp lay across my chest. I grabbed it. The shade had come off, but the bulb had not broken. I felt Ty heave his weight on me, about to throw more punches, and I jabbed upward.

It wasn't hard to guess where he was. The thin glass of the bulb shattered with a muffled *shink* sound, and I pushed.

I heard Ty back away, cursing. The bulb was broken almost down to the socket, with a couple of nasty glass shards sticking out. I'd expected to see blood on them, but there was nothing, just a faint, slimy sheen. I tossed it aside and sat up off the bed. Ty didn't come at me again.

He cursed again, and I oriented myself on the sound. The left side of my body below my arm was bruised, and

I had several spots on my face and head that felt painful and inflamed. If he'd been planning to beat me to death, it would have taken him a long time, but he was capable of it.

Ty cursed again, and this time his voice had gone high with fear. Had I hit a vital spot like a throat or an eye? I couldn't say I was sorry if I had, but I didn't want to deal with the consequences of killing him here. I wasn't ready to face four drapes, or to defend Dale from them.

Ty let out a wordless cry, then said: "It's like a tongue!"

"What's happening?" Dale cried.

"Ty!" I said. "Show yourself."

He did. There was a tiny drop of blood on his shoulder. It didn't look serious to me, but Ty shuddered and twitched back and forth. "Ah! Omigodomigodomigod . . ."

I moved toward him at the same time Dale did. There was still a delicate sliver of glass protruding from his skin. While I watched, it slowly backed out of the cut as though pulled by an invisible hand, then fell. I picked it up off the carpet. There wasn't a drop of blood on it.

Dale grabbed Ty's bare arm, then let go with a hiss. Ty grimaced and turned his face to the ceiling. The cut on his shoulder didn't look serious. It barely seemed to be bleeding.

"Shit!" Ty gasped. "It's digging in and squeezing—Ah, God!" He grimaced and staggered as though the right side of his body was paralyzed. "It's milking the blood out of me!"

I grabbed his gloved hand. It was bone dry, while my clothes were soaked with sweat. "This way," I said. "Quickly."

Dale struck my hand away. He was stronger and faster than he seemed. "You're the one who hurt him! Get out! Get the fuck out!"

"I'm the only one who knows what's going on!" I

shouted, surprising myself with my sudden anger. My face was in pain and felt swollen. Not to mention, I was trying to help a guy who had been beating the crap out of me a minute earlier.

"This is my place!" Dale shouted, and he was angry enough to let a Georgia accent show. "Mine!"

"Stop fighting," Ty said, "and do something about this leech."

Dale and I looked at each other. I waited for him to lay out a plan, but it was pretty obvious he had nothing. After a couple of seconds, I turned to Ty.

"All right, asshole," I said. "That thing on you is starving."

"Jesus, *shit*!" Ty said, as the blood welled up around his little scratch and vanished. "It's *drinking* my blood?"

"It won't be satisfied with your blood. It wants your skin and your guts and all the thoughts in your head, too. It wants everything, and like I said, it's starving. Now, it can't feed on you while Wally's spell is in place, but—"

"But it's taking the parts that come out of me. I'm not stupid."

I led the two of them into the other room, fighting very hard against the urge to tell him just how incredibly stupid he was. It was hard to raise my left arm, and my upper left incisor felt loose in my mouth. Ty parked himself on a chair at the little dining room table. Dale said he was going to the bathroom for bandages and disinfectant. I went into the kitchen, set a small cast-iron skillet on the stove, and turned the gas under it as high as it would go.

"Ray." Ty's voice came from the other room. I didn't think he could see what I was doing, because I don't think he could have been so calm. "I'm sorry."

I told him what he could do with himself.

"Then why are you helping me?"

There were gel packs in the freezer. I took two, pinning one against my ribs with my elbow and laying the other on the side of my face. "Because you may be a selfish, self-justifying asshole who thinks he can buy his way out of this mess, but that thing on you is worse."

"It's really alive, isn't it? It's a monster."

I sighed and closed my eyes. Predators killed people, and so did I. "It's an animal," I said. "And it's probably a person, too. I think it's smart—maybe as smart as a human, but in a different way." The dry skillet had begun to smoke faintly.

"I don't even know what you're talking about. Listen, if it's hungry, and it can't eat me, can't I get it to go to someone else? You know? Agh!" He paused while the drape worked on him. "Why can't I just, I don't know, transfer it?"

The packs were too cold. I tossed them into the sink on top of a pair of tiny bowls. "We don't do that," I said as I went into the other room.

Dale returned with a roll of bandages and a squeeze tube of disinfectant. He crouched in front of Ty and tried to squeeze gel onto the cuts. Ty looked me in the eyes, and for the first time I saw desperation there. "Ray, there's got to be a way."

I looked directly at Dale. "Ty, who do you have in mind?"

"No," Ty said. "There has to be someone else. Some bum off the street maybe. Somebody worthless." He winced and clutched at his shoulder. "Hey! There's a guy at the gym who smacks his wife around sometimes. He's the one."

"Even if I knew a way, I wouldn't do it," I said.

"Why not?" Ty demanded, as Dale flung the squeeze tube onto the table with an annoyed hiss. The drape was not letting him put the disinfectant on. "Why does it have to be me? If this thing is going to kill somebody, why can't it be him? Why me?"

I thought about the rape souvenir Lenard kept in the locker at the Bigfoot Room, and Maria's endless talk about finding a job, and Ty himself holding me down while he was hitting me. Why do any of us do anything? It's not like we put a lot of rational thought into things. "You two have slept together in the last few days, right? I mean, in the same bed."

Ty saw what I was saying immediately. "Shit."

Dale laid a bandage over Ty's shoulder and placed some tape on it. Then he looked back at me. "What?"

"This thing's been on him for days, waiting for the chance to feed. If it was going to jump to another un-protected victim, it would have done that already while you were sleeping. Wally didn't put a mark on you, did he?"

"I don't know any Wally."

I turned my attention back to Ty. "It has a meal and it's not letting go. Ever."

"Goddammit!" Dale said. The bandage had slid to the side and bunched up, and the tape had peeled away. He started to lay another one in place, and Ty helped him hold it still.

I went into the kitchen. The skillet was smoking hot now, and slightly grayish at the center. I wrapped an oven pad around the handle and picked it up.

"What's that smell?" Dale asked as I came back into the room. I shoved him aside and jammed the hot metal against Ty's wound.

He screamed. Oh, how he screamed. His voice almost covered the sound of the meat hissing against metal, but nothing could mask the smell of burning flesh and poly-ester shirt.

After a couple of seconds, I took it off him. Then I

grabbed Dale by the elbow and pulled him back. If the drape killed Ty, I wanted Dale and me to be far enough back that we didn't fall into the Empty Spaces.

It didn't kill him, though. Instead, Ty slid off the chair onto his knees, cursing and promising to kill me.

Dale tore out of my grip and rushed to him. "Oh my God, you—"

"At least he won't bleed to death from a scratch," I said. Of course, he would die soon enough anyway, but now I figured it was safe to take him outdoors. I went into the bedroom and slid open the closet doors. Half a dozen belts hung from a hook. I chose an army-surplus web belt.

And there on the floor was the open suitcase. I picked up a packet of hundred-dollar bills. The wrapper helpfully told me, in ink the color of spicy brown mustard, that the bundle was worth ten thousand dollars.

A suitcase full of money was a new thing for me. I'd always stolen cars, not cash. At least, not in piles. I didn't have a job and I'd just taken a beating from a friend—I wanted this money so much that it made me angry. I tore the wrapper off and stuffed the folded bills into my back pocket. I could have made things hard for Ty and Dale by tossing the wrapper behind the bureau where the cops might find it, but I dropped it into the suitcase instead. I wasn't put on this earth to help cops.

Back in the other room, Ty was smearing aloe on his shoulder. Dale stood between us, a butcher knife in his hand. I'm sure it was the biggest one he could find.

"You're leaving," Dale said. "Now."

"I know. And I'm taking Ty with me."

"I don't think so."

"What are you gonna do? Stab me so my guts fall out on the carpet? Right here in your own apartment, with a suitcase full of stolen money in the other room?"

That was all he needed to hear. He sagged and turned

toward Ty, letting the knife hang low at his side. "Ty . . ." His voice had an air of finality about it.

"Don't say it," Ty said. "I already know." He stood. "I tried to do things the right way. I tried a regular job and taxes and everything, but I just couldn't work it out."

"Are you going to be okay?"

"I'm not going to go down without a fight." Ty turned to me. "How much of the money did you take?"

"Less than all of it, but enough that I don't feel like killing you anymore."

Dale was staring at me. "Can you . . ." He couldn't finish the question. I didn't think he was even sure what he was asking for.

"I don't know, but no one else is even going to try."

Ty laid his hand on Dale's shoulder. "Take the money and get out of town for a while. Take a week, drive up the coast. Use up some of that vacation time. If you spend the money slowly, no one will notice."

"Tear off the wrappers," I said. "Order something at a drive-through McDonald's or something. Take the food out of the bag, stuff the wrappers into the bottom, and roll it up tight. Then stuff the bag into a trash can right there at the restaurant."

Dale moved toward Ty. "Don't," Ty said, and stepped back. "It'll burn you."

Dale kissed him.

I looked away, but I didn't turn my back. Dale still had that damn knife. After a short while, I heard Dale go into the bathroom. He closed the door and turned on the water to wash.

I wrapped the belt around Ty's right wrist and tightened it as far as it would go. He let me. We left the apartment and went down the rough concrete stairs. I held the end of the belt like a leash. It made me feel like an asshole.

"I'm through playing games," I said. "If you take

that belt off or"—I couldn't say it on a public stair-well—"do your thing, I'll kill you, and to hell with the consequences."

"I was the one who beat the hell out of Justin Gage, you know."

I couldn't remember who he was talking about, and I said so.

He laughed a little. "Guess you wouldn't. He's a big figure in *my* life, but . . . He's the Cardio-eira guy at the gym where I work. You know, like Tae-Bo, but with ca-poeira? Never mind. It's a new fitness thing that's been getting pretty popular, even though it's really stupid. Ev-eryone who went to the gym wanted Gage—I couldn't even pick up the guy's sloppy seconds. And to make it worse, he was always being nice to me about it. Encour-aging me that I was good enough and telling me how it all takes time . . . like I needed attaboys from him. Do you know how much the gym charged me to work there?"

"No." I tried to sound like I cared, but I failed. He glanced at me. He could see how I felt, but he was too busy feeling sorry for himself to drop it.

"Well, it's a lot. After I kicked his dancey little capoeira ass, I took over a bunch of his clients, but I could tell they weren't going to switch permanently. It was just a waste. Maybe I should have killed him. He was just lying there, at the end—I could have stamped on his neck, you know? But I wasn't desperate enough for that. That's what I told myself. I wasn't desperate enough. I thought I could be a straight arrow, you know? Like Dale. Such a waste, man."

He didn't sound sorry about what he'd done. I guess that would have been too much to expect. We reached my Escort and I opened the door for him. He sat and I shut the door. I went around to the driver's side and climbed in.

"I should have taken that money," he said. "I had hopes for it."

"Wally doesn't need your money."

"Maybe he wants it."

"For God's sake! It should have been obvious to you a long time ago that you cannot pull the usual shit here. You can't buy off or bully these people. There's no way to blackmail them. They have their own little world, and it only comes into contact with ours when they need to kill someone or find a patsy."

"Fuck you. I'm nobody's patsy."

"Fuck me? You have a living stomach lining over your whole body, and it's going to start eating you soon. You're a patsy. Deal with it. Whatever Wally really needed, he tried to get it with Luther. You weren't involved."

Ty turned toward me suddenly. "Tried? At that house?"

I didn't like the look on his face. "Dude—"

A Range Rover screeched to a halt right in front of my car. I jammed the key into the ignition at the same moment that Ty opened the passenger door and turned invisible. The engine started as I lunged toward Ty but missed him. He was gone.

The doors of the Range Rover swung open. Meatheads One, Two, and Three piled out.

To hell with this. I threw it into reverse and tried to back out of my spot. One of the meatheads fired three rounds into my engine block.

Immediately, the engine started grinding and lost power. I cut the wheel, backing up anyway, but I didn't have the space to make the turn, and I plowed into the street-side taillight of the car parked behind me.

By then, a man was standing by my window, tapping a pistol against the glass.

I turned off the engine and opened the door. Their ugly faces were all around me, thick, pouchy, scarred with acne. Hands pressed me against my car and patted me down the way a cop would. They found my cell and ghost knife, and this time they kept both. They also found the ten grand. Damn, I hadn't even gotten to the end of the block with it, and now I had to listen to them laugh as they split it between them.

A woman on the sidewalk held up her cellphone and snapped a picture of us. I stared straight at her, knowing my face would be recorded. Too bad I was on the twisted path; by the time she showed the photo to someone, it would no longer look like me.

"Let's go," one of the men said. They dragged me into the Range Rover and shoved me into the back, where I sat squeezed between two guys who smelled like sweat and enchilada sauce.

Potato Face sat in the front seat. He looked me over and turned away. He'd caught me, but he didn't look happy about it.

We pulled away, leaving my car with the money under the floor mats jutting into the street. An embarrassing pang of grief went through me. I'd killed too many people to be moved by the loss of an old vehicle, but I was anyway.

We drove on Beverly Glen Boulevard much too fast. The windows were open, but the freeway air blowing into my face was dry and hot—there was nothing cooling about it. I asked for water, but no one acknowledged me. I was forced to sit quietly and wonder how I was going to track down Ty again, not to mention the others, and how much time I had before he fell out of this world and let more predators in.

We pulled up to Francois's big white house and parked at the curb. There was a blue panel van in the drive, and its back doors swung open as we got out of the car. Two more meatheads climbed out, with Arne and Lenard at gunpoint.

Arne had a nasty smile on his face. "God, it's a beautiful day. Am I right?"

Lenard snorted. I wondered why the two of them let themselves be captured. Were they trying to keep their power a secret? I thought I was the only one concerned about that.

The three of us let ourselves be herded up the front walk toward the house.

CHAPTER THIRTEEN

Each of us had two meatheads assigned to him, with two more in back and Potato leading the way. When we entered the clean white house, the air-conditioning was so startling that I gasped aloud. It must have been 65 degrees inside, and the sweat on my face and back immediately chilled.

Lenard turned toward me, smiling at the way I gasped. "I know, huh? Let's move in."

One of the meatheads shoved him roughly, and we ran out of things to say. I could feel my ghost knife nearby, in the pocket of one of the men, but I didn't call it. If Arne and Lenard were hiding their tricks, so would I.

We were taken to the same room as the last time. The sliding doors were closed, and blinds were drawn across them. The only light came from a pair of lamps in opposite corners, and they cast a sickly yellow tint over the white furniture.

Swizzle Stick sat in a plush chair in the corner. She wore the same purple bikini, but her legs and arms were crossed, and her chin tucked low, as though she didn't want to be noticed.

Beside her chair, Francois paced back and forth. His suit this time was midnight black—maybe it made him feel tough.

He never took his eyes off Arne. Potato stopped us five feet from him. The meatheads were all around, standing so close together they were practically in one another's way. There was a door behind Francois, another that we came through, and of course the sliding doors. The meatheads would catch me if I bolted toward Francois, and there was too much heavy flesh to shove aside to get to either of the other exits.

"Well?" Francois suddenly barked.

"Yeah," Swizzle Stick answered. Her confidence had drained away. "It was the middle one." She lifted her chin toward Lenard. "He was the sp—"

"Watch your fucking mouth," Francois said. "Now get your things and call a cab."

Her crossed arms and legs slid apart. "What?"

Francois spun toward her. "What did you think would happen? Get out!"

She pushed her long, lanky body out of the chair. I stepped to the side to give her room to pass—and to better position myself to rush the door—but the meatheads took hold of me in a very convincing way. Swizzle went out the far door anyway.

"Bad enough," Francois said to us, "that you steal my fucking car and try to sell it back to me, but you had to put that fucking video on the Internet? And then you tell *my wife*?!"

Arne was still smiling. "That's Web two point oh, baby."

Francois stepped up close to him. "You think I'm being funny?" There was something unconvincing about Francois's performance. He wasn't used to threatening people, and he didn't have the knack. I snuck a glance at Potato Face. His expression was not quite blank, and he had turned his body away from his employer. I didn't think he'd be murdering anyone for this boss.

Francois shifted his feet. This wasn't turning out how he'd planned, and he was growing frustrated. "Do you know what I do to people who cross me?"

I said: "You make them leave this air-conditioned room?"

Arne and Lenard both laughed. Francois spun and came toward me. He got very close to my face. "You think you're someone, don't you? But you're nobody, and I'm going to prove it.

"What's the matter, *gallito*?" Lenard said. "Are you a man or not? Tell your wife you wanted to fuck somebody new for a change, and if she don't like it, tough."

"The only problem with that," Arne said, "is that most of the money is hers. Right?"

"That's bullshit! I have my own money. All my own."

"That's good," Arne said, his voice full of bad ideas. "It's good for a man to have his own."

"For now, at least," I said. "I hear your wife is one hell of a lawyer."

Francois licked his lips. "You guys are nothing. Mosquitoes. You have no idea what kind of enemies I have."

Arne grinned at him nastily. "Baby, *you* don't even know what kind of enemies you have."

He turned into a silhouette and vanished.

Francois shrieked—actually shrieked like a little girl—in shock. The meatheads shouted curses or little prayers, and suddenly no one was holding me at all. Lenard smiled and shrugged, then he vanished, too.

Potato suddenly grunted and doubled over as though he'd been kicked in the crotch. The door behind me banged open, and I could hear heavy footsteps stomping through it. Potato staggered toward Francois and fell against him, pinning him against the door and shielding him with his body. "Shut that damn door!" Potato rasped, and his heavy, low voice had the authority to stop everyone still. I heard the door slam shut.

My ghost knife was still nearby. I *called* it and it zipped out of one of the meatheads' breast pocket into my hand. He gaped at me, but no one else seemed to notice.

There were five of the meatheads left, plus Potato, Francois, and presumably Arne and Lenard. And me. Three meatheads backed against the glass doors blocking them. One stood against the door we'd come in, and the last one kicked the back of my knees and drove me to the floor.

I hated kneeling, but before I could do anything about it, Potato yelled, "Guns!"

The meatheads drew their pistols. Everything suddenly fell silent. We all listened for some sign of Arne and Lenard but couldn't hear anything. Were they being completely still, or had they already left the room?

Potato fished a Zippo out of his pants pocket and tossed it to one of the men at the sliding doors. "Newspapers," he said. The meathead grabbed a section off the coffee table and set fire to it, then held it out in front of him.

"Wave it around," Potato said. "Spread that smoke." He turned to me. "How the fuck are they doing this?"

"They were bitten by a radioactive chameleon."

He scowled at me but didn't press further. He had other problems to focus on.

The smoke filled the room quickly. I stared at it, eyes unfocused to take in as much as possible, looking for swirls that didn't have any obvious source. I couldn't see any.

"Let me out," Francois said, his voice a low, terrified whisper. "Let me out. Let me out."

"When I'm sure we have both of them trapped in here, I'll open the door. Until then, shaddup."

The central air-conditioning suddenly turned on with a low hum. Smoke swirled in every direction, and at the same moment, the guard holding the burning paper grimaced and clutched at his chest. Blood welled up under his left breast, and he collapsed forward onto the carpet, smothering the flames with his body.

"No, no!" one of the other men yelled, but Potato hissed at him. He shut up.

"Do you know what kind of enemies I have?"

It was Lenard's voice, and it came in a low whisper, making it hard to trace. I had a strange feeling, though, that he was very near me—just a couple of feet away. It was the same feeling that had led me to the spell on Sugar Dubois's back, a lifetime ago. It felt like magic, pulling me toward him.

"Gimme those," Potato said, pointing at the newspapers. One of the men tossed him a couple of sections. He shook them out, letting the pages fall onto the carpet around him. His men did the same.

Within seconds, each was surrounded by four or five feet's worth of paper.

"All right," Potato said. "You guys don't have guns. I know, because I took them from you. And I got your buddy right here." He pointed a pistol at me. "You can't get close to us without stepping on the paper and giving yourself away. And getting shot. So I'm gonna count to three, and if you don't show yourself, I'm putting a bullet in your pal here."

Potato aimed the gun at my forehead. Why couldn't he have chosen a part of me that was bulletproof?

"Go ahead," Lenard whispered. "So what?"

The smoke alarm suddenly went off; everyone winced except Potato. "Fire department's on its way!" he shouted. "Time is running out!"

"You're right, it is!" Arne shouted. He suddenly became visible just behind me. Damn if he didn't have a gun of his own in his hand, although I had no idea where he got it.

He pointed his pistol at Potato or Francois—it was hard to tell which. The meatheads all pointed their weapons at him. He was outnumbered and outgunned, and I couldn't figure out what his play was supposed to be. If he had the gun . . .

"Lenard!" Arne shouted. Lenard became visible just a few feet in front of me, crouching beside a low table. He shrugged, his smiling expression suggesting that he was playing along in a game that was beneath him. The meathead who'd been standing guard over me moved toward him.

Arne shifted his aim and fired a single shot at Lenard. The meathead jumped back. Lenard looked at his old friend in shock. There was a bloody hole in his shirt over his heart. Behind him, red was spattered against the wall; the drape was strong, but not strong enough to hold an exit wound closed.

Arne laughed and vanished again.

"No!" I shouted. There was a loud cracking sound, and beneath the piercing alarm I could hear a droning buzz.

It took a moment or two for Lenard to drop. I grabbed the meathead who'd been guarding me and pulled him away from Lenard's body. He twisted, thinking I was attacking him, and laid a heavy, door-busting right hook to the side of my face. I tried to roll with it, but it still had enough power to bounce me off the wall and lay me flat.

The noise was oppressive, but the awful mix of sounds helped me stay conscious. I struggled up onto my elbow, trying to clear the blinking white spots from my vision. Two meatheads moved toward Lenard—damn, they were close. I tried to warn them back, but all I could manage was a harsh croak and a vague wave of my arm.

Potato stepped toward them. "Back!" he shouted over the noise. He pulled one back and the other moved, too, as though they were tethered. Just then, the floor turned dark and vanished. Lenard's corpse dropped away into the void, and the meatheads began screaming.

Five drapes floated through the opening like balloons

rising out of a manhole. The yellow light from Francois's lamps made them look like phlegm. The meatheads gaped, frozen in place.

Potato Face stepped back, and the first of the drapes rushed him. It flopped over him like a net, and he struggled for a couple of moments before toppling to the floor.

The two men he'd pulled away from Lenard's body turned to run, but drapes were on them before they could take a second step. One fell against a lamp and end table. The other landed on the middle of the floor.

One drape moved toward the guard who'd laid me out, and he fired four quick shots into it. The bullets tore through the predator's body, looking like clean spots on smeary glass, but the holes sealed over immediately. I tried to stand and push him away, but I was too slow. The man had time to scream once before it wrapped itself over his face and head.

The opening into the Empty Spaces disappeared. The couch jolted to the side as one of the guards thrashed against it, but Potato and his three men had vanished. I reached toward the space where the fourth man had fallen. He was there, invisible and trembling, just like Melly after her protective spell wore off.

Where was the fifth drape? I tried to remember how many men had fled the room and how many should have been here still. The only other person I could see was a lone blond beefhead crouching by the French doors. He stretched his hand out and touched the air at the base of the glass, then yanked his hand back and wiped it on his polo shirt.

Was that the fifth? I touched the one that fell near me, then crossed the room to touch that one. One man had fallen closer to me than I thought, and I nearly tripped over him in my search. Then I found Potato by the back door and the last beside the broken end table.

That was five. If one of the drapes had escaped the

building, I didn't know what I'd do. Luckily, it hadn't become an issue. There were enough victims right here when they attacked.

And I'd had my ghost knife in my hand the whole time. I'd failed them all.

Worse, now I had to find a way to kill them safely.

That last guard stood. "You!" I shouted, trying to be heard over the blare of the alarm. "Stay here so we can help your friends!"

He stared at me for just a second, then barreled out the door. So much for my leadership abilities.

The alarm set my teeth on edge, and I suddenly remembered what Potato had said about the fire department coming. I rolled to my feet, bumping against one of the invisible bodies. My arm started to itch from the contact, but I pushed it toward the wall anyway. If firefighters chopped the door down and tripped over one of these invisible bodies . . .

I couldn't think with that damn alarm going, so I pushed a chair to the middle of the room and stood on it. The alarm was mounted on the center of the ceiling, and the cover came off with a quarter-twist.

It was nothing more than a thirty-dollar drugstore model. I yanked out the nine-volt battery, and the unit fell silent. There were no wires connecting it to the rest of the house, and no way for it to call emergency services when it went off. Potato had been bluffing.

First things first. I went through the open door into the kitchen, which looked like a smaller version of the kitchen at the Sugar Shaker, but without the men in white caps. I rinsed off my hands and searched the house as quickly as I could.

Francois was gone. So were Swizzle Stick, the two guards, and the Bugatti. Had Arne taken Francois and the car, or had one of the others? I wouldn't have a chance to drive it after all.

Beside the blank space where the Bugatti should have been parked was an H2 Hummer in a grotesque blue-green color. It was a big, stupid vehicle, but it was perfect for what I needed. A set of keys hung from a hook by the door.

There were also gardening gloves in the garage, but nothing I could use to move those bodies. Damn. I needed to find something, because there was no way I could leave those drapes and their victims here in the house.

Even if the fire department never came, *somebody* would. Maybe the guard would come back, or Swizzle, or even a process server for Francois's soon-to-be-ex-wife. Eventually, someone was going to want to know what happened to Francois—in fact, they could be placing a call to the cops right now.

These drapes couldn't be left here; I had to take them with me. I would either have to find Annalise and hope that one of her spells—the green fire?—could kill the predators without opening a passage to let more in, or I was going to have to figure out where they'd been summoned.

I didn't have what you'd call encyclopedic knowledge of predators or magic, but I had seen a couple of summonings. They took place inside circles—usually—sometimes painted, sometimes made of a particular material. They were like the circle around Wally King's cabin, only not usually so huge, and they could imprison the predator in our world.

I needed to know where Wally had summoned the drapes for Arne and his crew. Maybe, if I was lucky, the circle would still be intact. If a guard died inside it, the next group of predators—more than five of them, I guessed—would be contained.

I needed to catch up with Arne or one of the others. I needed a way to get that information out of them, and I needed to get them inside the circle, too.

The first thing I did was search the invisible bodies. One of them had taken the cellphone Annalise had given me, and I couldn't contact her without it. The drapes, strangely, seemed to be both under and over the guard's clothes. I could touch and move the fabric freely, but it was completely hidden by the predator's invisibility.

I searched all five bodies and couldn't find the phone. Damn. It was probably forgotten in the pocket of that meathead speeding toward Mexico.

That meant I would have to find Annalise or the circle—not an easy thing to do with ten million people in L.A. County, but I had a couple of leads.

There was a little shed out by the pool, but when I opened it I found nothing but towels and water toys. Apparently, Francois was too rich to own a wheelbarrow.

I took an office chair from a back bedroom, laid the bodyguards into it one by one, and wheeled each of them into the garage. The cargo area of the H2 was huge, but so were the guards. I had to slide out the last row of seats to make room for them.

Damn, they were heavy. At least they hadn't gone limp—each man was still fighting the effect of the predator, and all their muscles were clenched. I wished the blond guard hadn't run off. I could have used help getting the bodies up into the SUV.

I stopped myself. They weren't *bodies*. Not yet. They were still living men, and I wanted to treat them that way, not least of all because if one of them died in the back of this SUV, I was going to have drapes all over me.

I tried to lay them side by side; if one of them was pinned at the bottom, the weight of the others might suffocate him. The last two went into the backseat, tipped at an angle to fit.

By the time I was finished, I had slime all over my arms and on my neck. The burning and itching was intense. I skipped the sink and the shower and went straight out to the pool. After dropping my wallet and ghost knife on the grass, I toppled into the water.

I climbed out dripping wet, feeling like a guest who'd overstayed his welcome. I made a last stop at the fridge to steal six finger sandwiches, then it was time to go. I opened the back of the H2 to tap around the interior with a broom handle, just to reassure myself that everyone was still there. Then I climbed dripping wet into the driver's seat.

A button above the rearview mirror opened both the garage door and the driveway gate. I pulled out into the street, threw the switch to close them both again, and drove away.

There were more predators out there for me to find.

CHAPTER FOURTEEN

There was only one place to start my search: Ty had been much too excited to hear about Lino Vela's house. I didn't like the idea of Ty—or anyone in Arne's crew—finding a spell book. I didn't even want them to hear the words "Book of Oceans."

I drove toward Hancock Park, trying to be careful on the highway. The Hummer felt as wide as a traffic lane, and I didn't want to get into a fender bender in a stolen car. Luckily, other drivers assumed I was a jackass and gave me a lot of space.

I pulled up outside Lino Vela's address. Everything seemed quiet, but of course the greenery hid most of the property. I found a parking spot a block away and around the corner and pulled in.

Annalise's Dodge Sprinter sat parked across the street from Vela's gate. I tapped on the window. Annalise was in the passenger seat. She opened the driver's door and I climbed behind the wheel.

I didn't fit. The seat had been moved forward as far as it would go. Annalise had driven herself. "Talbot didn't come with you?"

"No," she said. "Have you accomplished anything?"

"I have five predators in the back of an SUV." She seemed surprised. "They have victims. Want to destroy them?"

She looked uncomfortable. She wanted to, always, but she didn't want to leave her post. I told her the drapes take a long time to feed, and what happens when the victim finally dies.

She asked how long we had until they actually killed their victims. I thought about the garbage stink in Melly's house, and the big pile of mail, and I said it seemed to take time, maybe a day or two.

Annalise nodded. "Normally I wouldn't wait to take out a couple of predators, but this is an unusual circumstance. If Wally King thinks there's a way to get a spell book from this house, he'll be back. I have to be here when he shows up. I can't let him get a lead on the Book of Motes or the Book of Oceans."

There was a note of desperation in her voice. Was she worried that Wally would become a primary? I was sure of it. But that wasn't all. The original spell books were a tremendous source of power, and she wanted them for herself.

But that was above me. I was just a guy with some invisible monsters in the back of his stolen Hummer. "Boss, these guys are dying slowly and badly. We need to . . . Wouldn't Wally have needed a circle to summon these things? A barrier, like the one in Canada?"

"Yes. Get one of your buddies to tell us where it is. If we can find that, we'll kill them there. If we can't, we'll try to get our hands on his book; it would have instructions on making the circle ourselves. If that falls through, we'll have to risk it. We won't have a choice. And yeah, those guys are suffering, but we're not here to make things easier for people."

She was looking away from me as she said it, and I was glad. She wouldn't have been happy if she'd seen my reaction—and maybe that's why she was looking away. Because in a sense, she was right; the most important thing was stopping the predators. Still, the suffering those men were going through had to count for *something*.

"So you're just going to sit here, waiting for Wally King?"

She still didn't look at me. "Looks that way."

"What if one of the invisibles turns up? How will you know?" She shrugged. "What if the guy who lives here is in danger?"

She turned and looked me in the eye. Her pale face was serene and still. "We're not here for him, either."

Before I had a chance to think about it, I was pushing the car door open and climbing out. I didn't want to be near her right then. Annalise had the power to kill predators *and* help people. The only thing she lacked was the will to do it. She just didn't give a shit.

I jogged across the street and went through the gate. The grounds were as overgrown as they'd been before, and it was quiet. The sun was still burning hot, and my clothes were drying quickly. I jogged toward the door. It was closed.

As I came closer, I saw a tall patch of natural wood on the painted green door. It had been repaired while I was in Canada, then broken open again. Someone had kicked the door in.

I could have gone back for Annalise, but I didn't. Ty might be in there, and who knows how many others from my old crew. They had predators on them, yes, and they would have to be killed, yes—and damn if that wasn't a hard thought to take and hold—but I didn't want Annalise anywhere near them. She didn't care about making things easier for people. She didn't care, period, and I didn't want her anywhere near my people.

I laid my hand on the door but didn't open it. Maybe there would be a better way. I went back down the steps to the narrow path between the bushes and went around the house.

It was impossible to move without rustling bushes, and the noise made me feel incredibly exposed. The windows were as high as my shoulder, and the bushes had grown slightly higher than the sill. There was no way I was getting through a window, or even getting a good look inside.

I went around a tall tree to the next set of windows when someone walked past the glass, moving away from me.

I ducked low. It was Bud, and while his face was turned away, I could see his jaw moving. He was also scratching furiously at the back of his neck. Was he talking to Lino or to one of the guys in the crew?

I crouched low, squeezing between some sort of thorny bush and the tall wooden fence that marked the edge of the property. I reached the backyard and the lush vegetable garden. It was empty. A rain barrel sat beneath a back window, with a PVC pipe leading out of the house and through the lid. I moved toward the back steps.

"Good to see you, Ray."

Damn. I turned toward the sound of that voice and saw Summer sitting on a little bench by the tomato vines. She held a gun on me. For a moment, I thought it was a toy ray gun, then I realized it had a silencer on it.

With her empty hand, she rubbed at her nose. My ghost knife was in my pocket, but could I reach for it without being shot?

"Don't," she said. "I can see your spongy little brain working—it's right there on your face—and if you try something stupid, I'll kill you and make my excuses to the new boss."

"Who's the new boss?" I asked. I already knew the answer.

"He can introduce himself."

She nodded toward the back door and stood. I went up the steps with her behind me. I pulled the door open, thinking I might spin around and snatch the gun from her, but when I looked back she'd gone invisible again.

I couldn't steal what I couldn't see. I wondered whether the predator would feel pain when the bullet left the barrel, or if the gun became very hot. I went inside.

The house was stuffy; Lino needed to turn on his air-conditioning. There was a small entryway with a long room off to the side—it held gardening equipment, piles of sports gear, and the laundry machines. The door behind me didn't swing shut right away; Summer was staying close enough to catch the door, but not too close. I went up the next step into the kitchen.

As I entered the room, I let my hand fall on the door and slammed it shut behind me. I twisted to the side, bumping against the stove and the handle of a bubbling pot of water as a single gunshot punched through the door. My ghost knife was in my hand, but I couldn't use it. Not unless I wanted the drape to kill Summer and bring more of its kind.

I took the handle of the pot—there were three eggs bubbling in about a quart of water—and lifted it off the stove.

As the door swung open, I threw the water into the gap. I felt like a monster as I did it, but that didn't stop me. The steaming water passed through the open space where she should have been but struck the wall beyond. Summer was too smart to rush through a door face first; I'd missed. She became visible and glared at me, her teeth bared.

She lifted the gun.

"Stop!" someone shouted. Fidel stood in the doorway to the next room. He wore a green silk suit that I guessed was tailor-made. It looked sharp, but how could he stand it in this heat?

"Fuck that," Summer said. "I owe him a bullet."

Fidel put his finger into a hole in the cabinet. "You gave it, now knock it off. The boss wants to talk to him."

Summer made a face when she heard the word *boss,*

but she didn't pull the trigger. Fidel waved at me and I
followed him, wishing I could keep the bulletproof tattoos on my chest toward Summer.

We went into the dining room, where the statues and
other antiques lined the walls. Ty was standing beside the
window, and Bud entered from the front hall at the same
time I did. The table was on its side against the wall, and
Lino Vela was sitting in one of the chairs. He looked exposed and vulnerable, and he was sweating freely. His
thermal coffee cup lay on the floor beside him, and I was
absurdly glad it wasn't leaking. *Focus, focus.*

"You brought these people here?" Lino blurted at me.

Wally King was standing in the corner. "Hi, Ray," he
said without looking at me. He stared at the little statue
he'd tried to steal, running his fingers along the place
where the little figure's head was coming off. "I have to
say I'm disappointed."

Was he expecting me to sneak up in a ninja costume?
Drive through the front wall in a half-track? I didn't
care; I wasn't in the mood to play his games.

And damn if Annalise wasn't just a few dozen yards
away. He'd gotten here without her noticing, or before
she'd set up her stakeout. I needed to get to the front
door and shout for her—somehow—as soon as I found
out where Wally's summoning circle was, and whether
he'd erased it.

I turned away from him toward the others. "You can't
be working with this guy," I told them. "You don't realize what he's done."

"I think we got a pretty good idea," Bud drawled.
He scratched at a spot on his leg.

"He's killed you."

"You're the one who wants to kill us," Ty said. "He
explained it."

Fidel cut in. "Why we gotta be your enemy? You re

member the old times, don't you, Ray? Shit, I feel like an old man just talking this way, but we have history."

"I remember. It's good stuff and bad, just like any family. That's why I'm here." Fidel scratched the back of his hand, and I couldn't look away. "What he's done to you is going to get bad soon. Very bad. And after it kills you, it'll bring more of those things into L.A. I have the proof right outside—"

"Outside where your peer is?" Wally said. He looked at Fidel. "She's the killer he works for, and she'd burn down this whole city block, killing all the kids and mothers and old people, to get to us. That's what they do."

"She's here for *him*," I told Fidel. "I want to help you."

Wally laughed. "I don't think they believe you, Ray."

I looked at their faces and knew he was right. They'd seen through me, but I had to keep trying. "We can go outside without her seeing you. I have something to show you in the trunk of a Hummer. Guys, you don't realize what he's done."

"Yes, we do," Summer said. "We're not stupid."

Ty held out his arm as though he wanted to show it to me. "We know these things are like a poison. But he's the only one who can offer an antidote."

Fidel was still smiling. "We aren't into euthanasia, baby."

I reminded myself that none of them had seen a drape as it fed. "Lenard is dead," I told them.

That hit them hard. There was silence for a moment, until Bud said: "How?"

"How do you think?" I snapped back, because I didn't want to put the finger on Arne, not even now. "The creature that was wrapped around him opened a hole in our universe and carried him off. He's gone."

"Opened a hole . . . ," Summer said with contempt. "What bullshit."

I spun on her. "How perfect is this: Vanishing Girl doesn't believe in magic. Wake the fuck up. There's more going on here than you understand, no matter what he's told you." I spoke to the group of them. "It killed Lenard and carried him back to its home, and more of them came through the opening. I have them, *and the people they're eating,* in a car outside. All I need is for you to be willing to look at what's going to happen when the symbols he put on you wear off."

"Crazy," Lino muttered. "You're all crazy." Wally laughed again.

The others thought about what I'd said. Summer's face was closed and angry—she didn't trust me, but she was willing to let the others think things through. Fidel smirked at me; he'd been trying to win me over, talking about old friendships, but that didn't mean he was open to what I was saying. Just the opposite, really.

Before I could judge Ty and Bud's responses, Wally broke in. "Why don't you tell them why you're here, Ray?"

I turned to him. He looked so grotesque that I wanted to look away, but I didn't. "Because a friend came to my apartment in Seattle and told me that you'd killed her."

"I don't mean why you're in *Los Angeles.*" Wally sounded annoyed. "I mean why you're here in this house. Surrounded by all this crap."

"Because I knew Ty was coming here, and I needed to find these guys."

"You're a liar and you're not even good at it." He reached out to the head-chopping statue, wrapped his hand around it as though he was going to pick it up, then let it go. "You're here for the same reason I am, for the same reason your boss is. For the same reason your own secret society pays the people across the street to keep video security cameras pointed at this house at all times."

Lino glanced up at that. "What?"

Wally liked being the focus of attention. He kept talking. "Georges Francois, the owner's great-great-something-grandfather, had a real spell book. One of the three originals. And when he vanished, he left behind this collection."

If he was talking, he wasn't killing me. I gave him a prompt. "A collection that can't be broken up."

"Nobody can break apart this collection. I have some wild and weird outsiders in here with me, but not even they can resist the compulsion to leave it all alone. You think the sapphire dog sold for a high price? This stuff would bring treasure beyond imagining at auction. At least five of the richest men in the world would literally give everything they own for it."

"Beyond imagining?" Ty asked. He looked around the room.

"Try to steal something," Wally said. "See how far you get. Anyway, the real point is that Francois—the original—had one of the three most powerful magical items in the world, and it's been missing and presumed lost for over two hundred years.

Ty tried to pick up an old candlestick shaped like a gas-lamp post but apparently decided against it. His hand fell to his side. He tried to touch it again, didn't, then shrugged and walked away. The compulsion was strong.

"But this," Wally continued, waving his arms around. "This is a clue farm right here. I think Georges Francois hid the Book of Oceans, and I think this unbreakable collection contains the clues we need to find it. What's more, I think this head-chopped statue is the key to the mystery."

I stared at him. "What the hell are you talking about?"

"It's true, man! I'm sure of it! It's how these people think! They want to pass their power to someone who's earned it. And I'm not the first person to believe this, let me tell you. Not by a long shot."

"Why would he hide it and leave clues? You said he vanished, right? How do you know it didn't vanish with him?"

"Then why would he create this collection, huh?"

"Because he was an egotistical asshole." I turned to Fidel, Summer, and the others. "You're signing on with this guy?"

They looked dubious. "Apparently," Fidel admitted.

"Ray, don't doubt me." Wally shuffled his bulk into the center of the room. "I know you think you're hot shit, but I gotta tell you, I haven't seen it. Neither have these guys. I have no idea how you got this rep as a bad-ass killer, but I suspect you're just a front.

"And I admit, I'm not really big on thinking up plans. But you know what? I don't have to be. I am damn good at finding out secrets. I solved every version of Myst without ever looking at a walk-through."

I couldn't help it. I laughed at him.

He smirked and shrugged. "Go ahead, buddy. Have a chuckle. But I'm telling you, I see things in ways you can't understand. These objects are all bound together, and they're all connected to him." Wally waved a hand at Lino. "I know a little desert retreat that's going to be abandoned soon, and I *was* going to ask you to join me while I worked this out. Why should you be killing all these people for the Twenty Palace Society when you could be killing for an old friend? Huh?" He sounded almost hurt. "I was hoping that, if nothing else, your rep would keep some of those assholes off my back while I figured these clues."

"Why would you think I'd help you?"

"The King Book of Oceans," he said. "The Lilly Book of Motes." He moved toward the statue, his expression blank.

"No."

"I know. It's too late for that anyway. Kill him."

I held up my empty hands, thinking my old friends might hesitate to kill me in cold blood.

Summer raised her gun.

I *reached* for the ghost knife and it zipped out of my back pocket. Summer sighted on my chest and fired two quick shots. Then I had my spell in my hand.

I whipped my arm down as I lunged at her, slashing the ghost knife through the barrel of her gun. It cut at an angle, slicing it close to her hand but not touching her. The silencer and front end of the barrel thunked to the floor, then the slide shot toward me and bounced off my leg.

Summer gaped at the ruined weapon in her hand, then at the two holes in my shirt.

I spun on Wally. He stepped backward, passing through the wall like a phantom. I threw my spell at him.

The ghost knife plunged through the plasterboard after him, zipping right between the head-chopping statue and a brass cow rearing up like a lion. It couldn't have missed, I was sure, and a moment later I was proven right when a jet of flame burst through the wall, blasting plaster, wood splinters, and knickknacks toward me.

I stumbled, struck something with my heel, and fell backward onto jagged wood and broken plaster. Lino was on the floor next to me, curled up on his hands and knees and covering his head.

Wally screamed as the flames roared out of him and through the hole in the wall. I must have hit one of his little iron bugs and ignited the others. They tumbled, still burning, out of a hole in his belly.

I grabbed Lino's flabby biceps and hauled him to his feet. "Let's save your life." I dragged him from the room.

Summer was still standing by the back door with Ty beside her. Fidel was standing in the doorway with Bud right behind him, almost ready to push his way into the room. Only Fidel was looking at me; he gaped at the bullet holes in my shirt.

"Shit, Ray," Fidel said. "Are you bulletproof?" I could see the hunger in his eyes.

His expression made me furious. I threw a punch at him, but he retreated toward the front door and vanished. My fist slammed into the doorjamb, and I cursed at the pain. I'd split my knuckles wide open.

Stupid. I moved toward the hall. I couldn't see Fidel or Bud; they had to be between me and the front door at the end of the hall. There were stairs on the right, and I shoved Lino toward them. We stumbled up.

The knowledge that Fidel or Summer could be inches away from me with a knife made me so shaky that I could barely lift my legs. Lino pounded up the steps, and I did my best to follow him.

"Front room," I said, but he was already headed there.

I entered after him and slammed the door. At least we'd know when one of the invisibles tried to come in.

Lino ran to the bedside table and yanked open a drawer. He pulled out an old revolver with a carved pearl handle. I grabbed it and twisted it out of his hand. "No."

"How can you say *no*?" His voice was high with stress. "These criminals broke into my home! If I can't shoot the hell out of them, please explain why not!"

The bedroom we were standing in was carefully arranged and covered with a thin layer of dust, like a museum exhibit. I went to the window and looked out. The greenery was heavy, but we were pretty high up. I could see the Dodge Sprinter parked across the street. There was also a sloping roof just outside the window, with a low gutter at the edge.

"Because nothing they're doing here is worth you losing your life." I snatched a baseball off the bureau. It felt small in my hand—it had been many years since I played ball, but in my freaked-out adrenaline high, the long throw felt entirely natural. The ball punched a hole in the window, soared out through the tree branches, and struck the side of Annalise's van.

"That was Mr. Francois's Mickey Mantle!"

"Well, why don't you go get it, then?" I opened the window. There was glass on the shingles, but he was wearing shoes. Lino hesitated. Just as I was about to point out the tree he should climb down, the bedroom door burst open.

I tore the curtain rod off the wall, then spun and threw it toward the door. The curtain fell on an invisible form there, and I charged at it, knowing I couldn't use my ghost knife or Lino's gun. I drew back my bloody right hand, hoping that the punch I was about to throw wouldn't hurt too much.

"I have a gun!" It was Bud's voice. I stopped where I was. The curtains bounced to the floor, and I heard him move away from me. Damn. I stepped toward the sound, but Bud shouted, "Don't!"

"Show me the gun."

He obliged by becoming visible. I had no idea why he did what I told him, but he definitely had a gun, which looked so ungainly because of the silencer. He was pale and trembling, so scared I thought he might crap himself. I knew how he felt.

But he didn't squeeze the trigger. Wally had been completely casual when he told them to murder me, but Bud wasn't a killer. He was a tough thief and a little mean, but killing someone in cold blood was deeper waters than he liked. I could see that he was trying to work himself up to it.

"Happy now?" he asked. "I'm bringing this loser back downstairs. Him, we want alive."

"Bud, you have to let me go downstairs to meet my boss. She's on her way into the building"—in fact, she should have arrived already. Where was she?—"and she's coming for Wally. I need to tell her to lay off you guys."

Bud scratched at the side of his neck. The pale skin there looked red. "They have guns."

I pulled at the holes in the front of my shirt. "So what?"

"You ain't bulletproof," Bud said, as if trying to convince himself. "Not with that face."

"Bud, you have it all wrong. We need to get you—all of you—back to the place where you got this creature." There was something at the back of my mind, something I was missing, but now wasn't the time to think it out. "We—"

"Shut up, Ray," he said through clenched teeth. "You think I'm going to listen to you? *You stole my truck!*"

He was working himself up to pull the trigger, and he was very, very close.

Lino stepped up from the side, almost from behind Bud, and slammed a golf club down on his forearm.

The gun didn't go off. I rushed Bud and slammed my right elbow into his mouth while I groped for the gun. I clamped my left hand onto his right, but it was empty. He'd dropped the gun and I hadn't even heard it hit the floor.

I spun him around and pushed him against the wall. The fight had gone out of him, and when I grabbed his forearm, he hissed sharply in pain. Lino must have broken a bone.

"Sorry, Bud," I said, although I was suddenly unsure how much that apology was supposed to cover. I looked down to pick up the gun, but it was missing.

So was Lino. Had he gone out the window? Somehow I didn't think he was spry enough to get out and down so quickly. The bedroom door was standing open.

There was a loud crash downstairs. Annalise had finally arrived.

A sound like water flowing through a tunnel came from the first floor, and I shoved Bud through the door toward it. He let me. An eerie orange light shone up the stairs; was the building on fire? I hurried toward it. Bud curled his arm across his body and moved his feet as fast as I pushed him, but the vitality had gone out of him.

At the foot of the stairs, we found the ground-floor hall blocked by a weird twist of the air, an orange glow that made the air seem to flow toward the front of the house. I didn't know what the hell it was, but it felt fundamentally *wrong*, the way some predators do when I get too close.

Bud drew back, not wanting to touch it. The weird flow was close to the bottom step, but I couldn't judge how close. It was coming from somewhere in the front room and flowing toward the front door—from Wally toward Annalise, I assumed—but I didn't want to get close enough to look down the hall to confirm it.

Then the flow reversed and I felt a weird pressure wash over me. I started rethinking all my thoughts of the last few seconds, but backward. I fell against the stairs, disoriented, feeling unmade in some odd way I couldn't understand.

My skin crawled. Whatever strange magic had been flowing toward the door, it had been turned back on itself, and I'd felt the effects. The flow faltered and stopped.

I tried to raise my hand, but it swung downward instead of up and I banged my wrist against the edge of the stair. The spell Annalise had used to turn Wally's magic back on itself was still affecting me, making me move in the wrong direction and sporadically think backward.

Bud's drape must have shielded him from the effects, because he stepped off the bottom stair, turned toward the front of the house, and raised his good left hand. He was holding a tiny pistol, and I had no idea where he'd gotten it. He looked tired and sad, as though he'd given up any hope of living out the day. Annalise strode into view. Bud aimed the gun at her throat and, from barely six inches away, shot her.

She didn't even flinch. She swatted his hand away, and his face came alive with sudden, startled pain. Annalise grabbed him by the belt and collar, then raised him over her head.

"Boss, no!" I hadn't gotten the words out of my mouth when she threw him down onto the floor with such force that the whole house shook and the floorboards cracked.

Bud suddenly turned crimson—all the blood that would have splashed out of his shattered body washed over his skin, held in by the drape. Someone was screaming and the wooden floor kept cracking, although part of my disoriented brain knew the sound wasn't coming from the floor.

Annalise stared at Bud's corpse, her brow furrowed as she watched his blood disappear. A buzzing noise grew louder and I struggled to my feet. Annalise reached toward her vest.

I tried to move toward her but took two steps back instead. Damn, her reversal spell still had me all turned around. I let myself fall toward her—she grew larger in my vision, at least—just as the floor vanished.

Bud and Annalise both dropped into the darkness below. Annalise gasped in surprise just before I caught her sleeve. The Nomex was slick; for a moment I thought it might slip out of my injured hand, but it didn't.

I jammed my foot between banister posts so I wouldn't slide in after her. Annalise slid out of the oversized jacket—it wasn't fastened, and she didn't fit into it anyway—but she caught hold of the hem and swung out over the void. She looked up at me, and God, for the first time ever she looked genuinely afraid.

And there, below her, was a huge mass of drapes moving toward us.

Just as I was about to start hauling Annalise in, she did it herself, scrambling hand over hand up the length of her jacket, then over me. She hopped up onto the stair behind me and said: "Don't lose my jacket."

The drapes were coming, and not in small numbers. Not five, not six . . . This was a swarm of thousands. I scrambled to the side, trying to get away, but I was too slow. Too slow! The drapes were already here.

The predators burst up through the opening in the floor just as a ribbon zipped over my head and burst into a huge bubble of green flame.

There was no keening this time, no death cries. The drapes died suddenly and violently.

When the green flames faded, I saw the predators swirling around the opening—close enough that I could have rolled over and slapped one—but not coming through. Then the floor reappeared and became solid, sealing over the opening.

Thick wads of gray sludge covered the baseboard and wall. Damn if we hadn't just found a way to kill the drapes without letting more into our world. I saw Annalise pluck another green ribbon from her vest. It was her last one.

"Boss, don't kill the ones who can turn invisible."

"He didn't look invisible to me." Police sirens grew louder. "Remember what I said about the police."

She stepped onto the hall floor, one hand on the banister just in case the portal reopened. It didn't. I stepped out behind her. Wally stood at the end of the hall, with an open door behind him that led to the backyard. The front of his shirt was torn, and his swollen belly had burst open. I could see dark, wet things moving inside.

He held Lino Vela beside him. Lino looked at me, gasping for air. He was so freaked out that any of us could have controlled him with a gentle word. At the edge of the room stood Summer and Fidel, and they looked just as shaken and helpless as Lino. Flickering light from a fire I couldn't see played against their faces.

"This guy," Wally said, his voice quavering a little, "can help us find the Book of Oceans. We can make a deal. Your people are looking for it, too, and—"

Annalise lowered her shoulder and ran through the gray sludge at him.

Summer and Fidel vanished.

Wally shoved Lino in front of him. "Listen! Wait!" he said, but that wasn't going to stop Annalise. Lino cringed.

"Boss!" I shouted, moving toward her, but it was too late. She threw a ribbon into the room. A greenish black tentacle whipped out of the open wound in Wally's gut and slapped Lino toward it.

Lino and the ribbon touched. For an instant, green fire lit his terrified expression. He didn't scream. He didn't have time.

Wally, though, screamed high and loud. Annalise charged into the room just as the flames died. Lino's smoking bones hadn't even had time to fall to the floor before she knocked them around the room.

I followed. Wally stumbled and fell onto his side. He raised his left hand to protect himself; everything from the middle of his forearm to the tips of his fingers had burned down to a stiff, gleaming, resinous bone.

Annalise grabbed him just above the elbow and stomped on his thigh.

His leg flattened and buckled. Wally shrieked, and the sound of it stopped me in my tracks. I stood in the doorway, horror-struck at the noise he was making. Goose bumps ran down my back, and I flushed with shame. hated Wally, but no man should ever be reduced to making a sound like that.

Annalise, her face utterly blank, like that of a skilled worker with a complicated job, twisted Wally's burned arm like a chicken wing and tore it off at the shoulder.

There was no blood for some reason, but I could see the awful knobby end of Wally's upper-arm bone. Annalise crammed that raw bone into his open, screaming mouth.

I didn't want to see any more. I didn't want to see the breaking teeth or the way she nearly pushed the bone out the back of his head. This was her work. I didn't want to see any more, but I couldn't look away, either.

This was who *we* were.

Something greenish black inside Wally's body lashed out at Annalise, but she caught it with her other hand. More tentacles flashed out at her, battering her and knocking her away, but she had hold of her victim and there was no way she'd give up now.

God, she was winning.

The strange orange flow erupted out of him, and Annalise was thrown back and her body curled to the side as though gravity was bending around her. The distorted flow suddenly changed direction, shredding the tentacle in her hand.

Annalise staggered. The torn flesh on Wally's belly opened again, showing more of the formless, writhing thing inside him. A limb flashed out, slapping Annalise away. The flowing orange distortion struck her again, lifting her off her feet and blasting her into the living room.

I rushed after her to keep her in view. She flew in a straight line, smashed through the plate-glass window, and passed through the greenery out of sight.

Damn. I ran toward her as though she had me on a leash. I had to make sure she hadn't been turned inside out or something.

She lay tangled in the bushes by the front gate, and

two LAPD uniforms struggled toward her, guns drawn. Her expression was furious and frustrated.

A cop turned toward the house, and I ducked out of sight.

Wally was gone.

CHAPTER FIFTEEN

I ran into the kitchen. Ty, Summer, and Fidel were gone, and so was Wally. Had they carried him away? I doubted it. They wouldn't have stuck around for the whole of that beating.

Lino Vela was still here—his bones were all over the floor. And there was his coffee thermos, and the little statue that Wally had wanted so badly. A burning piece of table lay against the wall, and there was a small fire on the wooden counter. Goose bumps ran down my back as I went near it, but it wasn't spreading like the fire that had burned me a few days earlier. No polyester.

I picked up the statue. The urge to return it to the shelf was strong, even though the shelf didn't exist anymore.

Someone pounded on the front door. The cops were about to bust in, and here I was standing in a ruined house beside a dead man's bones. Even better, Lino's gun lay in the corner.

I picked it up and fired two shots into the floor. The pounding changed to cursing and retreating voices. That may have bought me a few seconds, but when the cops came, they were going to come in force.

The compulsion to put the statue down was strong. Instead, I laid the edge of my ghost knife against the cut part of the man's neck.

And damn if that wasn't the easiest thing in the world. The enchantment on the statue demanded that I ignore it, but the ghost knife cut right through all that. The ghost knife *wanted* to cut the statue. I slid it through the metal, and the head fell, thunking to the ground.

I picked up the head—there was nothing usual about it—and set it on the counter. On the statue, there was a tiny hole on the cut stump of the neck.

It was small, less than half the size of the mouth of a soda straw. I angled it toward the window, hoping daylight might show a sliver of paper inside, and something blue spilled out.

The liquid dangled from the statue like a long, thin line of mucus. I righted the figurine and the stream zipped back up into the opening. Damn. What was that?

I grabbed Lino's coffee thermos off the floor and spun the lid off.

The liquid poured out of the statue in a thin, milky-blue stream. I tossed the statue away, and the spell's effects faded. The compulsion had been laid on the statue, not on this strange fluid. In fact, there was an odd feeling to the liquid—an absence, almost, as though it wasn't really there.

Whatever. I twisted the lid on tight. Time to go.

I snatched a big bottle of corn oil off the counter and splashed it onto the floor, then onto the hall carpet. In the other room, the phone rang. I tossed the oil onto the floor beside the spreading fire. Then I grabbed an antique lantern off the floor and smashed it against the burning wood. Firelight chased me out the back door.

No one shouted, "FREEZE! POLICE!" I vaulted over the back fence into the next yard. A huge brown mastiff raised his head to look at me, then lowered it again. It was too damn hot to bark.

I ran around the side of the house and let myself through the gate onto the sidewalk. There were no cop cars racing down the block, although I could hear more approaching.

I crossed the street and walked to the corner, keeping

my pace slow and steady. People were coming out of their houses, and I stood at the curb in a knot of them as a cop car went by, sirens screaming. Sweat ran down my back, and my mouth was dry.

An old lady gave me a suspicious look as I stepped off the curb—I'd taken too many punches to be truly anonymous. I crossed the street, slipping through a crowd of lookie-loos, then I got into the Hummer and drove away. I took a deep breath for what felt like the first time in hours.

If those patrol cars had gotten there a few minutes sooner, I would have been trapped. For once I'd had a bit of luck.

But something was nagging at me, and I couldn't figure out what it was. Something Arne had said? I turned my attention to other things to let my subconscious work on it. Ty, Summer, and Fidel were on the loose, and whatever was left of Wally had gotten away. I couldn't even catch a thought, let alone predators . . .

In a panic, I pulled into a strip mall and parked. I threw open the back door and poked into the empty cargo space with the base of the thermos. It wasn't empty after all; the bodies of the guards were still there. All of them, I hoped, but I couldn't tell unless I climbed in and started moving them around with my bare hands, and I wasn't going to do that.

I took another deep breath and pressed my trembling hands on the back door. Annalise wasn't around to burn the drapes to ash, which meant I needed to find the circle Wally had used to summon them, if it still existed. If it didn't, I didn't know what the hell I'd do. Could I stash them somewhere until Annalise got herself released? Although I was pretty sure she had run out of green ribbons and had no idea how long it took her to make new ones.

I leaned against the bumper and wiped my face with

my shirttail. God, I hated sweat on my face. And I was thirsty, too. Of course Wally had come here in August; it was like he wanted to give me extra reasons to hate him. Why couldn't he have holed up in that cabin in the woods? The breeze was cool there.

There was a Starbucks in the shopping mall, so I ducked inside and bought a bottle of water. It cost too much, but a little sign by the fridge promised that some of the money would go to help people somewhere get something. Clean water, apparently.

I was happy to spend some money on a well or whatever. I sure as hell wasn't doing any good as a wooden man. Wally had gotten away, and so had all the others. I went back out to the car and sat behind the wheel, drinking the cool water slowly and thinking about all the things I didn't do to stop them. I hadn't threatened anyone's children or torn someone's limbs off. I hadn't burned an innocent man to death.

Annalise was as ruthless as ever, and remembering what she'd done to Lino and Wally made me shiver in the sweltering car. Then again, next to Csilla she was practically a hero.

Damn, I was tired. The thermos lay on the seat next to me. I unscrewed the cap. The liquid was the same milky-blue color I'd seen in the fire-lit kitchen, even though it was at the bottom of the dark thermos. It was as though it had one color, no matter what light hit it.

For a moment I was tempted to gulp it down. Wasn't that what people did on hot summer days? I swirled it around the cup instead. Whatever this was, it had been sealed in an iron container for decades, possibly longer, and I didn't even like to drink a Coke that had been left out open overnight.

I poured a little into my cupped hand. It pooled like mercury—although it obviously wasn't that—but even stranger was the thin line of milky blue that connected the stuff in my hand with the stuff in the now upright thermos.

It wouldn't be divided. It flowed like a liquid but held together. I was glad I hadn't drunk it. I still had my ghost knife, of course, but I left it in my pocket. I suspected that using it against this "clue" was another bad idea.

Now that I was touching the stuff—looking at it, too—I could feel the weird absence of it again. It was almost as if it wasn't really there.

Actually, that wasn't quite right. Just as the drapes' portals were openings to another place, this liquid looked like an *intrusion* from another place. It felt oddly like it was pressing against me—against everything around me.

I was getting used to receiving strange impressions from magic, but I wished I understood them better.

The tiny pool of liquid in my hand swirled and rippled. I peered closer, trying to see what was making it move. Was something alive in there, but so small that I couldn't see it?

I should have poured it back into the thermos, but I didn't. There was something about the way it flowed upward from my hand to the thermos and back again that captured my attention. I was entranced.

My thoughts began to run free, growing and changing into something alien. It was as if they'd broken out of shackles that I hadn't known were there. My mind felt huge and monstrous . . .

Then the world turned to darkness.

For a moment I thought I'd gone blind. A strange whistling trill of panic blasted at me from somewhere, and the weird echo it made told me I wasn't in the Hummer anymore. I made myself still, trying to figure out what had happened. Where had that sound come from? What was I seeing?

Because I was seeing *something*, but I couldn't get a mental grip on what it was. I could feel myself floating.

Once, years before, I'd cast a spell that had sent me into the Empty Spaces. I'd floated then, too, but I could still see dark mist against an even darker background, huge predators gliding past, and whole worlds spinning below, obscured by darkness.

This wasn't that. I could hear a continuous, confused trilling, and there were moving shapes nearby. I tried to reach forward with my hands, hoping to grab the steering wheel of Francois's stupid Hummer, but there was nothing in front of me.

The shapes moved away, and I realized I was perceiving them with senses that were completely new. It was as though I was seeing and feeling them at once, and not just the edges, either. I almost laughed, and the trilling suddenly changed.

The noise was coming from me; with a sudden, dreamlike certainty, I understood that it was an expression of my own thoughts—my confusion, analysis, and emotional responses. I was broadcasting like a radio tower.

I forced myself to be silent, which wasn't easy. My "arms" wavered in front of me like the tails of kites, if kite tails had large hooks on their ends. The other shapes had long arms with hooks for hands, but they kept them around their middles.

The shapes were round and soft, and they floated by without paying me much notice. Only one, darker and more dense than the others, approached me. It trilled a greeting, and hearing its voice was like thinking its thoughts. I knew my vision had changed, but obviously my hearing had as well.

It was surprisingly easy to send a greeting in return; I only had to think it without trying to hold it back. The sound left me and became a thought in the other creature's head.

I was dreaming, obviously. Only a dream—and a

fucked-up one at that—would have this kind of absurd certainty.

The dark, dense creature opposite me thought a warning into me, letting me know that calling someone unreal or absurd was a serious insult. I sent back an apology.

It moved away from me, trilling a burst of notes that told me it was my host and I should stay close. I complied without hesitation. Having someone else's words appear in my mind as though they were my own thoughts made for a damn compelling request. After a moment of trying out my new body, I floated in its trail.

I was getting used to my new perceptions. I sensed that my host was dark and dense because he was scarred. I realized, with the sudden certainty that you get in a dream, that he'd fought in a war. My host had hooked arms, too, but only six of them. I had nine. I felt a twinge of envy at that, but it felt like someone else's emotion and I held it in.

I willed my arms to wrap around my midsection the way my host wrapped his, tucking them in place. It was probably bad manners to walk around with sharp blades at the ready, like walking through a shopping mall with a bowie knife in your hand. Other creatures like us floated by, trilling conversations about math that I couldn't understand.

A sudden stabbing pain in my guts startled me. Was I sick? I slowed down. My host matched my new pace and played a short melody of sympathy. I knew immediately that this body was dying, and it was impossible to tell the difference between my host's pity and self-pity.

What kind of screwed-up dream turned other people's opinion of you into your own thoughts? I didn't want to be here anymore. Maybe it would be better to wake up in the Hummer now.

We quickly reached a narrow opening in the ground.

To my dream senses it was as impenetrable as any well or cave. My host told me to enter. Before I realized that it had been his thought, not mine, I was too close. Suction caught hold of me and dragged me inside, into the darkness.

Then I popped out like a kid at the bottom of a slide. I scuffed along the gritty stone floor and painfully managed to rise into the air again. My host popped out of the tube behind me with more grace. I felt clumsy and vulnerable, and that made me angry.

My host asked if I was well, and I snapped back that I was fine. It wasn't offended. Maybe that's what it meant for one of these creatures to go to war; it'd had other people's dying thoughts in its head without dying itself.

It led me down a tunnel into a room as large as a tennis court. I stopped just inside the entrance at the top of a long slope. Indirect "light" shone through gaps in the wall, but the room was dim to my dream senses.

Then other creatures like me entered the room, although the dim light made them little more than silhouettes. They filed in from somewhere, casually falling into ranks like soldiers.

God, it was so much like the food bank in Washaway that I couldn't breathe. My dream body wanted to broadcast my panic but held it in. I'd had dozens of nightmares about the pets—no, *people*—I killed in Washaway, but none of them had been like this. This was too much. I backed toward the entrance.

One of the creatures moved toward me just the way the pets had, and I lost control.

The hooks around my torso untwined, and a loud trill whistled out of me. I knew I was beaming fear, fury, and the memory of what I'd done in Washaway directly into the minds of the creatures below me. I backed away from them, holding my "arms" out like a cobra's hood to warn them away.

They fell into a panic, crowding toward the exits and trilling in fear.

My host came toward me and, over the blare of panic and confusion, unleashed a single blast of noise. It was almost above my range of hearing, and it turned my mind into a still, dark nothingness.

I awoke in the same alien body, feeling myself being pulled down the hall. I felt the gritty stone floor and suddenly knew that this wasn't a dream—it wasn't a vision. I was here, somehow, in this body and in this place. The liquid I'd found in that statue had transported me here, and . . .

My host loomed above me. It placed a single barb on the center of my body and at the same moment made a sound like a soothing, sustained note. It was telling me I had nothing to fear, unless I lashed out. I understood and was still.

Then it asked for the story at the source of my fear, and the tones it used were impossible to resist. I answered, and the sounds that came out of me told everything—every nuance—in a startlingly short time. It felt like opening up my mind.

My host kept putting questions into me, and I kept responding. I couldn't hold back. These creatures didn't seem to understand secrets, and they certainly didn't understand shame.

It stole my entire life story within ten minutes, maybe less. I tried to make it stop, but it pressed its long spike a little harder against my flesh and urged me on. It couldn't understand that it was *taking* something from me.

Then it promised to "fix" me.

It told me that I could keep my memory of the pets—of the *people* I'd killed, but it was going to erase the awful feelings that came with it. It couldn't grasp why humans felt guilt or shame, and it was certain I'd be better off without it.

The Twenty Palace Society would make me its new poster boy.

No, I told it. No. I was a human being and I didn't want to be changed into something else.

It said I was too damaged to make this choice for myself.

I swung one of my hooked arms at it, aiming for its center. I knew my attack was feeble, but I didn't expect to kill the creature. I expected the creature to kill me.

And that's what it did. There was a sudden sharp pain as the hook went in, then I was back inside the Hummer, staring down at the milky-blue liquid in my hand.

I carefully poured the liquid into the thermos and twisted the lid back on. I set the thermos into the cup holder. Spilling any of it would be a terrible thing. Terrible.

Then I began to scream.

CHAPTER SIXTEEN

I didn't scream for long. For one thing, it didn't make me feel better, not even a little bit. For another, it was a waste of time. I had predators in the back of my car. I didn't have time to freak out.

I looked over at the thermos on the seat next to me. What the hell had just happened?

There was a sudden knock on my window. A chubby guy with a thick Vandyke was standing by my door.

The windows on the Hummer were electric, and I didn't want to fumble with the controls trying to lower them—that would be a sure sign that the vehicle wasn't mine. I opened the door a crack.

"Hey, man," he said. "You okay?"

And here I thought nobody in L.A. cared. "No," I answered. "I just got fired."

"Oh. Um . . ."

"Thanks for asking."

He accepted that and, his good deed accomplished, walked away. I was going to have to be more careful where I had my meltdowns.

I put my hand on the key in the ignition, then put it back into my lap. Where was I going to go? I had no plan, and no idea where to find Wally, Arne, or the others. I picked up the thermos again.

The liquid inside had sent me to some other place. Not the Empty Spaces, though—there was no air, no stone chambers, no caves there. It was all mists and nothingness. Another planet? This planet in the distant past or far future? I had no way to know for sure. What I did know is that those creatures were going to put thoughts into my head.

I have the Book of Oceans. The realization hit me like a medicine ball in the gut. The statue wasn't a clue; it was a container. Every sorcerer and wannabe sorcerer in the world was looking for this, and 98 percent of them would be willing to nuke the city and sift the ashes for it.

Annalise wanted it most of all. The Twenty Palace Society was fading without its spell books; it was losing ground against sorcerers who summoned predators. If Annalise got her hands on this, she'd share it with the other peers. She'd share it with Csilla.

And she'd killed Lino without a second thought. She'd threatened the boat captain's son. She wasn't as big an asshole as Wally or Ansel Zahn, but could I hand over the spell book to her?

Hell, no.

I gripped the steering wheel with my left hand, rubbing it against the leather. That was my skin, touching. My face itched from the sweat and heat. My hair was damp. It felt good to be back in my own bones, and I was tempted to step out into the parking lot to dance, just to make sure everything worked. And yet, I could still feel those nine hooks wrapped snug around my middle, like phantom limbs.

I closed my eyes and tried to remember how I'd "seen" in my vision. Those alien creatures had been about to tell me something important. They'd brought me to that private place, and they were all about to share something with me at once.

Maybe that's how the original spell books worked— they didn't really give you visions, they sent you out of your body, where those *things* dumped the knowledge of the universe into your brain the way I'd throw old newspapers into a recycling bin. And Christ, they'd almost given that knowledge to me.

I set the thermos on the seat next to me, but when I realized I was about to belt it in, I moved it to the cup holder. The L.A. River was just a few blocks away. I could dump the contents of the thermos into the thin stream and watch it flow out to the Pacific. Hell, I could take the advice I gave Dale and stuff the whole thermos into a trash can by the curb. The book would vanish into a landfill somewhere.

Would that be enough to get it away from everyone, including myself? Part of the reason I wanted to trash it was that I wanted it so much. "Reading" the Book of Oceans would turn me into a primary, one of the most powerful sorcerers in the world. I would live for centuries. I could go back to Hammer Bay and destroy the predator I'd left behind. I could do things I couldn't even imagine.

But if I didn't trust Annalise with that much power, I certainly didn't trust myself. Not that I was sure those aliens would accept me if I tried again. I laughed, and the sound echoed in the confines of the SUV. I hadn't lied to the chubby guy after all. My alien host had taken me into a room to become a full sorcerer, and I'd gotten myself fired.

I was going to have to get by on what abilities I already had . . .

And suddenly I knew where to go. Wally had said: *I know a little desert retreat that's going to be abandoned soon.* Arne had "broken into" a building in the desert—a building with security cameras on the outside—to steal that Bugatti, but he hadn't bothered to go invisible first. The building must have been his.

And once Arne vanished into the Empty Spaces . . .

I started the engine and pulled out of the parking lot. I drove aimlessly for ten full minutes, trying to remember the best way to get to the 15. Francois had been right all along; Arne was ransoming the man's car back to him, not recovering it.

I followed the 15 through Barstow into the desert. Somewhere out here was the turnoff to that little dirt road and metal warehouse, and I spent at least twenty minutes convinced that I'd missed it when it suddenly appeared in front of me.

To my right was the Mohave. To my left, across the median and the westbound lanes, was the dirt road. If I was lucky, I'd also find the circle Wally had used to summon the drapes. It was the only way he'd know about the building. I hoped.

Traffic was thin. I slowed and swerved onto the dirt median. When the way was clear, I drove across the westbound lanes onto the raised gravel pathway. Once I passed the rough ground by the dry stream, the gravel gave way to a dirt track.

After about a mile, I passed the spot where I'd spied on Arne, then came to the fenced gate. It was standing open, always a bad sign. A battered sign on the chain-link read QUAKEWATER REFRIGERATOR RECYCLING. I drove straight to the run-down sheet-metal building.

A piece of yellow metal stood out from the far corner, and I decided it would be best to drive around the building once, just in case a SWAT team was hiding back there. As I came closer, I saw that the cameras were pointing right at me, and that the front doors, each as wide as an airplane-hangar door, were wide open.

I drove down the path and coasted by the open doors. It was dark inside, unsurprisingly, and all I could see was a concrete floor and a row of unlit headlights.

Then it was once around the building. On the far side from the gate, I saw a digging machine, almost certainly stolen. There was a scraper on one end and a scoop on the other. Behind the building was a low berm that prevented me from driving out into the desert, which I didn't want to do anyway. The dirt out there had been disturbed in a few places, as though someone was digging for treasure.

At the front of the building, I turned the Hummer around and backed in. I was barely inside before a tremendous anxiety washed through me—I couldn't turn my back to all that darkness. I jumped from the vehicle and wandered into the room, wishing I had kept Lino's gun. I kept my hand close to my ghost knife.

Once I was out of the sun, the room didn't seem so dark. Against the far wall was a row of cars, mostly German makes. Those were always popular in South America, and Arne made most of his real money with them. In the dimly lit corner at the far right of the building was a small workbench and a radio playing norteño music. God, I hated those accordions.

To the left was a set of desks and tables, including a much larger bench covered with tools. There was also a huge blue plastic water jug mounted atop a cooler.

Against the right wall, off into the darkness, was a red circle on the floor.

I moved toward it. It had been made with red paint—in fact, an open bucket was set in the corner—and it was much bigger than I'd anticipated, more than fifteen feet across.

There were sigils along the inner ring. I compared them to the ones on the back of my hand, but they were not the same, of course. These were rounder and more filled with open space . . . which was appropriate, I guessed.

This was it. This was where Wally brought the drapes into our world, and killed my friends.

Time to work. I went to the tool area and found a long-handled shovel. The blade was sharp and heavy; it could kill someone if I put my back into it, but it was too crude. I kept searching, but the best option I found was a long flat-head screwdriver. There was duct tape, too, which would suffocate someone, but no. That's an ugly way to die.

Then I noticed a little shelf loaded with soup cans and packages labeled MRE. They were army rations; I could only wonder where Arne had stolen them. Beside them, in the back corner, was a knife block. I found a long, sharp boning knife there. It would have to do.

I got into the Hummer and backed it closer to the circle but not too close. I didn't want any part of it extending over the red paint when I opened the back hatch.

I opened the rear door and laid my hand on something I couldn't see. I caught hold of it—it felt like an arm—and pulled it toward me. My skin began to itch, but that couldn't be helped. I jostled the body until I managed to roll it onto its back and grasp it under the arms. As I dragged it, it whispered.

I jumped back, startled. Had the drapes learned to talk? I heard the sound again, and it didn't sound like something a drape would make. It sounded terribly human.

I leaned in close to listen. It was Potato Face's voice, and he was begging me to kill him.

I hauled him out of the vehicle, doing my best to keep him from flopping onto the concrete floor. He still fell heavily, and I apologized to him. I knew he was in terrible pain, and maybe thumping his heels on the ground was minor by comparison, but I owed him a bit of dignity before I did what I had to do.

I dragged him across the red circle, then set him down and checked the paint. It was undamaged. My brain was working quickly, and I didn't try to slow it down. How much time did I have before these men started dying? It could have been two weeks, or it could have been two minutes. I had no way to know, except that they'd been stuck in the back of a car for hours in desert heat, so probably not two weeks.

But I couldn't put them all into the circle at once. If I did, the first to die would drag the others into the Empty Spaces. If Wally was right about there being no death there, those four men would never have an end to their suffering.

So it would have to be one at a time. I taped the knife to the butt of the shovel handle. I probably used more tape than necessary, but I didn't want it to fall into the void.

Then I took a handful of dirty rags out of a bucket. I was ready, even though I really, really wasn't.

I laid my makeshift spear on the ground outside the circle. Then I found Potato's body and felt around for his throat. Once I had that, I laid one of the dirty rags near it, pointing away like a beam of light from a kindergartener's drawing of the sun.

Then I went outside the circle and hefted the shovel. The first time I'd killed someone in cold blood, Annalise had been standing over me. This time, I couldn't even see the guy's face. It didn't make things easier.

I slid the knife forward just above the ground. I suddenly felt resistance and shoved forward, sawing back and forth. I hoped I was hitting him just below the ear—that's where I pointed with the towel, at least. But I couldn't see blood. I couldn't see anything.

There were no sounds, either. I yanked the shovel handle back, pulling it outside the circle. The blade was clean, but . . .

A portal suddenly opened. There was no buzzing or cracking noise this time. The entire floor inside the red circle just vanished. The shop rag fluttered down into the Empty Spaces.

A swarm of drapes flooded up through the hole, swirling at the edges of the circle but unable to cross it. I stepped back to see how high they could go. It looked to be about twelve feet, well below the ceiling above.

I stepped back farther. It was like looking at a giant aquarium filled with drapes instead of water—minus the aquarium. I didn't want to be anywhere near it.

With my ghost knife in hand, I watched them swarm, hoping the circle could hold them all and knowing there was little I could do if it didn't. It held, and after a few seconds, the drapes dropped out of our world and the floor reappeared. From off in the corner, a man sang in Spanish about love and death, with accordion and sax accompanying him.

The next man wasn't easier, but it was quicker. I made sure to turn him the other way so the knife would enter below his left ear rather than his right. I had the idea that that would make it quicker, and I was right.

When the drapes swarmed in again, I turned my back on them and went for the third man, because fuck them. They scared the crap out of me, and I was tired of being afraid.

My hands were itching badly. The watercooler was just across the room, but I didn't wash the slime away. It seemed right that I should suffer during this job. These men were. Somewhere, somehow, I'd acquired a taste for penance.

Once the last man had vanished into the Empty Spaces, I walked to the back of the room toward the watercooler. It was half full. I dribbled the water over my hands and forearms; the slime the drapes left behind vanished at the water's touch, but my skin was still raw. Sweat ran down my back. The radio played another song with lyrics I couldn't understand. I felt terribly, painfully lonely and, at the same time, grateful to be alone while I worked.

"Is that what you plan for us?"

I yelped and jumped to the side, backing against the wall. A push broom and other long-handled wooden tools clattered to the floor.

It was Fidel. He was three feet from me, scratching

furiously at his neck. He'd stripped down to a sleeveless undershirt and those fancy green linen suit pants. I didn't like the bitter, desperate smile on his face.

Summer and Ty appeared beside him. Summer's expression was fierce, but her eyes were red, as though she'd been crying. Ty gaped at me.

"Let me ask again, Ray." Fidel's voice was quiet. "Is that what you planned for us all along?"

"We could see them," Ty said. He held his injured shoulder high and his arm close to his chest. The burn must have been bothering him badly. "Mostly. We know what they were."

"And you killed them," Fidel said. He scratched furiously at his arm. Summer did the same. "I didn't think you had it in you, baby. But why did you put them in that summoning circle, hey? You calling up more of these creatures?"

"That's not what the circle is for," I said, but Summer didn't let me continue.

"You tried to stop that woman from hurting Bud, but you weren't trying to save his life. Right? You just wanted to kill him here so you could call up more of these things."

"Summer—"

"I'm right, Ray. Just admit that I'm right."

"You don't understand," I said. "As soon as that symbol wears off, you're going to be like those guys I pulled out of the SUV. How long have you been itching?" Summer stopped scratching her arm.

Ty glanced at Fidel. "He said they would start eating us."

"What bullshit," Fidel said.

"Once you're dead, they carry you away and let more into our world. If you die outside the circle—"

"This is bullshit, Ray!"

"They get loose!" I shouted at him. "And they do this to other people!"

"Fuck other people!" Fidel leaned into my face. "I got to watch out for myself!"

I almost said: *There's nothing left of you to see,* but I didn't. He'd backed himself into a dangerous spot, and he couldn't see a way out. I sympathized.

Ty's expression was uncertain. I thought I'd had him convinced that the drape was killing him, but it was pretty clear he wanted to be unconvinced. He was still looking for a way out. "Did Arne tell you to say that?"

"Where is Arne?"

Fidel and Summer rolled their eyes. Ty said: "He said we should meet him up here. He said he could make things right."

Arne had brought them running to him by giving them false hope. Maybe I should have done the same thing. Maybe I should have lied. It would have been easier than this.

But what had I expected? They weren't going to line up inside the circle like victims of a firing squad.

"Ray." Fidel's voice was low and urgent. "Did your good friend Wally make you bulletproof?"

"No," I blurted out with more anger than I'd intended.

"It wouldn't work anyway," Ty said.

"What wouldn't work?" I asked.

"Ain't nobody else offering another plan, so why not?" Fidel said. "Where did you get that magic, Raymundo? Hey? How did you get so well protected? Who hooked you up?"

Damn. He wanted a closed-way spell to protect him from the drape. "It won't work, believe me."

Fidel sighed and turned to Summer. "He don't know how to answer a question."

Summer glared at me. "Maybe we should raise our voices."

"Guys, these creatures are in your mouths and down your—"

"I got a better idea," Fidel said, raising his voice to talk over me. "Ray might be bulletproof, but we can all see he'll still take a beating, hey?" He stepped over to the table and picked up a hammer.

Oh, shit. He snatched a screwdriver off the work-bench and tossed it to Summer. She caught it, and they both vanished.

Ty gave me a helpless look, and he vanished, too.

I grabbed a tool from the wall behind me—it was a curved metal piece at the end of a twenty-foot wooden handle—and swung it. The metal tip struck something soft, and I backed along the wall. I swung the handle again, this time not hitting anything except wall.

The radio at the far end of the room suddenly switched off.

In the silence, I listened for footsteps. Nothing. I moved toward the middle of the floor, which maybe wasn't a good idea, but it was the only way to get to the Hummer.

I swung the handle again. They were keeping their dis-tance. Good. I glanced at the metal piece and realized it was used to open and close the transom windows at the top of the wall.

Not that it mattered. I swung again, struck something at two o'clock, then swung overhand at that spot.

I hit nothing but concrete, breaking off the metal tip. The splintered wood and metal end flipped up and over my shoulder—too high to hit me, but I ducked away from it just as something struck the outside edge of my ear.

I snapped my head to the side; it felt like my ear had been torn off. I didn't pause to check it, though. I swung the broken handle, and it moved much faster now that it was shorter. I struck something and heard Fidel grunt in pain.

Then something dull scraped against my shoulder blade.

I stabbed backward with the splintered end of the

wood, but I missed whoever it was behind me—Summer? Which was a good thing, since we weren't even close to the red circle yet.

I sidestepped, swinging the handle low in a full circle. Summer hissed when I hit her shin. Contact. I charged at her, my arms wide to make sure I caught her.

I did, by her hair. She yelped in pain and I felt a sudden rush of shame. I had to kill her, but I didn't want to hurt her. Was this how Wally felt?

Whatever. I caught her around the neck and knocked her to the floor. I couldn't see her, but I could feel that she was facing away from me. I guessed she had the screwdriver in her right hand and grappled for it blindly. It clattered to the floor.

Scuffling footsteps approached from behind. I wrenched Summer off the floor and spun to put her between me and whoever was getting close. Nothing bashed my skull open.

Sweat stung my eyes as I backed toward the red circle. If I could get her inside, I could use my ghost knife on her. The drape would kill her, quickly, and that would be that. It would almost be like mercy.

But she was struggling furiously, and even though I was stronger and heavier, I couldn't contain her. She was fighting for her life, and in my heart I wanted her to win.

Ty became visible in the middle of the room; his expression had so much sorrow in it that it stole my energy away and I stopped fighting.

Summer tore free of my grip. "Fuck!" she shouted, letting herself become visible. "This is bullshit."

"Yeah," Fidel said from just behind her. He became visible, too. "Let's try shooting some more."

Summer moved her hand toward her lower back. I grabbed her and half lifted, half shoved her into Fidel. We were too far from the red circle for me to try to wrestle her inside, not if people were drawing guns.

I sprinted toward the open door. The Hummer was right there, but there was no time to get in, start the engine, and pull away.

A barrel beside the door suddenly toppled on its side, and a wash of dirty black oil flowed toward me. I jumped, clearing it before it spread too far, and landed in the doorway.

I went through the doorway and turned the corner out of sight. A gunshot went off, but I didn't feel any sudden, crippling pain, and I didn't fall over dead.

At the corner of the building, I crouched behind the digger. No one came out of the building—not that I could see, anyway—but if someone did, the machine would give me some cover.

Who had tipped over that barrel? I hadn't seen anyone, but Ty had been at the other end of the room, by the toolbench, and I'd just left Summer and Fidel behind me.

It had to be Arne. If it wasn't, there was another person running around with a drape, and I didn't want to think about that. Had he turned off the radio, too?

Was he helping me?

I still couldn't see anyone leaving the building, and I thought I would at least see a smear of oil or loose dirt stirred up by their footsteps, even if they were invisible.

There. A smear of black appeared on the concrete lip of the building foundation, then a scuff of dirt.

The footsteps headed toward the gate, away from me. I scrabbled toward the back of the building.

The ground was packed hard with a fine layer of dirt on top. I sprinted across the open area in back of the building, my feet scraping through the faint tracks Francois's Hummer had laid down. Would they be able to find me with those footprints? They looked pretty faint, but I didn't like the idea of leaving a trail. Not that I had a choice.

I scrambled over the top of the berm and slid down the other side. This dirt was loose, as though it had been moved recently, but it was the nearest cover. I left huge footprints, but the dirt would stop a bullet.

There was a deep, broad hole in front of me. I hopped over it, but the dirt crumbled. I tipped into the hole, landing on my hands and knees.

I heard flies buzzing, and that smell . . . The hole was just a bit over five feet long, and right beside me was someone stretched out, lying in wait.

CHAPTER SEVENTEEN

My throat was too tight to let me scream; instead I hissed like a leaky bicycle tire. I panicked for a moment, convinced that Ty or Summer had gotten here before me and was stretched out with a gun trained on me.

But they weren't. The figure beside me wasn't moving at all. I leaned closer to it, to the smell and the flies, and I saw that it was Francois. He had been shot once in the head.

"You're lucky," Arne said from somewhere nearby. I spun and saw him crouching in the open space above me. "Some of the older holes have rattlesnakes in them."

He extended his hand. I clasped it, letting him lift me out of the hole. He stood upright, visible above the top of the berm beside us. I stood upright, too.

He slapped a .38 revolver into my hand. "Don't get busted with this."

I opened the cylinder. One round had been fired—and I was pretty sure I knew where that bullet was—leaving five shots. For all the good it would do me.

"I can't use this."

"Oh no?" Arne gave me a look that was difficult to read. "I thought that was what you did now."

"It is," I said, hating the words as they came out of my mouth. I had never admitted it aloud before. Arne was still giving me that look. "But I can't kill them unless I can get them in the circle first. Otherwise—"

"No need to explain. I know. I was in the building,

too." He scratched at his neck, then lowered his hand with a visible exertion of will. "I saw."

"You can see them when they're invisible?" It was hard to believe he was really on my side. It seemed impossible that he'd help me, knowing that I would have to kill him, too.

He broke eye contact, looking toward the building as though scanning for the others. "Yeah, if I really concentrate." If he saw something, he didn't say. "Well, I said I would help you with your thing when I was done with mine, didn't I?" He waved toward Francois's corpse. "I have one more problem to bury, but I guess I won't have time for that."

I looked away, determined not to think about patches of disturbed dirt behind me. "I didn't know," I said.

"I didn't want you to know. There are some problems that can only be solved by a grave in the desert, but I couldn't trust you with that. Don't take that hard; I couldn't trust anyone."

Graves. And I had thought that disturbed dirt had come from digging for treasure.

We heard the sound of an engine, a low-horsepower motorbike approaching. I grabbed Arne's elbow and pulled him low, so we were just peeking over the berm. The bike came into view and passed through the gate. It was a small thing, baby blue, with the minimum cc's necessary for highway travel.

Wally was riding it. His green sweats had been replaced by a pair of huge purple M. C. Hammer pants and a gigantic dashiki. His left hand was encased in a mitten, and he had a pair of expensive mountain-climbing shades on

I pulled Arne all the way down out of sight. He resisted at first, then turned invisible. I caught his elbow and looked at him, shaking my head at where I hoped his face was. *I can see with more than just light.*

I sat with my back against the dirt, silently cursing a

myself. I'd known Wally wasn't dead—yeah, his injuries would have killed most people, including me, but I had learned to expect a certain *toughness* from the people the society went after.

But I didn't want him here. I still didn't know what I was going to do about Fidel and Summer—putting Wally on the to-do list just made me feel tired.

The scooter engine idled. Was Wally coming over the berm at me? I took my ghost knife from my pocket and held it in my right hand. Arne's gun was in my left. I was as ready for him as I'd ever be, and that wasn't ready enough.

Then the engine started again, and I heard the bike putter away. The sound became muffled as it moved to the other side of the building, then shut off.

I turned to Arne, who had become visible again. "Shall we?" We stood.

"Ray, two things." Arne took a deep breath and scratched furiously at his neck for a second or two. The drape must have been getting to him. "First, I saw the way you did those five guys in there. I want you to make it quick for me, too. Humane. Okay?" I nodded. He looked out over the desert. "Second thing, about Jasmin . . ."

Damn. Was he going to apologize, finally, for stealing my girlfriend while I was in prison? It didn't seem like the time, but part of me was hungry for it.

"She's relying on you to stop these things." He wouldn't look at me. "You're the guy who handles this stuff, right? That's what Wally said, anyway. Jasmin—my daughter—needs you to clean this mess up, okay?"

I almost laughed at myself. Had I really expected him to apologize? Shame washed over me like a wave. Arne didn't give a damn about my hurt feelings; he had more important things to think about.

So did I. "Okay," I answered. He vanished.

And so did I, in a way. My fears, my guilt over the

crimes I committed in Washaway, my desire to do the right thing, whatever that was, all seemed to shrink down so small that I couldn't even tell they were there.

Arne's clarity had copied itself onto me. Wally was here, along with all my remaining friends, and best of all, they'd brought their predators with them. It was as if they'd gathered together in one place as a gift, to give me another chance to murder them all.

There was a scuff of dirt to my left; Arne was circling the building.

I crept toward the back corner. The radio and workbench should have been just on the other side of that wall, along with the line of stolen cars.

I took out my ghost knife and cut a horizontal stroke across the sheet metal an inch above the ground and again two feet higher. Then I sliced two vertical lines and caught the panel gently as it fell to me.

I ducked low and eased myself inside, nearly hitting my head on the rear bumper of a black Lexus LX 570. I stayed low, creeping along the bumper toward the bench. The red circle was a few feet from the front fender, just ahead on my left.

People were talking. I raised my head to peer through the Lexus's windshield. The driver's-side window was busted, and I caught the faint, nasty stink of old cigarette smoke.

Wally stood in the center of the room, facing away from me. The red circle was several yards to his left. Fidel, Summer, and Ty all faced him. Any of them could have seen my silhouette just by glancing over at me, but they were too focused on Wally.

The high, metal ceiling created muffling echoes; I couldn't make out what they were saying, but it sounded as though Fidel and Ty were trying to convince Wally that they could be useful to him. Wally's answers were mild and the others seemed to find them frustrating.

I backed away from the window and bumped against the bench. Jars behind me rattled like wind chimes, and I dropped to the concrete floor.

The Lexus had a high clearance, but the car beside it was a Dodge Viper. A pair of black sneakers—Summer's, I was sure—moved toward me, then stopped. If she took a few paces to her right, she would see me.

After five long seconds, Fidel spat out a string of curses, and she went back to the others.

I eased into a crouch and turned around. A disordered row of mason jars stood on the long, pressure-board table. I took two of them, choosing ones that were empty and had lids. Then I set them carefully on the concrete.

I edged a little higher, peeking into the Lexus. There, in the cup holder behind the gearshift, was a Bic lighter.

I wanted it, but there was no way to open the door and get it without everyone hearing. And although the window was already broken, the lighter was out of reach. I was going to have to lean in with my whole head and shoulders.

Summer and Ty were focused on Wally, but I could see their faces. If I made too big a movement, I'd catch their attention, and I wasn't ready for that. I crouched down, unsure what to do.

"You're being ridiculous!" Wally suddenly said in a loud, clear voice. "I can see you, you know."

My hands immediately went to Arne's gun in my waistband and my ghost knife. But it was Arne who spoke next. "So you can. So what? You're still an asshole."

I peeked through the SUV's windshield again. Arne was standing by the doorway, and everyone had turned their backs to me to face him.

I lunged through the open window, grabbed the lighter, and ducked out of sight again. No one yelled out my name or shouted "What was that!" I snatched a rag off the floor, grabbed both jars, and scurried behind the Lexus.

Arne stood in the sunlight, talking shit at Wally. The urge to stop what I was doing and listen was strong. It was stupid, too, so I ignored it.

The underside of the Lexus had skid plates on it, for reasons known only to the idiot who'd bought them, and I couldn't remember where the gas tank was. Beside it, the Viper was too low to the ground to fit the large jars beneath it comfortably. The third vehicle was a silver Audi A8. I unscrewed the lids and set them aside, then crawled under it. At the other end of the building, Arne talked a fast patter of insult and abuse at Wally, who only laughed in response.

With my ghost knife, I cut the corner of the Audi's tank. Gas streamed into a jar. The noise seemed unbearably loud to me, but Arne raised his voice, seemingly in anger.

Damn. He was holding their attention. He was acting as my wooden man.

It didn't take long for the first jar to fill. I swapped it for the second, then used my ghost knife to cut a small gap in the metal lids. I slashed the rag in half and began stuffing the pieces into the gap.

The gasoline slowed to a trickle and ran out when the second jar was two-thirds full. The tank had less than half a gallon in it. Arne must have drained the tanks after stashing the vehicles here. I screwed on the lids.

I was still afraid. I hated to admit it, but I was. But Arne was running out of time, too, and I couldn't let Wally kill him, not outside the circle. I set jars beside one another so the rags would touch, then I lit them.

"For God's sake!" Arne yelled, his tirade getting louder. "You should have gone and gotten yourself laid, you stupid shit!"

I stood and threw the ghost knife.

It zipped across the room silently. Wally, Fidel, Ty, and

Summer had no idea it was coming, but Arne saw it and, not knowing what it was, jumped aside at the last moment.

The spell struck Wally in the back of his neck. His skin split open, and from the other side of him where the exit wound would be, a huge splatter of thick green gushed out of him.

I *reached* for the spell. It passed through Wally's chest, causing another splash of nasty green liquid. He started choking, then collapsed onto his knees.

The ghost knife returned to my hand all slimy. I stuffed it into my pocket, knowing I'd be burning these pants soon.

"No!" Fidel yelled. "We need him!"

Fidel ran at me, reaching into his waistband.

I bent down and reached around the flaming wick. The fire was scorching, but I wouldn't be holding it long. I straightened and threw the jar across the room.

It landed just short of Wally's foot. Flaming liquid splashed up onto his back and sloshed around his leg. I grabbed the second jar—not so carefully this time, because Fidel was getting close—and threw it on instinct.

This time my throw was perfect. The jar shattered between his calves, and the fire roared under his crotch and belly. Wally went up like a bonfire.

I couldn't see Fidel, but I could hear his scuffling shoes nearby. A tiny black hole appeared in front of me, and just as I realized I was looking at a gun barrel, it went off.

I didn't feel the bullet strike. Fidel did, though. He turned visible, not three feet away. There was blood on the front of his shirt, and his mouth fell open. His bullet had hit me over my heart, then ricocheted back through his breastbone.

He dropped the gun and collapsed onto the floor. I shouted his name and grabbed his shirt, hoisting him up again. His eyes grew dim, but he had enough life in him

to look at me hopefully, as though I could save him somehow.

I lifted him as high as I could, his drape eating at the
skin of my hands, then bum-rushed him between the
cars toward the red circle. I bumped against something I
couldn't see, but it only took a moment to regain my
balance and momentum.

Fidel sighed and his eyes closed just as I crossed the
line with him. I dumped him onto the concrete—not
gently, but he was already dead—and leaped back across
the red line.

The drape carried him away and brought another
huge swarm into our world. The red circle held them
until they fled.

God, I was tired. I was drenched in sweat and had no
energy left.

Ty stood by the grill of the Viper, Fidel's gun in his hand.
He bared his teeth at me. "I didn't want this, Ray."

"I know you didn't."

He walked across the front of the car toward the
Lexus, circling me and scowling. He could lift that gun
in a moment, but my ghost knife was in my pocket and
Arne's gun was back in my waistband. We weren't going
to have a quick draw.

I glanced at the others. Arne had turned invisible
again—or he'd run. Wally was rolling in green slime, trying to extinguish the flames. It was working, too, a little.
Summer stood in the middle of the room, a look of blank
shock on her face. She'd gone as far as she could go. She
was done.

I turned back to Ty just as he stepped across the edge
of the red circle. I reached for my waistband, hungry for
the chance to kill my friend.

Ty pointed Fidel's gun at his head.

"I didn't want this," he said. "I had plans, Ray! I had
plans!"

"We all give up our—" The gunshot cut me off. He didn't hear me. He'd already pulled the trigger. I watched his drape carry him away.

I turned to the others. Wally was on his feet. A long black tentacle stretched across the room and pulled the watercooler tank off its base, then held it over his head. Stale water gushed over him, extinguishing most of the flames. His left hand burned like a torch at the end of his arm. He slapped at his shoulder with it, trying to put it out. He looked smaller.

Wally's face was a horror of blackened flesh. "Dammit, Ray," he said, his voice as clear as ever. "You really are a pain in the ass."

I had no idea how he was talking with that scorched and ruined throat. Maybe his voice was a hallucination and had been since we met at the Sugar Shaker.

"Well, your ass is such a big target—"

"Shut up, dude. Seriously. I had to eat a *whole family* to heal the injuries your boss gave me. Now I'm going to have to do it again, and that's on you."

A tentacle suddenly shot out of his belly and wrapped around Summer's neck. She squawked as Wally yanked her off her feet. Wally's belly split open like a huge mouth, the roasted flesh tearing, and a green, puckered funnel that looked like a large flower petal pushed toward Summer. She tried to scream as the tentacle stuffed her into the funnel, but her neck snapped. More bones broke as Wally crammed her inside.

I backed away, goose bumps running over my whole body. It didn't seem imaginable that Wally could stuff a hundred and thirty pounds of human being into himself, but I had just seen it. His flesh seemed to fill out, and some of the blackened skin began flaking off. No portal opened beneath him. It wasn't just Summer he had killed and eaten; he'd gotten her drape, too.

"Better," he said. He rolled his neck around once to

loosen it up. More black flakes fell. "Better, but not enough."

He took another step toward me.

I backed toward the Lexus, then around it to the work area. There were plenty of things there I could use as a weapon, but not against someone like him. I took out my ghost knife.

Wally laughed at it. From under his shirt, a half-dozen tendrils appeared, coiled like snakes. Would they catch my ghost knife or slap it away? I wasn't sure which would be worse.

Wally floated upward as though he was being lifted off his feet. He looked pretty startled as he tumbled onto his side. At the same moment, Arne dropped his invisibility.

Wally fell inside the red circle. Arne fell on top of him.

I already had Arne's gun in my hand. He turned toward me—maybe he wanted to say something, or maybe he wanted to meet my gaze one last time, the way friends do.

I didn't give him the chance. I put a bullet into his head.

Skull and brain splashed out of the exit wound onto Wally's ruined face. He laughed. "Oh, gross," he said, "but it's just what the doctor ordered," then made as if to lick it.

He realized his error a moment too late. The floor vanished. Wally gasped as he fell into the upsurge of drapes. I could see his gaping expression of horror dropping away, distorted through a filmy screen of fast-moving predators.

Gone. Thank God.

Suddenly, a tentacle shot out of the swirling mass of drapes, crossed the red circle, and slammed down on the hood of the Lexus. The breeze it made as it zipped by my face ruffled my hair. I stumbled back, almost falling, as a second limb shot out of the dark and lodged itself on the undercarriage.

The Lexus lurched forward, knocking me onto the

ground. One of the tentacles had punched through the underbody at just the right spot to grab the front axle. A third punched through the grill and secured itself against something inside.

I jumped to my feet and slashed the ghost knife through the nearest tentacle. It parted like smoke, then joined together again. A fourth tentacle snaked under the body, and all of them flexed, pulling themselves out of the Empty Spaces.

I ran to the passenger door just as the Lexus slid forward again, straining against its brakes. Damn if I wasn't on the wrong side of the car, but there was no time to run around.

I yanked the door open and dove inside. I slammed the gearshift into neutral, then grabbed the parking-brake release.

I pressed the button and slammed it down; it let go and the Lexus wrenched forward. Metal under the hood strained and groaned. I scrambled backward, the idea of falling into the Empty Spaces in this ridiculous car giving me frantic speed. My feet hit the ground and my upper body spun as the SUV glided forward, the frame scraping across the concrete lip as the front wheels fell into the void.

Then I was out, on my hands and knees on the concrete, as the Lexus tipped into the opening and disappeared. The drapes retreated and the floor became concrete again.

Alone. I began to laugh.

CHAPTER EIGHTEEN

My laughter didn't last long. It only took a few moments before a terrible lonely silence came over me. I rolled onto my back and stared at the ceiling overhead. It would be full dark soon. Maybe I could shut my eyes and sleep on the concrete.

I stood and walked out into the center of the circle. My feet scuffed against the concrete. A sudden bout of vertigo made me stagger, as if one misstep would topple me into the void after my friends.

But of course that wasn't going to happen. The hole had sealed over and they were gone. Arne, Ty, Robbie, Summer, Bud, and, oh God, Melly . . . They had all gone down into a grave as deep as the universe, into a darkness where I could never follow, and I was left standing there breathing parched air and squinting against the light of the setting sun. The ground beneath me was unyielding, and I was alone.

Wandering through the building, I found, among other things, a suitcase with a bunch of clean unfolded laundry inside and a case of bottled water—Arne's jump bag? I stripped off my pants and tossed them aside in favor of a pair of long plaid surfer shorts. They looked stupid, but they didn't have Wally's predator puke all over them.

I rinsed the ghost knife with a couple of bottles of water. The green goop stuck to the plastic, but I managed to wipe it off on a clean spot of my ruined pants.

When that was done, I tossed my pants into the oil Arne had spilled.

Arne had said he'd run out of time to finish what he had to do, and now he was dead. I walked around the building to the digger and started it up. I had no idea how to use it, but a little trial and error made the basics clear.

I lurched the machine around to the back of the building and spent the next half hour scraping loose dirt out of the berm over Francois's body. It was hard going at first, but I managed to finish just before sundown. It wouldn't fool the cops if they decided to search, of course, but I thought it would pass a casual inspection.

The building was metal and concrete; I couldn't exactly burn it down the way Annalise always did. Sure, there were plenty of flammable liquids, and cars burn real nice, but it wouldn't totally wreck the place. It would, however, draw firefighters and cops.

I found an oil pan and slid it beneath the Audi, then cut the brake line and collected the dripping fluid.

There was a shop broom by the front door. I dipped the bristles into the brake fluid and scraped it over the painted floor. While I couldn't burn the place down, I didn't have to leave a functioning circle. I scraped at it until it was nothing but faint smears of red. Then I threw a bunch of Arne's old clothes onto the floor and pushed them around with the broom until they were ruined and the circle was barely visible.

After that, I swept the spilled oil from the barrel across the floor until it washed around the green glop Wally had puked on himself. Cement building or not, that crap would have to burn. I tossed my ruined pants into the pile.

What was left?

Nothing. Nothing was left.

I went outside. The sun was well below the horizon by now. Only a faint red glow in the west remained, but the moon was overhead, and its dim white light was soothing.

I didn't want to take Francois's SUV back into town. The bodyguards who'd fled the house should have notified the police hours ago, and I didn't want to be caught in his car. Arne's Land Rover was there, and so were Fidel's and Summer's cars. There were no keys, though; those would have been in their pockets when they fell into the Empty Spaces.

The Dodge Viper, however, had the keys inside. I got behind the wheel and drove it out of the building. I siphoned enough gas from Arne's SUV to fill the tank halfway. Once I got back to the city, I'd ditch it somewhere. The cops would return it to the guy Arne stole it from—hell, I'd be doing someone a favor.

I took the coffee thermos from Francois's vehicle. The Book of Oceans was still in the bottom, but I didn't look at it very long. I wasn't ready for another "dream."

I tore the boning knife off the shovel and dropped it into the oil. Then I set fire to the oil and shut the huge doors. The building wasn't visible from the highway, and the darkness would hide whatever smoke the oil gave off. Sure, the smell would be strong, but the wind seemed to be in my favor.

Not that it mattered. The last of the green crap would be burned up by then. The rest was just details.

I drove the Viper along the gravel bed back to the highway, wondering how Arne had managed to steal gravel.

About forty feet from the shoulder of the highway, I waited until I couldn't see any headlights in either direction, then pulled out. In no time, I was up to sixty, headed back to L.A.

I went to Violet's place, partly because I didn't want to see anyone from the society right away, and partly because I wanted to see what I'd done to her life. The building was still there, and it still had a gaping hole in the side, as though a giant had put a fist through the wall.

Violet was there, too. She was leaning against the hood of her own car, smoking and staring up at the ruined apartment. I parked at the end of the block and walked up to her.

Her cigarette smelled rank, so I walked to her upwind side. "You okay?" I asked. "Where's Jasmin?"

"With my mom. They're hiding with a friend of a friend of a friend. I don't even know where they are."

"I'm glad they're okay." It was a stupid thing to say, but it felt like an obligation.

She threw her half-finished cigarette away as though it wasn't doing what she wanted. "Mom said she asked you to find Mouse."

"We shouldn't talk about it here."

She got into her car and I got into mine. I followed her out to Cahuenga Pass. In one of the sharpest bends of the road, she swerved up someone's driveway. I thought she'd jumped the curb for a moment, until she parked. I pulled in beside her. Lino's thermos stayed in the cup holder, but I got out.

Vi held a package under her arm as she led me inside.

The house was small but tasteful—wood paneling, dark couches made of fake leather, and hunting rifles on the wall. Very male. As I followed her into the kitchen I wondered whose place this was. New boyfriend? I realized I didn't care.

Then I laid my hand on the couch and realized that the leather wasn't fake.

Violet dropped the package onto the counter. "Come here," she said, and led me to the bathroom. "Get yourself showered up. I'll get you some clean clothes." She shut the door.

I showered in a stranger's tiny tiled bathroom. I lathered up with translucent blue soap and dried off with rough white towels. The clothes were too big for me, but there was a belt, too.

Violet was in the kitchen when I returned. There was a lot of glassware and copper. She opened the fridge, took out two beer bottles, and popped the caps on them. She set one on the counter for me.

I walked close to the package to examine it. It was a brown leather folder with a black ribbon tied around it. SHIMMERMAN & PENOBSCOTT had been printed in gold leaf along the edge. I didn't touch it.

"Whose place is this?" I asked.

"Mine, if you can believe it. Arne gave it to me this afternoon." She held up her bottle. We clinked them together and drank.

"He did, huh?" My brain was racing through the events of the previous few days. Arne had a house? Like this? I never would have guessed.

"He really fixed it up. He got it from a guy who owed him money. That was right before I got the court order. Did you know I had a restraining order against him?" Violet's voice was soft. "He kicked my door down once, the second time I broke up with him. The cops came and everything. All those crimes he did, over all those years, and he'd never been picked up by the cops before. He was furious with me, as though it was my fault he had a record."

"He was always careful."

"I always thought he was too careful." She took a long pull. "And I thought he should grow up and get something legit. But he used to laugh at that."

"Why did he give you the house?"

"The guy explained it to me. Penobscott, although I think it was Penobscott's kid, really, not the one with his name in gold. Arne said he was going away, shedding all his worldly possessions and simplifying. He was going to find himself. It's all in a trust or something. I don't know. This snotty-faced kid was sitting behind a big desk in a suit that cost more than I earn in a month, and he's telling me all about the terms of the trust and what I have to do to maintain it for Jasmin. But I couldn't hear a thing he said. We must have talked for half an hour, and I walked out of there like I'd been hypnotized to forget it all. But Arne left me and Jazzy a bunch of offshore accounts, properties, and stocks."

I had no idea how to respond to that. I'd been living above my aunt's garage carrying rocks down a hill, and Arne had been squirreling it all away.

I wondered how much he'd gotten from Francois before he killed him.

"Vi, how long has the Bigfoot Room been at the Roasted Seal? When was the last time he moved it?"

She shrugged. "Years. A few weeks after your sentencing, actually. When you were busted, he pulled up stakes and didn't set them down again until he was sure you were going to do the time without naming him."

"He didn't pull up stakes when Mouse disappeared, though, right?"

"Right. Now, what about him? Where is Mouse?"

"In the properties Arne just gave you, is one of them out near the Mohave? A little patch of desert and rock, maybe, with a prefab building on it? A place called Quakewater."

"Maybe," she said. "I think . . . maybe."

"Don't go out there, understand? Not if you want to keep what Arne left for you and your daughter."

She set the bottle down and picked it up again. In one long pull, she drained it. She understood what I meant, and she wasn't surprised. "Oh, God, Ray," she said, her shoulders slumped and her head bowed. "What did I do?"

I went around the counter and put my arms around her. She cried against my chest, soaking Arne's shirt with her tears. When she was done, she grabbed a fistful of his shirt and pulled me into the bedroom.

Arne's bedroom, and it hadn't even been five hours since I'd put a bullet through his brain. I kissed her, then she pulled his clothes off me. Arne was dead and gone, and there was nothing left of him but memories and a lot of expensive crap. Violet and I were still alive, and together again.

Whatever she and I had was in the past; this was something new. Everything between us was different except the sounds she made. It felt like new life, and a new chance at happiness.

But when we both had finished and she lay against my shoulder, I knew I was not about to get a new life. I had a life already, and it was inescapable. A few moments later, when Vi rolled away from me, I didn't try to draw her back.

"I think I'm going to move away," she said. "I think I'm going to meet with that guy in the suit again, get him to explain everything again, and then get the fuck out of here."

"You want to leave L.A.?" I was surprised to hear it. People leave the city all the time, of course, but I didn't think Vi would be one of them.

"I mean leave America. I've never met any of my mother's family in Oaxaca. I could . . ." Her voice trailed off. I waited for her, and eventually she said, "Better yet, we could go to Canada. They let you in if you have enough money, right? Live up in Canada with all that cold, clean snow."

Something about the way she said that made me think that *we* didn't include me. I rolled out of bed and began to dress again. They were Arne's clothes, and she was the mother of his child, but I'd never had any qualms about stealing things before.

"Ray . . . ," she said, as though she was about to make a confession.

"I already know," I said as I pulled on the shirt.

"No, you don't."

"Yes, I do." I sat in a little cloth chair in the corner and put on my socks. "You're the one who connected Wally with Arne, and with Caramella and Luther and Fidel and the rest. Wally wouldn't have known about the Bigfoot Room or about Arne, but he would have been able to find you, the girl I was living with when I was busted. You're the one who told him how to find the Bigfoot Room."

Violet pulled the blankets off the bed and wrapped them around herself. She didn't turn toward me.

"Wally as much as told me so himself," I continued. "He was disappointed by our waitress at the Sugar Shaker. He wanted to sit in your section. I'll bet he was, actually, and you asked the other girl to take his order, yeah?"

"Yeah."

"Wally wanted me to know he was connected to you. And Arne . . . well, Arne moved the Bigfoot Room when I went to prison because he was afraid I'd turn him in. He didn't move when Mouse disappeared, though, did he? You knew your brother was dead. You didn't exactly gasp in surprise in the other room when I told you. I think I must be the only idiot who didn't realized that Arne had a place to dump the bodies of people who were dangerous to him. That's why Fidel tried to have him killed before striking out on his own; Arne didn't like the idea of his crew getting busted for stupid jobs and easing their sentences by naming him.

"So, Wally must have looked you up. You didn't know

him, but anyone who took one look would know the guy was trouble. You thought about your missing brother, and your suspicions about what happened to him, and you pointed Wally King straight at—"

"Do you think Arne knew what I did?" she asked, breaking in as if she couldn't stand to listen anymore.

I remembered the expression on his face as we stood out behind the berm. Hell yeah, he knew. "No."

"Okay," she said. Vi had always told me I was a terrible liar, but she seemed to believe me now. Maybe she wanted to. She still didn't turn around. "But what does that make me?"

I almost answered *Nothing*, but I held it back. She would have misunderstood. "Someone with a secret. A secret you should never ever admit to anyone."

And that was all we had to say to each other. She was silent and wouldn't even turn her head to look at me. I finished tying my shoelaces and stood. She slowly tipped sideways until she nestled on the pillow. Maybe she was going to sleep.

I let myself out. The stolen Viper was still parked in her drive, and there were no cops clustered around it, checking the plates. There was only one place to go. The thermos and I went back to the supermarket.

I parked the Viper a block away, making sure I overlapped the marked fire-hydrant zone. The car would collect tickets until someone ran the plates. I tossed the keys under the seat. Even if I couldn't find Annalise, I didn't want to drive it again. I didn't feel sporty.

I wandered out to the bus shelter where I'd called the society and spoken with Mariana. No one was there. I sat on the bench and waited.

It took about five minutes for Annalise to pull up in her van. She must have been nearby, watching for me.

She opened the driver's door and climbed into the passenger side. I got behind the wheel, adjusted the mirror and seat, then started the engine. The thermos went into the cup holder beside me.

"Where have you been?" she asked me.

"Finishing a job."

"Tell me about it when we get onto the freeway."

"What about Csilla? What about Talbot?"

"Csilla is gone, back to wherever she goes. And we're not going to see Talbot again. He's out."

"Out?" I couldn't hide my surprise. "I don't understand. Why is he out? Because he ran?"

"No," Annalise said. "Because you said he was useless."

That wasn't how I remembered it.

I didn't much like Talbot, but I hoped whoever caught up with him killed him quickly. "I don't know, boss. The guy probably needs a little training. Hell, he could probably design the training. He might still be useful."

She grunted as though I'd made a good point. And that was all I could do for Talbot. Maybe she'd send word not to kill him. I hoped so.

Annalise hadn't told me where to go, so I got on the 10 heading east. She didn't object. Maybe she didn't care. As we rolled along with traffic, I told her everything that happened after she went through Lino Vela's front window. The only thing I left out was finding the Book of Oceans inside the statue, the vision I had, and the fact that it was sitting in the thermos between us.

By the time I'd finished, we were northbound on the 15, heading for Barstow. She told me briefly about her time with the cops. They'd been gentle with her from the first moment they'd fished her out of the bushes. She told them that she was trying to reach Steve Francois to convince him to donate to her foundation, and within half an hour they'd received confirmation that she did exactly that with her time. She gave them a statement and asked to be released. They let her go.

I shook my head in disbelief. Even with her tattoos, she still got the middle-class white-woman treatment. Or did she have help from one of the spells on her body?

"Boss," I said. "What would you have done if we had found the Book of Motes? Or one of the other original spell books?"

Her response surprised me. She sighed heavily. "That's a hard question. The long-standing rule of the society is that anyone who finds one of the three original spell books is to bring it to the peers directly without 'reading' it first. All the peers would gather together and decide what to do."

"You wouldn't want to check it out before you turned it over? Become a primary yourself?" She didn't answer right away. "Boss?"

"You're damn right I would. I want to finish the job in Hammer Bay *myself*. I want to . . . We're falling behind in this fight, Ray, because we're losing focus and power by the year, while the predators are as dangerous as ever. But the peers want to decide as a group who should have access to it."

"I'm guessing you don't think they'd let all the peers have a turn."

"I know they wouldn't. A few of them don't even think a woman can become a primary. They're sure the visions would corrupt her and maybe damage the book. Also aside from me, one Brazilian, and one Arab, the other peers are all white Europeans; they don't trust the rest of us with that kind of power."

"What if you read it anyway, then gave it to them?"

She sighed again. "Civil war? Again? The problem is that I *believe* in the work the Twenty Palace Society does. I couldn't live with the terrible things I've done otherwise. But the society itself has become a nest of serpents. If I could do this work without them, I'd kill them all."

"I saw the letter you gave to Captain." Dammit. I didn't want to go there next, but the words had slipped out.

"Who? Oh, our friend who took us to Canada? Is that why you've been such a crabby bastard? The letter was for her protection in case we were arrested, genius."

"Okay."

"I know this is leading somewhere, Ray. Get on with it."

"When I asked you if you wanted to become a primary . . ." *You blinked.* I wasn't sure how to ask Annalise if she was frightened or uncertain, and it turned out I didn't have to.

"I hesitated. I know. Ray, what was that guy's name? You know the one I mean."

I did. "Lino Vela."

"Lino Vela. As apprentices, we're trained to attack rogues at the first opportunity. No matter where we are, or who's in the line of fire, we *go*. Becoming a primary, having all that power, well, that would make things easier. But there's a part of me that doesn't think what happened to Lino Vela should ever be easy."

Well, damn. I knew she trusted me enough to share information, but not that she was ready to share this.

She kept talking: "So, you asked, and I hesitated. But the answer is always going to be *yes*, because there's too much at stake."

We drove in silence for a while.

I needed to be careful with this next part. "What if we—I mean, just us two—went out to find one of those original spell books? What if you had the visions, and to hell with the society? You'd be a primary, right? Couldn't you take over? Change the training? Couldn't you just . . ." *Wipe them out?* I couldn't finish the sentence.

"Fight the whole society? Take on not just all the peers but the allies, too? Plus whatever rogues they decided to point at me? Without support? I don't know. I don't think so. And the society has financiers, lawyers, and investigators, too. They can strip away an enemy's resources before a fight, if they know who they're targeting, and they know me. I'm not saying it's a terrible idea. I'd be happy to get my hands on a spell book just to keep it away from assholes like your—like Wally King. But if I became a primary, I think the Twenty Palace Society would kill me—would kill us both. And even if we won the fight, we'd lose the infrastructure of the society. As a primary I'd kick ass, yeah, but I'd need investigators to tell me where to go, and financiers to cover the bills, and so on. *If* we won, and I doubt we would."

"What if the peers got their hands on a book?"

"Incredible power for the most vicious serpents in the nest. These aren't men who worry about the job being easy; it's already easy for them, because they love it. They love the brutality. They pride themselves on their willingness to kill. With society resources backing them, they'd have the world behind the world under their heel."

"You've thought about this."

"Of course I have. This is my life and my future. Either the society loses this fight and the world is overrun with predators, or I become a primary and lose a fight with the society, or the assholes become primaries and I get demoted to . . . what? Wooden man? Errand girl? None of them are good options, but the last one is the least awful."

"To hell with that." I picked up the thermos and swirled the liquid. I couldn't hear it over the rumble of the engine, but I could feel it slosh around. "Boss, here. I found the Book of Oceans."

She stared at me silently for a moment, trying to judge if I was being serious or if she was going to start breaking my bones for playing a prank. I pushed the thermos at her, and she took it. She screwed off the top.

"Oh" was all she said.

I laid my hand over the top. "You're not going to go back on everything you just said, are you?"

She gently moved my hand away and looked into the bottom of the thermos for another few seconds. Then she screwed the cap back on and held the thermos in her lap. "You bastard." She sounded almost as though she wanted to laugh. "You goddamn son of a bitch. You're really good at this job, aren't you?" I shrugged. "Where are you driving us?"

"East," I said.

We drove to Barstow in the dark, and I switched to the 40. "The Mohave Desert?" Annalise asked.

"Can you think of a better place to hide the Book of Oceans?"

"Death Valley."

I laughed. I couldn't help it. "Don't be annoying, boss."

"We're going to hide it?"

For a moment, she sounded unsure of herself. I hadn't thought that was possible. "You said it wouldn't be safe for us to use it, and I sure as hell won't give it to the serpents. I have a better idea."

We took the 40 to the 95. The sign said that Las Vegas was 103 miles away. As we passed the freeway entrance sign for the westbound on-ramp, I made note of the odometer. We counted off a random number of miles, then pulled onto the shoulder.

"Shovel's in back," Annalise said.

We climbed out into the darkness. I couldn't see a car in either direction.

There was a shovel mounted on a rack in the back of the van. Only one, though. I knew who would be using it. I took it down and followed Annalise into the desert.

We walked at least a quarter mile away from the asphalt before Annalise pointed at the ground. "Here."

I dug a shallow hole. She tossed the thermos in without hesitation. It was long life and power beyond anything I could imagine, but I shoveled dirt over it. Annalise picked up a rock as large as a beach ball and set it down to mark the spot. Then she found two more large flat rocks, each the size of a trash-can lid, and laid them beside the beach ball.

"I think we'll be able to find it now, boss. If we have to."

She nodded. We started back to the van. No other cars passed by on the road. "Ray, this only works if we trust each other. You understand? Because either one of us could come back later and move that thermos. Either one of us could cut the other out."

"Boss, if I wanted to cut you out, I wouldn't have handed you that thermos. The truth is, I need your help. It's not enough to hide the Book of Oceans from the Wally Kings of the world—or from the other peers, either. There are two more books out there, and I don't trust anyone with that power—"

"Neither do I."

"Not even the two of us. I don't think we're ready for it."

Her answer was quieter this time. "Because of what you did in Washaway. And Lino Vela."

"Yeah. We will be ready for it, someday, but not yet. Like I said, stashing one book isn't good enough. We need to hunt down the other two."

"That's all, huh? Just go out and find them?"

"That's all."

"And what then? You and I form a new, kinder, gentler society?"

"Yes. We clean the serpents out of the nest. This whole legion-of-brutal-killers thing isn't working. It's a losing strategy. We can do better."

She didn't respond, and I couldn't read her expression in the dark. We returned to the van.

"Ray, this is incredibly dangerous. You don't even understand how dangerous it is. You're just my stupid wooden man."

"All they think about is their limitations," I said to her.

"Don't throw my own words in my face—"

"Some things should never be easy."

"Dammit, Ray! I'm the peer and you're my wooden man! You belong to me!"

"I know I do, boss. You're in, though, right?"

"Fuck, yeah."

I started the engine and pulled onto the highway. It took a long while to get up to speed.

"Where to, boss?"

"Straight through to Vegas," she said. "You look like you could use some sleep. Then we're headed east. You're going to the First Palace. The peers want to meet you."

"Um, really?"

I wasn't sure if I should be pleased about that or not, so I changed the subject. "Can you convince the society to work with Talbot? He's an asshole, but he saved my life."

"I'll make a call. It probably won't do any good, but I'll call."

"Damn. He was really looking forward to living a century or three."

"Not everyone earns a golem-flesh spell."

I turned to her. "What?"

"Not everyone earns that spell," she snapped, annoyed at having to repeat herself. "Especially in the last few years. Only older peers like Csilla can even manage it anymore."

I touched the spell Csilla had put under my left arm,

the one that healed me when I ate meat. Annalise had called that mark golem flesh.

For once, she understood my expression. "Didn't I explain that part?"

"Jesus." I wasn't sure what to say. I was going to live to be, what? Five hundred? Older? "How long until I talk gibberish like Csilla?"

"Gibberish? She was telling you the secrets of the universe."

Be sure to check out the first two novels
of the TWENTY PALACES series,
Child of Fire and *Game of Cages*!

CHILD OF FIRE

Ray Lilly is the lowly driver for Annalise Powliss, a high-ranking member of a secretive group of mage hunters known as the Twenty Palace Society. When Annalise is injured on a mission, Ray must carry on in her stead and defeat a powerful sorcerer who is sacrificing dozens of innocent lives. As if that wasn't tough enough, Ray only knows one spell! Can Ray best the virulent wizard and destroy the source of his inhuman magic?

"Excellent reading . . . delicious tension and suspense."
—JIM BUTCHER, author of The Dresden Files

GAME OF CAGES

A small town in the North Cascades is the site of an unholy auction in which a shadowy group of wealthy collectors gathers to bid on a dangerous creature that could exterminate all life on earth. Ray Lilly is assigned only as backup to the Twenty Palace Society investigator, but all hell breaks loose when the creature escapes and Ray, armed with his single spell and a mean left hook, is forced into survival mode.

"Will enthrall readers who like explosive action and magic that comes at a serious cost."
—*Publishers Weekly* (starred review)